Born in Worcestershire in 1968, **Jasper Kent** read natural sciences at Cambridge before embarking on a career as a software consultant. He also pursues alternative vocations as a composer and musician and now novelist.

The inspiration for Jasper's bestselling début, *Twelve* (and indeed the subsequent novels in *The Danilov Quintet*), came out of a love of nineteenth-century Russian literature and darkly fantastical, groundbreaking novels such as *Frankenstein* and *Dracula*. His researches have taken him across Europe and to Saint Petersburg, Moscow and the Crimea, including three days on a train from Cologne to the Russian capital, following in the footsteps of Napoleon himself.

Jasper lives in Brighton, where he shares a flat with his girlfriend and several affectionate examples of the species *rattus norvegicus*.

www.rbooks.co.uk

Also by Jasper Kent

TWELVE

For more information on Jasper Kent and his books,
see his website at www.jasperkent.com

THIRTEEN YEARS LATER

Jasper Kent

BANTAM PRESS

LONDON · TORONTO · SYDNEY · AUCKLAND · JOHANNESBURG

TRANSWORLD PUBLISHERS
61–63 Uxbridge Road, London W5 5SA
A Random House Group Company
www.rbooks.co.uk

First published in Great Britain
in 2010 by Bantam Press
an imprint of Transworld Publishers

Copyright © Jasper Kent 2010

Jasper Kent has asserted his right under the Copyright,
Designs and Patents Act 1988 to be identified as
the author of this work.

This book is a work of fiction and, except in the case of historical fact, any
resemblance to actual persons, living or dead, is purely coincidental.

A CIP catalogue record for this book
is available from the British Library.

ISBN 9780593060650

Addresses for Random House Group Ltd companies outside the UK
can be found at: www.randomhouse.co.uk
The Random House Group Ltd Reg. No. 954009

The Random House Group Limited supports The Forest Stewardship
Council (FSC), the leading international forest-certification organization.
All our titles that are printed on Greenpeace-approved FSC-certified paper
carry the FSC logo. Our paper procurement policy can be found at
www.rbooks.co.uk/environment

Typeset in 11/15pt Sabon by
Kestrel Data, Exeter, Devon.
Printed and bound in Great Britain by
Clays Ltd, Bungay, Suffolk.

2 4 6 8 10 9 7 5 3 1

Mixed Sources
Product group from well-managed
forests and other controlled sources
www.fsc.org Cert no. TT-COC-2139
© 1996 Forest Stewardship Council
FSC

For
H.E.C.

AUTHOR'S NOTES

Distances
A verst is a Russian unit of distance, slightly greater than a kilometre.

Dates
During the nineteenth century, Russians based their dates on the old Julian Calendar, which in 1825 was twelve days behind the Gregorian Calendar used in Western Europe. All dates in the text are given in the Russian form and so, for example, the Decembrist Uprising is placed on 14 December, where Western history books have it on 26 December.

Names
Names used are transliterations of the Russian spellings. For historical figures, these transliterations can be unfamiliar to readers used to the more common Western renderings. The main examples are:

Pyotr Alekseevich – Tsar Peter I (the Great)
Yekaterina Alekseevna – Tsaritsa Catherine II (the Great)
Pavel Pyetrovich – Tsar Paul I
Aleksandr Pavlovich – Tsar Alexander I
Nikolai Pavlovich – Tsar Nicholas I
Aleksandr Nikolayevich – Tsar Alexander II

I would like to say a sincere thank you to Mihai Adascalitei for his help with the Romanian language.

Selected Romanov Family Tree

Reigning tsars and tsaritsas shown in **bold**.

Dates are birth–*[start of reign]–[end of reign]*–death.

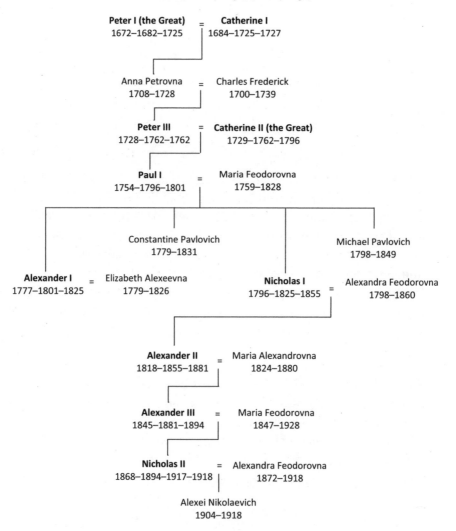

Peter I (the Great) = **Catherine I**
1672–1682–1725 1684–1725–1727

Anna Petrovna = Charles Frederick
1708–1728 1700–1739

Peter III = **Catherine II (the Great)**
1728–1762–1762 1729–1762–1796

Paul I = Maria Feodorovna
1754–1796–1801 1759–1828

Constantine Pavlovich Michael Pavlovich
1779–1831 1798–1849

Alexander I = Elizabeth Alexeevna **Nicholas I** = Alexandra Feodorovna
1777–1801–1825 1779–1826 1796–1825–1855 1798–1860

Alexander II = Maria Alexandrovna
1818–1855–1881 1824–1880

Alexander III = Maria Feodorovna
1845–1881–1894 1847–1928

Nicholas II = Alexandra Feodorovna
1868–1894–1917–1918 1872–1918

Alexei Nikolaevich
1904–1918

THE DECEMBRISTS

On 14 December 1825 (26 December) a crowd of three thousand men – overwhelmingly members of the military – assembled in Saint Petersburg's Senate Square to oppose the succession of Tsar Nicholas I. The origins of the revolt lay in 1814, when victorious Russian troops, led by Nicholas' predecessor Alexander, occupied Paris, having pursued the French all the way from Moscow. The nation that they found, even in defeat, seemed to many a utopia of liberty and enlightenment – at least in comparison with their own country. At the same time Alexander, who had once been hailed as a modernizer, began to turn towards more conservative policies. For a decade resentment festered. Revolutionary societies formed and re-formed, but took no action. The death of Alexander, a thousand miles away in Taganrog, was the flashpoint. With confusion as to which of Alexander's brothers – Constantine or Nicholas – was to succeed, the revolutionaries seized their one, slim chance.

The uprising was quickly suppressed. Loyal troops, at the tsar's direct orders, opened fire on the rebels, scattering them into flight across the capital. Many were killed and more arrested. Five of the leaders were hanged and a further 284 were exiled to Siberia. Ever after, Nicholas referred to them as *'mes amis du quatorze'*. It was only after Nicholas' death in 1855 that the exiles – those who were still alive – were allowed to return to the west.

In 1925, one hundred years after the uprising, Senate Square was renamed Decembrists' Square, in memory of that first Russian revolution. In July 2008, the name was changed back to Senate Square.

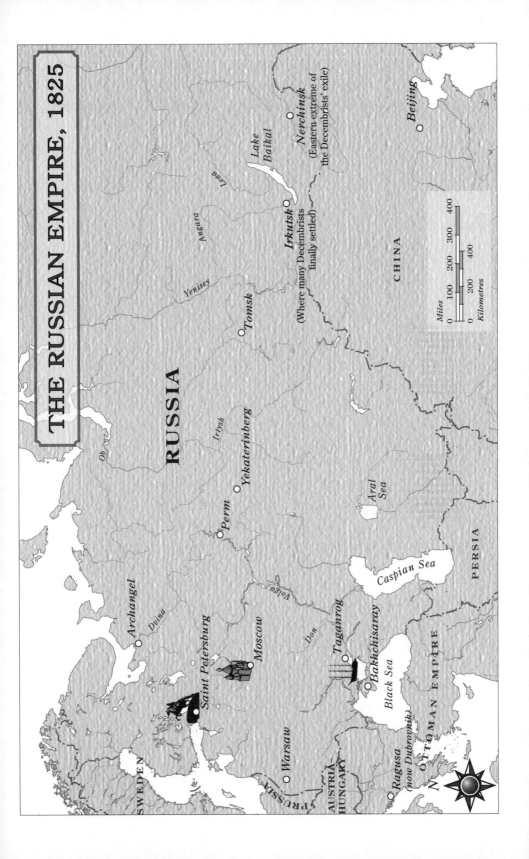

THE RUSSIAN EMPIRE, 1825

RUSSIA

Archangel

Dvina

Saint Petersburg

Moscow

Warsaw

PRUSSIA

AUSTRIA-
HUNGARY

Ragusa
(now Dubrovnik)

OTTOMAN EMPIRE

Black Sea

Bakhchisaray

Taganrog

Don

Volga

Caspian Sea

PERSIA

Aral
Sea

Perm

Yekaterinburg

Irtysh

Ob

Yenisey

Angara

Lena

Tomsk

Irkutsk
(Where many Decembrists
finally settled)

Nerchinsk
(Eastern extreme of
the Decembrists' exile)

Lake
Baikal

CHINA

Beijing

SWEDEN

Miles
0   100   200   300   400

Kilometres
0   200   400

N

PROLOGUE
Saint Petersburg – 1812

The metropolitan spoke:

'*He that dwelleth in the secret place of the Most High shall abide under the shadow of the Almighty. I will say of the Lord, He is my refuge and my fortress: my God; in Him will I trust.*

'*Surely He shall deliver thee from the snare of the fowler, and from the noisome pestilence. He shall cover thee with His feathers, and under His wings shalt thou trust: His truth shall be thy shield and buckler. Thou shalt not be afraid for the terror by night; nor for the arrow that flieth by day.*

'*Nor for the pestilence that walketh in darkness; nor for the destruction that wasteth at noonday. A thousand shall fall at thy side, and ten thousand at thy right hand; but it shall not come nigh thee.*'

Suddenly the chapel seemed empty; empty of noise, empty of its congregation, empty of the metropolitan himself. Aleksandr perceived only the words, surrounding him not as sounds but as creatures – angels sent by God, sent to convince him of what he must do. And what he had to do was so simple: to trust in God.

That the metropolitan had chosen this day to read those words hinted that God had not trusted Aleksandr to understand His meaning. He had read the exact same words yesterday, quite by chance – or, as he now realized, by design. A clumsy accident had caused a Bible to be dropped to the floor and to fall open at that same text, the ninetieth psalm. And the psalm was but the last of three signs. Aleksandr had read it even then with understanding.

Nor for the pestilence that walketh in darkness; nor for the destruction that wasteth at noonday.

'The destruction that wasteth at noonday.' It was clear what that was: Bonaparte – a man who had laid waste to the whole of Europe and who now planned to destroy Russia too. Planned to? He had already made himself a home in the Kremlin.

'The pestilence that walketh in darkness' was something different, something Aleksandr had almost forgotten, but never completely. He had learned of the pestilence at his grandmother's knee, and had never doubted her, as other enlightened grandsons might have doubted stories told them by their frail *babushka*. Yekaterina had never been frail. She had said that a traveller would come to avenge the Romanov Betrayal, and one such had come, just a week before.

That had been the second sign.

He had called himself Cain, but he was merely the emissary of another. Simply to mention the name of that other – a name Yekaterina had whispered to her grandson many years before – had been enough to allow Cain a private audience with Aleksandr. It had caused consternation amongst many, that this stranger should be so trusted by the tsar even at his country's darkest hour. It was not trust, though, but fear that had persuaded Aleksandr.

And yet he had discovered that in truth he had little to fear from Cain or his master, just as his grandmother had assured him. All that Cain had to offer was a bargain – a bargain that

14

promised to save Russia from Bonaparte. And Aleksandr had no reason to doubt that it could. But the cost would have been too great. Yekaterina's strength flowed through Aleksandr, flowed in his veins, and he found it easy to resist, easy to spurn perhaps the last hope that his country had.

Cain had taken the news calmly but he had promised Aleksandr that the offer would be made again, in circumstances when the tsar would be more inclined to agree. More inclined than now, when his country was overrun by a foreign invader? It seemed unlikely, but he doubted Cain as little as he had doubted his *babushka*.

The first sign had come in a vision.

Aleksandr had expected a visitor, but Cain's had not been the face he had been anticipating. Alone in his study he had been forewarned, even before Bonaparte had reached Moscow. It was not the first time he had seen through the eyes of another, but it was, so far, the most vivid.

It began with his hands. He had merely glanced down at them, but even a glimpse was enough to tell him that they were no longer his own. His fingers had become broad, squat and coarse, with dirty nails – something that for Aleksandr was inconceivable. Then he noticed he was not alone, nor was he any longer in the palace, but in a dimly lit corridor. There were four men with him but, still gazing at his own fingers, he did not see them clearly. He held the hand of one of them in his, and soon looked up to glimpse the man's face before kissing him on each cheek, perhaps bidding him farewell.

He perceived the man's jaw tighten as his lips came close, as if he were resisting the urge to recoil from some fetid stench. For the first time Aleksandr noticed a foul, metallic taste on his tongue, and wondered if it might not be his own breath that was so repellent. As he stepped away, he saw the man's face in detail for the first time. He was a little younger than Aleksandr, in his early thirties, clean-shaven, with blue eyes and brown hair that extended in sideboards a little way down his cheeks. The jaw was square and solid. It was an unremarkable face, but one which Aleksandr would never forget.

He stepped back, releasing the man's hand and again glancing at his own. It was now that he saw what Yekaterina had so long ago told him to beware: a ring, in the form of a dragon with a body of gold, emeralds for eyes and a red, forked tongue. Its tail entwined his middle finger. Aleksandr mouthed the name his grandmother had whispered to him, the name of the man through whose eyes Aleksandr was now seeing, just as his great-great-grandfather had once seen.

He reached out to touch the dragon ring, but as he did so, it vanished. His fingers were once again elegant and slender. He was in his palace.

Aleksandr understood what he had seen – or thought he did; a master sending away his servant. It would not be long before that servant came to Aleksandr. And so a servant did come, but when he did, his face had been nothing like the one Aleksandr had seen in his vision. He had been mistaken, but it made no difference. He had sent Cain away, and now he knew that he had done the right thing – the psalm told him so.

The metropolitan carried on reading, but Aleksandr no longer paid him any heed. Instead, he gazed at the floor of the chapel and made a silent promise to the Lord. What he had been, he would be no more. God would deliver him – would deliver Russia – and Aleksandr would make Russia into the country the Almighty wanted it to be. He would be delivered from the destruction that wasteth at noonday, and from the pestilence that walketh in darkness – the terror by night.

Within days, the good news arrived. Bonaparte and all his men – what was left of them – had abandoned Moscow and were heading west. The Russian army would deal with them, with the help of the Russian winter. And the Lord would ensure, Aleksandr felt certain, that the winter would be a bitter one. Far more than ten thousand would fall at his right hand. Aleksandr no longer had to fear the destruction. Now he could do God's work.

And as for the pestilence, Aleksandr still feared that and awaited its advent, but it was not a threat that was to be faced by him, or by Russia, until thirteen years later.

PART ONE

CHAPTER I

'IT MUST BE BY HIS DEATH.'

Ryleev spoke quietly, hiding neither his passion nor his distaste for his own words.

'It's not personal; it's *what* he is, not *who* he is,' he continued. He looked around the room, judging the reactions of the dozen or so men whom he was addressing, reactions with which he must already have been well familiar. 'He's the tsar.' It was an unnecessary clarification, but it added to the enormity of what Ryleev was suggesting.

Some in the room nodded with hesitant acceptance. Some avoided his gaze. Others faced it, demonstrating by the fact they had the stomach to look their leader in the eye that they also had the stomach for his plan.

Aleksei Ivanovich Danilov was among those who allowed Ryleev's eyes to fix on his. He revealed nothing – years of deceit had taught him how to make his eyes the barrier, not the window to his soul. In his time he had stared into eyes behind which there lay no soul whatsoever, and learned from that too. Ryleev's gaze lingered momentarily longer on him, as though he were aware that he would detect nothing, but then moved on. Still no one commented on what he had said.

'It's changed him, being tsar – changed his nature,' he continued.

'It was the war that did that,' said a voice from the back. 'We all went to France and saw what liberty really meant. Aleksandr saw it too. Saw what it would mean for him. He was terrified by it.'

'He *should* be terrified by it,' said another.

'He will be.' This time Aleksei recognized the quiet voice as belonging to Pyotr Grigoryevich Kakhovsky. He had only recently returned to Petersburg, but had quickly become involved with the Society.

Not for the first time, Aleksei noted how much older he himself was than all the others gathered in the room. It was true they all remembered the fall of Paris in 1814, and most could recall Napoleon's occupation of Moscow in 1812, but it would have been their first campaign. By 1812, Aleksei was already a toughened warrior.

'But you raise the problem yourself, Kondraty Fyodorovich,' he said, addressing Ryleev. 'It's not who he is; it's what he is. We may kill Aleksandr, but the tsar will still live. The serfs will still serve. The censor will still censor. We won't have a *duma*, we'll just have Tsar Konstantin instead of Tsar Aleksandr – and for all his faults, I know which I'd prefer.'

Even as he spoke, Aleksei was glancing around his confederates in the comfortable, decadent salon and wondering which of Aleksandr's failings it was that caused them most offence. They were not serfs themselves – nothing like it. Many had estates upon which hundreds of men were bound in labour. Nor were they aristocrats, for the most part, though there were princes amongst them. They were dressed either as gentlemen or as soldiers, and all sat on the elegant French chairs or leaned against the expensively papered walls with the air of men who fitted into society. What they shared was a simple conviction – almost a sense of embarrassment – that compared with the rest of Europe, Russia was still in the Dark Ages.

'We're lucky that Aleksandr has no children – only brothers to succeed him,' said Kakhovsky. Aleksei shot him a questioning look. Kakhovsky smoothed his moustache in a way that hinted at a repressed anger. 'I'd have less stomach to kill children,' he explained.

'Even the death of Grand Duke Konstantin may be unnecessary,' interjected Ryleev. 'If we can act quickly enough, we can take power – either with Konstantin as a puppet, or without him. And then we'll free the serfs, and set up the *duma*, and publish whatever the hell we please.'

'Why wait then, for God's sake?' exploded Kakhovsky. 'The tsar's had his chance. They all have. We have to act! You think Brutus sat around like this, discussing what would happen after Caesar's death?'

Aleksei suspected that was precisely what Brutus had done, but didn't mention it. It was a bad analogy anyway. 'And did it do Brutus any good?' he asked. 'Who took power in the end? Augustus was Caesar's nephew. Brutus helped to found a dynasty, not destroy one.'

'And there lay Brutus's error,' said Ryleev, his manner calming the mood. 'It is not "we" who will be doing the killing. Whoever carries out that task will be a *garde perdue*; a separate body able to take the blame for what has to be done and allowing those of us who envisage a new order to take power.'

'Taking the blame,' said Kakhovsky, his wrath now expressed as a growl rather than a roar, 'but what about the punishment?'

'To be forever devoured by Satan, like Brutus was?' asked a voice. Aleksei smiled to himself; whatever the politics of this group, it was pleasant – and, in Russia, rare – to be amongst a group of men who would have no trouble understanding the reference to Dante.

Ryleev smiled too, but his expression was enigmatic. 'Those who claim power will be magnanimous to those who brought about their rise to power. But in the eyes of the people, the two must be separate.'

It was Aleksei who asked the all-important question, though he had already heard rumours as to the answer.

'When?'

The room quietened. All eyes turned to Ryleev.

'It's too late for this year,' he said. 'In the next few days, the tsar will be leaving for Taganrog.'

'Why's he going there?' asked Kakhovsky.

'We don't know,' admitted Ryleev. 'He claims it is for the tsaritsa's health, but I find that hard to credit. There are some secrets that even our most well-placed sympathizers are not privy to. But he'll be close to the Crimea and the Black Sea. My guess is he wants to strike a deal with the Turks.'

'Not standing by the Greeks, then?' said Kakhovsky. 'They're Christians at least.'

'They're revolutionaries,' explained Ryleev. 'If he helped them to throw off the Ottomans – well, what example would that set?'

'One more reason to get rid of him quickly.'

Ryleev nodded. 'It will happen,' he said. 'And it will happen next year. We may be thirty-seven years behind the French, but no one will blame us for that. 1826 *will* go down in history as the year of the Russian Revolution.'

The meeting broke up early and Aleksei headed home. The sun was bright and warm, as befitted a city like Petersburg, and served only as a reminder of how unRussian a place it was. He walked home along the bank of the Yekaterininsky Canal, his path meandering with that of the waterway. He knew that his wife, Marfa Mihailovna, was expecting him not to be late and that the party which she had planned required his presence – if not his active participation – for its success, but even so, he did not walk too briskly. The reason for the party added a certain irony to the discussions that had just been taking place. Today was 30 August; the feast day of Saint Aleksandr Nevsky, and hence Tsar Aleksandr's name day. Many houses in Petersburg would be holding similar soirées.

The meeting of the Northern Society, as it styled itself, had taken place at the home of Prince Obolensky, in the shadow of the golden domes of Saint Nikolai's. Aleksei had been a member for a long time, almost from its foundation in 1816, when it had gone by the name of the Union of Salvation. Many of the members had come to the organization through Freemasonry, having been initiated into lodges in Paris, but Aleksei had little enough stomach for genuine Orthodox ritual, let alone the pseudo-religious twaddle that was practised in the lodges. It had not been a bar to him joining the Union. The name had changed many times since then, but the aspirations had not – they had merely become more focussed. Once, its political aims had been vague; progressive, certainly, but with the intention of having some influence on the reforms which, back then, Aleksandr was still believed to be planning. For many, Aleksei among them, philosophy and literature had been favoured over politics as matters of debate, and discussions of Brutus and Dante and the like had abounded. When the subject matter of the discussions had changed, many had left, but Aleksei had chosen to remain.

'They're the three greatest heroes of Christianity,' said Maksim Sergeivich, his voice kept low.

He had said it a long, long time before, but Aleksei could place it precisely. They had both been lying on their stomachs on a hot, dry hillside a little to the west of Smolensk, in August of 1812, just days before the city would be abandoned to the French. Maks had died scarcely a month later. 'Maks had died' – expressing it that way made it all so simple. 'Aleksei had left Maks to die' was more accurate. 'Aleksei had left Maks to be slaughtered' was the phrase that best fitted the facts.

But in Smolensk, neither of them would have dreamed of the eventual manner of Maks' death, nor of its proximity. They had been observing the French lines, Aleksei peering through his spyglass, looking for signs of the advance they knew would soon come. Somehow the conversation had turned to Brutus, Cassius and Judas, the three traitors who, in the ninth circle of Dante's Hell, were each consumed throughout eternity by one of the three faces of a Satan himself encased up to his chest in ice. That any of these three could be a hero of Christianity was patently ridiculous, and yet Aleksei knew Maks would not have made the statement without there being a compelling argument behind it.

'I don't think many theologians would agree with you there,' Aleksei had said, looking down and making a brief note of what he could see of the enemy's deployments.

'Really?' said Maks. 'Perhaps I'm wrong.' Anyone who did not know him might have been convinced.

'Go on then,' said Aleksei. 'Start with Judas.'

'That's the easy one.' Maks turned on to his side, instinctively sliding a little way down the hillside to avoid any chance of being seen. 'Without Judas, there would have been no arrest at Gethsemane. Without the arrest, no trial. Without the trial, no crucifixion. Without the crucifixion, no resurrection, and without the resurrection, no Christian religion.'

'That doesn't quite make him a hero. He didn't act for good reasons.'

'His reasons are debatable,' Maks explained, characteristically pushing his spectacles up over the bridge of his nose. 'The gospel of John even has it that Christ *selected* him as the betrayer, and that Satan only entered into him after that, which looks like collusion to me. And yet Christ sits up there at the right hand of God, and Judas ends up in Hell.'

Aleksei had heard this line from Maks more than once over the years since they'd first met; both recruited by Vadim Fyodorovich to a small band to carry out 'special duties'. It was Vadim who had sent them out there, and was waiting back in Smolensk for their report, along with Dmitry Fetyukovich, the final member of the group.

'So what about Brutus and Cassius?' pressed Aleksei. 'Weren't they dead before Christ was even born?'

'When I was a kid,' replied Maks, though Aleksei questioned – would always question – whether he wasn't still a kid, 'I used to marvel at the coincidence that the establishment of the Roman Empire and the birth of Christ were separated by less than thirty years; the political foundation of the Western world and its religious foundation, at the same instant in historical terms. What an age to have been alive! But, of course, it was no coincidence. Rome conquered Europe and delivered both its politics and its religion. OK – Christianity was lucky to be one of the several Roman religions to gain ascendancy, but it wasn't luck that got it spread across the empire. That was military might. And there wouldn't have been a Roman Empire if Brutus and Cassius hadn't tried to prevent there being one.'

'So again, they're heroes, but not by their own intent,' said Aleksei.

'Dupes, really. We know Christ's plan was to die. Maybe Caesar decided it was best to go out on a high note and engineered things the way he wanted them. For both, death made them greater than they had been in life.'

'For Christ, perhaps, but Caesar's death was pretty final.'

'*Julius* Caesar's was, but Caesars have been doing well enough out of it ever since; and kaisers, and tsars.'

'Maybe,' said Aleksei, 'although you can't put the spread of Christianity down just to the Romans. Christianity goes beyond Europe, which they never did.'

'Carried by the British Empire to the north of America and by the Spanish to the south. It's still the same mechanism.'

'And what about the Russians? The Roman Empire never got this far.'

But Maks never answered. He had crawled forward once more to examine the French camp, and had seen something which Aleksei had not. 'My God,' he said. 'They're moving.'

The canal disappeared beneath Nevsky Prospekt, under a bridge far wider than it was long. Aleksei turned off the embankment and on to the city's wide thoroughfare, heading westwards into the setting sun. Ahead of him the yellow-plaster walls of the Admiralty marked the end of the Prospekt, and behind him – several versts behind him – the Nevsky Monastery stood at its beginning. Maks came to his mind less often these days, but was still a frequent visitor. Maks would have been at that meeting tonight, Aleksei was certain – had he lived. He would have been a founder member of the Union of Salvation and would have stuck with it through thick and thin. Some even said he'd have been in charge today, instead of Ryleev. He'd certainly have better understood the implications of what they were planning. Ryleev was just a poet playing at politics.

But Maks had not lived long enough to join with the rest of them in the occupation of Paris in 1814, though he had probably seen the city earlier. The reason Aleksei was so sure Maks would have been a member of the Northern Society was the same one that had condemned him to death in 1812: he was a French spy. The irony of that particular recollection of him – the discussion of Judas and Brutus and Cassius – was that his execution had been carried out by a man who had taken on the name of Christ's betrayer, albeit in its Russian form – Iuda.

But Iuda too had died, a few months after Maks, and the eleven monstrous creatures that had accompanied him – *voordalaki*, who drank the blood of Russians and French alike – had perished also. Iuda himself had been no vampire, but he had been in good company with them. Whatever it was that had driven him to inflict suffering on his fellow man was something more perverse than the mere need for blood, but just as despicable. He was dead though, long dead, and his name was no longer of any interest to Aleksei. He turned off the wide avenue and into Great Konyushennaya Street, where his apartments stood. He could see the light from the tall first-floor windows, and the sound of voices already spilled from within.

He climbed the stairs up from the street and entered his home of almost twenty years, dismissing thoughts of the name Iuda from his mind and turning to a different name which, today at least, was of more concern to him. That name was Vasiliy.

*   *   *

28

It took Aleksei more than a moment to recognize either his drawing room or his wife. Both had undergone a transformation that was evidently intended to please the evening's guests. On consideration, Aleksei preferred what Marfa had done with herself to what she had done with the room. Usually their home was tidy and simple, its comfortable size and central location being expression enough of the degree of wealth required to maintain it. Today, however, it seemed everything they owned was on show. The best crockery and cutlery covered every available flat surface, far more than was needed for the number of guests expected. The only exception was the harpsichord, which neither he nor Marfa would ever dare sully with such clutter.

Marfa herself had opted for simplicity, and a beautiful simplicity at that. She wore a cream satin dress, decorated with only a few tasteful blue ribbons. Her hair was up, adorned with a silver tiara. She was going to be forty in a month's time, but few would suppose it. The fact that she was a little plumper than when he had first known her only served to hide any wrinkles she might have developed. Her hair was still the same dark chestnut it had always been, and few other than her maid and Aleksei himself would have guessed at the efforts she made to keep it so.

He bent forward to kiss her on the cheek and she stepped away from the woman she had been speaking with – whom Aleksei did not recognize – to talk to her husband.

'Have you seen Dmitry?' she asked.

'Is he not here yet?'

'I wouldn't have asked if he was.' Her voice revealed the mild, familiar irritation born of a long marriage.

'He'll be here,' said Aleksei, kissing her again. 'He loves his mother.'

He almost pushed her back to her conversation and turned to eye the room, ostensibly looking for anyone to talk to, but in fact looking for one guest in particular.

My Darling Vasya . . .

The rest of the letter had made clear that there could be no mistaking what Marfa had meant by 'darling'. Aleksei had found the letter, unfinished, folded inside a copy of Diderot's *La Religieuse* in her writing desk two nights before. It was not the kind of book he would have expected her to read – and he knew she would never have expected him to glance at it, which was perhaps why she had trusted it as a safe hiding place. He had not been deliberately spying on her – in fact, he'd been trying to find inspiration for a gift for her upcoming birthday – but espionage was his profession, and so when he had found the letter, he had not hesitated to read it.

There were three Vasiliys at the party, though Aleksei did not know the names of all the men present. He had known none of them ever to use the diminutive 'Vasya'. Vasiliy Pyetrovich was a soldier, like himself – a major in the Moskovsky regiment. He had married only six months before, and his wife, who clutched his hand and never moved from his side as they circulated amongst the guests, was clearly showing the rapid results of their union. Vasiliy Andreevich was a *chinovnik* in the Admiralty, with a reputation as a womanizer. Indeed, Aleksei had met his latest mistress; she was twenty-two years old and stunningly attractive. With all respect to Marfa, Aleksei doubted that she would have caught Vasiliy Andreevich's eye. Vasiliy Borisovich was a striking fifty-year-old of no profession. He lived off his family's estate of five thousand souls – described in the Russian manner of the number of serfs owned, where in the West, as Aleksei well knew, his wealth would be measured by area of land. But however wealthy and attractive he might be, he was an unlikely match for Marfa; he was – as most in the room knew and few cared – a homosexual.

Besides, Marfa's letter had given Aleksei no reason to suppose that Vasiliy would be attending the party. That she wrote to him at all might imply that he did not live in Petersburg, though there had been no clue as to an address.

'You know Yelizaveta Markovna, don't you, Lyosha?' Marfa's

question distracted him from his thoughts. He turned to see the woman he was being introduced to.

'Of course I do,' he replied with an enthusiasm that belied the haziness of his memory of the woman. 'Delighted to see you again.'

'You too, Colonel Danilov. You must be so proud of Dmitry Alekseevich's commission,' said Yelizaveta Markovna, in a voice whose pitch wavered randomly, as though she were almost uncontrollably excited. 'We always said he'd make a soldier – just like his father.'

Aleksei smiled and nodded politely. 'Very proud,' he said, wondering why his voice so utterly failed to convey the sincerity of his feelings. Perhaps it was Yelizaveta Markovna's mistaken conception that Dmitry was entering the same profession as Aleksei. Aleksei knew he had not been a real soldier for a very long time. He noticed both Marfa and Yelizaveta Markovna looking at him, expecting him to say more, but suddenly their heads turned away from him, across the room, to the source of a sound.

It was the harpsichord; the first notes of a sonata by Mozart. The fingers that danced over the keys, deftly sounding melody and countermelody, belonged to Dmitry. He had not announced himself to his parents, but had headed directly for his favourite seat. All in the room gravitated towards him. Aleksei stood at the back of the crowd, scarcely able to see his son, but listening intently. It was a beautiful sound, but what impressed him even more than the music was the easy charm with which Dmitry engaged his listeners. Aleksei was no musician, but if he had been, then playing even the simplest piece would have taken his attention utterly. In contrast, Dmitry smiled at his audience, laughed at their comments and even replied to their questions. When he moved to a new piece – Scarlatti this time – he did so as if it had been a request rather than his own choice, though Aleksei had heard requests only for more Mozart and a few for Beethoven. He was, Aleksei knew well, a showman – something

31

Aleksei could never be. He envied his son for it, but also saw how it could be a weakness, how it would mean that Dmitry would never be a great musician.

When Dmitry stopped playing, an hour and a half later, so the party stopped too. Many had left already, but a core had remained to listen. It was still early, for Petersburg – not yet two in the morning. Aleksei caught in his wife's eye a hint of disappointment that their party did not go on as long as the 'real' parties in the city. The reason was known to both of them, but not discussed. The guests at those parties did not have to work in the morning. Tomorrow – today – was Monday, and government departments had to be run, shops opened, troops drilled. Even those who did not have to work – men such as Vasiliy Borisovich, whose serfs would be set to their tasks by other, more honoured serfs – knew that there were still better parties to be visited before dawn.

'You were superb,' said Marfa to her son, when only the three of them remained.

'Absolutely,' said Aleksei, but he knew that his voice again sounded unconvincing. His sentiment was sincere, but he had never been good at giving compliments, even to – especially to – his own son. 'I don't know where you get it from,' he added, for want of anything to say.

The implication struck Aleksei immediately. His wife had been unfaithful to him with this Vasiliy. How far back did that go? How many others had there been before? Dmitry had been born in 1807, less than ten months after Aleksei and Marfa had married, at a time when Aleksei had been almost constantly on the march. When he had made it home, it had been only for a few days at a time.

But there was no doubt that Dmitry was Aleksei's son. To look at them now, even though Dmitry was eighteen and Aleksei forty-four, the similarities were unmistakable. Both had the same square face and flat chin. Their nostrils flared when they laughed or became angry in a way that caused many to remark upon the resemblance. Dmitry wore his hair shorter and it was naturally darker and straighter. He was considerably taller, taller than most of his countrymen, while Aleksei had a heavier build, though at eighteen, he remembered, he too had been skinny. A life in the army had forced muscle and sinew on to those bones. He hoped the army would do the same for his son – he knew that a life sitting at the harpsichord would not.

It was only Dmitry's eyes that were his mother's. They were the same dark brown that expressed everything that his – or her – face tried to hide. Aleksei's own eyes were blue and – he prided himself – inscrutable. Only one man had ever seemed capable of divining his thoughts, and that man was long dead, his frozen corpse lost amongst so many others as it floated down the Berezina. Even then, Aleksei knew, Iuda had not been able to see into his soul, simply to think like him. From the same starting point he had unerringly managed to reach the same conclusion. That was even more frightening. As for Dmitry, perhaps his eyes too would become opaque as he learned with time to hide his innermost self from others. Aleksei hoped he would never need to, but if he did need to, that he would succeed.

'But you know what you're going to allow me to do with it,' came Dmitry's voice bitterly. He had replied to Aleksei's statement almost instantly, and yet even in that instant, Aleksei's mind had wandered. Dmitry brought him back to a conversation that he never enjoyed, not in any of the dozen times they had had it.

'Mitka, don't start this again,' he said.

'Why not? Because it's something that *you* never dreamed of doing?'

The 'why not?' of it was clear enough to Aleksei, though he would never say it. 'We're not rich, Mitka,' he explained instead. 'You have to live.'

'I'm not asking you for money,' insisted Dmitry. He paused. Money was precisely what he had asked Aleksei for a few months earlier, when this great decision of his life was being made. If Dmitry had been older, or if the two of them had been less close, then a smile would have broken out. Aleksei thought of another

Dmitry, Dmitry Fetyukovich, after whom his son had been named. They had had some terrible arguments, but the last expression that had ever passed between them had been a smile.

'Beethoven's made money,' said Dmitry, changing tack. Aleksei had met Beethoven, briefly, in Vienna in 1817, and heard him play, even though by then he was totally deaf. He knew from that encounter that fame and wealth are all too easily associated in the public mind. Beethoven was not poor, but much of his income came from constant work in both composition and performance, both of which became ever more difficult as his deafness increased. But it was not that which convinced Aleksei that his son could not be a success as a musician. He had heard Beethoven play. He had heard his son play. There was no comparison. Dmitry might scratch a living as a performer in some hostelry. He might even make it to the heights of the pit of an Austrian opera house. Either way, he would earn his real living – a meagre one at that – by teaching. There was nothing wrong with that, but the disappointment would destroy Dmitry, Aleksei was sure. Better to nip it in the bud.

But he explained none of this to his son. 'Beethoven's German. So was Mozart, more or less. Germans and Italians have a chance. The West's like that. You're Russian, for Christ's sake.'

'Have you *heard* of Frederic Chopin?' asked Dmitry, in the way that Aleksei had observed so many children do, in hopeful expectation of their parents' ignorance. Aleksei had heard of him, not least through Dmitry's obsessive reverence.

'He's not Russian.'

'He's Polish,' shouted Dmitry, 'which is as good as – for now. He played for the tsar when he was just eleven. He's destined to be a new Mozart.'

'Mozart was buried in a pauper's grave,' said Aleksei to his son. 'Do you want to spend your life in poverty?'

Dmitry slammed the lid of the harpsichord shut. 'There are some things more important than money!' he shouted, and stormed out. Aleksei heard the door close behind him with a thud.

'He only says that because he's never been short of it,' said Marfa. 'That's thanks to you.'

But Aleksei knew his son was right. There were plenty of things in Aleksei's own life that were more important than money – that was why he spent so many roubles trying to keep hold of them.

Marfa put her arm round his waist and rested her head on his shoulder. 'Let's go to bed,' she said. 'He'll have calmed down in the morning.'

Aleksei considered, but he was too annoyed for sleep. 'You go,' he said. 'I'll be with you soon.' He watched her depart and understood that it was not Dmitry with whom he was angry. Nor – justified though he might be – was it with Marfa. The bitterness inside him could only be directed at one cause, not even at a person, but merely a name: the faceless Vasiliy.

Aleksei gazed out across the Neva. He was at the very heart of Petersburg. This was the point where the river split into two, the Great and Lesser Nevas, part of many divisions as it formed a delta and flowed into the Gulf of Finland. It was a magnificent site. In almost every respect, Aleksei preferred Moscow to Saint Petersburg, but compared to the Neva, the Moskva was a mere ditch. The late-summer sun glistened on the rippling waters that stretched out in a vast azure expanse. The Danube itself could make no claim to be blue in comparison with this. Directly in front of him, at the point of the fork where the rivers divided, stood the two red lighthouses that guided ships into port. Beyond that, north of both rivers, was the Peter and Paul Fortress, founded by Pyotr the Great 122 years before, giving birth to the city itself. Rising from within the walls of the fortress was the yellow-and-gold spire of the Cathedral of Saint Peter and Saint Paul, beneath which lay the tombs of the tsars.

Aleksei turned and looked around. He could see all along the English Quay, the Winter Palace in one direction and the Admiralty and Senate Square in the other. The city was busy, but he did not see the man he was expecting. He looked at his watch. It wasn't quite four in the afternoon, so his contact was not late. Aleksei turned back to the river, leaning forward and resting his hands on the low wall, his fingers splayed out to support his weight – five on his right hand and three on his left. He had been without those two fingers of his left hand now for fifteen years – almost the whole of his son's life.

Dmitry had finally come home in the early hours of the morning, but they had not spoken. There were only a few weeks left to do so before Dmitry had to go and join his regiment in Moscow. Perhaps it would be better to leave things. Dmitry would enjoy the army life, Aleksei was sure, and with luck his resentment would evaporate as he began to immerse himself in it. But Aleksei had often failed to understand his son's character. For the first nine years of his life, Aleksei had only been home briefly and occasionally. Marfa and Dmitry could only know part of the reason.

Up until the French invasion, Aleksei had been a member of an élite band: himself, Maks, Dmitry Fetyukovich and their leader, Vadim. That much was no secret, nor was, in general terms, what they did, though Aleksei rarely shared the details of the spying and the sabotage he undertook, sometimes with his comrades, sometimes alone; never of the assassinations. Then Dmitry Fetyukovich had introduced twelve new allies to the cause. The Oprichniki – that's what they'd called them, after Russia's once-feared secret police. Aleksei had soon discovered their true, inhuman nature, but by then it was too late. Aleksei had been the only survivor – out of either the Oprichniki, or his three friends. He had returned to the regular army, but there was little work left to be done. Bonaparte was already routed.

Peace in Europe had allowed him to spend more time in Russia and, of that, more time in Petersburg, but Aleksei wondered whether even by then it had not been too late. He tried to recall his own father, but the memories were foggy. He had been young – much younger than Dmitry was now – at the time of his father's death. But at least there was a memory of someone; someone who had been present almost every day amongst Aleksei's earliest recollections. He regretted that he had not ensured such a place in his own child's memories. At least he might learn from his mistakes with Dmitry.

'Aleksei Ivanovich.' The voice came from his right. He glanced sideways, to confirm who was speaking.

'Yevgeniy Styepanovich,' he said, looking out across the water and making no further movement to acknowledge the presence of another. Yevgeniy Styepanovich looked upwards, switching his gaze between the high buildings around them, and then squinting, as if trying to focus on the clock on the Admiralty tower. Aleksei suspected that anyone who saw them would not be in the slightest doubt they were talking to one another, but Yevgeniy insisted on at least the formalities of a secret rendezvous.

'Well?' said Yevgeniy.

'I need to see him,' replied Aleksei.

'In person?'

Aleksei nodded. 'I'm afraid so.'

'The official line is that he's already left.'

'And has he?'

Yevgeniy paused. Aleksei could sense his eyes glancing towards him, assessing him. Yevgeniy's fingers fiddled with the braid of his uniform before he spoke. 'He's left the city, yes, but he's still nearby.'

'Where?'

'Right now, he's in Pavlovsk, visiting his mother.'

'And later?'

'He'll be at the dacha on Kamenny Island, but he won't want to see you there.'

Nor I him, thought Aleksei. There would be far too many people. 'Anywhere else?' he asked.

'He'll visit the monastery before he goes.' Yevgeniy blurted the words out quickly, as if it lessened his betrayal.

'Which monastery?' asked Aleksei.

37

'Which monastery?' The sarcasm of Yevgeniy's voice betrayed a hint of scorn. '*His* monastery,' he said.

Aleksei nodded again. It was an odd way to describe it, but it made sense. And Yevgeniy had been right to be sarcastic – there was no question as to which monastery. 'When?' he asked.

'In the early hours. Can't you just give me a message?'

'No,' said Aleksei thoughtfully. 'I have to speak to him.'

Even before the words had left his lips, Aleksei sensed he was alone again. He turned and saw the tall figure in the uniform of a lieutenant general making its way back towards the Winter Palace. Aleksei himself chose to head in the opposite direction, walking downstream alongside the Neva. He had plenty of time before he needed to be at the monastery. He passed the Admiralty and found himself in Senate Square. The Isaakievsky Bridge, floating on the river on its pontoons, stretched north over to Vasilevskiy Island. Aleksei turned away from the river and strode into the square.

He stood at the foot of the statue and looked up. The massive block of granite – the Thunder Stone – that formed its pedestal towered above him. The horse's bronze hooves kicked at the air. Here was Pyotr the Great – founder of the city. That, to Aleksei's mind, as a lover of the old capital, had been his only error. Beyond that, the epithet 'great' truly applied. He had dragged his reluctant country out of its miserable isolation – dragged it both to the West and to the future. Subsequent tsars and tsaritsas had wavered, but none had been able to halt the momentum which Pyotr had begun.

Trampled under the feet of the horse upon which Pyotr rode was a serpent. It symbolized – so the sculptor, Falconet, had claimed – treason, crushed by Russia's rightful emperor. But for Aleksei, the whole image seemed designed to pose Pyotr as Saint George slaying the dragon. True, Saint George had little specifically to do with Petersburg. He was the patron saint of Moscow – but the images and icons of him that were scattered throughout the old capital generally took the same basic form: the saint on horseback, victorious, as the beast writhed in its death throes beneath. Admittedly the beast would have wings and the saint would carry a spear, but these were mere details. Aleksei's mind turned inevitably to Zmyeevich – the 'son of the serpent', if his name was taken literally – who had led the twelve Oprichniki to Russia in 1812. Aleksei could picture the ornate ring that Zmyeevich had worn – a golden serpent with green eyes and a protruding red tongue. He would have liked to compare himself to Saint George, or to Pyotr, but he had never defeated or even confronted Zmyeevich, who had slithered back to his own land.

Aleksei looked up at the statue again, at the tsar's small features. Perhaps the similarity to Saint George was unintentional. Why should Pyotr, the founder of this city, be associated with the patron of Moscow? True, the saint appeared on the escutcheon of the Romanov coat of arms, but again that was due to the connections with Moscow. Anyway, Pyotr had had no choice in the design of the statue; that had been down to his successor Yekaterina, again given the epithet 'great', who had commissioned it. But the same question could be asked of her. That the serpent represented treason made more sense – that, after all, was what every tsar and tsaritsa should fear. And not without reason.

Aleksei walked away, going south across the square, his thoughts set upon that evening's rendezvous.

'They plan to kill you, Your Majesty.'

The voice spoke quietly, but did not whisper. It came from the darkness to the left. The man who uttered the words must have been an arm's reach from the tsar, but he had not seen him. Aleksandr had deliberately let the metropolitan get ahead of him, so that he might be for a moment alone in the bowels of the monastery – a moment of solitude being all that a man in his position could ever hope for.

'Show yourself,' he said firmly. The confidence in his voice was real, born of years of power. Some might think it foolhardy, but it was here that he felt safest of all. This was the monastery of

Saint Aleksandr Nevsky, a saint whose name the tsar bore, in the place where the Lord had revealed Himself to the tsar, through His word, at the time of Russia's direst need. If God was going to protect him anywhere, it would be here.

A face appeared from the gloom. It was a face that was familiar to him, though he could trace its changes over the years. The jaw was still broad, though the skin had gained some wrinkles. The man still wore sideboards, but the light-brown hair was now flecked with grey. When Aleksandr had first seen that face, through monstrous eyes that were not his own, he had felt sure it was the image of an enemy. He had seen it in the flesh many times since, and was now convinced that it belonged to an ally.

'Colonel Danilov,' he said, offering his hand.

Danilov bent forward and kissed it. Aleksandr looked down on him with a certain distaste. He was, after all, a spy. It was not a gentleman's profession, but it was a necessary one. It was best to treat such a man, much like any other soldier, as a tool, to be directed rather than embraced. And yet the vision of him that Aleksandr had seen in 1812 proved that Danilov was more than just a soldier or a spy. Time would reveal the truth.

'I had to speak with you before you left,' said Danilov.

They first had met, in the flesh, just days before Napoleon's abdication – his initial abdication, in 1814 – on the recommendation of Aleksandr's deeply missed field marshal, Prince Barclay de Tolly, who had told him that Danilov, then a captain, had been one of those who had helped to save Moscow. Aleksandr had flinched as he saw that face for a second time, but had not mentioned his recognition of it, nor had he done so since. Danilov had said nothing either, though his presence in Moscow at its darkest hour, just when Aleksandr had seen the apparition, could have been no coincidence. He spoke French perfectly – not the way Russians spoke it perfectly, even the tsar could manage that, but the way the French themselves spoke it. Aleksandr had wanted to get a feel for how the people of Paris were thinking, and Danilov was the ideal man to discover it. He had done his job well, and had continued to work directly for the tsar ever since – though the enemy had changed.

'It's certain then?' said Aleksandr. 'Assassination?'

Danilov nodded. 'It's too late for reform now. It won't assuage them.'

The man was no politician. Aleksandr had learned long ago that reform only encouraged revolutionaries and he'd learned also that reform was not what his people wanted. Above all, they – the Russians, the whole of Europe – craved peace. Aleksandr had given them that, for a decade now. For all but a few of his subjects, it was reason to love him.

'Who will do it?' he asked, leaning forward slightly and tilting his head to listen; since childhood his left ear had perceived almost nothing.

'They talk of a *garde perdue* – a separate group to do the job, without those in charge taking the blame.'

It was sensible – that was how Aleksandr would have done it. Somewhere inside him a voice commented that that was how he *had* done it, but he dismissed the idea. He had never dreamed it would be necessary for his father to be killed.

'How long do I have?'

'At least until next summer.'

'They won't attempt anything while I'm in Taganrog?'

'I doubt it,' replied Danilov. 'The Southern Society is based mostly around Tulchin and Kiev, and that's still a long way away.'

'Can we be sure they trust you? They could be feeding you a line.'

'If they are, you'll know soon enough.' Aleksandr found Danilov's grim sense of humour distasteful at the best of times, but he understood it had been forged out of experience. From what he had heard, Danilov had been part of a squad of sixteen when the French invaded – four officers and twelve men. By the time Napoleon had departed, he was the only survivor.

They fell into silence. Aleksandr pondered the implications of what he had been told. He'd allowed these societies to grow – both in the north and in the south – when he could have crushed them at any time. But to destroy them too soon would have been fruitless. They would have scattered and re-formed. Now, though, the time was approaching when he would deal with them all – before they could move against him.

'I will act when I return from Taganrog,' he said. 'I'll need names by then.' He didn't reveal to Danilov just how many names he knew already. What would be the benefit?

'Unless I can diffuse the situation.'

It was understandable that Danilov saw hope of redemption in these men – he had fought alongside many of them. For Aleksandr a quiet resolution seemed neither probable nor desirable. But if that hope was the price of Danilov's loyalty, it was unwise to disabuse him of it.

'I think you'll find that impossible, Colonel,' said Aleksandr, 'but my prayers will be with you if you can.'

Danilov saluted and the tsar returned the gesture, then he turned and disappeared into the darkness of the passageway. The sound of approaching footsteps came from another direction. Aleksandr turned to see that the metropolitan had come looking for him. He straightened his jacket and marched briskly along the corridor to the front of the monastery.

Outside, his calèche was waiting for him, its three horses shaking their manes as if impatient. It was a humble carriage, but best suited for the journey. His wife, the Tsaritsa Yelizaveta, would follow later in grander style. A small crowd of monks had gathered, and was now joined by the metropolitan.

Aleksandr leapt nonchalantly on to the calèche and hid the pain it caused in his legs and back. He rarely forgot his forty-seven years, but on those occasions when he attempted to, his body soon reminded him. He raised a hand and waved at the assembled holy men.

'Pray for me,' he said. 'And for my wife.'

With that, he heard the sound of the driver's whip and the

carriage began to move. Amongst the crowd, he noticed the shadowy figure of Colonel Danilov observing the departure. There was a man he hoped would do more than pray for his safety.

The tsar remained standing as the calèche drove away. His escort was small and did not block his view. Behind him, the Nevsky Prospekt led straight to the centre of Petersburg, just five versts away. Ahead of him, almost fifteen hundred versts hence, lay Taganrog, and what else, he knew not.

He remained upright, with one foot inside the carriage and one on the running board, looking back the way they had come. Only when the towers of the monastery, lit solely by the stars and the candles that shone dimly from its windows, had vanished from view did he sit down.

The writing was in French. The destination was Ragusa, on the Dalmatian coast. The message was brief:

I have heard from Saint Petersburg. He is on his way.

CHAPTER II

DMITRY FELT THE KEYS BENEATH HIS HANDS. ONLY HIS TWO ring fingers did not make contact. The chord was C minor: C-E♭-G-C in the left hand, the same in the right. He had not chosen it for any particular reason, but his hands came to rest there naturally. He closed his eyes and waited.

He sat still at the harpsichord for over five minutes, in complete silence, his fingers touching the keys but not striking them. Music danced through his mind, as clearly audible as if it were being performed in the very room in which he sat. Orchestras poured out their melody, along with pianofortes, church organs, even human voices. Tunes never before played leapt from instrument to instrument, sometimes imitating familiar styles, sometimes in forms that would scarcely be thought of as music.

It was no special gift; he knew many other musicians who spoke of the same sensation, something they could call to themselves almost at will. Lying in bed at night, it always came, but even in daylight, as Dmitry walked down the street, or in the middle of a conversation that did not interest him, he could summon it. The summons was his, but after that, the music was not his to master. He knew that it was a creation of his own mind, but he made no conscious decision as to its path or pattern. The composition was instinctive, as instinctive as hunger or lust or anger. He could neither prevent it nor control it.

But whenever the music came, it came only to tease him. In

his life, Dmitry must have heard hundreds of hours – thousands – played inside his head, never repeating, never disappointing. But not a single note had ever made it out to be heard by any human ear. It was not influenced by consciousness and so, just as he could not direct it, neither could he analyse it, remember it, or even slow it down to a manageable tempo.

He had tried playing it at the keyboard; he had tried writing it down on paper. He had even attempted to sing it out loud so that another could transcribe it. But the music could not be contained. It fled on at its own pace, oblivious of the fact that in so doing it destroyed its own chances of immortality. Of course, he could pick out a note here and there, but what did that help? There were only twelve notes to choose from in total; the beauty did not lie within them but in their combination and permutation.

He pressed down on the keyboard and the chord sounded. It was a pleasant sound – melancholy, as a minor chord should be, but still harmonious. But it was not a new creation. It had no context, no before and no after to make it more than itself; a tableau that failed to tell the story of the play.

Dmitry lifted his fingers from the keyboard and the sound stopped. The music inside him had stopped too, not as he released the keys, but as he had first pressed them, banished as a ghost by its living cousin. It was always that way. But it must have gone somewhere. If only that place could be his fingers. He moved his right hand down the keyboard, still forming a C minor, but in a different inversion. All he needed to do was forget himself, to stop trying to listen to the music, to intercept it and capture it, instead simply to let it flow from him. He had attempted it so many times before, but he knew it would work one day – had to work. It didn't matter if it was never written down, just to make the air vibrate for a few brief minutes to the sound of his music would be enough. And if that barrier could be broken, perhaps the rest would come easily.

He closed his eyes again and played. C minor. Then the same chord again. His hands moved up the keyboard – he had not asked them to – and played a G. Then C minor again, a diminished C and another G. His fingers moved as if they knew where they were going, through no direction of his; a diminished A$^\flat$ now. The music began to smother him – control him. It was as if the harpsichord were dragging his creation from him, as though his blood were being drained from his veins, as though he were experiencing a slow, drawn-out orgasm that would leave him empty, as if the production of that music would kill him – and yet he did not want to stop. And the sound that he produced was wonderful. More than wonderful, it was sublime. It was brilliant. It was beautiful.

It was Beethoven. His hands moved of their own volition not out of inspiration but through repetition. He had played it so often during his life that now his hands knew it better than he did. Sonata in C minor, number 8 – the *Pathétique*. Of course it was wonderful, and brilliant, and beautiful. But it was not Dmitry's. The one concept followed inescapably from the other.

He let his hands play on, drowning out the possibility of any of his own music entering his mind. His right hand scurried over the high notes while his left thumped out the low, rhythmic chords. It was not really a suitable piece for a harpsichord. His left hand frequently stabbed for a low note that didn't exist on the short keyboard, but beyond that, the tone of the instrument was quite unsuitable for this stormy piece. He moved on to the *allegro* and played it far too fast, deliberately pushing himself to the limits of his technique. His left hand flickered over the bass tremolo like a trapped butterfly, while his right appeared merely to slap the keyboard repeatedly, but each time his fingers found the correct notes.

As he played he cursed his father, cursed him for being too mean to replace this ancient instrument with a pianoforte, cursed him for forcing him into the army, and above all for not believing precisely what Dmitry himself did not believe – that he could make a career as a musician.

His fingers moved ever faster, ignoring the faults in the

instrument beneath them and the cramp that was developing in his forearms. At least, while they played, the sound of his own music could not return to taunt him.

Aleksei lay back in his chair and listened to the muffled sound of the harpsichord from across the hallway. Dmitry was showing off, he could tell, playing at that sort of speed. And what was wrong with that? He had plenty to show off with – enormous accuracy and dexterity. It wasn't enough to make Dmitry into a great musician, but Aleksei hoped it was enough to make him happy. The very sound of it made Aleksei happy, made him for a moment forget those things that caused distress in his life.

He looked across the room at Marfa and smiled. She had been reading, but noticed his movement and looked up at him. She seemed embarrassed at his stare, and he was reminded of how she was more than twenty years ago, before they were married, when his glance at her across a crowded room would have caused her heart to pound and her face to flush behind the powder, little though he had been aware of it. Memories of his feelings for her back then began to push themselves into his mind, passionate feelings that had long since been replaced by mere affection – still more than many couples had left between them.

She returned his smile, and he wondered whether it was now in response to Vasiliy's glance that her heart beat faster and her cheek reddened. When he was younger, when he had been in love with her, the thought of Vasiliy – of anyone with her – would have enraged him. He would have challenged Vasiliy to a duel and – had he survived, which he little doubted – he would then have cast Marfa aside, unable to forgive her. Did that show how much or how little he loved her? Would he have gone further? Had he loved her enough to kill her? Aleksei had faced that dilemma once, not with Marfa, but with another woman. He had not killed, but not for want of love.

Today, he had no urge to face a duel with Vasiliy, no desire to cast Marfa out of his home. Was he too forgiving, or was it mere indifference? He knew he should confront Marfa, if only to discover which of those two it was, if only to show her that he cared enough to object. But with Dmitry's music filling the house, he felt too relaxed to be concerned with it now.

Even his concerns for the tsar's safety seemed far from urgent. It had been almost two weeks since he had spoken to Aleksandr in the Nevsky Monastery. He smiled to himself. The last time he had gone there, it had been for a very different reason. He'd heard the story of an old monk who lived there – a monk who slept each night in a coffin. The implication was obvious, but Aleksei had been wise enough to test the theory before acting. A glimpse of the old man kneeling in prayer outside one of the chapels in the full glare of the sun had been ample evidence.

It wasn't the first time since 1812 that he had gone in search of a *voordalak*. In the intervening years he had investigated every rumour he had come across that might just hint at the presence of a vampire. All had proved to be false alarms. He had not gone out of his way in search of them, had not travelled deep into the Carpathians – where he knew he would find them – to hunt them down. If they did not come to him, he would not go to them. Most people were lucky enough never to encounter a *voordalak* in their whole lives. It would be unkind of fate if he were to meet such creatures twice.

As for the tsar, he would be almost at his destination by now. He should be safe for the winter. And there was more that Aleksei could do to make his safety permanent.

Five menacing chords in sequence ended the first movement of the sonata. It was not suited to the harpsichord, thought Aleksei. He would do something about that. In the meantime, he relaxed as Dmitry began the *adagio cantabile*.

The small black calèche had come to feel like home. It had been a speedy journey – just thirteen days to travel from the top of his country to its bottom. To have traversed Russia in the other direction – from west to east – would have taken months. He had been joined soon after leaving Petersburg by a small entourage, amongst them his chief of staff, Baron Diebich, two doctors – Tarasov and the Scotsman Wylie – along with his valet, Anisimov, and other personal staff.

A larger court would arrive with the tsaritsa. She had departed the capital only a few days after Aleksandr, but would travel at a gentler pace. Her health had, for Aleksandr, been only an excuse to come to Taganrog, but it was an issue nonetheless. It had been easy enough to persuade Wylie to suggest the town as a suitable location for a winter convalescence. She certainly could not stay in the capital. The flooding of the Neva the previous winter had been the worst that any could remember, and much of the city had not recovered. It was not the place for a woman in his wife's frail condition. Nor would she be able to face a recurrence of the deluge this year, which was a strong possibility.

The whole way from Petersburg, at each post house they called at, Aleksandr had checked that the accommodation would be suitable for the tsaritsa and sent a note back to her describing the best route to take. Moreover, he had left her in the care of Prince Volkonsky, despite the degree to which he would have appreciated the companionship and counsel of Pyotr Mihailovich himself. They would both be with him in a week or so.

It had been seven years since he had visited the town of Taganrog, and then only briefly. It had not changed much. Aleksandr looked out over the Sea of Azov. It was calm today, but he had heard it could grow stormy. To the east, though he could not see it, the river Don emptied into the sea, having risen in the heart of the country. To the south, the narrow Strait of Kerch opened into the Black Sea, and beyond that lay the whole world.

The accommodation was humble for a tsar and his consort, but he was satisfied with it. In his youth he might have raised hell, demanding that some more appropriate residence be found – or built – but not today. Whatever he thought of it, it was a palace, by simple virtue of the fact that he inhabited it. It was just one storey high, with fewer than twenty rooms, though the basement

49

had additional ones for the staff. Aleksandr wandered through the building, selecting half a dozen or more rooms that could be allocated to the tsaritsa. He then looked for the room that he would make his study. There was a possibility on the north side of the house, but as soon as Aleksandr glimpsed the view he dismissed it. The skyline of Taganrog was dreary. He could count only six spires and a couple of domes which broke the monotony. How unlike either of his two capitals.

The room on the south side was smaller, but it would suit him. He could see the garden and, beyond that, the sea. He sat down and gazed across the water once again, with but one question on his mind. Why had he come here?

News travelled rapidly, even on the borders of the empire. It was less than a day before reports of the arrival reached the Crimean peninsula – the eastern shore of the Sea of Azov. This letter was just as brief as the last, written in the same hand, to the same address in Ragusa.

He is here. Come at once.

Aleksei had heard nothing for over half an hour, though in truth he had no way of determining how much time had passed. The cupboard was windowless, and although a dim light had for a while seeped under the door, once that had been extinguished, it was impossible for him to see his watch, or even his own hand in front of his face.

He had been glad to leave the meeting early. The same arguments had been churned over once again, with no new conclusions being reached. Pestel was by far the smartest amongst them. Aleksei had read his manifesto, '*Russkaya Pravda*' – 'Russian Justice'. There was plenty of it that Aleksei did not agree with, such as the expulsion of the Jews to Asia Minor and the forced Russification of every nationality in the empire, but at the very least it did show the vision of someone genuinely planning to create a new form of government for the country. There were real plans for how to abolish serfdom – without leaving millions of former serfs to simply starve – for freedom of expression and for the equality of all before the law. Ryleev and Muraviev and the others had no such clear plans. They were just romantics who wanted to imitate Byron. They risked meeting the same fate, and would probably revel in it.

Fortunately for the tsar, for anyone who would prefer to let Russia remain in its current state, Pestel was leader of the Southern Society, not the Northern, and while that might put him within striking distance of Aleksandr, the real struggle for political power would take place in Petersburg. It was lucky for Aleksei too; Pestel was one of the few who might be smart enough to see through him. In the north, there was no one, except perhaps the newcomer, Kakhovsky. He was not smart, but he had a certain animal cunning.

Kakhovsky had been the last to leave, from what Aleksei could hear. Having given his excuses, Aleksei had made his own way out of Prince Obolensky's house. It was usual practice not to be seen out by servants, whose tongues might in gossip give away their names. Thus, it had been a simple matter to slip into the small cupboard, full of winter clothes that would not be needed for a month or two. The meeting had gone on for another hour or so, the members occasionally raising their voices loud enough that Aleksei could make out individual words, but mostly just producing a quiet hubbub that revealed they were still there. Then they had begun to leave. Finally, Aleksei had heard Kakhovsky talking alone to Obolensky, just on the other side of the door. He caught only one sentence.

'I will do it, if need be.'

Then there was a pause, with no sound of movement. Aleksei pressed himself back against the wall, hiding amongst the furs, for fear that, operating on some sixth sense, Kakhovsky would open the door of the cupboard. Within moments, he heard their footsteps begin again, followed by farewells and the slamming of the front door. There were a few more noises as Obolensky pottered around before making his way to bed, and then silence.

Aleksei stepped out into the corridor. A patch of moonlight that had entered through the window above the front door was the only illumination. He crept over to it and checked his pocket watch. He had been in the cupboard almost two hours. Obolensky's study was to the left, beyond the room in which the meeting had taken place. The door was closed, but made no sound as Aleksei turned its handle and pushed it aside. Here, on the other side of the building, there was no moonlight. Aleksei could just make out a lamp on the desk, which he lit, keeping the flame guttering at its lowest, for fear that even the slightest brightness in the house would attract attention.

Aleksei knew what he was looking for. Ryleev had waved it in front of them earlier that evening.

'We are not alone,' he had said. 'We are not an enlightened few standing against the masses. The people, we know, are with us, for we are with them. But even amongst the nobility, we have many friends. This list' – and this was the moment he had shown them the papers – 'contains the names of all our friends in the north. In Kiev, Pestel has a similar list, twice as long. When the time comes, we will be the *bolsheviki* – the majority will be with us.'

Aleksei had caught a glimpse of Ryleev taking it into Obolensky's study and returning empty-handed. It did not take him long to find. It was in the right-hand drawer of the desk, beneath an invoice from a tailor's shop. There were five sheets in all – over one hundred names – the entire organization in the north. Aleksei folded it into three and slipped it into his pocket. Of course, he knew he shouldn't take it, he should copy it. Vadim Fyodorovich, his mentor in the world of espionage, had taught him that much. Even if there was no time for that now, he should copy it at home and return the original before it was missed.

But Aleksei's plan was not as straightforward as that. He did not simply desire a list he could hand over to the tsar. He wanted the absence of the list to be noted. If Ryleev, Obolensky and the others realized that their organization was compromised, that at any moment they might expect a visit from the gendarmerie, then they might abandon the whole ill-founded idea of assassination and return to doing what it was they knew best. Aleksei had no desire to see the tsar murdered, but there were many ways in which he might prevent it. Vadim would have admired the ingenuity of such a double effect, though they would have argued as to which was the intended consequence and which the side-effect.

Vadim was another of Aleksei's comrades who had died badly in 1812.

Aleksei extinguished the lamp and left the room, closing the door quietly behind him. The light of the full moon still illuminated the front door at the end of the corridor. He walked rapidly and silently towards it, but then stopped. The grey moonlight was not all that he could see. It had been joined by an orange glow, which became gradually brighter. He stepped back into the shadows, just glimpsing the figure which descended the stairs carrying a candle.

As the man came past him, he recognized it to be Obolensky. He was more than ten years younger than Aleksei, but Aleksei had no doubt he could beat him in a fight – it would be better than trying to outrun him. But if he were to take him on, Aleksei would have to do it without his face being seen. While it served his purposes for the conspirators to know they were discovered, he did not want them to know who it was who had betrayed them. He could, of course, kill Obolensky, but to do so would be unnecessarily cruel.

Obolensky had walked past without noticing him, and continued down the corridor. A sudden fear gripped Aleksei. If Obolensky went into his study now and discovered the theft, he would raise the alarm. Whilst Aleksei could easily have defeated him on his own, taking on the entire household would be a different matter. But Obolensky turned away from the study, heading towards the kitchen. Aleksei gave him a few more moments to get suitably far away, then made for the door. He was out of the house in seconds, and walking through the streets of Petersburg.

His journey home followed the same route as that of several weeks before. The broken image of the moon shone up at him from the dark waters of the Yekaterininsky Canal. Once out of Obolensky's house, he had no need for stealth; the city was not bustling, but a lone figure making its way home as if from some decadent soirée would not seem out of place. His thoughts turned once again to Vadim. Even though they had both been dead now for thirteen years, and they were not on his mind as once they had been, he thought often of Maks and not infrequently of Vadim. Dmitry Fetyukovich came to his mind less regularly. It was hard to determine why. In many ways, he and Dmitry had been closest of all. In 1805, on the eve of the Battle of Austerlitz, Dmitry had saved Aleksei's life. That was why Aleksei had named his own son Dmitry, in honour of his friend.

But still, Aleksei's memories of his friends were biased by how he had last known them. Maks he had discovered to be a spy, but had forgiven. Vadim had never changed – a rock by which Aleksei could navigate his whole life. But Aleksei had come to doubt Dmitry and had only just started to become reconciled to him before his death. Dmitry had brought the twelve creatures they had known as the Oprichniki to Russia – eleven creatures and one human, each taking his nom de guerre from one of the twelve apostles.

Dmitry had eventually come round to see the horror of the mistake he had made in trusting the Oprichniki, but even when he died, frozen by the cruel winter that had taken such a toll on Bonaparte's retreating army, Aleksei had not been quite sure where his loyalties truly lay, beyond the suspicion that Dmitry's loyalties ultimately had always lain with Dmitry.

Vadim, Aleksei, Dmitry and Maks; they had been quite a team. Or just В, А, Д and М, as they'd identified themselves in the brief messages they had used to coordinate their activities across Moscow and beyond. Aleksei realized he had never worked in a team since; not in that way. He had fought as part of the regular army as Bonaparte retreated across Europe, but as far as espionage was concerned, he had always worked alone. At the Winter Palace, Yevgeniy Styepanovich was an informant, not a colleague. And the members of the Northern Society might see Aleksei as a *tovarishch*, but they would one day discover the truth.

Aleksei reached his front door. He could still smell the mould and damp from last year's floods. Fortunately, he occupied none of the ground-floor rooms in the building. There were good reasons the upper storeys were more expensive. Many of the shops at street level were still unoccupied. The smell barely penetrated into his own home. He climbed the steps to his apartment and went inside. He did not feel tired, so went to his study and lit the lamp before going over to the cabinet and pouring himself a brandy.

It was only when he turned around that he saw it.

It was odd that he had just been thinking of the coded messages they used to leave for each other in Moscow. This was different, of course. The characters were as tall as he was, and scrawled in red across the wooden panels of his study wall. But the style of the message was chillingly familiar.

$$9 - 22 - 14 - Ж4 - М$$

CHAPTER III

DMITRY'S FATHER WAS SITTING IN HIS CHAIR WITH A STRANGE rigidity. His knuckles were white as his fingers dug into its arms. He stared directly in front of him. Dmitry had only glanced into the study on his way to bed after a night – yet another night – of saying goodbye to his Petersburg friends. He was slightly drunk, but few would notice – that was something he shared with his father. He stepped into the room.

'Are you all right, Papa?'

Aleksei did not reply. The slightest nod of his head indicated to Dmitry that he should follow his father's stare. Dmitry stepped further into the room and turned. He could not miss the writing.

$$9 - 22 - 14 - Ж4 - M$$

It covered two walls, the corner of the room lying between the number 14 and the letter Ж. Dmitry approached it, reaching out his hand to touch. The lettering felt dry, and smeared when he rubbed it. He suspected it was some kind of pastel. He stepped back again to view the text as a whole. It was clearly intended to mean something, but he could not fathom what.

'It's from your Uncle Maks.' His father's voice cut through the room, louder than was necessary, monotone and grating, as if he was trying hard to keep it under control.

Dmitry did not remember his Uncle Maks. He'd been told by

his parents that Maks had been a frequent visitor to their home when he was young, but he could not have been more than four years old at his last visit. Both his mother and father had shown a great affection for him, but they had not spared their son the truth about him – he was a traitor, a French spy. The other thing Dmitry remembered with certainty about Uncle Maks was that he had died in 1812.

'Maks is dead,' said Dmitry.

'I hope so,' said Aleksei. Dmitry glanced round at him, but Aleksei did not explain what he meant by the comment. 'The trouble is,' he said instead, 'that everyone who knew what that code means is dead: Vadim, Maks, Dmitry Fetyukovich, and the others – all of them, except me.'

'What *does* it mean?'

'It's very simple. Those first three numbers are a date and time: month, day, hour. Then there's a letter and number combination indicating a place, then a final initial, by way of a signature.'

Dmitry looked at the message again and spoke his thoughts out loud. 'So that's 22 September, the fourteenth hour – two in the afternoon. And it's from Maks. How do you decode the location?'

'There's no real system there,' said Aleksei. 'It was just a list – dozens of places in Moscow, and all around it.'

'Do you still have it – the list?'

'We destroyed it once we'd memorized it.'

'Forgotten now, I suppose,' said Dmitry.

'Mostly. But I remember Ж4. It's a woodsman's hut, near a town called Desna, south of Moscow. At least it was – it's been a long time.'

'Why do you remember that one?'

Aleksei paused. Dmitry had always thought his father an un-emotional man – a temperament quite different from his own – but the fact was that Aleksei did not lack emotions, he merely concealed them, desperately. Dmitry only understood that now, as he saw that concealment beginning to break down. Finally, Aleksei spoke.

'Because that's where Maks is buried – where he died. That's the only place he could meet anyone.'

'It's not from Maks, Papa.'

Aleksei's rigid posture relaxed suddenly, as though Dmitry's assertion had at last brought rationality back to him. He leapt to his feet. 'You're right. It can't be from Maks. So who is it from?'

'You said everyone who knew about the code is dead – except you.'

'I believe so, but that doesn't mean no one told anyone else. Not one of us – one of them.'

'Them?' asked Dmitry.

'The Oprichniki – that's what we called them. Twelve mercenaries from Wallachia. But they betrayed us. Maks was the first to see what was happening.'

'So Uncle Maks wasn't spying for the French?'

'Oh, he was. And at the time, that's all we could think about – all I could think about. I left it to the Oprichniki to execute him.'

'In Desna?'

Aleksei nodded. 'Later they killed Vadim.'

'And Uncle Dmitry?'

'No, the Russian winter killed him,' said Aleksei, 'but it was still down to them.'

'Who might they have told?'

Aleksei shrugged. 'Perhaps their leader, Zmyeevich.'

'He survived?'

'We only met him briefly. He delivered them to Moscow and then returned home – I presume. They wouldn't have had a chance then to tell him, but they could easily have sent him the information. But why would he want it? And why use it now?'

'You're going to go and find out, aren't you?' Dmitry might have resented his father's willingness to abandon his family in

58

pursuit of adventure, but he knew him well enough to understand that he could not change it.

Aleksei gave his son a smile that Dmitry didn't think he'd seen since he was four years old, not directed towards him at least. 'Do you want to come with me?'

Dmitry scarcely needed to think about it. 'I have to go to Moscow anyway.'

Aleksei smiled broadly. 'Good,' he said. 'Now go and get some water and a couple of brushes.'

'What?'

'I don't think we want your mother to see this, do we?'

It took almost two hours to get the walls completely clean. Dmitry had not felt as close to his father for many years.

Aleksei had been in a hurry to set out for Desna, but his appointment was set for the twenty-second, and no rushing across the country at breakneck pace would change that. For him, a sudden departure from Petersburg such as this was nothing unusual. For most of his life he had been prepared and able to pack up the most meagre selection of his possessions and leave one city for another without more than a moment's consideration. An emergency supply of gold coins sewn into his belt provided for most things he could not bring with him.

And so if it had just been down to him, Aleksei would have been happily ready to depart within hours of reading the message – and happier still that such haste would give him even more time to spend in Moscow. But he knew that for his son the departure from his home was a much more serious step. Dmitry had spent the last two days visiting his tailor, traversing the city saying goodbye to friends and attempting to console his dismayed mother. Now that there were only a few hours remaining before their departure, he was doing what he should have been doing all along – packing.

Aleksei went into his son's room. Dmitry was on his knees, bent over an old trunk full of books and toys and childhood memories which, in truth, probably evoked greater feelings of nostalgia in the father than they did in the son. Dmitry heard the footsteps behind him and turned briefly to smile at Aleksei.

Aleksei walked closer to peer over Dmitry's shoulder and into the box. There was a model boat, a wooden whistle – his first musical instrument – and a book of Perrault's fairy tales. Each item brought a different smile to Aleksei's lips. He bent forward to see more, squinting to focus on the dark mass of items. Suddenly his blood ran cold.

'My God, Mitka. What are you doing with that?'

Dmitry turned again. In his hand he clutched a sword – a short, wooden sword, no longer than a large dagger. The tip was whittled to a point which time had blunted, but which could easily be made once again fit for purpose. The guard was merely another short strip of wood lashed to the blade with twine, intended less to protect the wielder's hand than to allow it to apply greater force. Aleksei had made and used such a tool before. It was designed to kill, but not to kill a man.

'Don't you remember, Papa?' said Dmitry, standing up. He began fencing with the sword against an imaginary opponent. 'You made this for me, years ago – when I was a kid.'

The recollection came back to Aleksei. When he whittled away at those vampire-killing swords, he remembered having made a similar one as a toy for his son. The form was much the same, however different the purpose.

'You loved the idea of being a soldier back then,' he said.

'I grew up,' said Dmitry, then relented. 'But I'm sure I will enjoy it.'

'If I'd been better at woodwork, I'd have made you a piano.'

Dmitry smiled, but said nothing.

'Are you taking it with you then?' asked Aleksei.

'I think I'm old enough for a real one now.'

'Do you mind if I keep it?' The request was not a sentimental one. Aleksei had no idea what he would find in Desna, but he knew it had some connection with the creatures he had met thirteen years before. It was reassuring that the meeting was to take place in daylight, but with such a weapon he would feel far more comfortable. 'Just as a reminder,' he added, for his son's benefit.

Dmitry studied his father, but saw nothing beyond the obvious in the request. 'There you are,' he said, handing the sword over with a shrug and a smile.

A few hours later, they said their farewells to Marfa. It was a tearful occasion, on her part at least, and Aleksei thought he perceived a glistening in Dmitry's eye too. For himself, he felt no especial emotion beyond what was normal for his departures from home, beyond that feeling of giddy anticipation he had felt about visiting Moscow since even before he had any specific reason to and whose causes had multiplied over the years. His goodbye to Marfa was no different from what it had always been, and as for Dmitry, they were not yet to part.

Marfa had recomposed herself by the time she kissed her husband's lips, stroked his hair and let his fingers linger briefly in hers. There had been no tears between them for many years, and her kisses had long since lost the passion of a soldier's new bride. Aleksei had always supposed she contained her emotion for his sake, so that he would not feel so callous in leaving her, but now he knew that the cause was different.

How long after his departure, he wondered, would it be before Marfa found herself in the arms of Vasiliy, her lover?

Most likely no longer than it would be before Aleksei was in the arms of his.

The journey to Moscow took four days. Aleksei complained all the way that they would have travelled more quickly on horse-back, but Dmitry suspected that, at his age, his father was quite happy to be driven in the comfort of a carriage. Even if the two men had chosen to ride the whole journey, they would still have required a carriage of some sort to follow them, bringing Dmitry's copious luggage. It amazed Dmitry that his father could travel with so little, but the explanation offered was that Aleksei was such a frequent visitor to the old capital that he kept all that he required in terms of clothing and other essentials at his usual residence there.

It was not Dmitry's first visit to Moscow, but he was by no means familiar with the city. As they approached, and increasingly as their carriage trundled through the outskirts, Aleksei sat up, his head pushed out the window, resembling nothing so much as an excited pet dog recognizing its environs and realizing it will soon be home. At almost every turn he would point out a brand-new building, a newly reconstructed one, or one that he had never seen before, or perhaps only seen once or twice. Many of them were simply houses or shops, but he seemed to observe every detail that had changed since his last visit.

'Of course, it's the theatres that everyone's talking about,' he said as they drove down Tverskaya Street to the centre of the city. 'The Bolshoi only opened in January. I've seen it, but I haven't been in yet.' His eyes tracked sideways for a moment, gazing down a small lane to the left as they passed, then returned to the road ahead. 'We'll see them both in a minute.'

'It's hard to believe it was ever how you described it,' said Dmitry. He had been just five years old when the fires – caused, directly or indirectly, by the invading French – had destroyed two-thirds of the city's buildings. His father's passion in describing both the horror of that carnage and the joy of the subsequent resurrection was always a delight to hear. Dmitry knew, of course, that there was some exaggeration in it. Aleksei described the fires as if he had been standing right in front of them, as if he could feel their heat on his face. But Dmitry knew his father, along with the rest of the Russian army, could not have been in Moscow at the time of the occupation. At best he could have witnessed the conflagration from several versts away. That was just part of the skill Aleksei had in telling the stories.

'When did we first come here?' Aleksei asked.

'1820.'

'Even by then, there had been so much done. Most of the private homes were rebuilt within a few years.'

'There are still some that haven't been,' said Dmitry, pointing to a gap between two new buildings where rubble and charred wood were still visible. Not even a fence separated it from the street.

Aleksei nodded. 'Some people just decided not to come back home,' he said wistfully. They rode on in silence for no more than half a minute. Dmitry had just caught sight of one of the Kremlin towers, though he did not know which one, when his father pulled his arm and pointed in the other direction.

'There it is! Look!' he exclaimed excitedly. The Bolshoi Theatre was certainly impressive. The stone colonnade of the entrance, topped by a bronze quadriga, gave exactly the impression that was intended – exactly what the tsar had paid for. Beyond it, the Maly Theatre was less ostentatious, but presumably served its customers just as well. 'Worthy of Paris,' said Aleksei.

The coach turned right, past the Kremlin, and headed down towards the river. Aleksei leaned over and pointed out of the right-hand window. 'That's the manège. You'll be spending a lot of your time training in there.'

Dmitry smiled. His father had pointed out the half-finished riding school to him on his first visit. Now it was complete. 'You said exactly the same thing to me when I was thirteen,' he said.

Aleksei seemed too enthralled with his surroundings to listen. 'Of course, there used to be a river flowing down here,' he explained, pointing back out of his side of the carriage, to the gardens at the foot of the Kremlin wall. 'The Neglinnaya. Just a sewer really – stank to high heaven. Still is a sewer, I suppose. At least now it's covered over. I wonder if we can see where it comes out.'

As the carriage clattered on to the Stone Bridge, Aleksei leaned far out of the window and looked back the way they had come. They were almost halfway across when he sat back down.

'No, couldn't see it,' he said with a brief shake of his head.

He was smiling broadly, in a way that Dmitry had rarely seen in Petersburg.

'You like it here, don't you?' Dmitry asked.

'So will you, Mitka. So will you.' His father's tone did not suggest that this was an attempt to persuade him – just a statement of the obvious.

The coach drove over the river and over the canal and into Zamoskvorechye. Soon they pulled up outside a hotel. It was not the grandest the city had to offer. Aleksei jumped out on to the street. The coachman dismounted more slowly.

'So this is where you usually stay?' asked Dmitry. On their visits as a family, they had stayed in a somewhat grander residence, north of the river.

'Yes, since the war.' The coachman gave Aleksei his single leather bag. 'Before that it used to be a place in Tverskaya, but that half burned down. They demolished the rest, eventually.'

The coachman had remounted, and shook the horses' reins. 'And we'll meet here, tomorrow?' said Dmitry, as the coach pulled away.

'Yes. Eight o'clock,' shouted Aleksei after him. 'And then on to Desna.'

Dmitry watched his father's image recede for a few moments before settling back into his seat. Before long he would be at his barracks, and a new life would begin for him. He smiled. His father's enthusiasm had infected him. Perhaps an army life wouldn't be so bad.

Aleksei had unpacked, changed his clothes and was out of the hotel again within eight minutes. He chose to walk. It wasn't far; back across the Stone Bridge and then west towards the Arbat. One might have thought Aleksei had chosen his hotel, back in 1816 when he first stayed there, for its convenience, but that was not the case. Back then, the house for which he was now heading had not even been built. The proximity which he had sought had been in the opposite direction, to a street in Zamoskvorechye occupied almost exclusively by milliner's shops, and to one shop in particular.

But that was in the past. Today, as he had done within moments of his every arrival in Moscow in the last four years, he strode purposefully west. He recalled how, many years before, he had always teased himself as to where he might go the moment he arrived in the city. Later, after 1812, he had abandoned such pretence, not because his sense of guilt was any less, but merely because he had become better at suppressing it. Since 1821, he had felt no guilt.

He walked up the five stone steps to the door of the house in a wealthy street in the south of the region, and rapped on the heavy iron knocker with three short, close reports. Then he waited. From within he heard the sound of slow, steady steps making their way towards the door, quickly overridden by lighter, less careful footsteps racing down a flight of stairs.

The door was opened and the face of an elderly butler was revealed behind it. Within an instant, the door, along with the butler, had been pushed further aside by the energetic advance of a pile of unkempt black hair which topped an unsuitably tall, unsuitably lean body.

'Aleksei Ivanovich!'

A year or two before, the boy would have leapt into Aleksei's arms, but today, regardless of how socially inappropriate that might have seemed for a boy who was almost a man, the physical action itself would have sent them both tumbling down the steps and back on to the street. Instead, Aleksei walked into the house, his arms widening as he responded to the greeting.

'Rodion Valentinovich! Haven't you grown?' There was a time in Aleksei's life when he would have despised such an inane, rhetorical question, both as its source and its recipient, but he was old enough to know that that period began some time after the age of thirteen and ended before the age of forty-four. For Rodion, it was an issue that had not yet arisen. They embraced briefly, but Rodion was soon rushing away towards the back of the house. Aleksei handed his overcoat to the servant who still stood at the door, and then turned in pursuit of the boy.

He remembered the way to the drawing room perfectly well, and entered to find the figures of four people whom he knew and loved, four figures that seemed to make, much as the thought displeased him, a perfect family. Rodion stood – unable to remain quite still – behind the sofa on which his parents were seated. His father, Valentin Valentinovich, rose to greet Aleksei as he entered. Yelena Vadimovna remained seated, but grinned broadly. Beside her stood the tiny figure of Tamara – four and a half years old now, but seeming less changed since Aleksei had last seen her than did Rodion. Her red hair, curling tightly down to her shoulders, had perhaps darkened a little, but beyond that, she was the same. She looked at Aleksei nervously and attempted to smile.

'Aleksei Ivanovich,' said Valentin. 'It's good to see you. We only got your letter yesterday.'

'Yes, it was all rather sudden,' said Aleksei. 'Some business came up and so I thought I'd accompany Dmitry here to join his regiment.'

'You should have brought him with you,' said Yelena after Aleksei had gone over to kiss her offered hand. Valentin shot her a look.

'Which regiment is he in?' asked Rodion.

'The Izmailovsky,' said Aleksei. 'So he should be back in Petersburg once he's finished his training.' He paused and stared directly into Rodion's face for a few seconds. Then he turned to Yelena. 'He looks more like Vadim Fyodorovich every time I see him.'

She smiled warmly. 'I know.'

Yelena herself, thankfully, looked nothing like her father; his broad features had skipped a generation.

'Tell me another story about Granddad,' said Rodion. 'Please.'

Aleksei's mind drifted back, as so often, to the events of the autumn of 1812. Vadim had died in Moscow, on 18 September, as well as could be guessed – killed by Iuda. Rodion had been born less than two weeks earlier, in Petersburg. Vadim had never known that he had a grandson. Aleksei had never told them the exact manner of Vadim's death, but in all his stories, Vadim Fyodorovich was a hero. That required no embellishment.

'Give him a minute,' said Yelena. 'He's only just arrived. He hasn't said hello to Tamara yet.'

Aleksei squatted down, his eyes level with those of the little girl. His heart began to pound in his chest and he felt the urge to wrap her in his arms. Instead, he lifted her hand and kissed it.

'Good afternoon, Toma,' he said.

Tamara grinned, revealing her bright white teeth. Then she turned away, breaking his contact with her hand and pressing her face against the arm of the sofa, so that it could not be seen. Yelena stroked her head.

'I think she's tired,' she said. 'Nanny will put her to bed. Do you want to take her, Aleksei?'

Aleksei looked at Yelena. She had been somewhat older than Tamara was now, perhaps thirteen or fourteen, when she and Aleksei had first met, but in the twenty intervening years they had come to understand each other very well – not least through their mutual love of her father. Many, perhaps even her husband, would have missed the glint in her eye as she spoke, and Aleksei knew, much as he tried to suppress it, that she would have seen the same glint in his. It was a game with which they were familiar.

'I'd love to,' said Aleksei. He held out his hand, and Tamara took it, then he turned and led her to the door.

'You know the way,' he heard Rodion add from behind him. It was a game for all of them.

Almost as soon as they were out of the drawing room, Tamara seemed to gain a little more confidence, and it was she that began to lead more than he. He deliberately walked more slowly, giving her the chance to run on ahead, although he knew where they were going. They arrived at the door and Aleksei raised his hand to knock, but Tamara did not wait; she opened the door and rushed inside.

The little girl ran straight across the room and over to the slim, dark-haired woman who stood silhouetted in the light from the window. The woman opened her arms as she saw the girl's approach, and as the child leapt into them, she lifted her up to the level of her face for a kiss. It was only then that she noticed Aleksei's figure standing in the doorway.

'Lyosha,' she said in a whisper.

She put Tamara down and Aleksei strode over to her. He had not seen Domnikiia for over six months. It was not the longest time they had ever been apart, but even if it had been only a day, the passion of their reunion would have been little different. Her arms held him tightly and he squeezed her body in return. His grip was so strong that he feared he would hurt her, but even as he relaxed his hold the merest fraction, her arms only pulled harder, imploring him not to lessen the expression of his desire. After only a few moments, he had to release his hold, had even to push her away from him, simply to be able to look at her face and let his lips fall on hers. They kissed deeply, not even breathing, lip dragging across lip, tongues circling one another in a silent waltz.

Eventually, it was Domnikiia who separated their embrace. She squatted down and spoke to Tamara. 'Are you ready for bed?' Tamara nodded. 'Well, run into your room and get changed. I'll be in in a bit.'

Tamara scurried off, but before reaching the door to her room, turned. 'Will *you* still be here?' she asked Aleksei.

'Oh, yes. I'll be here.'

She turned again and ran into her room. Aleksei sat on the couch. Domnikiia sat down beside him, but immediately turned and leaned backwards, her shoulders in his lap, her eyes staring up at him. He clasped her hand. She was thirty-two now, but even more desirable than when he had first met her. She had been nineteen then, and he had been struck by her similarity to Bonaparte's second wife, the empress Marie-Louise. With Bonaparte's downfall, Marie-Louise had, thanks to her father's position as Emperor of Austria, been fortunate enough to be appointed Duchess of Parma. Aleksei had not seen any recent portrait of her, and did not know whether her appearance had diverged from Domnikiia's. He doubted she could be more beautiful.

'Yelena Vadimovna said you were coming,' she said.

'I'm sorry it's been so long.'

'I know you are. You have "business" to attend to, I'm told. You still think of it as "business" with me?'

Aleksei smiled. For the first months of their relationship, money had changed hands each time they met. In all honesty, it still did, but now he had the pleasure, and pleasure it was, of paying out even when they were apart.

'I have to go to Desna,' he said.

'Desna?' she asked, the concern showing in her voice. 'Isn't that where . . . ?'

'That's right,' interrupted Aleksei. Of those who knew of Maks' fate, only a few would remember the name of the place where it occurred thirteen years on. Only Domnikiia would make the association immediately. She knew his mind. He corrected himself. There was one other person who made the connection – whoever had summoned him with that message.

'I'm guessing that's not a coincidence,' she said.

Aleksei shook his head. 'No,' he said. 'I was sent a message. It was signed by Maks, ostensibly.'

'My God. You don't think . . . ?'

'Thankfully, no. I saw Maks' corpse, two months after he died. Vampires don't rot.' That was speculation, but it fitted the facts he knew. The image of Maks' putrefying face – the rim of his spectacles sinking into his yielding cheek – filled Aleksei's mind. But there was more than that. Aleksei had been told that only a willing human can become a vampire. Maks would never willingly have done that. He looked into Domnikiia's eyes and remembered another occasion when he looked down upon her. He chose not to mention the idea of a human volunteering to become a *voordalak*.

'So who else?' asked Domnikiia.

Aleksei shrugged.

'You never saw his body, Lyosha.' Domnikiia did not use the name, but he knew who she was talking about – Iuda.

'He drowned, or froze.' Aleksei pictured his left hand forcing Iuda's head beneath the icy surface of the Berezina, his three fingers entwined in the long blond hair. He recalled feeling the body writhe and spasm as the freezing water hit Iuda's lungs, but realized that he had never in truth experienced that feeling – his own hand had been too numb. He'd kept the few strands of hair that were all he found when he pulled his hand from the water.

'Those were a long six months,' she said. She was referring to the time between his departure from Moscow to pursue Iuda and his return in 1813, after the Russian defeat at Lützen.

'There was a war,' he said. 'And I did write.'

'I know.' This was not the first time they had discussed it. All his explanations were reasonable, and yet between the Battles of Berezina and Lützen, Aleksei had found time to go home to Marfa.

'The landlord was ready to throw me out,' she said.

'He knew my credit was good.'

'And then you set me up in the hat shop.'

'The family trade – you must have inherited your father's skill.'

'My father went bust. I would have – more than once – if it hadn't been for you.'

'You miss it?' asked Aleksei.

She smiled. 'How could I?'

A call came through from the doorway to the other room, small but piercing, demanding their attention.

Domnikiia stood up. 'Come on,' she said, taking Aleksei by the hand. They went through to Tamara's room. Toys, on shelves and on chairs, surrounded the bed. Aleksei recognized some as being gifts from him. Tamara had tucked herself in. Only her red hair and her small, pale face peeked out of the sheets. Domnikiia sat

70

beside her on the bed and took her hand. Aleksei knelt down on the other side, resting his elbows on top of the blankets.

'Are you tired?' he whispered.

'Yes,' said the little girl, with certainty.

'Are you going to go to sleep?'

'Yes,' came again, in the same tone.

'Do I get a kiss goodnight?'

Tamara nodded. He leaned over and kissed her lightly on the lips. Domnikiia bent forward and did the same. Then she began to sing a lullaby.

'*Bayoo, babshkee, bayoo,*
Zheevyet myelneek na krayoo,
On nye byedyen, nye bogat,
Polna gorneetsa rebyat.
Vsye po lavochkam seedyat,
Kashoo maslyenoo yedyat.
Kasha maslenaya,
Lozhka krashenaya,
Lozhka gnyetsa,
Rot smyeyetsya,
Doosha radooyetsya.
Bayoo, babshkee, bayoo.
Bayoo, babshkee, bayoo.'

It was a meaningless song, about a miller and his children at carnival. Aleksei had never heard Domnikiia sing until Tamara was born. She had a sweet voice. He listened and watched Tamara drop off to sleep.

'Yelena Vadimovna and Valentin Valentinovich have been very good to me,' said Domnikiia, picking up their earlier conversation as she stroked the sleeping child's hair. 'They must owe you a great deal.'

'Owe me? It's not really like that. You never met Vadim, did you?'

71

She shook her head.

'He did everyone favours,' Aleksei continued, 'without asking for anything in return – though he often got it. After he died, I think, those of us who knew him best realized if we couldn't pay him back, the closest thing to do was pay each other back.' That explained some of it, explained Yelena's attitude, but it had taken more to bring Valentin on side.

'It sounds like the Freemasons,' said Domnikiia. Aleksei nodded. Because of its involvement with the revolutionary societies, he knew something of Freemasonry, but the Society of the Friends of Vadim Fyodorovich was infinitely more exclusive. 'So how have you paid them back?' asked Domnikiia.

'It doesn't work like that,' said Aleksei, realizing he had heard the phrase years before, but unable to remember where. 'They don't even have to know that I will. As long as they know that I would.'

'Don't they think they owe anything to Marfa Mihailovna?' It had taken years for Domnikiia even to go beyond the deliberately distant 'your wife', but she still stuck with the formal combination of name and patronymic.

Aleksei laughed briefly. 'Morally, I'm sure, but she hardly knew Vadim.'

'So they're not doing it for me?'

'Absolutely not,' said Aleksei. He leaned over the bed and kissed her. 'But you'll never be able to tell the difference.'

'I wish I had met Vadim,' she said thoughtfully. 'I'm glad I met Maks.'

You fucked Maks. The thought blurted itself out in Aleksei's mind, but he did not give voice to it. Their brief relationship had meant nothing to either. For her, it was work; for him, nature.

'I met Dmitry, too,' she added ruefully. 'Dmitry Fetyukovich, that is.' It was strange how they could both remember in precise detail conversations they had had years before, and also how they could each be confident that the other remembered too. In 1812 she had toyed with him as to whether she would rather meet

72

Dmitry his friend or Dmitry his son. She had met his friend, and it had not been a pleasant experience.

'Shall I ever meet Dmitry Alekseevich?' she asked, just as teasingly as all those years before.

'I don't think it's a good idea.'

'Wouldn't he like me?'

'He'd probably like you,' replied Aleksei, 'but he loves his mother.'

'Wouldn't he love his sister?'

They both gazed down at the tiny figure of Tamara Alekseevna, asleep in the bed, the child whom, with neither intention nor regret, they had conceived together five years earlier, whom Vadim's daughter and son-in-law had agreed to secretly raise as their own, with her true mother never far away. Aleksei bent forward and kissed her cheek, then squeezed her mother's hand.

'Who couldn't love her?' he said.

CHAPTER IV

ALEKSEI SPENT THE NIGHT IN THE HOME OF YELENA AND Valentin Lavrov, sleeping entwined in the limbs of his lover of almost fourteen years, just a few steps away from their beloved daughter. He crept away a little before dawn, having kissed Domnikiia, who awoke, on the lips and Tamara, who did not, on the forehead.

He glanced around as he arrived back at his hotel, but Dmitry had not shown up early. He slipped inside and emerged within half an hour, shaved, changed and carrying a knapsack which contained, amongst other necessities, the wooden sword his son had given him. The two horses he had ordered stood ready for him, and he had to wait but a few moments for Dmitry to arrive.

'So, how was your first night in Moscow?' asked Aleksei, as they trotted south out of the city.

'Somewhat quiet,' said Dmitry. 'I'm not officially expected until next week, so until then they're just giving me a bed to sleep in. There are only two others there so far.'

'So did you all go and see the sights last night?'

'We had a drink,' said Dmitry cautiously. 'How long will it take to reach Desna?'

Aleksei could easily tell that Dmitry didn't want to go into any detail about his first night in the army, nor would he, for many years, want to go into detail over any other night. The reason was simple: he had no standards to judge his own behaviour by. Whilst Aleksei, like any military father, had not held back in telling his stories of both valour and defeat, his descriptions of army life outside of battles, both in those long intermissions known as peace, and in those snatched moments of darkness when the enemy must pause for sleep, had remained sanitized. There was no need to tell any son about the whoring and the drinking and the inescapable vomiting. At least, that was Aleksei's thought. He knew other fathers who told their sons the whole truth, and knew too how odious those sons grew up to be. But it meant that, for Dmitry, any story he told his father of his army life would be a stab in the dark, risking, in the one extreme, shocking his sensibilities, and in the other his silent contempt.

'A couple of hours, at most,' he replied, 'though I've done the return journey quicker.'

'You never told me what happened,' said Dmitry.

'You never needed to know.'

'I think I do now.'

Aleksei nodded. 'It was before Bonaparte reached Moscow – around the time of Borodino. We'd all headed out west to do what we could to stop him. The twelve Oprichniki and me, Dmitry, Vadim and Maks, divided up into four groups. We got separated, but made it back to Moscow. I met up with Dmitry, who told me that Maks was a French spy – that he'd handed three of the Oprichniki straight over to the enemy.'

'Did you believe him?'

'I don't know if I did at the time, but he was quite right. Maks got a message to me through . . . well, it doesn't matter – through a contact. It said to meet him at the place we're going to now. I went there, more slowly than we're going, making sure I wasn't followed.' He looked around. They were out of the city now. 'Not much has changed,' he added.

'And when you got there?'

'And when I got there, I found Maks. He confessed to everything – everything he thought I knew. Told me he'd happily handed over the Oprichniki to be executed by the French; told me he'd been spying for them since Austerlitz – that was in '05.'

'I know that, Papa.'

'Sorry,' said Aleksei, momentarily brought back to the present. 'Of course you do. The thing is, what Maks didn't tell me was that he'd discovered the Oprichniki had their own agenda.' They were vampires; that was the simple, straightforward way to put it. But even if he hadn't wanted to protect his son from such dangerous knowledge, the very word, spoken out loud on this sunny autumn morning in an era when modernity had expelled all such notions from educated people, would have been greeted with laughter.

'They weren't on our side, then?' asked Dmitry, forcing his father to continue the story.

'Up to a point, but when there were no more French for them to rob' – 'rob', that was a nice way to put it – 'they turned on the Russians.'

'I can't imagine many Russians had anything worth taking at the time,' said Dmitry.

'"From him that hath not, even that he hath shall be taken away from him,"' replied Aleksei. 'They were very devout.'

'But Maks told you everything?'

'About himself, but not about them. And before he could, they arrived.'

'They'd followed you?'

'Your Uncle Dmitry had found out where Maks was, and told them. They got there soon after I did.' After dark.

'They wanted justice?'

'They wanted revenge,' spat Aleksei, adding more calmly, 'but it's a moot point. I was outnumbered – I couldn't stop them. But I should have stayed.'

'You wanted to see him die?'

'I wanted to see him live, just a little longer. But I wanted to live myself, and that seemed more important at the time. Eventually I came back – to bury him.'

'When was that?' asked Dmitry.

'About two months later, when your Uncle Dmitry and I travelled side by side down this very road, just as you and I are doing now.'

'So you'd reconciled with Dmitry by then?'

Aleksei was about to answer, but found he could not. Had he ever truly accepted Dmitry's complicity with the Oprichniki? He felt now, in 1825, that he had, but he had only reached that acceptance in the years after Dmitry's death. 'Just about,' he answered, rather than be forced to explain.

'I guess he was as much in the dark as you were as to what the Oprichniki were really up to.'

'Oh, he knew all right.' Aleksei paused to recollect, but realized he could not leave the issue hanging. 'Don't worry, Mitka, you're nothing like your namesake.' Aleksei spurred his horse on a little, and pulled away from his son.

'I never thought I was,' muttered Dmitry.

He is here. Come at once.

The letter had taken nine days to reach Ragusa. The uprising of the Greeks against the Turks made all communication hazardous, but they had chosen their couriers with care. Now there were only a few final preparations to be made, but little could be done immediately. A heavy curtain hung over the window and behind it were wooden boards, but still it was obvious that the sun had risen outside. The atmosphere was oppressive, nauseating. Sleep was the best escape. He would have slept already, but for the anticipation – for the last three mornings – that the letter would arrive.

He screwed it up and threw it into the unlit fireplace. It would burn when the next guest stayed in this room – one who needed the comfort of physical warmth. Even if it was found and read, it did not matter. He would be long gone and no one would know where to follow him.

Sleep: that was the thing for now. At sunset he would make

things ready. Even then, there would be no need to rush. The journey would not begin until the small hours of the morning. That was the safest way. And for now, sleep. Patience came easily after so long an existence as his. He had waited over a hundred years and soon he would claim what he was rightfully owed.

Over a hundred years, and yet as he lay down, he felt he could still taste that noblest of blood on his lips.

They arrived at Desna before noon. Not quite at Desna – the small, abandoned wooden hut was a little north of the village.

'We're early,' Dmitry said.

'I know,' his father replied.

Aleksei tied up his horse, using a tree some way from the hut. Dmitry did likewise, then strode across the open patch of dusty ground that stood between them and the wooden building.

'Stop!' hissed Aleksei. There was an urgency to his voice that demanded instant compliance. Dmitry paused, the toe of his left boot barely kissing the ground where he had begun to lift it. He looked around him, turning only his head, expecting to see some snake sidling towards him through the dirt, if not worse. There was nothing.

Aleksei came up to him quickly and knelt down beside him, staring at the ground as though he were a doctor attending to a patient prostrate on a couch. Then his eyes scanned the surrounding area, glancing at trees, and often at the hut – at the landscape itself. He stood and walked a few paces back the way he had come, picking up a stick of wood from the ground before returning. He scanned his surroundings again, in the same way as before, and then began to draw markings in the soil. It was a very simple shape.

Four straight lines, forming a rectangle, slightly taller than the height of a man, and slightly wider than a man's shoulders.

Aleksei stood and stared silently at his work for a few moments, then headed towards the hut, skirting around the rectangle rather than walking across it. Dmitry, still poised in his frozen stance, relaxed and let his foot return to the ground. Then he followed his father – followed his route exactly. He could easily guess what those lines in the earth represented.

'It hasn't changed,' said Aleksei.

He stood in the doorway of the hut, his hand clutching the loop of rope that served as a door handle. His eyes scanned the walls and ceiling. He stepped inside, and Dmitry followed. The strangeness in his father's mood that had gradually come upon him during the last few versts of their journey had not abated. There was a madness to him – to the look in his eyes – an almost deliberate madness that he had brought upon himself so that he might confront his fears; as if he had reasoned that only a madman would return here.

'He's not here yet,' observed Dmitry.

'Who?' His father turned his head, bringing those crazed eyes on to Dmitry's own.

'Whoever wrote the message.'

'Oh, Maks you mean? Maks is still here. He *was* there.' Aleksei pointed to the centre of the room. 'There was a chair.' He walked in a small circle around the room, as if searching in its dark corners. 'Can you see a chair?' There was nothing. Dmitry did not comment on the obvious.

'Then he was there,' Aleksei continued, now pointing to a corner of the hut, across from the open doorway. 'Of course, he didn't need a chair then. He was dead. And now he's—' Aleksei stopped abruptly. His back was turned to Dmitry, and his body scarcely moved, even to breathe.

'And now he's buried outside,' said Dmitry.

Aleksei turned and nodded. His eyes were no longer insane, but frightened, like a child's.

'We marked it with a cross,' he said, 'but that's gone – just like the chair.'

'We'll make another one,' said Dmitry.

Aleksei walked over and placed his hand on the side of his

son's face. 'You're a good lad, Mitka,' he said. Dmitry could feel his father's thumb and two fingers stroking his hair, and felt the stubs of the two others against his cheek. He could not remember a time before Aleksei had lost them. He must have been about three, perhaps older. There had been an occasion around that time when his mother had been distraught, and he associated that with her hearing the news, but that was the rationalization of an adult. He remembered – it could not have been very much later – being surprised that other boys' fathers had five fingers on their left hand, and remembered Aleksei trying to explain it to him. He remembered Aleksei allowing him to touch the gnarled stubs. It had fascinated him. His father had said that it didn't hurt at all, but as he grew older, Dmitry began to wonder if that was not just one of the things fathers say. No man wants to let his son know that he can cause him pain.

The contact lasted only a moment, and then Aleksei walked away.

'We've got plenty of time before whoever it is is due here,' said Dmitry. He instantly regretted the implication – that the making of a new monument for Maks' grave would be simply a way to pass the time. But before he could make amends, his father spoke.

'I don't think he's coming.'

Dmitry turned. The room had darkened slightly, and Dmitry now saw that it was because his father had closed the door. Aleksei was looking at the wall revealed behind it, and Dmitry followed his gaze.

$$9 - 8 - 13 - M - \Pi$$

Dmitry stared at the message. As far as he could tell, it was in the same hand as the one daubed on the walls of their home in Petersburg. This, however, was much smaller, intended simply to inform, not to impress. Again, the same red pastel had been used.

'That's the same place Maks put his message,' said Aleksei.

80

'The eighth of September, one o'clock in the afternoon,' said Dmitry. Aleksei nodded. 'But that's before he even wrote the message at home.'

'That's why I don't think he's coming,' explained Aleksei. 'He put the message here first, then gave us the second message so that we'd come here. Not to meet him, but to see this.'

'But what's the point of that? Just to tell us he was here? It's like something some schoolkid scratches in the bark of a tree.' Dmitry thought for just a fraction of a second; when he spoke again, his voice had an air of hushed realization. 'Or maybe it wasn't just to tell us he was here, but to tell us he wasn't alone. That's not just signed "M", but "M" and "П". So the question is, who was, who is, "П"?'

'He *was* alone,' said Aleksei, walking away from the door back towards the centre of the hut. He was completely himself again now, a puzzle of the present having dismissed the ghosts of the past. 'П is not a person; "П" is for "*peesmo*".'

'A letter?' said Dmitry.

'Precisely. Give me a leg-up.'

Dmitry did not follow exactly what was meant, but his father mimed the action, and Dmitry copied, bracing the fingers of his two hands together to form a stirrup. Aleksei stepped into it, his head now almost touching the low wooden ceiling. Dmitry was quite able to take the weight, but resented his father nonetheless, not for this, but for his arrogant dismissal of Dmitry's line of reasoning moments before. He was not to know that П meant '*peesmo*', but his father was happier to show himself as right rather than complimenting Dmitry on having a good idea. It had always been so.

'Here we are,' said Aleksei, jumping to the ground and clutching a small envelope he had plucked from between one of the rafters and the sloping planks of the roof.

'How did you know it would be just there?'

'Because that is where Maks placed *his* letter. So the more important question is . . .'

81

'Is, how did whoever it is know where Maks put it?'

'Exactly,' said Aleksei. 'Only Maks and I knew that.'

'And Uncle Dmitry.'

'True. But he's dead too. So, logically, only I could have placed this envelope there.' He grinned, and tore open the thin paper. Inside was a single stiff piece of card. Dmitry could not see what was written on it, but it took his father only moments to read. His eyes flicked up and met Dmitry's.

'Another appointment,' he said.

'The same code as before?'

'No, somewhat different. Hardly a code at all.' He handed the slip of card over for Dmitry to read.

The Imperial Bolshoi Theatre of Moscow
presents
Cendrillon
by
Fernando Sor
26 September 1825. Row 5. Seat 15.

'You said you wanted to go,' observed Dmitry.

'I don't think I'll have my full attention on the ballet.'

'Do you want me to come with you?'

Aleksei thought for a moment before replying. 'Probably best not. I don't think he means me any harm – here would have been a much better place for that. And there'll be plenty of people about.'

'He may still come here,' said Dmitry. 'It's not two yet.'

'We'll see.'

Aleksei went outside. Dmitry followed. They spent the next few minutes searching for wood and making a cross, embedding it in the ground at the head of where Aleksei had marked out the grave and piling stones around its base. Aleksei said that it was a much better effort than the first one. Even so, Dmitry suspected it would vanish just as quickly. He said nothing.

'I think we can be sure no one's coming,' Aleksei finally stated, looking at his watch. 'It's past four.'

'We should head back.'

'You go. I want to stay here for a while.' Aleksei glanced down at the grave as he spoke.

'Do you think it's safe?'

Aleksei shrugged. Dmitry recalled how it was fear for his safety that had made Aleksei leave Maks alone here before. He clearly wasn't going to let history repeat itself. Anyway, Dmitry doubted there was any danger – otherwise why arrange to meet at the theatre? And if there *was* trouble, his father was quite capable of dealing with it.

He shook his father's hand, then walked over to his horse and untied it. He mounted and began to ride slowly north. He looked over his shoulder to see his father standing, watching him go.

He had scarcely turned his head back in the direction he was travelling when he heard his father's shout: 'Dmitry!' He turned back again. His father still stood there, and after a moment he raised his arm in a broad wave. Dmitry returned the gesture, but he suspected the call had not been meant for him.

After a minute or so he turned and looked again, by now probably out of earshot. He could just make out his father, sitting cross-legged in front of the hut, staring down at the patch of ground he had marked out.

CHAPTER V

'BUT THAT'S THE POINT, ALEKSEI. I THOUGHT YOU UNDERSTOOD. They're not—'

The back of Pyetr's hand dashed against Maks' jaw, knocking his head sideways and silencing the word 'human' that had been on his lips, replacing it with a brief yelp as Maks' breath rushed across his vocal cords.

'Aleksei's gone, Maksim.' It was Iuda who spoke. 'Left you all alone with us. And even if he were here, do you think he would care about that?' Maks looked up at him. Blood ran from the corner of his mouth. 'Did Dmitry?'

'Aleksei isn't like Dmitry.'

'They're neither of them like *you*. They both love their country.'

'Love is a relative concept. They love their fellow man more.'

'Do they?' Iuda raised an eyebrow as he spoke the question.

'Aleksei does.' Around the hut, the other five Oprichniki had stripped to the waist. Varfolomei was coiling a length of rope. 'When he finds out what you are, he'll destroy you. He'll hunt you down across the face of the earth.'

Iuda gave a brief nod to Pyetr, who hit Maks again, on the other side of his face. Pyetr looked at his hand. There was blood on it – his own blood. He licked it clean, and the wound healed in seconds. Looking at Maks, the cause of the injury was obvious.

His glasses were broken. They hung off one ear, one lens intact, the other shattered.

Iuda leaned forward and gently took them off Maks' face. 'I think we'd better put these somewhere safe, hadn't we?' Maks' head jerked up. He looked around, his eyes unseeing. He was virtually blind without his spectacles, as Aleksei well knew. 'Don't worry,' said Iuda, as though speaking to a child, 'you can have them back afterwards.' He popped them into his inside pocket and patted the breast of his coat reassuringly.

Varfolomei walked over and tied the rope around Maks' wrists, binding them together. Then he flung the other end into the air. From his vantage point, Aleksei could not see the roof of the hut, but there was evidently something there to hook the rope over. Varfolomei and Andrei pulled in unison, and their combined weight hoisted Maks out of the wooden chair on which he had been sitting. Pyetr kicked it with the inside of his foot, and it hurtled towards Aleksei. He flinched, pulling back from the side of the hut, but immediately realized that the chair had not been aimed at him. He knelt back down and pressed his eye once more against the thin gap between the panels, observing what went on inside.

Pyetr knelt down behind Maks and rolled up the leg of his breeches until it was above the knee. Then he opened his mouth, pulling back his lips to reveal his fangs. His mouth seemed too large to fit into his skull, as though it should protrude like a dog's snout. His jaws snapped shut and his teeth sank into Maks' calf. Maks' head whipped back, and his mouth opened in an agonized scream, though Aleksei heard no sound. Andrei stepped forward, and pulled up Maks' shirt. His teeth, even larger and more gruesome than Pyetr's, sank into the side of Maks' abdomen. Blood gushed out, staining Maks' skin and flowing into Andrei's mouth. Soon it was full and the blood overflowed, dribbling over his chin and on to his own clothes.

Iuda walked over towards where Aleksei watched. He knew

Iuda could not see him; he was simply coming to retrieve the chair. But as he bent down to pick it up and his face came level with the tiny slit through which Aleksei watched, he narrowed his eyes and gave what looked to all the world like a wink. An expression of cheerful cunning fleeted across his face, but then he disappeared from view. The next Aleksei saw of him was his back as he strolled away towards Maks, dragging the chair behind him.

Maks' feet swung only inches from the ground on to which now dripped the blood from the wounds to his leg and stomach. Effectively, this made him taller than Iuda, and that was why Iuda needed the chair. He placed it on the ground and stepped on to it. Now his head was, as it would normally be, above the height of Maks'. He bent forward and placed his lips on Maks' throat. Aleksei noticed, concealed in Iuda's hand, the double-bladed knife that was his preferred weapon. He was wise to hide it, lest the other Oprichniki should see and realize that Iuda was not one of them – that he was not a vampire. Even as the thought crossed Aleksei's mind, he wondered how it had come to him. How did he know that Iuda was not a *voordalak*? How, indeed, did he know that the others were? He would not discover that for weeks.

Iuda lifted his head from Maks' neck and placed his lips beside his ear. He whispered something and Maks' response was to grin ecstatically and nod his head with vigorous approval. Iuda smiled and stepped down from the chair. He walked behind Maks. With a swift stroke of his knife, he cut Maks' shirt in two. With a couple more strokes under Maks' arms, which cared little whether they cut linen or flesh, he had removed the garment from Maks' body, except for the sleeves, which still clung to his up-reaching arms.

Iuda stepped back and eyed his victim's body. He glanced back in Aleksei's direction, and Aleksei could have sworn that he winked again. Then Iuda issued an instruction to the others, which Aleksei did not understand, and the vampires gathered around Maks, pressing against him, their exposed flesh rubbing against his as their teeth penetrated his body. Aleksei looked up at

Maks' face, but the expression on it was one of laughter, not pain. He looked back at the creatures that swarmed around him. There seemed to be more of them now. They were hard to distinguish, even if their faces could be seen, but the hair on two of them was distinctive. One had long, dark brown hair, almost to its waist. This one had gone further than its comrades, and had stripped completely naked; the tips of its long tresses danced over the top of its buttocks. The figure next to it was much smaller, with hair distinctive not for its length but for its colour – a rich, deep red.

Iuda issued another command, and these two figures turned, revealing their faces to Aleksei. One was Domnikiia, the other Tamara. He looked up again at Maks' face, a face that was still laughing – but it was no longer Maks. In front of them all, Iuda crouched down and stared directly at Aleksei. He winked again, but did not reopen his eye, staring ahead of him with just the other, on a level with Aleksei's as he half walked, half crawled towards him.

Aleksei glanced up once more. The laughing figure hanging from the roof had not changed back. It was still himself – Aleksei Ivanovich Danilov, laughing in ecstasy as his lover and his child devoured his flesh. Iuda's single eye came ever closer until it filled Aleksei's vision. Aleksei tried to join in with his own laughter as Iuda's eye pressed up against the wall from the other side, gazing into Aleksei's own, but as he opened his mouth it was not laughter that spewed forth, but a long, deep, terrible scream.

Aleksei's scream filled the dark wilderness. He sat up. The fire he had made had gone out, but as he reached his hand towards it he felt the warmth of its embers. The high half-moon made it easy to see, but cast eerie shadows through the trees. He had not had that dream for many years. It was a dream he might have avoided if he had actually stayed to witness Maks' death. Knowledge of the reality of what had happened inside that hut, however terrible, would at least be a certainty into which no macabre speculation could creep. But Aleksei had not stayed; he had ridden away, just as Iuda had told him to. Could he not then dismiss the whole thing as the fantasies of his guilty imagination? How he wished it were that simple, but though he had not witnessed Maks' death, he had seen enough elsewhere to know that the images in the dream were based on truth.

A few months after he had left Maks to die, in a town south of here, he had witnessed a very similar scene. The victim had been no one he knew, just a serf, whose wife had already met the same fate. Aleksei's eye, pressed up to a crack at the edge of a barn door, had seen the Oprichniki do to that peasant much what they had done to Maks in the dream.

But what of the end of the nightmare? It had been over five years since Aleksei had last dreamt it, but even then it would end with Domnikiia. Did he still doubt her? Such was the power of the games Iuda had played with him that even now – thirteen years after his death – Aleksei could still be asking himself that question. Iuda had presented Aleksei with a scene: two bodies entwining; a woman exchanging blood with a monster; Domnikiia choosing to abandon all that was good and to become a vampire; Domnikiia choosing to abandon Aleksei.

But the scene had not been what it seemed. Domnikiia had not become a vampire. The woman had not been Domnikiia but her friend Margarita. Iuda was not a vampire, but a mortal man. As each page of the story turned, Iuda had ensured that Aleksei's view changed, until Aleksei was so familiar with change he could no longer cling to any certainty. He knew he had been wrong, but he could not know precisely how, nor could he ever fully determine the truth of that one, vital concept: that the woman had not been Domnikiia. Whether it was true or untrue, either possibility fitted the facts with equanimity. That was the eternity of doubt that, even in death, Iuda had planned for Aleksei.

Aleksei's solution had been simple, and one that men have turned to throughout history – faith. Where he could not be sure he would choose to believe what he wanted to believe. And what he wanted to believe was that Domnikiia had never desired to be a vampire, had not been the figure Aleksei saw in the window that evening, had never tasted Iuda's blood on her lips. It was easy to believe, and over the years it had become easier with every hour he spent with her. But faith was still different from certainty, and his dream was a reminder from somewhere deep in his unconscious mind that there was another possibility.

There was still no way of knowing. Domnikiia might have been the woman at the window and later been distraught to discover she was not a vampire, and again to hear of Iuda's death, but she would never reveal the truth to Aleksei, if that truth was what he did not want to hear. And he did not. He imagined, sometimes, a deathbed confession from her, telling him what had happened, telling him that she had regretted her mortal life ever since. But were there any prospect of that, he would avoid her deathbed. It would have been one thing to learn the truth soon after the events had taken place, but to learn it later would reveal the hollowness not only of Domnikiia, but of the whole edifice of faith he had created over the years. What devout Christian would want a priest to whisper in his ear at the moment of death, 'It's all a lie'? Who knew? Perhaps that's what priests did.

And so the truth for him, in his heart at least, was that Domnikiia had always been faithful. And over the years the doubts – and the dreams of doubts – had become fainter and less frequent. It was only the fact of being here, of seeing once again the place where Maks had died and of sleeping virtually alongside where his body lay, that had brought the nightmare back to him.

And yet, there was something new in that nightmare – Tamara. In the five years since he had last dreamed it, he and Domnikiia had had their daughter. She was being raised by her mother. If Domnikiia could not be trusted, how might she form her daughter's character? What lies that had passed from Iuda to Domnikiia during their brief moments together might be passed on to the next generation in Tamara?

Such were Aleksei's deepest fears, as expressed to him in his dream, but they were not his beliefs. These thoughts were but temptations to test his faith. He had kept his faith for thirteen years. Had he not, there would have been no Tamara. Such goodness came out of faith, not truth.

But the truth always sat there at the back of his mind, impenetrably disguised, watching him, taunting him, waiting. He did not know how he could remove that disguise and discover what had really happened. If he did know how, he doubted he would do it. But still the truth was there, waiting to be revealed.

He lay back down on the ground, closing his eyes, though he knew he would not sleep, and awaited the light of dawn.

It was pitch dark when the ship finally sailed from Ragusa. The crew was small and trustworthy – none of them locals. The Dalmatians knew enough to fear their passenger, but that fear might be so great as to tempt them, in the safety of the midday sun, to slip both him and his cargo overboard, turn round and head for home. Instead, he had chosen a crew from amongst his own people, further inland to the north-east. They were less skilled as sailors, but the journey would be short and the waters were calm.

The ship was not noteworthy, scarcely more than a large yacht. She went by the name of *Răzbunarea*, but that could easily be changed if anonymity were required, as could the flag she flew. At the moment, she was French, but there were a dozen other nationalities stored below deck.

Though small, *Răzbunarea* was swift. There were only two items of cargo. On her return she would be a little lower in the water, but few would notice. She sped down the Adriatic, towards the Strait of Otranto, though that was not her final destination; that was many days away.

Her sole passenger stood and stared at the night sky and inhaled the sea air. He had no fear of the water, as some thought he should. Even so, he would not spend much of the journey on deck. When he arrived, he would have work to do, and that work would require concentration, and concentration required rest.

Aleksei mounted his horse soon after dawn. He took one final look at Maks' grave, and hoped he would never return. He had no need of a memorial to remember his friend, and he had never felt the urge to return here in all the years since his death. He had only come now because he had been led here. He reached into his pocket and pulled out the theatre ticket. He had three days until the performance. He enjoyed ballet, and though he knew the story of *Cinderella* well, he had not seen this version. Perhaps this whole journey had been an elaborate way of giving him a present, though his birthday was long past. Perhaps it was just a ploy by Domnikiia to bring him to Moscow.

He laughed at the thought. She needed no such ploys, and whatever the reason he had been invited to the theatre, it was not for entertainment.

He spurred his horse and headed back to Moscow. He did not look behind him again.

Aleksandr could see the small cortège from quite a distance. It had surprised him how much he had missed the company of the tsaritsa. It had been his grandmother Yekaterina who had arranged their marriage, more than thirty years before, as she had arranged everything in his life. She had brusquely decided that neither Aleksandr's mother nor his father – her own son, the future Tsar Pavel – was fit to raise their child. Yekaterina had controlled every aspect of Aleksandr's upbringing, from his education to his marriage to Yelizaveta at the age of just fifteen. He had quickly learned to hate his wife, but had grown to despise his grandmother more. He had learned from her too, though. Her reign had been founded on the untimely death of her husband; Aleksandr's similarly, on the death of his father. Both had successfully kept their hands clean; the *garde perdue* was not a new idea.

But time had changed Aleksandr's attitudes, towards both his wife and his grandmother. Russia was a difficult country to rule, and Yekaterina had known that it needed a tsar who emulated his *babushka* more than it needed one who loved her. He could almost sense her approval of his plans for dealing with the rebels back in Petersburg.

And he had grown to realize the wisdom in her choice of Yelizaveta Alekseevna as his consort. What had seemed at first merely an unhappy political union had evolved into a mutually supportive friendship. He was not restricted to the concept that a man's wife should be his only lover – Grandmother, of all people, would not have espoused that. Even so, they had had two children, daughters, who had both died before their second birthdays. It seemed too long ago now to think of their deaths as tragedies. Aleksandr had lost another child far more recently. Sophia, his daughter by Maria Naryshkina, had died of consumption in 1824. She had been eighteen. His other daughter with Maria, Zinaida, had died at the age of just four. He had other children by other mistresses, the youngest only four years old, but he thanked the Lord on all their behalves for blessing them with the gift of bastardy. None would inherit from him the heavy yoke that was the crown.

None of this was a secret to the tsaritsa; nor were her infidelities to him. When Sophia died, Yelizaveta had been a great comfort to him, and her own illness had in turn proved to them both how much they cared for each other. For Aleksandr, the future – these next few months in particular – was unclear. To have his wife with him, perhaps for the last time, would be a consolation.

The carriages were closer now. He stood impassively, not wanting to appear over-eager to see his wife, even though he had ridden out specifically to accompany her on the final leg of the journey. She had arrived only ten days after him, and he hoped she had not tired herself. In Taganrog that evening, their first port of call would be the monastery, where the abbot and the monks would line up to greet the tsaritsa, and then a service of thanksgiving would be performed. Her rooms in the palace were all prepared.

But as much as Aleksandr would be pleased to see his wife again, he was impatient for the arrival of another in her party, Prince Volkonsky – a man who was indispensable when it came to matters of state. Volkonsky had been one of those who had overthrown Aleksandr's father in 1801 – one of the few whom Aleksandr had subsequently allowed to remain close to the throne. Wylie had been another, though he had been less involved – less involved even than Aleksandr. The Scottish doctor had merely signed a politically acceptable death certificate for Pavel, blaming the death on apoplexy. It was strange how those two men remained so close to him. The dispersal of the others to various backwaters of the empire had not been the outpouring of Aleksandr's guilty conscience; it was simply wise to make it clear to the world that one was unlikely to prosper by daring to overthrow a tsar. *Babushka* would have been proud.

The retinue of coaches and horses finally drew up. Aleksandr went over to his wife's carriage and held out his hand to help her down. As she smiled at him, and he at her, he worried that she would notice the swelling tear that had formed in his eye. If she did, he hoped she would take it as an outward sign of the emotion he felt at their being reunited. In truth, that was not the cause. The tear was merely a sign that the tsar's thoughts had once again turned to his beautiful, young, departed daughter Sophia.

'Mama!'

Domnikiia turned from the window and looked over to Tamara. Tamara grinned, but could detect a falseness in the smile that her mother returned. She had had no reason to call out, except to cause a reaction. It was simple, safe and reliable. Call out 'Mama!' and Mama would reply. It was a confusing word though; sometimes people – visitors to the house – would think that Mama Yelena was Tamara's mama, and she was told not to contradict them. That's why she thought of her as Mama Yelena, so, when she spoke to her, she just had to remember not to say 'Yelena' and everyone was happy. But she didn't call her mama 'Mama Domnikiia', even though she knew Domnikiia was her name. She was just 'Mama' because she was Tamara's mama. That part was simple.

'Papa' was a really difficult word. She never called Valentin Valentinovich Papa, although Rodion did. And Rodion called Mama Yelena Mama. She'd made the mistake once – calling Valentin Valentinovich her 'Papa' – and he'd scowled at her, but hadn't shouted. She remembered him shouting once before at her, when she was very young, and Mama Yelena had said something about Aleksei being *her* friend and this being *her* house, and Valentin Valentinovich hadn't shouted again.

Aleksei was the man who had started visiting again. *He* was the one that Mama said she should call Papa. She'd told her that before, last time he was here, but Tamara had forgotten. Papa was very nice, whenever he was here, unlike Valentin Valentinovich, who was sometimes nice and sometimes wasn't. But he was here most of the time, and so, overall, he was nice more often than Papa was. So 'Papa' didn't just mean a different person to her and to Rodion, it also meant a different thing. She preferred her person, but she preferred Rodion's thing.

'Mama!' she shouted again.

Domnikiia turned again. 'Yes, my darling?'

'Do you miss Papa?'

Domnikiia smiled, more genuinely this time. 'Whenever he's not here. Don't you?'

Tamara shook her head firmly. 'I don't see him enough. If he was here more often, I'd probably miss him when he wasn't.'

'He'll be here for a while. He came back from Desna, didn't he?'

Tamara nodded. When Papa had left again, so soon after arriving, she'd been upset. She'd woken up early and run into her mama's room to find her alone and sad. She'd explained that Papa had had to go to Desna, but would be back soon. Tamara vaguely remembered being told he'd be back soon last time he went away, but he hadn't been – not soon.

But this time, he had. He'd come home on Wednesday and he'd been there, with Mama, on Thursday morning and this morning.

'Will he go away again?'

'You sound like me.' Tamara frowned. She didn't understand what her mother was saying. 'Like a little voice in my head, when I first knew him. "Will he go away again? When will he be coming back? *Will* he be coming back?" But I know now. Lyosha always goes away – and he always comes back. To both of us.'

'Lyosha?'

'Lyosha – Aleksei – Papa.' Domnikiia squatted down and held her arms wide open. 'Now come over here and give Mama a hug.'

Tamara ran over to her mother. She was not as good at running as some people – certainly not as good as Rodion – so she concentrated on keeping her balance, looking at the floor just in front of her, rather than at the thing she was running towards, as grown-ups do. She knew she had arrived when she felt her mother's arms around her and felt her own legs dangling beneath her as she was lifted into the air. She wrapped her arms around her mother's neck and pressed her face into her chest.

'That's a good girl, Toma,' whispered her mother.

'Will Papa be back today, then?' asked Tamara.

'Yes, darling.'

'Will he be back soon?'

'I hope so.' Tamara guessed those last words were spoken to comfort them both.

Domnikiia turned back to the window. Tamara lifted her head and followed her mother's stare. Down below, towards the end of the street, stood a man. He was too far away to see his face clearly, but stood like a young man does – older than Rodion, but not by much. His hands were buried in his pockets. He was gazing down the main road, but as they looked, he glanced up at the window, then quickly looked back down, seeming to pay close attention to the horses and carriages that drove past.

'Who's that, Mama?' asked Tamara.

'I don't know,' she replied. There was something in her voice that made Tamara think she was afraid.

CHAPTER VI

SEAT FOURTEEN WAS EMPTY. IT HAD BEEN FOR OVER AN HOUR, since the ballet began. Seat sixteen was occupied when Aleksei arrived, by an elderly woman whose bony fingers clutched an old military spyglass, most likely a relic of the Patriotic War. They were quite close enough to the stage for her not to need it to view the performance, but the performance was not the object of her attention. She spent the evening scanning the boxes around and behind them. From time to time, she would nudge her husband – who attended neither to the dancers nor to the audience, but spent most of his evening attempting to catch up on his sleep – and keep him abreast of who it was she had recognized, and sometimes waved to, in the vain hope that, had they possessed a spyglass of equal magnification, they would have recognized her.

In truth, Aleksei's attention was not much captured by the ballet itself either. In general, he preferred ballet to opera. A ballet was a symphony with performers added to keep the eyes from wandering. An opera was a play with music added to please the ear. He would always prefer the case where music was the primary concern. Moreover, he found the stamp of the dancers' feet less of a distraction than the warbling of the singers' voices. The only other work he had seen by Sor had been an opera: *Il Telemaco nell'isola di Calipso*. That had been a long time ago – before Austerlitz. He could scarcely remember it. Tonight he listened to the music, and enjoyed it – he promised himself to come again and to bring Dmitry – but his eyes rarely settled on the stage.

At first, he constantly glanced around the auditorium, anticipating the arrival of whoever had invited him. Three or four times he made eye contact with someone, half suspecting he had seen some flicker of recognition in their eyes, but it had come to nothing. His presumption was that the person, when they came, would be a stranger, but he kept an eye out for a face that he knew. He had dismissed the possibility that he might really be dealing with Maks, the memories that had returned to him in Desna finally having convinced him that his old comrade was truly dead. But one other face haunted his mind, though he felt sure that it too was the face of a dead man. Nevertheless, he prepared himself to confront once again the tall, blond figure of Iuda.

But as the ballet began and the hubbub of the audience's conversation died down, the empty seat next to Aleksei became an ever more obvious presence. He had been invited to one particular seat, and the only empty space he could see in the whole theatre was that beside him. He felt sure it would be filled before the evening was out. If not, then perhaps there was a further missive already hidden somewhere beneath the seat, or beneath Aleksei's own. Aleksei would search them at the end of the evening, along with seat sixteen, if the lady with the spyglass did not hang around for too long.

In the meantime, Aleksei's attention was captured by the architecture of the theatre itself. He had seen the exterior frequently enough, and indeed had seen it growing up over the years, far grander than the original Petrovsky Theatre it had replaced, which had been reduced to ashes some two decades before. The interior, however, was utterly new to him. The stage itself was wide, high and deep. The scenery for the ballet was impressive enough, but Aleksei mistrusted all such façades, knowing they were only cardboard and paper, and could be gone

98

by the following evening. He would rather have seen the stage empty, to see its construction instead of having it hidden.

The auditorium was another matter. Like his friend with the spyglass, but with only his own eyes to observe, Aleksei spent much of the evening craning his neck to look at the space around him. He, however, did not look at the audience, but at where they sat. Surrounding the stalls, six circles rose up, layer upon layer, like stacked horseshoes. The highest – and cheapest – was above the level of the massive chandelier which dominated the chamber, illuminated by a hundred candles. Flights of stairs, through which the audience could enter and exit, cut through the rows of seats, great cavernous tunnels that might lead one to who knew where. That this vast room existed in the centre of Moscow, surrounded and hidden by brickwork indistinguishable from that of the buildings around it, was difficult to imagine. Those stairwells were like gateways to another world – to Dante's Hell. There there had been nine circles, not six, and they were true circles, connected through a complete 360 degrees, and yet Aleksei could easily imagine the audience in each of those balconies as pagans, lechers, gluttons, misers, sloths, heretics, sodomites and panders. He himself was at the very pit of the theatre, the lowest level of hell – that reserved for traitors. He glanced around, but saw no sign of Brutus or Cassius. Neither was his worst fear fulfilled: he did not see Christ's betrayer – he did not see Iuda. He returned his eyes to the stage.

'It's been a long time, Aleksei Ivanovich.'

The voice came from his right. He knew before he had turned his head that the seat next to him was now occupied. He knew also, the realization dawning upon him even as his eyes fell upon the face beside him, both that the voice which had spoken was not Iuda's and that in his heart he had been utterly convinced it would be.

He saw it first in profile. It was a young man, scarcely more than a boy – perhaps older than Dmitry, perhaps a little younger. He turned, and Aleksei saw something familiar in him, which he could not place. Aleksei opened his mouth to speak, but the man placed a finger to his lips to silence him. He then pointed to the stage, indicating that they should pay attention to the ballet.

Aleksei turned his head forward, but his attention was not focussed on the exertions on stage. His mind tried to grapple with the possibilities, eliminating first the impossibilities. This was not Maks. He had never thought it would be, but the messages had ostensibly come from him, so it had to be included as a possibility. Any such pretence had now been abandoned. Moreover, it was not Iuda, nor was it Zmyeevich, nor any of the other Oprichniki. And there Aleksei's logic ran out of facts which it might process. The initial flash of recognition had now vanished, but it had been there. The few words the man had spoken implied they had met before. Perhaps they had, in some fleeting moment Aleksei had long forgotten. But in connection with Maks and Maks' death, Aleksei could think of no one.

The end of the act came quickly – too quickly for Aleksei, still desperately trying to understand who the man beside him could be.

'Let me introduce myself.' The man turned to him again as the hum of conversation in the theatre grew. He offered his hand. 'My name is Innokyentii Sergeivich; Innokyentii Sergeivich Lukin.'

The Christian name meant nothing to Aleksei, and the patronymic could easily have been a coincidence, but combined with the surname, it was shockingly familiar. Even so, as they shook hands, with Aleksei momentarily as if in a trance, Innokyentii made the connotation clear.

'I'm Maksim Sergeivich's brother.'

'Maks . . .' gasped Aleksei. Again his mind raced, supplied with this new information. Maks' brother. Did that explain why Aleksei had seen something he recognized the moment he saw Innokyentii's face? He could not see anything in it now. Had Maks even had a brother? He had sisters, Aleksei recalled, but could not remember ever hearing of a brother. This man was around Dmitry's age – much younger than Maks. He would have been about five when Maks had died. Perhaps a half-brother? If so, the name would suggest that it was their father whom they shared, and yet Aleksei was sure that Maks' father had died when he was very young. Of course, what did Aleksei really know of Maks? He had never met any of his family, and had only Maks' descriptions of who they were – the descriptions of a man who had lied for as long as they had known each other about the very matter of his national allegiance. Perhaps he had been hiding his brother, protecting him from the revelation that he was also a French spy. How little did that matter today? France was a monarchy again – an ally of Russia. It made no real difference where Innokyentii's loyalties lay. Nor Maks'.

'I didn't know Maks had a brother,' said Aleksei directly. 'You must have been very young when he died.'

'I understand your suspicions, Aleksei. I could be anyone. Perhaps this will convince you.' He reached into his pocket and pulled out a folded letter, handing it to Aleksei. As soon as Aleksei opened it, he recognized the handwriting – it was his own. The date at the top was 29 August 1812. It began:

My dear Yelizaveta Malinovna . . .

Aleksei understood immediately what the letter was, but self-indulgently read through it, down to his own signature at the bottom. It told a mother the story of the heroic death of her son on the field of battle. The detail was invented, but the sentiment was true, truer than Aleksei had first realized when he had written the letter to Maks' mother.

'Mother gave it to me to help prove my *bona fides*,' said Innokyentii. 'Of course, I scarcely remember my brother, but he often spoke to Mama of you, and she in turn has told me much. Maks had a good friend in you.'

Aleksei refolded the letter. It meant nothing. It was certainly genuine, but it could easily have been stolen. Maks' mother might not even be alive any more – the letter could have been picked up in an auction room disposing of her possessions. He was about to hand it back, but decided to call Innokyentii's bluff.

'I'll return this to Yelizaveta Malinovna when I see her,' he said.

'That's very kind of you. She'll be so glad to meet you after all these years.'

The orchestra struck up again and the dancers returned to the stage. Aleksei lowered his voice, his whisper adding to his tone of mistrust.

'You'll forgive my suspicion, Innokyentii Sergeivich, but I fail to see why, if you are Maks' brother, you've been so contrived in approaching me.'

'Please, let's not be so formal. You called my brother Maks – call me Kyesha.' Aleksei made no reply. 'And as to my caution?' continued Kyesha. 'I felt it wise to be circumspect. You did murder my brother, after all.'

The music rose in a sudden crescendo, becoming too loud for Aleksei to speak over. He looked over at Kyesha, whose eyes were fixed on the stage, as though his only reason for being there was to take in the entertainment, as though the last words Aleksei had heard had never passed his lips.

Aleksei turned back to face the ballet as well. Kyesha's silence gave him time to consider. The first possibility was that he – Aleksei – had gone mad. Accusations that he was responsible for Maks' death had been levelled at him before, but only by his own mind, awake and in dreams. This did not feel like a dream, but could it be that Kyesha was just a projection of his own conscience? Aleksei smiled to himself. It was possible, but unlikely. Anyone who knew of the circumstances of Maks' death could twist them in the same way as did parts of Aleksei's own mind. So how had Kyesha learned of the circumstances? Not through Aleksei's letter. But all the Oprichniki knew what had happened. Beyond that, Aleksei had told Vadim and Dmitry Fetyukovich. And Domnikiia. Even Marfa knew something of it. However the details had reached Kyesha, no mystery was needed to explain it.

'I'm sorry.' Kyesha's voice whispered in Aleksei's ear, as if commenting on the performance. '"Murder" is too strong a word. But you were responsible for Maks' death.'

Aleksei had no reply to make. He sat in silence, his eyes fixed on the stage. It was not long before the ballet came to its end, and the audience erupted in applause. Many of them rose to their feet, Kyesha included, his hands beating together rapidly to express his apparent pleasure. Aleksei stood and joined him. He had paid little attention to the quality of what he had seen that evening, but the rest of the audience had clearly found it superb.

'We'll meet again,' shouted Kyesha over the noise. He was a little shorter than Aleksei, who bent forward to hear him. 'Each evening for a week. I'm sure you can guess the time and places.'

As Kyesha was speaking, Aleksei's eyes had been on the stage, not out of a particular interest in the curtain calls, but simply as a result of his stooped posture. He stood upright and then turned to ask Kyesha what he meant, but he had gone. Aleksei looked into the aisle, but already others were leaving their seats and heading out of the theatre. Aleksei could not distinguish the figure of Kyesha amongst them and, even had he been able to, he would have had to fight his way through the crowd to reach him.

Besides, he already understood what Kyesha meant. The clue was where he was that very night: the Bolshoi Theatre – or, at least, the theatre in Petrovsky Square – on a Saturday night. It was the first, or perhaps the last, on a list of seven days and seven locations within Moscow itself. During Bonaparte's occupation, Aleksei and his comrades had needed a way to keep in touch as they worked to undermine the strength of the invading forces. To meet at the same place every evening would raise suspicion, but seven locations on subsequent nights – each at nine o'clock – should, and did, prevent their being detected. Kyesha had already been careful to replay the events of that terrible autumn, so many years before, with the coded message, the hidden envelope at Desna and now a Saturday meeting at the theatre. It could only be that he intended to keep to the list.

And so would Aleksei. It surprised him how easy it was to remember not just where those places were, but which one corresponded to each day. And that, of course, led on to a more intriguing question, similar to those which Aleksei had already asked himself: how did Kyesha know the list? He certainly hadn't learned it from his brother Maks. For when Vadim, Dmitry and Aleksei had drawn it up, in the desperate hiatus before the arrival of the Grande Armée, Maks was already dead.

The Archangel Gabriel had not held aloft the cross that topped Menshikov's Tower for more than one hundred years, not since a fire – it was always fire in Moscow – had almost razed the whole building. Today, the tower looked little different from when Aleksei had last stood beneath its orange-plasterwork walls thirteen years before, waiting to meet Vadim. Vadim had not shown up; Aleksei was soon to discover, as he even then had feared, that Vadim was already dead. Then, the small alleyway between the tower and the Church of Fyodor Stratilit had been quiet and gloomy. Tonight it was relatively busy. It was odd to find two churches so close to each other, but the Russians were a religious people. Aleksei himself had attended mass that morning. Not here, but over in Arbatskaya, at Yelena Vadimovna and Valentin Valentinovich's regular place of worship. They made a happy family – the parents, the son and the little daughter – and it did not seem odd that they should be accompanied by the girl's nanny and an old family friend.

Few of those who were now heading into either of the two churches paid much attention to Aleksei. It was dark now, and autumn was giving way to the beginnings of winter. There was no moon, and only the candlelight from the windows illuminated anyone's face. Aleksei peered to see if he could recognize Kyesha amongst them.

'I see we understand each other, Aleksei.' Kyesha's voice came from behind him, and to the left. Aleksei knew he was getting old. When he had been at his peak, it would have been difficult for anyone to creep up so close to him – any human. He turned to face Kyesha.

'How did you know about the list?' he asked.

'We can't talk here,' said Kyesha. 'Let me get you a drink. Do you know anywhere decent?'

Aleksei wasn't in the mood to socialize, but he was in no position to control the situation. It was too late to pretend now that he wasn't hooked, and besides, he did need a drink.

'This way,' he said.

The tavern he took them to wasn't far, and was pretty rough. As he glanced around, he recognized a few of the faces he'd been hoping to see – men he'd at one time or another either bribed for information or paid to do what would be too risky for Aleksei to be caught doing himself. He wouldn't call any of them friends, but if he got into trouble, he guessed they would be on his side, in the expectation of further payment to come.

He ordered a bottle of wine; red and French – this sort of place made little further distinction, and even then the borders of France could be pretty vague at times. They went to a booth and began to drink.

'I think you'd better tell me what it is you want,' said Aleksei.

Kyesha reached into his pocket. Aleksei could see his fingers searching around inside. When he withdrew his hand, it was clasped shut. He looked down at it, considering whatever was hidden within. Then, with a quick shake of his wrist, as though he were throwing dice, he cast what he was holding on to the table: six small stones, roughly cylindrical in shape, but not smooth or even. At the ends, nodules protruded with a randomness that hinted at a natural formation. They varied in size. The largest was almost the length of Aleksei's thumb, the shortest smaller than a one-copeck coin. All six had fitted comfortably into Kyesha's closed fist.

'Do you know how to play knucklebones, Aleksei?' he asked.

It was an incongruous thing to ask, but Aleksei nodded, taking the question in his stride. The game was common enough in the army, where anything that could be bet upon was popular. Knucklebones had the added benefit that they could be easily transported – or replaced. 'Aren't there usually just five?' he asked.

'Always pays to have a spare,' said Kyesha. He took the smallest of the bones and put it back in his pocket. Then he cupped the remaining five in his hand and scattered them across the table. He picked out the largest. 'I'll stake five roubles on two. Will you take the bet?'

Aleksei said nothing. Kyesha threw the bone in his hand into the air. Aleksei's eyes followed it, but Kyesha's did not. Aleksei looked down again. Kyesha's hand darted over the table, grabbing two of the bones and then twisting his palm upwards, opening it to catch the one he had thrown into the air just before it reached the table.

'That's five you owe me then,' said Kyesha. Aleksei did not move to pay him. 'Don't worry, I'll keep a tally.' He produced from his pocket a pencil and paper and noted down Aleksei's debt. 'We can settle up later.' He poured the three bones from his hand to join the two left on the table, and then pushed all five over towards his competitor. 'Your turn.'

Aleksei eyed the knucklebones. He had no idea what this was leading to. It seemed silly and trivial. Perhaps it was, but Aleksei doubted that Kyesha's true reason for being here was either of those things, and if this was a necessary preamble, then so be it. He took a swig from his glass and then picked up the bones. They were smaller than those he had played with before. Traditionally, they would be made from the anklebones of sheep or goats. These certainly seemed to be made of bone – not stone as he had first assumed – but if they were from a sheep's ankle, the creature had been very small. Clearly Kyesha had played with them a lot; they were well worn, but even so, Aleksei could see that one end of each of the longest two was smooth, as if the bone had been deliberately worked, or perhaps cut.

Aleksei dropped the five bones on to the table, with the slightest of downward force from his hand. They bounced off each other and spread in an almost perfect circle. He selected the largest, as Kyesha had done and presumably for the same reason – that it was closest in size to what he was used to playing with.

'Two for five,' he said.

Kyesha nodded.

Aleksei threw the bone up with a flick of his fingertips. This time, his eyes did not follow it into the air. As part of the same motion, his hand turned over and he reached for the bones on the table. He picked up one and then a second, and realized he had made the bet too easy. It didn't matter. In his peripheral vision, he perceived the first beginning to fall. Now his eyes did fix upon it, but he did not turn his palm upwards as Kyesha had done. He curled his fingers around the two he held, rather than grasping them in his fist, and kept the bottom joints of his fingers straight, effectively increasing the area of the back of his hand. Just as the falling bone touched his hand, he dropped it slightly, and the bone came to a steady rest. Aleksei raised his hand to eye level, looking at Kyesha across the back of it.

'You pay double for that where I come from,' he said.

'And where I come from.' Kyesha noted down the tally.

'And where's that?'

Kyesha smiled and said nothing. He threw down the bones again, and picked up the largest, as before. 'Five roubles for two,' he said.

Aleksei shook his head.

'For three?' asked Kyesha.

'OK.'

Kyesha threw the bone upwards. He picked up two, but it was obvious he had no time for a third. He plucked the falling bone from the air moments before it hit the table. If he had picked up three but dropped the one he had thrown then – at least according to Aleksei's rules – he would have paid double; it was always better to fail by not picking up sufficient bones than by missing the catch.

They played several more rounds. Aleksei fared better, but not by a huge margin. Eventually he was owed thirty-five roubles.

'What say we make this more interesting?' asked Kyesha.

'What do you have in mind?'

'I don't know. We could' – Kyesha gave half a smile – 'play left-handed?'

Aleksei smiled too, though without any humour. His left hand was resting on his thigh, under the table. Kyesha was unable to see the two stumps where his fingers once had been. He began to lift it up to show his opponent, but he was interrupted.

'I'm sorry,' said Kyesha. 'That was in poor taste. Maks told me what happened.' Aleksei placed his left hand on the table any-way, his thumb and two fingers splayed out widely, in a way that would have been impossible if his hand had been entire. 'I was thinking more that we change the stakes,' continued Kyesha.

'I'm not a rich man,' said Aleksei.

'In monetary terms, perhaps not, but I'm sure neither of us is too concerned with material wealth. What we both seek above all else is knowledge. And we each have knowledge which the other would delight in possessing.'

Aleksei considered. There was certainly much he would like to know about Kyesha, but the one question that stood out – why had Kyesha gone to all this trouble to find him – had been answered. He wanted some information that Aleksei possessed. Or was even this just another ploy, obscuring some greater final goal? There was a simple way to find out – to play Kyesha's game, and win. And if he lost? There was little he knew that he would not be quite willing to tell Kyesha, and if the questions strayed into territory in which he was less comfortable, he felt no compunction about lying. There, though, he was at some disadvantage; Kyesha was clearly prepared for this. He would have researched Aleksei and had a fair chance of spotting any untruth. Aleksei would have to be careful. But what did it matter if Kyesha did know he was lying? At worst it would mean the game was over – and it was Kyesha who wanted to play.

'Very well,' said Aleksei.

He reached out for the knucklebones, but Kyesha was quicker, sweeping them off the table with his hand and slipping them back into his pocket.

'But not tonight, I think,' he said.

Aleksei looked over at the clock. It was past midnight. The wine bottle was empty, and only a mouthful was left in his glass. He knew he had drunk the majority of it. He had never seen Kyesha's glass more than half empty, and had topped it up only out of politeness as he repeatedly refilled his own.

'Tomorrow then?' he asked.

Kyesha nodded. Neither man bothered to confirm where they would meet. Kyesha rose to his feet. 'Until tomorrow,' he said, then turned and left. The thought briefly occurred to Aleksei that he should follow, but he didn't act upon it. A decade ago, perhaps he would have done, but what did he hope to find out? If he wanted to discover where Kyesha was staying, all he needed to do was win a round of knucklebones and ask the question. He only had to wait until tomorrow. Not even that – tomorrow was today.

He lifted the glass to his lips for a final taste of wine, then stopped. He reached across the table and picked up Kyesha's, pouring its contents into his own. That at least would give him something to savour. Even then it did not last long. Within a minute he was out of the tavern and heading back to the Lavrovs' house, where both Domnikiia and Tamara would already be asleep. Domnikiia would not mind being woken.

The Northern Society was not as well represented in Moscow as in Petersburg, but Aleksei knew enough to know where like-minded officers would gather. The two leaders in the city were General Fonvizin and Count Orlov. Aleksei could well remember hearing reports of the meeting at Fonvizin's home in 1821. He had himself desperately tried to gain access to the meeting, but only a trusted few were allowed to attend. There had not been a Northern and a Southern Society then. The Union of Salvation that preceded them had not lasted long. Its hierarchical structure deliberately imitated the Masonic lodges from which it had sprung, dividing the membership into four degrees: Boyars, Elders, Brethren and Friends. The Union of Welfare cast all that aside, but was soon known to be infiltrated by government informers – Aleksei himself was by no means the only one. And so in 1821, the decision had been taken to dissolve the Union of Welfare, and give up all plans for revolution or even reform.

It had all been play-acting. Those in the know knew that the society would be re-formed – they just had to keep in touch with their former comrades. If Aleksei had been under any suspicion before, then it had disappeared somewhere during this re-formation, the assumption being that those who were aware of and joined the newly formed Northern Society must have been approved of by someone in a position to have confidence in them. The fact of the split between the northern and southern factions becoming more formalized was something of a side-effect. It pleased both groupings to be able to follow their own agenda – the radicals of the south unfettered by the moderates of the north and vice versa. The division pleased the government even more.

Thus 1821 had been a momentous year, though few Russians had known it. For the majority, it was 23 April that had been most celebrated that year – not simply for being Saint George's day, but because it was the day on which Napoleon's defeat, begun in Moscow in 1812, had reached its conclusion. The former emperor of the French had died in humiliating exile on the island of Saint Helena. To Napoleon himself, and to the Western world, the date was 5 May, but to Russians it was more than a quirk of the calendar that his death should come on the feast of the patron saint of the city which had begun his downfall.

Aleksei, however, had been celebrating 23 April 1821 long before the news of Bonaparte's death had reached Russia. 23 April 1821 was the day which had seen the birth of his second child, his only daughter, Tamara.

Now, Tamara was four years old, as was the Northern Society, at least under that name. Nowadays, meetings rarely took place at Fonvizin's house, or at Orlov's. But there was a club just off Lubyanka Square where sympathetic officers in Moscow tended to congregate. It was nothing formal, but a man on the door knew who should be let in and who should not.

Aleksei glanced around the room inside. It hadn't changed since he was last here. There were a few faces he recognized, but only one that he knew well: a captain from his own brigade – the Life Guard Hussars – by the name of Grigoriy Ivanovich Obukhov, who was sitting alone. Aleksei ordered a vodka and then went over.

'Colonel Danilov,' said Obukhov. 'What brings you away from Petersburg?'

There were many possible answers, none of which Aleksei chose to reveal. 'There's nothing going to be happening in Petersburg until the tsar returns,' he said. 'It's a chance to liaise with you down here.'

It was intended to flatter, and it succeeded. Aleksei was certainly more highly regarded in the Society than someone like Obukhov, but over the years he had managed to give the impression of being even closer to the heart of the plotting than he really was, not just to Obukhov, but to several junior officers. The more they thought he already knew, the more they might tell him. And in return he was prepared to tell them plenty. If he had his way, the whole of the Northern Society would turn into a sieve; information would leak out at every point and its leaders would abandon their plans before the government ever bothered to move against them and prove how hopeless their ambitions were.

'We're ready to serve,' said Obukhov, 'whenever the call comes.'

'It will be next year – the summer, I would guess; once Aleksandr returns to Petersburg. His death will be the signal.'

'His death?' For a moment, Aleksei wondered whether the idea was too much for the young officer to stomach. 'But how can we

111

predict that?' Aleksei gave him a stony look. It didn't take long for realization to dawn. 'Oh, I see,' he said. 'It's for the good of the country, I suppose.'

It was a debate Aleksei had had with Maks, long ago. He could not remember precisely when. Maks had spoken of the benefit to the country (for Maks, the country would as likely have been France as Russia), but he had seemed to forget that a country is only a grouping of citizens within a geographical boundary. The tsar was a citizen of Russia, but his death would not do *him* any good.

'Would you kill a serf, if it was for the good of the country?' Aleksei knew he shouldn't get into such discussions, not here, but it was likely that Obukhov would assume that he was simply playing devil's advocate.

'We're doing this for the serfs,' said Obukhov earnestly. Maks would have come up with a better answer. Would Obukhov, he wondered, kill ten million serfs to liberate ten million and one? Aleksei suddenly remembered where he had had that conversation with Maks. It was in that hut near Desna, moments before Maks had died. He gulped down his vodka and raised his hand to order another. He wondered whether he should press the point with Obukhov, but before he could, they were interrupted by a sound from the next room.

A piano had started playing, and after a few bars, voices joined it. The song was 'Where Are Those Islands?' Aleksei, like many of those present, was personally acquainted with the lyricist. He had spoken to him only days before. It was Kondraty Fyodorovich Ryleev, leader of the Northern Society, in whose house Aleksei had but recently discussed the very assassination of which he had just informed Obukhov. Ryleev was a poet of some standing, and works such as 'Where Are Those Islands?' were sung in the most conservative of establishments. Other pieces, which revealed more of his politics, were not. Sometimes he was mentioned in the same breath as Pushkin – in terms of politics as well as talent – but Pushkin was more idealistic, which not only benefited his poetry, but kept him away from serious revolutionary groups such as this one; that and exile to the south, though as far as Aleksei knew, he had not become involved with the Southern Society.

Along with most of the other officers in the room, Aleksei and Obukhov made their way through to join in with the singing. The adjoining room was much larger, with space in the middle of the floor large enough to dance, as two or three men were attempting to do, little though the tempo of the song suggested it. Most were thronged around the piano, obscuring it from view. They were drunk enough to sing and, for the most part, not so drunk as to sing badly.

Aleksei felt his lips moving in time with the words, and a few quiet notes formed in his voicebox. The idea of singing out loud did not appeal to him – certainly not the idea of others hearing him – but he enjoyed joining in, being part of the spontaneous choir. He had lost sight of Obukhov, but he gradually pressed his way through the crowd towards the piano. The pianist was doing a marvellous job, not simply accompanying, but introducing decorations and countermelodies, and yet never outshining the singers themselves.

At last, Aleksei got within sight of the man at the piano. As their eyes met, Aleksei felt the words of the song freeze in his throat. It would have been an acute ear that noticed the briefest of caesurae in Dmitry's playing, but after he saw his father, his accompaniment reduced in complexity to being simply that. The virtuoso flourishes that had previously adorned his playing vanished.

Aleksei had never suspected that his son might have anything to do with the Northern Society. For one thing, he was far too young. For another, he had never been out of Russia – excepting one brief visit to Warsaw – never to the West. The two reasons were really the same reason. It was in Paris that the soldiers who had fought Napoleon, routed him from their own land and pursued him across a continent, discovered the true nature of what they had been fighting. For many, particularly the young, it was paradise. For Aleksei it came close, but he had been old enough to understand that it was a paradise that could never be achieved in Russia. The idea of Heaven on earth brings with it, inescapably, the concept of the final destruction of earth. And Russia was the most earthly nation imaginable. More than that, Aleksei knew that even France was no utopia, for how could a utopia have produced the monster Bonaparte? He had dragged half a million men across Europe into Russia and returned with less than a hundred thousand. That didn't even take into account the Russians who had died. Whatever blessings the French Revolution had brought, it had not brought peace, and Aleksei had fought in enough battles to love peace above all things; even above freedom.

Thus, although there were a few in the Northern Society of Aleksei's age, and older, he was too old to be a typical member. Similarly, Dmitry was too young; too young and too Russian. But if Dmitry had somehow acquired revolutionary ideas during his short life, they could only have come from one source – Aleksei himself. It would be appropriate. Aleksei's own father had had little education, and yet his love of the idea of learning had been passed down to Aleksei to become in him a reality. Had Aleksei's talk of liberty similarly become in his son a concrete desire to bring that liberty about, no matter what the cost?

Aleksei's eyes locked with his son's for less than a second. He could see questions in Dmitry's face that were no less confused than those in his own mind. For Dmitry to learn that his father mixed with those who openly plotted to overthrow the tsar would be more shocking than anything Aleksei could feel at the reverse discovery. He did not wait for his son to ask those questions. He turned and fled – walking calmly and unhurriedly, yet still his action could only be described as flight – walking out of the room, out of the building and into the cool, darkening evening of Lubyanka Square.

*   *   *

Aleksei had not had far to walk to reach that evening's rendez-vous. Red Square was a very different place from what it had been when he first met the Oprichniki there in 1812. Before that – only days before – it had been different again, filled with shops and stalls that obscured the huge majesty of the open space that lay to the east of the Kremlin. By the time Aleksei had had his meetings there, during the French occupation, most of those primitive wooden buildings had been burnt to nothing, and the stone ones had suffered almost as badly. The rebuilt square was less cluttered. There were still shops on the east side, but nothing taller than a single storey. Nothing had been built that would hide Saint Vasiliy's or the Kremlin itself. Beyond the cathedral, on the hill down to the river, there was a mess of new buildings, but they were scarcely visible from the square. Even viewed from the south, Saint Vasiliy's managed to dwarf them.

It was a little after eight when Aleksei arrived. He preferred the square as it was now, though he would have liked it even more if it had been completely clear – of shops, at least. He would have broken down and cried if Saint Vasiliy's had become a victim of the fires. He stood briefly to look up at the statue of Minin and Pozharskiy taking pride of place in the centre of the square. This was the kind of clutter he appreciated, even though it was less than a decade old. The heroic events it commemorated were over two centuries old, back in the 'Time of Troubles'. Boris Godunov – one of the original Oprichniki after whom the monsters Aleksei had encountered had been given the epithet – had declared himself emperor, but the entire nation had come under threat from a Polish invasion, which had besieged the Kremlin. It was only when a prince, Dmitry Mihailovich Pozharskiy, and a butcher, Kuzma Minich Minin, had raised an army of Muscovites that the Poles were driven out. The year was 1612. It was always the twelves. 1612: liberation from the Poles, which led almost immediately to the foundation of the Romanov dynasty. 1712: the year Saint Petersburg became the capital – Aleksei might not have liked it, but he couldn't deny its place in history. 1812: the defeat of

Bonaparte – an event that had not merely changed Russia, but the entire world. What, Aleksei wondered, would happen in 1912 that would be so globally significant that it could compare with the happenings of a century, two centuries, three centuries before? Aleksei would not be around see it. Neither would his children – but his children's children? Perhaps.

There was still no sign of Kyesha, but the clock on the Saviour's Tower said that it was barely half past eight. Aleksei walked on towards Saint Vasiliy's, revelling in the new openness of the square. He had entered from the north, and the moment he had done so, the cathedral had called to him across the vast empty space, in a way it never could have when the area was built up. The Kremlin itself was ubiquitous, looming over the entire length of Red Square, but Saint Vasiliy's was like a beacon, small in the distance, but never insignificant, and ever growing as it was approached. Aleksei had seen Notre Dame in Paris. He had been inside and had climbed its towers. It was massive and beautiful, but it could never be as compelling as this ornate, garish symbol of all that it meant to be Russian.

'I never could work out quite where in Red Square you planned to meet.' Aleksei could not see where Kyesha had come from. It did not matter.

'It doesn't seem to have caused you any trouble,' he said.

'Are you ready to play?'

'Of course. Where shall we go?'

Kyesha looked around, then nodded towards the only object that interrupted the surface of the square between the cathedral and the statue of Minin and Pozharskiy – the Lobnoye Mesto. It was a round stone dais from which, traditionally, the ukases issued by the tsar had been announced. They climbed the steps up to it. The platform itself was more than a man's height above the square, and surrounded by a stone wall that came up almost to Aleksei's shoulders. It would not have been easy to attract attention when making a proclamation, but at the very centre of the large circular platform was another, smaller podium. Aleksei presumed it would have been on this that the herald actually stood.

But it was not Aleksei and Kyesha's intention to be seen by the people in the square, few of them though there were that evening. Once they had sat down, their backs against the outer wall, they were invisible to anyone who did not actually climb the steps and look inside. Even if someone had done, they would have had to look closely to see the two men through the darkness of the moonless night. But the dark would be an equal problem for them if they intended to play knucklebones. Kyesha had come prepared. He lit a candle. Its dim light didn't even reach the far wall, but it was sufficient. He took the bones from his pocket again and placed five of them on the stone floor between them.

'How shall we do this?' asked Aleksei. He was sure Kyesha would have worked out the details.

'The question is the bet,' he replied. 'You announce the question and the number of bones, and if you succeed, you're given an answer. We'll forget about doubling.'

'And if you don't succeed?'

'Then you lose control of the bones. We keep playing till we fail – then the other one gets a go.' He pushed the bones towards Aleksei. 'You start.'

Aleksei threw the five bones on to the ground. He didn't need to worry about catches on the back of the hand, and again he chose the largest to throw into the air. Then he had to think of a question.

'When was your brother's birthday?' he asked. 'For two.'

'I'd have thought you'd know that already,' said Kyesha, 'but I'll accept.'

Aleksei did know it already. It wasn't that sort of question. He threw the bone in the air and picked up two easily.

'13 April 1788,' said Kyesha. Aleksei still found it very doubtful that this was indeed Maks' brother, but he had done his homework. He threw the stones down again, perhaps a little too hard. They bounced wildly and spread further apart than usual.

117

'What's your mother's patronymic? For two.'

Kyesha accepted. It was a harder pick-up, but Aleksei managed it.

'Malinovna,' said Kyesha. 'But that was too easy, Aleksei; it was in the letter I gave you.'

Aleksei had realized that almost as soon as he'd asked the question. He threw the bones again. 'Your father's?' he asked. 'For two.'

'I don't accept,' said Kyesha. Aleksei smiled. It seemed that his opponent's research had not gone very deep after all.

'For three?'

'OK.'

The way the bones had fallen made three tricky. Aleksei threw the one in his hand higher than he had before. He picked up three from the ground easily enough, but had to reach out to catch the one in the air. He smiled as he felt his fingers grip it, and then looked Kyesha in the face, waiting for an answer.

'Our father's name was Sergei.' He paused, as if unsure, but Aleksei guessed now that he was merely teasing. 'Sergei Ilyich Lukin.'

He was right. It meant nothing except that he had come well prepared. Aleksei tried a change of tack. He threw the bones down again.

'Have we met before? For two.'

'No,' said Kyesha.

'We haven't?' asked Aleksei.

'I mean, no, I don't accept the bet.'

'For three?'

Kyesha shook his head.

'For four?'

Kyesha considered for a moment, then nodded. It did not really matter. Aleksei knew Kyesha would not have tried to avoid the question if the answer had been 'no'. His very resistance implied – though he might well have been bluffing – that they had met.

Aleksei had thought his face familiar that first evening in the theatre, but he still could not place it.

The large bone hit the stone platform with a gentle click just as Aleksei's fingers reached for the third one to pick up. He did not mind about not having his question answered, but it did mean that he lost control. He handed the bones over to Kyesha.

'I have no personal questions for you, Aleksei,' he said, throwing the bones down. 'I trust that you are who you say you are.' Aleksei noted, not for the first time, how Kyesha's calm and confidence appeared out of keeping with his youth.

'When did my brother die?' he asked. 'For two.'

Aleksei accepted. It was an easy bet, but Aleksei had no objections to answering the question. In fact, he realized, he would probably learn more from hearing what Kyesha had to ask than from any answers he might give to Aleksei's questions. Kyesha had no trouble picking up the knucklebones.

'28 August 1812,' said Aleksei. It was a date he would never forget.

'Was he a traitor? For two.'

Aleksei nodded his acceptance of the bet even as he considered what his answer would be. Again, Kyesha had no trouble snatching up the two bones, but Aleksei did not answer his question.

'Well? Was Maksim a traitor?'

'He was a French spy,' said Aleksei. 'He confessed that much to me himself.' The words were carefully chosen, and Kyesha did not press for a more direct answer. Instead, he cast down the bones again.

'Did you kill him? For one.'

Aleksei would have answered that question for none, as Kyesha had clearly guessed with the simplicity of the challenge, but they followed the routine.

'No, I did not,' he answered when the time came. The direct answer disguised more than it revealed.

'Did Dmitry? For two.'

For a brief moment, Aleksei felt a horrible pang of concern at the

119

sound of his son's name on Kyesha's lips, but he quickly realized that the object of the question was not Dmitry Alekseevich, but the long dead Dmitry Fetyukovich. Aleksei pictured the abandoned farmyard where he had last seen Dmitry – not the last time he had seen him alive, nor indeed the first time he had seen him dead. It had been the spring of 1813. At the first sign of a thaw, Aleksei had headed back to the burnt-out farmhouse north of Yurtsevo where he had left Dmitry's frozen corpse. Even then, the ground had been hard to dig – but easier than it would have been in the winter, when Aleksei had first found the body. It did not matter how hard it was; Aleksei had made a promise to himself. Dmitry was the third and last of the three comrades he had lost during Bonaparte's invasion. He had witnessed none of their deaths, but had buried them all.

'For three then?' asked Kyesha, misinterpreting Aleksei's silence. Aleksei nodded, and Kyesha collected the bones without trouble.

'No,' said Aleksei. 'Dmitry didn't kill Maks either.' It was as accurate as the answer he had just given concerning himself.

'There was a famous Dmitry died at this very spot, wasn't there?' said Kyesha. Aleksei said nothing, surprised by the change of subject. He glanced down at the knucklebones. Kyesha misread the gesture. 'You're not going to make me play for an answer to a question like that, are you?'

Aleksei smiled. 'I suppose not. You're right. That was 1606. The first "False Dmitry".'

'There was more than one?'

'There were three – each claiming, falsely, to be the missing heir to the late tsar, Ivan IV. All in the Time of Troubles. He didn't last long. When the mob had finished with him, they left his body here.' Aleksei was a little surprised that Kyesha didn't know all this, but Maks too had had surprising gaps in his knowledge of Russian history. On the other hand, Kyesha might just have been playing dumb. 'You know why they call this thing Lobnoye Mesto?' he asked.

'"*Ee, preedya na mesto, nazivayemoye Golgofa, shto znacheet: Lobnoye Mesto . . .*"' Kyesha recited the words in a monotone, as if he had learned them by rote, long ago, as any good Christian should have. 'Matthew 27:33,' he added.

'And they came to a place named Golgotha, which means: the Place of the Skull . . .' At least, that was how the French described it, presumably from the Greek. The literal meaning of the Russian term 'Lobnoye Mesto' was closer to 'the Place of the Forehead', though that sense was usually forgotten. It was now a phrase that, in reality, meant simply 'the Place of Execution'. Either way, it was just a description of a rocky outcrop near Jerusalem two millennia before which had a passing resemblance to a human skull, and whatever the etymology, this place represented to the Orthodox Church and to many Russians the spot upon which Christ was crucified.

Aleksei suddenly felt uncomfortable, sitting in the dark in this holy place, gambling with knucklebones, even if they weren't playing for money. 'Can we go?' he said.

'Just one more round,' said Kyesha. 'Look – I've already cast.' Four bones lay on the stone floor, and Kyesha had already picked up the fifth, ready to throw it. 'Who did kill Maks? For two.'

Aleksei shook his head. He had no reason not to answer the question, but he felt a sudden urge to make life difficult for Kyesha.

'For three?'

'For four,' said Aleksei.

Kyesha considered for a moment, then nodded. He threw the bone into the air, no higher than he had done for earlier rounds. His hand moved at tremendous speed across the stone slabs as it picked up the other bones, faster than Aleksei could have managed – faster than any human could have managed, and the implication was not lost on Aleksei. Kyesha had plenty of time to pluck the last, falling bone from the air before it was anywhere near the ground.

'So . . .' he said.

'Maks was killed by six Wallachian mercenaries, from a group that at the time numbered nine in total. We called them the Oprichniki, as a joke.' Aleksei could not recall a moment when it had been funny. 'Originally there were twelve of them, but Maks had handed three over to the French, who executed them. That's why the others wanted revenge.' There had been a time – a very brief period – when that was essentially the story as Aleksei himself had believed it, before he had discovered that all but one of those mercenaries were in fact vampires. He doubted whether Kyesha would have gone to all this effort if his concerns were not in some way related to that fact – it was more than conceivable that he was a *voordalak* himself; Aleksei had never seen him in daylight. But that sort of information could keep until Aleksei was more certain of its value.

'What were their names?' asked Kyesha.

Aleksei pushed the knucklebones towards him. 'That's another question,' he said.

Suddenly, the dais in which they were sitting was filled with light. They both looked towards it. Aleksei's eyes adjusted, and he saw that its source was no more than a lantern.

'You can't sleep here,' said a voice emanating from behind the light. Aleksei was taken back for a moment to the French occupation, when enemy soldiers had constantly harassed him and other Russians who had remained in the city. But this voice spoke in Russian, not French. It was one of the guards from the nearby Saviour's Gate of the Kremlin. Aleksei rose to his feet. He would have needed only to show the guard his identification papers for the man to be running back and forth between the Kremlin and the Lobnoye Mesto, bringing them tea and vodka and anything else they might ask for, but he preferred to let the evening end there.

He walked down the stone steps, back into Red Square. Kyesha followed him. The soldier stood above them, at the entrance to the platform, waiting to see that they left.

'Until tomorrow,' said Kyesha. He gave a half-hearted salute and then turned away, heading down the hill towards the river. Aleksei's journey took him north. When he was halfway across the square he glanced back and could see the glimmer of the guard's lantern as he stood waiting at the Place of the Skull. The next time he looked, the light had gone.

Domnikiia was not asleep when Aleksei slipped into bed beside her. He had kissed Tamara lightly on the forehead as she slept, and she had not woken.

'Where have you been?' asked Domnikiia.

It wasn't a question she normally asked. She knew the nature of his work, and knew therefore that there was much he could not share with her.

'Just . . . seeing people,' he said. 'You know.' He gazed up into the darkness, fixing his eyes on a ceiling he could not see. He felt Domnikiia roll over towards him. Her cool, naked thigh curled over his and he felt her cheek on his chest. Her arm reached across him and she squeezed him tightly to her. He stroked her long, dark hair. She said nothing. There was a melancholy to her that he had only known once before, many years ago.

'What is it?' he asked.

'They're back, Lyosha,' she said softly.

He was tempted to reply with a patronizing 'Who?', but Domnikiia knew him well enough not to be fooled by it. Ever since he'd seen that red lettering scrawled on the walls of his study in Petersburg, he'd known that, in some sense or other, they were back.

'How do you know?' he asked.

'Yelena Vadimovna told me. There's been a murder – at least, that's what they're calling it. A man. They found him out near . . . near where I used to work. But it wasn't murder. She told me about the body. The blood. The throat. It sounds just like Margarita.' The image of the corpse of Domnikiia's friend and colleague Margarita Kirillovna lying on her bed, naked, with her throat ripped open flashed into Aleksei's mind. Once he had had no further use for her, Iuda had slaughtered her. Of course, Iuda was not a *voordalak*, but in killing he had impersonated one. And though Domnikiia had not, Aleksei had seen the bodies of enough victims of true vampires to know that it was a precise impersonation.

'That could be just exaggeration,' said Aleksei. 'Someone's throat is slit and rumour blows it out of all proportion. It would have been at least third hand by the time it got to Yelena.'

'I'd have thought that, if you hadn't come dashing down here to see who left you that message. Did you find him?'

Aleksei had not told her anything since his visit to the theatre. She had not asked, but now that she did, she deserved an answer.

'He claims to be Maks' brother.'

'Maks didn't have a brother,' she said, with no pause for consideration.

'Are you sure?' Aleksei had thought the same, but did not share Domnikiia's glib certainty.

She got out of bed, and Aleksei heard her walk over to her dressing table. A light flared as she lit a candle. Aleksei watched as she bent forward and opened a drawer. She brushed her hair back over her shoulder, revealing her breast. He still felt thrilled by her. She turned her face to him, detecting his gaze, and smiled a short tight smile that said so much about their relationship. Then she delved into the drawer and pulled out a battered old notebook. She returned to the bed, placing the candle on the table beside him, and slipped back under the blankets. She flicked through the book, not reading in detail, but just glancing at each page, as if looking for something in particular.

'You know you were always impressed by my memory,' she said.

'I still am.'

'Well, I cheat.' She held the book out to him; it was folded back so that he could only see one page. It was a blur to Aleksei. He had not noticed many signs of old age encroaching upon his body, but his worsening eyesight was one of them. He pushed Domnikiia's wrist, moving the page further away from him, and held the candle close to it. The writing at the top of the page was largest.

Snowman.

He narrowed his eyes and read on.

Aleksei Ivanovich Danilov. Captain. Lyosha.

'What *is* this?' he asked.

'It's my client notes,' she said. 'Every man who ever paid me to lie back and convince him he was the greatest fuck I'd ever known. And to convince them of that, you have to pretend that they made an impression. And to do that, it helps if you remember things about them.'

'And Snowman?' he asked.

'I gave you all nicknames. Some didn't tell me their names at all. Most lied. A nickname is easier to remember.'

'But why Snowman?'

'You saved me from a vicious snowball attack, remember?'

He laughed and she bent forward to kiss him. He felt her lips touch his, but his eyes remained on the page. There was a huge amount of information, with little structure to it, just added as it was discovered.

*No uniform. Married. Son. Dmitry. Fingers. Marfa.
Two brothers.*

There were dozens of small details about his life, his habits, his interests. And amongst all that, with increasing frequency and candour, descriptions of activities which Aleksei could not even have begun to describe in words, and yet every one of which he recognized with a mixture of embarrassment and pleasure.

The last thing on the page was about halfway down – a single short phrase. The rest was blank.

Miss him.

Aleksei looked over at Domnikiia. Her eyes glistened. He stroked her forearm gently with his thumb.

'You were very professional,' he said.

'Mostly.'

'But I don't think we want anyone else to see this, do we?' he said, reaching forward and pretending he was about to tear the page from the book.

'Hang on!' She snatched the book from him. 'I still need to check things sometimes.'

He took hold of her wrist and pulled her down on to him. They kissed again, then he tried to grab the book off her, but she held it away at arm's length.

'Anyway, why are you showing me this now?' he asked.

She rolled off him and turned her attention back to the book. 'Because of Maks,' she said.

Aleksei was glad she had her back to him, so that she couldn't see the smile on his face deflate. It was no secret that she had slept with Maks, but it had for years been unspoken. There was nothing wrong in it. It was her job, but the depth of Aleksei's affection meant that it pained him even now; not his affection for Domnikiia, great though that was, but his affection for Maks.

'Here we are,' she said, showing him another page, but keeping her hand over the bottom half.

Robespierre.
Eyeglasses. Maksim. Maks. Lukin.

The nickname was apt. Domnikiia had shown an appreciation for Maks' true nature that Aleksei had only learned much later. He scanned further down the pages.

Mother in Saratov. Yelizaveta Malinovna. Two sisters.
Only brother died in infancy. Don't bring up. Innokyentii.

'Innokyentii – that's the name he's using. Or, at least, Kyesha.'

'So he's not Maks' brother, but he knows what he's talking about,' said Domnikiia. Aleksei had to agree, but his mind had already moved on from there. He'd never heard of Maks having a brother until Kyesha had mentioned it. Now he could see, almost at first hand, that the idea was based on fact. The question that now presented itself was, how had Kyesha got the information? He couldn't help wondering whether the answer was staring him in the face.

'Let me see the rest,' he said. Domnikiia's hand still covered the bottom of the page.

'No!' she exclaimed. 'You don't really want to see what it was that turned Maks on, do you?'

'Don't be silly. What I want to see is if there are any other details I can use to check whether Kyesha has got his facts right.'

Domnikiia reluctantly removed her hand. The paper beneath it was blank.

'There wasn't really anything very special about him,' she said, as though it were a confession. 'But I didn't have very long to get to know him before you scared him off.'

Aleksei could understand how she might want to protect Maks' memory by hiding how small an impression he had made on her, but it did not matter. Maks' greatness had lain elsewhere. The more significant discovery was that Kyesha had not got his information from this book. It was preposterous to think that he might have, but the seeds of doubt Iuda had sown could germinate at any time, however stony the ground might appear.

'So is he a vampire, this Kyesha?' asked Domnikiia.

'I don't know, but it's a possibility.'

'And will you kill him, if he is?'

Aleksei nodded. 'Oh, yes.' It was a conclusion he had come to within hours of first discovering that the *voordalak* was more

127

than a phantom from his grandmother's tales – that all such creatures must die. Nothing he had learned about them since had changed his mind. It had to be said, though, that beyond those he had encountered in 1812, he had not come across a single other example of the species. He had been on several wild goose chases since then – six, to be precise – but they had all ended in natural explanations, fortunately for the suspects in question. He would treat Kyesha with the same dispassion.

Domnikiia took the book and put it back in the drawer. Then she snuffed out the candle and crawled back into bed beside Aleksei. They lay in silence for several minutes, but her breathing did not slow down to the settled murmur of sleep.

'Do you have to?' she asked eventually.

'*He's* come after *me*. I have to do something.'

'What does he want?'

'I don't know, yet.'

'You were lucky before, you know that. And now you have Tamara to think of.'

'I had Dmitry then,' he said. She rolled over so that her back faced him and said nothing more, but he knew that she understood what he had to do, for both his children. He reached over and his hand found hers. Her five fingers squeezed his three.

Aleksei could not guess how long he had lain there. He had not slept, nor had he been wide awake, but as the day's events tumbled through his mind he had realized that there was one problem, quite unrelated to Kyesha, that he had to deal with. He pulled his hand away from Domnikiia. In sleep, her fingers did not try to restrain him. He slipped on his robe and went into the next room.

He had few possessions which he kept here; most were at the hotel in Zamoskvorechye, which he tried to visit at least once a day, if only to collect his mail. In the corner of the room lay a battered leather saddlebag – acquired even before Austerlitz – where he kept those things from which he dared not be parted. He lit the lamp and hauled the bag on to the desk. He knew that what he was after was in the small, left-hand pouch. Five thin sheets of paper folded into three: the list of members of the Northern Society he had stolen in Petersburg. He unfolded it and peered at the text. The writing was even smaller than Domnikiia's. He could make nothing of it.

He reached into the bag again, and his fingers felt what he needed. He brought out the spectacles. They had been Maks'. Aleksei had taken them from his body before burying it, all those years before. One lens had been broken, but Aleksei had had no practical use for them, not then. It had been soon after Tamara's birth that he first noticed he had trouble reading. He had tried the spectacles, but even the single lens that was intact did nothing to help – in fact it made matters worse. Aleksei had struggled to remember a long-forgotten conversation with Maks about them. Maks could not see at a distance, but he could see close up. Old people – that had been Maks' term, and Aleksei knew that it now applied to him – found it hard to see to read. A different-shaped lens was needed to fix each of the two problems.

'And what will *you* do when you're old?' Aleksei had asked. 'Two pairs of lenses?'

'I'll turn to Benjamin Franklin,' Maks had replied, with a smile.

'A long way to America. And isn't he a little . . . dead?'

'A man's ideas live after his death,' Maks had explained. 'And you're right: Franklin's invention was two pairs of lenses, bound together in a single frame. One for when you're looking out in front of you, one when you're looking down at a book. I know a man in Petersburg who can grind them for me – when the time comes.'

But for Maks, the time had never come, nor had any other of those signs of ageing that Aleksei had feared in his youth but embraced in his middle age as reminders of the fact that he had survived to grow old. He could still see at a distance, but he had gone, when reading had become too difficult, to that same optician in Petersburg, and had him make some lenses to fit Maks' old frames. He avoided wearing them in front of Domnikiia – that was why he had struggled on in the bedroom reading her book. But now he slipped them on and looked at the names on the list.

Fortunately, they were alphabetical. He found what he was after about two thirds of the way down page two.

Grigoriev, V. F.
Gusev, I. B.
Danilov, A. I.
Danilov, D. A.
Demidov, E. B.
Dmitriev, P. P.

So Dmitry was more than just the piano player; Aleksei had never really thought otherwise. Dmitry would never have got into the club if he had not been trusted, and the look Aleksei had seen in his son's eye had told him the truth. This was mere confirmation. But it left many questions unanswered. Simply being a supporter of the Northern Society did not mean being a supporter of all its methods – most, in fact, did not know the detailed plans. Only the inner circle into which Aleksei had insinuated himself was aware of the scheme, vague though it still was, to assassinate the tsar. That was, in part, why he had revealed the information to Obukhov, and intended to reveal it to others; in the hope that the realization of what was being planned would shock the Society into collapse from the roots upward. But Obukhov had not been shocked. Would Dmitry be, when he discovered the truth?

Another question that raised its head was why Aleksei had never heard a hint that he and his son were, ostensibly at least, working for the same cause. Of course, Dmitry himself would not have mentioned it, but why had there not been even a word of congratulation from Ryleev or Obolensky, who clearly knew? Perhaps they understood security better than they seemed to – that any unnecessary discussion of other members, even fathers and sons, was a potential risk. Perhaps they simply hadn't thought the issue important enough to raise.

It did not matter. What did matter was the list Aleksei held in front of him. He opened the desk drawer and found some paper. It did not match the paper on which the list was written, nor would he be capable of seamlessly imitating the handwriting on it. It was unimportant – it simply meant a little more work. Instead of replacing one page, he would rewrite all five. He could disguise his hand, and even if he was caught out, he could say he had copied the list.

It took him only half an hour to complete the task – simply to copy names from one sheet of paper to another. He should have looked at the list in detail before. There were a few names that surprised him, but none that he cared to do anything about, except for that one on the second page. He glanced at his work once he had finished.

Grigoriev, V. F.
Gusev, I. B.
Danilov, A. I.
Demidov, E. B.
Dmitriev, P. P.

Of course, it would take more than that to remove suspicion from Dmitry completely, but Aleksei would have to work that out when the time came. His hope was still that the entire plot would collapse and that the list would never be needed. He pondered for a moment whether he should have removed his own name as well, but it would have been foolish. Whoever he handed the list to – *if* he chose to hand it over at all – would clearly be aware of his membership and of where his true loyalties lay. If they saw that his name was missing, they would know the list had been tampered with, and if they knew that, they might well infer that it was not only Aleksei's name that had been removed. Better to keep the changes to a minimum.

Aleksei screwed the sheets of the original list together into a loose, crumpled ball, then lit them using the flame of the lamp. He dropped the burning papers into the grille of the fire and watched them writhe and curl. The flames quickly began to lessen, before all the paper was consumed. He poked it with the fire iron and it burst briefly into flame again. It went out a second time, with only a tiny patch of paper still unblackened. A glowing red line of flameless combustion worked its way slowly across the last few names, like an advancing army viewed from above, turning in on itself and forming a circle which shrank smaller and smaller before vanishing to nothing, finally exhausting its fuel supply. Even then, some of the paper, now as ashes, maintained the shape it had had before the flames reached it. The ink of the names was still visible, blacker on black. He stirred the remains with the fire iron, and the cinders collapsed to powder. Any information they might have carried was finally destroyed.

Aleksei turned back to the bedroom. He glanced in on Tamara as he passed. She was sleeping soundly. Today, Aleksei realized, she had a little more in common with her half-brother than she had had before. It was a strange world he inhabited that forced him now to make secrets of not one but both of his children.

CHAPTER VII

KYESHA PICKED UP THE THREE BONES EASILY AND CAUGHT THE fourth on the back of his hand, even though it was quite unnecessary by the rules they had formulated. He was merely showing off. His first question of the evening had been a simple one:

'What were their names?'

Aleksei happily answered. 'Pyetr, Filipp, Andrei, Iakov, Varfolomei and Iuda. They're aliases, of course. The three that weren't there were Foma, Matfei and Ioann.'

'How very pious,' observed Kyesha.

'What's in a name?' said Aleksei bitterly.

'What happened to them? For three.'

Aleksei nodded. The game was by now no more than a formality. Kyesha had no trouble picking up three or four, and probably more. It was an easy game for a vampire – with agile movement and an ability to see in poor light. But Aleksei would not judge him yet. Perhaps he was a mortal human who merely practised a lot. He succeeded easily in the task.

'They're dead.'

'All of them?'

Aleksei's eyes flicked at the knucklebones and Kyesha rapidly went through the motions of the game, as though it were some sacred ritual that by tradition had to accompany each question.

'All of them?' he asked again, when he had finished.

'All of them,' said Aleksei.

'Did you kill them?' Again the same action.

Aleksei considered before answering. Was this what Kyesha had truly come to find out? And once Aleksei told him, would he take revenge for the deaths of his fellow creatures? It seemed unlikely. Why be so scrupulous? A *voordalak* might kill two or three in a night simply for food – Aleksei had seen it himself. They could kill dozens if they had reason to. If Kyesha had come to take revenge on Aleksei, he would have just got on with it.

'Yes, I killed them all,' he said. There was a bragging tone to his voice, as he took pleasure in telling this *voordalak* what a dab hand he had been at dispatching others of his kind. Just as Domnikiia had reminded him the previous night, some of the deaths had been matters more of luck than design, but Aleksei had been there and made sure that luck had gone his way. Even so, he knew that his real good fortune lay in the fact that Iuda had found him more interesting alive than dead.

'It seems then that there's no need for me to avenge my brother's death,' said Kyesha. He reached into his pocket and pulled out the sixth and smallest of the knucklebones he had first shown Aleksei at the tavern, just nights before. They were in a tavern again. This one sat opposite the Church of St Clement, where they had met. Its red-plaster walls were visible through the window. 'This is getting too easy,' said Kyesha. 'And I think my next question is going to deserve five.'

He scattered all six bones across the table, and again picked up the largest.

'For five then,' he said. Aleksei nodded his agreement. Kyesha paused and then asked the question. 'Is it true that they were *voordalaki*?'

Aleksei did not even have time to accept or reject the question before Kyesha comfortably picked up all five bones and caught the sixth. It was a strange relief to hear the word on Kyesha's lips. It proved nothing about his nature, but it confirmed to Aleksei that this had little to do with one brother avenging the death of another.

'It's close enough,' said Aleksei. Kyesha raised a questioning eyebrow. 'Iuda was human, though the others never guessed. He was as foul a creature as any of them – I'm not sure there'll be any distinction made at doomsday.'

Kyesha cast the bones again. 'For three – are you sure Iuda was not a *voordalak*?' He picked them up without trouble.

'I saw him in daylight,' said Aleksei. More than he could say for Kyesha.

'For one. Did you kill Iuda?'

'I did.'

Kyesha gathered the bones again. 'For three,' he said. 'Did you kill Iuda?'

'I did.'

'For five. Did you kill Iuda?' Kyesha threw the large bone into the air, then picked up one, two, three, four and five off the table. He turned his hand over, opening his palm to receive the falling bone, but it did not reach him. Aleksei's hand shot forward and plucked it out of the air just inches above Kyesha's fingers.

Kyesha smiled. 'You can tell me tomorrow,' he said. With that he left.

It was surely mere coincidence that the route Kyesha had chosen to take away from his meeting with Aleksei at the Church of Saint Clement was exactly that taken by the Oprichnik Foma after a similar meeting at the same location in the autumn of 1812. Aleksei's desire to follow had been much the same on both occasions, though in 1812 he had had no idea what his pursuit might ultimately reveal; today, his intent was merely to confirm what he already suspected – that Kyesha was a creature of exactly the same nature as Foma. They were to the south of the city centre, and so to head north was a reasonable decision for anyone. It was just before the Vodootvodny Canal that Kyesha's path diverged from Foma's, turning to head west instead of continuing north.

Aleksei kept a safe distance. It was no surprise to him that he could remember the route along which he had pursued Foma, so many years before. There were few events of that autumn that had not been retraced and repeated endlessly in his mind in the intervening years. The process of following was different now. The city was free. It was crowded, even at this late hour, with Muscovites, and empty of occupying soldiers who would stop anyone who caught their interest and question them about their business. The benefits accrued more to the pursued than the pursuer. Aleksei still had to be stealthy, to avoid Kyesha seeing him, while Kyesha had nothing to slow his progress.

Kyesha turned north again and on to the Stone Bridge. Aleksei was forced to hang back. On the streets, it had been possible to get quite close to his quarry, to use buildings and alleyways to hide in if Kyesha happened to turn back. But now there was nothing. From the middle of the bridge, Kyesha would have a clear view all around him, the streetlamps providing ample illumination, despite the lack of moonlight. Aleksei could only wait while Kyesha moved further and further away. Eventually he would have to risk crossing the river himself, but he was fortunate. A group of three men – drunk, but not so drunk as to slow their progress – began to walk over the bridge. Aleksei followed, a few paces behind. Now he had mobile camouflage. He could easily step out to the side and look around the men and make sure that Kyesha had not got too far from him, but if Kyesha were to turn, all he would see would be the three revellers ambling along. Even if he did catch a glimpse of a figure behind them, he would not recognize it as Aleksei.

Aleksei was in the dead centre of the bridge when Kyesha stepped off its northern end. Aleksei could not see which way he had turned. There was no sign of him heading east along the embankment, or north along Manezhnaya Street, clearly visible as it ran alongside the Kremlin. Aleksei darted over to the left-hand side of the bridge and looked down. There he saw Kyesha heading west and about to disappear once again between the built-up

136

houses. Aleksei instantly abandoned all attempts at subterfuge and sprinted across the remainder of the bridge. He was unlikely to be seen by Kyesha, who was now out of sight, but unconcerned if he was. Kyesha's chosen route was precisely that which Aleksei would have taken had he decided not to follow Kyesha but return straight home. True, there were many turnings Kyesha could take in the tight web of streets he had just entered, but the one that figured greatest in Aleksei's mind was towards Arbatskaya, where Valentin and Yelena Lavrov lived as, more importantly, did Domnikiia and Toma.

Aleksei reached the end of the bridge and stared down the road where he had last seen Kyesha. There was no sign of him. But Aleksei's intention had now changed. Instead of determining where Kyesha went, his highest priority was to ensure that he did not arrive at one particular address, or that if he did, he would find Aleksei there waiting for him.

Aleksei ran home by the directest route. He saw no further sign of Kyesha, but made no attempt at stealth. Kyesha – or anyone trying to avoid detection – would have heard his approach a block away. He entered the house and went to Domnikiia and Tamara's rooms. Both were asleep. All was as it should be, but that only told him that Kyesha had not come yet, not that he would not arrive later. It was impossible to guard both Domnikiia and Tamara while they remained in separate rooms. He went into his daughter's room and pulled back the bedclothes. Only her head and feet poked out of her long nightdress. Even her hands were hidden, tucked into the sleeves. He picked her up and carried her across the room. She stirred a little, but did not wake. They entered the other bedroom and he laid her down on the bed next to her mother, pulling the blankets over her. Then he went back to their living room and, for the second night in a row, opened up his saddlebag.

He gripped the solid wooden handle of Dmitry's toy sword. It was well made, even though all those years ago Aleksei had had no idea what the real function of such a sword might be. He went

137

back to the bedroom and slipped it under the mattress on his side of the bed. Then he lay down. He reached across and rested his hand on Domnikiia's hair, listening to the sounds of breathing that came from her and from Tamara, easily distinguishing one from the other. It would have been a blissful way to spend the night, were it not for the fear that gripped him.

He knew it would have been safer to wake Domnikiia and warn her, but he refrained, not, as he at first told himself, to spare her anguish, but to spare him her reproach. It was he who had brought this on them; his inquisitiveness that had meant he couldn't resist Kyesha's bait. She would not have said anything directly; quite the reverse. She would have told him that they were in this together – there had been only a few months, at the beginning of their relationship, when they had not known and feared the *voordalak* together. More than dividing them, it was a part of what they were as a couple.

But Tamara made things different. Whatever Domnikiia might say about being unafraid for herself, she would loathe Aleksei for bringing her daughter into danger. And in those circumstances, it would be 'her' not 'their'. There was only one person in the world that Domnikiia would turn her back on Aleksei for – at least, he hoped only one.

But whatever Domnikiia's thoughts might be, it was easier to avoid the issue. He would explain Tamara's presence by saying she had had a nightmare – even if she had no memory of it herself.

Nightmare or no nightmare, it was not Toma who lay awake that night until the first orange light of dawn glowed behind the curtains and the birds struck up their announcement of the new day. Kyesha had not come. Moscow was a big city. There were many places towards which he might have been heading, and why should he know where Aleksei was living anyway?

The dawn meant he would not be arriving here, whatever his ultimate intentions; not until nightfall at any rate. If he was a *voordalak*, then in some dark cellar of the city he would be settling down to rest. The knowledge brought comfort to Aleksei, and he finally allowed himself to fall into a troubled sleep.

Dawn came to the Dardanelles an hour later than it did to Moscow. It did so just as *Răzbunarea* steered quietly out of the Aegean and into the strait. Its passenger hovered at the top of the ladder that led down to the hold. He had wanted to see them pass this place. An oddly mundane desire for a man of his stature, whose journey would change the face of Europe, but he was, nonetheless, a man with a sense of history. He gazed out at the coast of Asia Minor stretching away to the south. Somewhere there had stood Troy. Even he was not old enough to know where, but he was wise enough to know its existence was no myth.

The route that the ship was taking, at least for now, was that of Jason. Ultimately, their destinations were different, but Jason's goal of Colchis had not been so far from where *Răzbunarea* was headed. Jason's quest had been to bring back the Golden Fleece. That – unlike Troy – was surely a myth, certainly as far as its magical properties went. And it had been guarded by a serpent. If that were true, the passenger of *Răzbunarea* would surely have known about it. He glanced down at the golden beast that entwined his finger and smiled to himself. He was in danger of believing his own propaganda. But he, like Jason, would bring a great treasure back with him when he returned this way.

He gazed to the east, into the mouth of the strait, set against the backdrop of the morning twilight. He could sense to within a second of arc where the sun was. Normally, he would not have cut it so fine, but he had wanted to see the strait.

It was at the very moment the first sliver of the sun's disc appeared on the horizon that he slipped once more below deck.

'You must have been up and out very early.'

For the briefest of moments, the terrifying thought crossed Aleksei's mind that Kyesha had found him, accompanied by the far more astonishing concept that if Kyesha could be out and about at this time of day, he could not be a vampire. Both ideas were quashed in an instant as Aleksei recognized the voice as one so familiar to him – that of his own son.

He turned and saw Dmitry sitting in the hallway of the hotel reading a pamphlet.

'Well, you know me,' said Aleksei, smiling. It wasn't the smartest thing to say. Dmitry did know him, and knew therefore that early rising – certainly at his own volition – was not an obvious feature of his character. Perhaps Dmitry would take it as ironic. He had awoken particularly late this morning, due to not sleeping the previous night, and then spent an hour playing with Toma. After that he had come straight to the hotel to collect his mail and change his clothes. 'How long have you been waiting?'

'Almost four hours,' said Dmitry.

'You only just missed me,' Aleksei lied, hoping the hotel's patron had not over-elaborated his story to Dmitry. 'You should have left a note.'

'That's what I did yesterday.'

Aleksei had not come to the hotel at all the previous day. 'Yes, I'm sorry,' he said. 'I've been busy.'

'Me too. But I had to see you. I've been so excited since Monday.'

'I think we'd better walk,' said Aleksei, glancing pointedly over to the hotel keeper, who was unconvincingly pretending not to listen to their conversation. Dmitry nodded and stood up. Aleksei led the way out on to the street. They turned south, away from the centre of the city.

'I was as surprised as you are,' said Aleksei.

'You can't have been! I mean, no one's more loyal to the tsar than you.'

'I'm loyal to Russia. That's what we all have in common.'

'Well, I see that now. I always thought you saw them as one and the same thing,' said Dmitry.

Aleksei knew that he would have to lie to his son. He had lied before – to those he loved as well as those he despised – but this time was different. Each word he said against the tsar would be a lie that only made Dmitry admire his father more. What would become of that admiration if the truth were ever revealed?

'Aleksandr has changed over the years,' replied Aleksei. That was true enough, and for the worse, in Aleksei's opinion. It was the war that had caused it all, most agreed on that. In the first decade of his rule, leading up to Bonaparte's invasion, Aleksandr had had plans drawn up both for government reform and emancipation of the serfs. It had been his minister, Speransky, who had done the real work, but Aleksandr had been behind him. But with war, priorities had changed and Speransky had fallen from favour. And after the war, Aleksandr had suddenly begun to see himself as a peacemaker – he'd found an almost evangelical zeal for it – and seemed to forget the need for change at home. He was happier to be seen as a figure on the world stage, a wise older brother settling the disputes of his fellow kings, kaisers and emperors. And if he would not act as a force for transformation at home, others would, and the transformation would consume him. Aleksei could easily list the tsar's faults, but he could not share the rebels' ideas of how to address them.

'I should have known from the way you talk about Paris – and about Uncle Maks.' Dmitry wasn't really listening to what Aleksei said. He was carried away by what he believed his father to be. It almost made things worse – there was nothing now that Aleksei could say to disabuse his son, short of a full confession, and he wasn't going to risk that. 'Does Mama know?' asked Dmitry, coming to a sudden standstill.

Aleksei almost burst out laughing. 'God, no!' he said. 'Believe me, between a man and his wife, there are some things best left secret.'

'Really? It's just that . . . No. I see what you mean. But what would she think if she knew?'

'In politics, women follow their husbands,' said Aleksei. For him it was not a prescription of what should be, but a description of what was, not just in Russia but everywhere – even America.

It would certainly be the case with Marfa. Maks had once told Aleksei to read a book on the subject by an Englishwoman called Mary Wollstonecraft, but he never had. It was an issue over which Maks would have disagreed with the current leadership of the Society. '"Woman cannot be the subject of political rights; she is even barred from attending open sessions of the legislature."' Muraviev had written that.

'And their sons,' said Dmitry with a smile. No, thought Aleksei, not if it came to it. Marfa would stick with her husband.

'How long have you been with the Society?' asked Aleksei.

'Oh, not long. Two years. Ryleev may have graduated from the Cadet Corps, but he's not been forgotten. I bet you've been there from the start though.'

'Not quite but . . .' Aleksei paused. 'Look, Mitka, I don't think we should be talking like this. The Society is founded on secrecy – survives on it. We can't make exceptions, even between father and son.' Again, it wasn't a lie, but Aleksei knew that he would have to plan very carefully before prising his son from the clutches of the revolutionaries. To rush in now could ruin everything.

Dmitry nodded earnestly. 'You're right, of course, you're right.' There was a lot in him that reminded Aleksei of Maks, but the humourlessness so often found when the young discovered politics was a trait he'd never known in Maksim Sergeivich. Dmitry would grow out of it. 'Though you know they're trying to blame the murders on us?'

There was only one murder Aleksei had heard of recently. 'That bloke up in Tverskaya? What's he got to do with the Society?'

'It's more the Poles people are trying to pin it on. But it's the new one that's really got them talking.'

'Another one? When?'

'They found him yesterday morning. His throat ripped out just like before. Some people are saying it's part of a Masonic ritual – that points the finger at us too; at some of us.'

'Bollocks,' said Aleksei, a little too vehemently. Though what did he know? He had no doubt about the nature, even the identity, of the killer. But Freemasonry? Did they allow vampires to join? 'What's so ritualistic about having your throat cut?' he asked.

'It's part of the punishment – you know that.'

'And did he have his tongue ripped out and buried in the sand?' Aleksei despised and ridiculed it all in equal measure. In a way he regretted that the Union of Welfare had dropped the Masonic trappings of the Union of Salvation from which it had evolved. It was much easier to have an opponent that could be laughed at.

'No,' Dmitry conceded, 'but the place they found him was obviously ritualistic – if not specifically Masonic.'

'The place?' asked Aleksei, but even as he spoke, he understood what his son was saying. He'd been at the very spot, only two days before.

'They found him in the Lobnoye Mesto, Papa,' said Dmitry. 'At Golgotha.'

As Aleksei had noted the previous night, the midpoint of the Stone Bridge provided a fine vista of the area around it. But to see is to be seen, and any man standing at that position, even though the crescent moon was on the point of setting in the west, could not avoid being observed.

So although Kyesha had arrived early, and stood on the bridge staring down at the water that flowed below and occasionally glancing around, Aleksei had arrived earlier. Again, history was repeating itself. In 1812, on a Wednesday night, Aleksei had hidden away on the south bank of the river and watched as two of his friends met with two of his enemies – though he had not yet known them so to be. It had been that very evening, thirteen years and one month ago, that he had discovered the truth, by following the Oprichnik Matfei and seeing him feast on the body of a French soldier. Matfei had died that night by Aleksei's hand, as had another of them: Varfolomei. Tonight he would prove beyond his own doubt that Kyesha was a *voordalak* – a doubt which had already vanished to almost nothing.

The news he had heard from Dmitry of the body at the Lobnoye

143

Mesto – the body of a Kremlin guard whose colleagues had last seen him striding over from the Saviour's Gate claiming he had seen a flickering light – had convinced Aleksei of Kyesha's guilt. He had spoken to the guard, however briefly, and could almost pinpoint the moment at which his life was extinguished, along with the flame of his lantern. He should have begun tailing Kyesha that night, but now he would make amends. And when he caught up with the monster, he had ways of dealing with him.

He had his sabre, with which he might behead him, his wooden sword – newly sharpened – to drive through his heart and, most useful of all, the patience simply to wait until dawn and let the sun's rays do his work for him, at no risk to himself. The short wooden sword was easy enough to conceal, and his sabre hung from a loop of cloth around his shoulder, so it could not be seen beneath his long greatcoat. It was a technique he had devised when trying to hide the weapon from the French, but it would work just as well against a *voordalak*. If Kyesha got close enough to see it, Aleksei would be close enough to use it.

There had been some degree of rebuilding work along the Sofia Embankment, but Aleksei found a sidestreet, very close to where he had stood before, and watched the bridge, hidden by the corner of a house. Kyesha waited for over an hour, his movements becoming increasingly impatient. Aleksei felt the bizarre sensation that he was being rude. He'd arranged to meet Kyesha at a certain place and at a certain time, and now he was keeping the man waiting. The fact that their conversations had always taken place with almost complete politeness added to the feeling. Any antipathy had been only an undercurrent, and therefore could have been purely one-sided; Kyesha might feel nothing but friendship for Aleksei. It seemed unlikely, but years of being taught to behave properly were difficult to overcome.

Eventually, Kyesha walked irritatedly away. He headed north. Aleksei had betted against that – by placing himself on the south side of the river – on the basis that it was the direction he had gone the previous night. If he rushed back to the bridge now – and over it – he had little chance of catching up with Kyesha, and a lot of being seen by him. Instead he waited – there was still a possibility that he would be able to keep up with his quarry. He watched the figure reach the far end of the bridge and then disappear from view. A moment later, he could see him again, heading east along the embankment, dwarfed by the Kremlin's looming, red walls. Now there was no possible turn-off for him until he reached the Moskva Bridge, but it would do Aleksei no good to be seen running parallel to his prey along the south bank. He turned away from the river towards the canal. He would have to sprint; Kyesha was moving at a brisk pace. He passed Bolotnaya Square and then turned to run alongside the canal before heading north again to the foot of the Moskva Bridge. The curve of the river gave him a slight advantage, and when he reached the bridge, he could see Kyesha still some distance away, not yet clear of the Kremlin.

Now Aleksei had to take another chance. If he waited where he was to see which way Kyesha headed, he could well lose him. He would have to start crossing the bridge. But that in turn meant that if Kyesha did go south, they would undoubtedly meet. There was no real choice. If Kyesha had been going south, he would have done so immediately, when leaving the Stone Bridge. And even if they did come face to face, Aleksei could simply apologize for being late and say how pleased he was to have caught up with Kyesha. The wooden bridge did not provide much cover, but Aleksei would not stand out amongst the individuals and groups crossing in both directions, and it was unlikely that Kyesha would be looking that way.

He timed it so that he would not have to stop and wait for Kyesha to reach the other end. He was about three quarters of the way over when Kyesha drew level with the bridge, but he did not turn on to it. Instead he turned left and headed up towards Saint Vasiliy's. As he left the bridge, Aleksei glanced behind him. There was no one of note, but he felt uneasy. There was no time to worry about it; he carried on up the hill in pursuit of Kyesha. It was easy to lose him in the mass of small buildings that lay between the cathedral and the river, but unless his destination was actually within those buildings, it was a safe assumption where he would emerge. When Aleksei caught sight of him again, he was beyond Saint Vasiliy's and passing the Lobnoye Mesto. Returning to the scene of the crime, thought Aleksei, but Kyesha ignored the platform and turned out of the square to the east.

When Aleksei himself reached the cathedral, he looked back again. The positioning that made Saint Vasiliy's so prominent from the south also made it a good viewpoint. Aleksei could see the whole of the Moskva Bridge. One man stood at the near end, seemingly looking straight back at Aleksei. It was too far to see his face in any detail. Moments after Aleksei looked at him he suddenly turned his face to the ground and began to march purposefully up the hill, disappearing from view.

Aleksei turned quickly and followed the road Kyesha had taken. At first there was no sign, but as Aleksei headed on towards Kitay Gorod, he caught sight of him. He was standing on a street corner a little way ahead, in conversation with a well-dressed man a few years older than Aleksei himself. The contrast between them reminded Aleksei again of how young Kyesha was. When talking to him, his maturity made it easy to forget that, going by his appearance, he could only be seventeen or eighteen. It fitted perfectly with Aleksei's conviction that he was dealing with a *voordalak*, whose physical age would have been captured and frozen at the moment he ceased to be human, and yet whose experience of the world would continue to shape his character. The Oprichniki themselves, it had to be admitted, had for the most part displayed little in the way of character, but Aleksei had long held the suspicion that this was due to the breed of men they had once been, and not their nature as vampires. Odious though it was to admit it, Zmyeevich had cut a sophisticated figure, regardless of his taste for blood.

The man with whom Kyesha had been talking turned suddenly away from him and strode off, coming towards Aleksei. Kyesha himself continued on in the direction he had been heading, his gait far more casual in this relatively crowded street than it had been down by the river. Aleksei carried on too, and from the corner of his eye noticed a figure at the other end of the block of shops beside which Aleksei had paused begin to move, in parallel with him, one street away.

At the next junction, he glanced to the left again, and saw the same figure cross the road and apparently continue on his path, but Aleksei felt sure he was just out of sight awaiting Aleksei's next move. So now Aleksei had two challenges; to keep track of Kyesha, and to deal with whoever it was lurking in the shadows over to his left.

Kyesha had stopped again, and was in conversation with another middle-aged man, whose general description would have been indistinguishable from the first. It took no great leap of the imagination for Aleksei to guess what he was up to, particularly given the region of the city in which they found themselves. Aleksei held no particular disdain for it. He himself, admittedly when not quite so old, had been happy to pay for the caresses of young flesh, with little complaint from his conscience, despite the fact that he was married. That this gentleman preferred those caresses to be with a person of his own sex was of little interest to Aleksei, nor to many Russians of his class, provided it was kept in private. Only the Anglo-Saxons really seemed to care; and some of the more puritanical members of the Northern and Southern societies. They might liberate the serfs, but only to make them free in their own image. To be an enlightened female, to be homosexual – these were not the rights for which they fought.

Tonight, however, it was only pity Aleksei felt for the man he now watched, negotiating with Kyesha a fee he would never live to pay. It was a smart policy for a *voordalak* who had died young enough to retain his looks. Again, Aleksei could only contrast Kyesha with the Oprichniki he had known before. Few of them were in any state to offer themselves as enticing bait – to man or to woman. Brute force was their only tactic. Had Kyesha's first victim, the one that Domnikiia had described to Aleksei, been lured in the same way? The guard at the Kremlin had been prey Kyesha had fallen upon simply by chance. Did it matter who exactly died at Kyesha's hand tonight? Aleksei knew it was his duty to destroy this creature, but he would not play God and choose who his victim would be. If he could kill him tonight, all the better, but he would not, despite his instinct, shout out now to save this man. Kyesha would find a substitute before the night was over.

Again, Aleksei caught sight of the figure to his left. He wasn't doing a great job of tracking him unobserved, whoever he might be. But who was it? Some companion of Kyesha's, looking out for his safety? A government spy keeping tabs on a known member of the Northern Society? Or conversely, could it be a member of the Northern Society in pursuit of a suspected government spy?

The safest choice was to assume the most dangerous protagonist. If this man was working with Kyesha, then it could mean death for Aleksei. He had to be dealt with first. At the next junction Aleksei broke into a run. Kyesha was still some way ahead and unlikely to notice, but anyone keeping his eye on Aleksei would. As soon as he was beyond the junction Aleksei stopped and doubled back, turning down the road along which he had seen his pursuer. When he came to the next corner he could see the figure ahead of him, turning his head from side to side, attempting to relocate his prey. Aleksei also now recognized who it was. He walked briskly down the street towards him. The man set off at right angles, towards where he expected Aleksei to be, but it took little time to catch up with him. Aleksei put a hand on his shoulder and spun him round to face him.

'What the hell are you doing here?' he asked, his teeth gritted.

Dmitry looked at his father and stammered a few words, but could produce nothing articulate.

'Why were you following me?'

'I was worried.'

'Worried?' asked Aleksei, trying to appear angrier – and less fearful – than he actually was.

148

'Curious,' admitted Dmitry. 'You've hardly been at your hotel at all.'

'You'd have to have been spying on me to know that in the first place,' said Aleksei.

'No.' Dmitry remained flustered. 'But whenever I've called on you, you've been out.'

'And so once you did manage to find me, you followed me?'

'Yes,' replied Dmitry simply.

'Then you will have noticed I'm in the middle of something.'

Dmitry's face lit up. 'I can see. What's it all about?'

Aleksei suddenly realized how much time he was wasting. While his pursuer was unknown, it had been the better bet to find out who he was. Now he knew, there was no danger to him, but the danger to Moscow still existed.

'A man's life is at risk,' he said abruptly. 'I'll talk to you tomorrow.'

With that, he ran down the street towards where he had last seen Kyesha negotiating with his potential victim. He heard Dmitry's feet behind him, but there was no time to deal with that now. He emerged back on to the main street and looked in both directions, but saw nothing. Kyesha had escaped. To Aleksei, and to Kyesha, it meant little; just one night's delay before their ultimate confrontation.

But to the middle-aged man who had, as far as Aleksei could tell, gone with Kyesha, it would make all the difference in the world. There would be no more lying to his wife and family now. His secret life – his life itself – would shortly be at an end.

That, of course, was only one possible outcome. Kyesha could kill him, relatively swiftly, relatively painlessly, and give him the chance of bliss eternal, or at least of eternal nothingness. Or Kyesha could offer him one final temptation, and give him the opportunity to spend eternity, or what might seem like it, as a pariah; an abomination to all mankind. Aleksei prayed that Kyesha would choose to be merciful.

CHAPTER VIII

'WE LOST HIM?'

The voice was Dmitry's, speaking in undertones close to Aleksei's ear. Aleksei nodded.

'I'm sorry,' said Dmitry.

'Let's get a drink,' said Aleksei. There were plenty of places to choose from, but they were not far from Lubyanka Square, and so went to that same club where Aleksei had first discovered his son's true loyalties.

It was quiet at that time of the evening, but Aleksei acknowledged a few acquaintances, and noted his son doing the same. They found a quiet corner where they could talk. Aleksei drank vodka; his son, brandy.

'So who were you following?' asked Dmitry as soon as the waiter had left them with their drinks.

Aleksei considered. There was no question of him telling his son the truth. This terror should have ended thirteen years before, and Aleksei hoped it would end now, but above all he was not going to let it pass down to the next generation. Dmitry would die nobly on some battlefield, or better, old and in bed. But if it was within Aleksei's powers, he would never have to face, or even hear of, the horrors that the *voordalaki* could bring to mankind. So the question was not whether he should tell the truth, but precisely what lies he should spin. There was no pain in this kind of lie. He took a deep breath.

'I think it may be the murderer,' he said in a low voice.

Dmitry looked around, making sure that no one had heard. Aleksei hid a smile, amused at the idea that his son should be mimicking the precautions that he himself, out of years of experience, found almost instinctive.

'Really?' whispered Dmitry.

Aleksei nodded. 'I can place him at the scene of the murder in Red Square, and I think we can be sure that's linked to the one in Tverskaya.' Dmitry nodded. He seemed excited by the proximity to danger, which was another reason for Aleksei to keep him away from it. 'I'd expected there to be another murder last night, but I've heard nothing.'

'Me neither,' said Dmitry.

'Tonight's victim is probably dead already.' An image flashed before his eyes, an amalgam of all the deaths he had witnessed at the hands of a *voordalak*. What particular torture would it be that most whetted Kyesha's appetite? Blood and sinew and clenched jaws and the sound of screams filled his mind. Somewhere in the city, probably not far away, that was happening to the licentious man whose face Aleksei could clearly remember, and whose evening would be ending with so different a climax from the one he had expected.

'Who is he?'

'That I've yet to find out.'

'But it's connected with the message – and the meeting in Desna.'

Aleksei nodded. 'I can't really say any more,' he said.

'But whose side is he on? Is he one of us, or one of them?'

It was very, very simple for Dmitry – 'us' and 'them'; radicals and conservatives. But every 'us' and 'them' could eagerly form into a combined 'us' when faced by a new, dangerous, external 'them'. Thus the whole of Russia had become a united 'us' when faced with the invading French. And if only the French and Russians had known, they could have joined together to see off the threat of the *voordalak* 'them' for good.

'It's not as straightforward as that, Mitka,' he said. He realized he sounded condescending, particularly by using the diminutive, but it was how he felt. 'The man's an enemy of Russia – the whole of Russia, regardless of our petty squabbles.' The whole of Russia and beyond.

'So you're still working for the tsar?'

'For Russia,' said Aleksei. 'There'll still be a government after the tsar is gone. There'll still be criminals and spies, and they'll still have to be dealt with.'

'So you plan to keep your job?' There was bitterness in Dmitry's voice. Aleksei was tempted to ask whether he thought the over-throw of Aleksandr would leave him free to pursue his career as a musician, but he refrained. Instead he simply nodded.

'You sound like Talleyrand,' said Dmitry. 'Friend of Napoleon, friend of Louis, friend of Charles. Friend of anyone who's in power.'

'Talleyrand is a friend of France. I'm a friend of Russia.' He realized it was an odd way to put it. 'I'm Russian,' he added. 'And any man who can say that should mean by it the same as I do.'

Dmitry looked expressionlessly at his father for a few moments, then changed the subject. 'So, how are we going to catch him?'

'*You're* going to have nothing to do with it.'

'But I can help you.'

'Like you helped me tonight?' asked Aleksei.

'He's a dangerous man. You can't do this alone.'

'That may well be the case, Mitka, but – and I don't mean this to sound cruel – if I did want help, would you really be the best man for me to turn to? I've been in this business twenty years. If I need the help of someone to track down a man, there are hundreds of professionals I know to call on. If I need to kill a man, I know dozens who would help me.'

'But Papa . . .'

'It's not about me being your papa or you being my son. Would you ask me to play a piano duet with you?'

'I'd love you to, if that's what you wanted.'

'If our lives depended on my ability? If that piano had killed three, maybe four people in Moscow over the past week?'

Aleksei's lip quivered at the absurdity of his own analogy. He could not hide it from Dmitry, and both broke into laughter.

'My point is,' said Aleksei after a few moments, 'that certain tasks require expertise. Passion and loyalty aren't always enough.'

'After a few years in the army then?'

'If that's the path you want to go down. Is it?'

Dmitry considered for a few seconds. 'I don't know,' he said at last.

His father hoped to God it wasn't.

Aleksei climbed the steps to the door of the Lavrovs' house and raised his hand to knock, but he tensed the muscles of his forearm, and his knuckles never reached the door. He had been kicking so many ideas around in his mind as he walked home – concerning Dmitry, Kyesha, the Northern Society and more – that it was only now that his most immediate problem came to his attention.

Dmitry had been following him.

From that simple fact followed two vital questions. When had he started his pursuit, and when had he stopped? The second question could be posed more bluntly: had he stopped?

Aleksei glanced up and down the street, but saw no one. Dmitry had played a clumsy shadow earlier that evening, but that did not mean he could manage nothing better. Aleksei turned away from the door and carried on down the street, then to the right. He knew the layout of the area, had known it for over four years, though he could not specifically recall committing it to memory. Around the corner, there was only one house before a metal railing ran alongside the pavement, separating it from a private garden. Aleksei leapt over silently.

Of course, he had been visiting the area for several years. Yelena and Valentin had moved down from Petersburg in 1817. After

Vadim's death – and the general chaos the French invasion had provoked, even as far away as in the new capital – Yelena had become particularly close to her widowed mother. But she had died, brokenhearted, less than four years after her husband. Others of her children had remained in their home town, but Yelena and Valentin had moved away almost as soon as Yelena's inheritance had made it possible. Valentin had, some thought recklessly, left his government post to set up as an importer of textiles. Aleksei was one of the few who knew the full story behind it. Yelena had been happy to follow her husband, even though it was her money that paid for their new life.

Aleksei crept through the garden that surrounded the detached house – a rarity in that neighbourhood – and headed back towards the street in which the Lavrovs resided. It had been here he had come in 1820 on discovering the news that Domnikiia was pregnant. There was no way she could continue running the milliner's shop, following in the footsteps of a father she had seen only once in the last sixteen years. To raise an illegitimate child would not have been, even for a man like Aleksei and certainly for a woman like Domnikiia, an insurmountable stigma in Russia. It was to the north-west of Europe and beyond that such details of people's private lives were the concerns of others, and becoming ever more so. But Aleksei had always felt a visceral urge, with which his cautious mind on this occasion agreed, to keep all matters concerning his relationship with Domnikiia as secret as possible: secret from his wife, out of affection for her; from Dmitry, in consideration of his pride; from whoever or whatever lurked out there. Even though Iuda was dead, Aleksei still had enemies. The greatest safety for Tamara lay in no one ever knowing that she was his offspring. Even though Iuda was dead.

And so it had taken only a little persuasion for the Lavrovs to take her in. Whatever her acquaintance had been with Marfa in Petersburg, Yelena's primary loyalty had always been to her father, and Aleksei was Vadim's closest comrade. As for Valentin

– he was hardly in a position to deny Aleksei anything. And the extra money was a boon; the textile trade was not going well, at least under his helmsmanship.

Once this street had become the home of Domnikiia and, arriving soon after, Tamara, Aleksei had instinctively acquired an understanding of the lie of its land, as the leader of a wolf pack does of its territory. He had long known this garden to be an easy way to double back, unseen, into the street. He looked both ways, but saw no one. Here there were no shops or taverns, and the only people he would expect to see would be those who lived here, or were calling on friends who did. Perhaps in the old days, before the war, that would have still meant a street that was, if not crowded, something more than deserted, but tonight it did not.

He waited another quarter of an hour before emerging. It would seem that Dmitry had not followed him from Lubyanka Square – or if he had, he had very rapidly learned a whole new set of skills in the field of stealth and concealment. Aleksei went back to the door and knocked. The maid who opened it scarcely disguised her displeasure at being dragged from the warmth of her fireplace at this hour. No one else in the house kept the same hours as Aleksei, nor would anyone, except perhaps Domnikiia, have tolerated the servant's look with the same good humour.

'Well?' Domnikiia was standing in her nightgown when Aleksei entered. He had no doubt as to the meaning of her question.

'He got away,' he said.

'He saw you?' Her voice showed a concern that was little different from terror.

'No, no. He just got lucky.' He lay back on the bed, exhausted, choosing not to mention his son's involvement in the evening's fiasco. He'd left Dmitry at the club, and while he had established now that the boy had not followed him from there, he still could not tell when in the evening the pursuit had started and, more than that, whether Dmitry knew just how much of his time Aleksei spent here. And why.

He stretched out his leg and Domnikiia put her hand to the heel of his boot, pulling it off him. She did the same to the other boot. He began to take off the remainder of his clothes.

'So what are you going to do?' she asked.

'Try again,' he said, though he knew little more than that. How he would try, he had no idea, but there was no escaping that Kyesha was his responsibility. Even if one had to look back to 1812 to find the link, each of the deaths that had occurred and would occur in Moscow were Aleksei's fault.

'Did you find out for sure?' asked Domnikiia. 'Whether he's . . . a vampire?'

Aleksei shook his head. 'No,' he said. 'But I *feel* sure.'

'Then you must be right. You'd know, if anyone did.'

'You think so? I've seen half a dozen vampires over the past years, only to discover them to be human.'

'Not like this though.'

'No, not like this – but I have to be certain.'

He was naked now, and they stood face to face. He reached down and began to pull her nightgown over her head. She raised her arms, her long hair stretching upwards above her until it finally slipped from the neck of her dress and fell gently down on to her shoulders. They lay down on the bed, facing each other. Aleksei ran the three fingers of his left hand down the side of her chest, over her abdomen, her hip and along her thigh and then back again. Their eyes remained fixed on one another. She was still the most beautiful creature he had ever seen.

'What have we done to deserve this?' she asked.

He laughed. 'I think we both know that,' he said.

'Other men cheat on their wives. They get nothing worse than a guilty conscience.'

'Amateurs,' he said dismissively.

'What do you mean?'

'Other men may be unfaithful, but one has to be a true expert to select a paramour quite as perfect as you. If I'm being unduly punished, it's only for my excessive good taste.'

'That explains it for you, but what about me? It's not like *I'm* guilty of good taste.'

'Ha! Ha!' he said sarcastically, before leaning forward to kiss her. She responded and he allowed himself to be lost in the sensation of her lips, her arms, her body. He allowed all thoughts of Kyesha and of vampires and, more than anything, of his own guilt to slip from his mind, the concept of his adultery being smothered by its very enactment. It would work for a while.

'We're really in trouble now,' he said afterwards, as they lay side by side in the still darkness. 'If God caught a glimpse of half of that then the punishment's going to be harsh and swift.'

'Don't joke about it,' she said.

Aleksei fell silent. He had already seen one man that evening who would by now have paid the price for his adultery – presuming, as was likely, that he was married. It was an unjust payment for so trivial a sin.

Kyesha's sin – the path he had chosen to take when he became a *voordalak* – dwarfed those of them all: the man in the street, Aleksei, even those who planned to murder their tsar. But Kyesha would soon pay a fair price for his choice, and it would be Aleksei who would take the payment, before another twenty-four hours had passed. Tomorrow, Kyesha would die.

Another serpent, trampled beneath the hooves of another horse. This time the horseman *was* Saint George. The icon over the Resurrection Gate had not changed over the years; Moscow's patron saint had remained triumphant. Tonight, Aleksei would play the saint, and Kyesha, already a vile beast, would become the serpent. Again Aleksei had his two swords – one wooden, one steel – but this time he would abandon stealth. Tonight he would deal with Kyesha face to face.

'What happened to you last night?' As ever, Kyesha seemed to arrive from nowhere.

'Is that a question?' asked Aleksei. 'If it is, you have to win the right to ask it.'

'You already owe me one answer.' Kyesha had not seemed annoyed when he first arrived, but Aleksei's tone quickly made him drop the veneer of politeness. 'And I think the question is of greater import than the matter of how you spend your evenings.'

'Not here,' said Aleksei.

'The Lobnoye Mesto again?' suggested Kyesha.

'I don't think so, not after what happened on Monday. This way.'

Aleksei led Kyesha south, across Red Square, but past the Lobnoye Mesto and on to the grander building beyond – Saint Vasiliy's Cathedral. The name instantly brought another Vasiliy to his mind – his wife's lover, back in Petersburg. The very idea of jealousy seemed trivial when put in contrast with tonight's concerns; with what would be happening within the cathedral in just a few hours' time, perhaps less.

A bribe of a few roubles earlier in the day had ensured a promise that a side door would be left unlocked, and the promise had been kept. Even so, there was no guarantee that they would be left alone, although it was unlikely anyone would enter at this time of night, and if they did, the church was a maze of chapels in which it would be easy to hide. Aleksei knew full well that he did not need consecrated ground to carry out what he planned to do, but he knew also that some vampires had a slightly more reverent view of religious institutions than others. With luck, their location might unnerve Kyesha, if only a little.

They climbed the narrow stone steps and emerged into a candle-lit chapel. Aleksei had not gone into the cathedral by that entrance before, but soon found his bearings. They were in the chapel of Saint Nikolai, the southernmost of the ten chapels that formed the cathedral's labyrinthine interior.

'It's best if we move further inside,' said Aleksei, in a low voice. They stepped out into the gallery that surrounded the Chapel of the Intercession from which the cathedral took its official name. It stood at the centre of a square formed by the eight remaining

158

small chapels. The four larger of these, of which Saint Nikolai's was one, sat at the corners of the square, and the four smaller along the sides. A later addition of another chapel, to house the remains of Saint Vasiliy himself, not only served to disrupt the symmetry, but also to give the cathedral its more familiar title. Aleksei followed the gallery anti-clockwise. The dark, brick-lined passageway created by the walls of the chapels was only wide enough for one man at a time. Beyond it, the gallery opened out again, the plain walls giving way to floral tiling, and Aleksei led Kyesha into the Trinity Chapel.

The candelabras hanging above them were only partially lit, casting flickering shadows over the mixture of brickwork, murals and icons. High above, Aleksei could see the inside of the dome, whose hemispherical shape gave no clue as to the complexity of the onion dome outside it. The chapel domes and the central tower grew out of the base of the cathedral like a clump of mushrooms growing from a single root; there was no connection of any kind between the towers at the higher level, but the chapels and corridors below provided a route between them – for those who knew it.

'You seem more formal than usual tonight,' said Kyesha, gesturing at Aleksei's uniform.

'We had an inspection today,' lied Aleksei. 'I haven't had time to change.' The truth was quite different. Aleksei needed a way to conceal his sabre, and what could be better than carrying it in plain view where it would be overlooked as simply part of the uniform? Seen where it was expected to be seen it was far more innocuous, but just as deadly.

'You still owe me an answer,' said Kyesha, sitting down with his back to the wall and gesturing that Aleksei should do the same. Aleksei unbuckled his sword – it was impossible to sit on the floor with it on – and leaned it against the wall before sitting. He had no need to be reminded of Kyesha's last question.

'I think Iuda is dead,' he said.

'Think – but not believe.'

'He drowned. I held him under.' Aleksei could feel the cold numbness that had penetrated his left hand and arm. 'But I never found his body.'

'You let go?'

'I don't know. The water was freezing. I couldn't feel a thing.' He reached inside his shirt. Against his chest he felt two small pieces of metal; one oval, the other square. The first was an icon of Christ that Marfa had sent him during the darkest days of the Patriotic War. He pulled the second chain off over his head and tossed it towards Kyesha, who caught it with the same dexterity he displayed during their games of knucklebones. 'Open it,' he said.

Kyesha slid his thumbnail down the small crack between the two halves of the locket and it sprang open. He peered inside. Aleksei could clearly picture what he was looking at: twelve blond strands, coiled into a circle, unfaded by time.

'His hair?' asked Kyesha.

Aleksei nodded. There had been more wrapped around Aleksei's fingers as he pulled them out of the water to discover Iuda gone. He had slipped it into his pocket and only weeks later remembered it was there. Twelve seemed the appropriate number to keep.

'How strange that *you* should keep such a memento of a past encounter,' said Kyesha. Aleksei noted the stress on 'you', but before he could ask what it meant, Kyesha had continued. 'Couldn't you have looked for the body?' he asked.

Aleksei gave a short laugh. 'I wouldn't have had much trouble finding a body,' he said. 'It's just a question of whether it would have been the right one.' Aleksei saw the river flowing out in front of him, chunks of ice and the corpses of men carried along by it with equal alacrity. Thousands of French had drowned or frozen that day. A few had managed to swim across. The chances were that Iuda could be counted with the former group.

'I'm sorry,' said Kyesha. 'It appears we've been breaking the rules.' He tossed the locket to Aleksei, who caught it and put it

160

back around his neck. Kyesha produced the knucklebones from his pocket once again, all six of them. 'For five,' he said. 'Where was Iuda from?'

Aleksei pondered the question as Kyesha threw one bone into the air and began picking up the others. He had assumed that Iuda was from Wallachia. Why? Because Dmitry Fetyukovich had said they came from Wallachia. But Dmitry had not met them all before, certainly not Iuda. It seemed reasonable that the other eleven were Wallachians, but why assume the same for Iuda? It was as foolish as the assumption Aleksei had so blithely and speciously made that, because eleven were, then the twelfth must also be a *voordalak* – the sort of fallacy that Maks had more than once warned him against. Iuda could speak French perfectly and Russian better than many of the Russian nobility. He had also spoken Romanian to the others, which Aleksei did not understand at all, but which had apparently been good enough to fool them into believing he was their countryman. So, all things considered, the answer which Aleksei prepared to deliver to Kyesha was a simple and honest 'I don't know.'

The need never arose. Kyesha had picked up the five bones from the floor of the chapel and clutched them tightly in his fist, but he never reached out his hand to catch the sixth. It dropped to the brickwork floor, with the slightest of sounds.

'Oops,' said Kyesha. The comment was unnecessary. It was clear enough to Aleksei that the failure had been deliberate. Aleksei had not been in control of the bones for days, and hence had had no chance to ask a question. He'd been happy with it, knowing that he would learn more by hearing Kyesha's questions than by listening to his potentially deceitful answers. Perhaps Kyesha had worked out the same thing. He pushed the bones towards Aleksei and Aleksei knew that now was his chance to ask the sole question that mattered. He picked up the bones and cast them down on the floor, then selected the largest to throw. He looked Kyesha in the eye.

'I think this one's a five, don't you?' said Kyesha.

Aleksei nodded. 'For five. Yes-or-no question. Are you a *voord-alak*?'

Aleksei threw the large bone high in the air. The others had not scattered too broadly, and the first four were easy to pick up, but the fifth had fallen between two of the red floor bricks, where the mortar had worn away slightly. It was the smallest, no bigger than the tip of Aleksei's little finger. Aleksei scrabbled, trying to retrieve it from its hiding place, and eventually it yielded, but the bone in the air had almost reached the floor. He had no time to turn his hand to catch it. Instead, he brought his hand sharply upward, batting the bone back into the air again. It flew off at an angle, heading towards Kyesha. Aleksei leaned forward and pushed with his legs, launching himself across the room. He kept the bones in his hand pressed against his palm with his smallest two fingers and reached out with the remaining three, the handi-cap of his left hand momentarily mimicked in his right. The side of his hand hit the ground at the moment his two fingers and thumb plucked the bone out of the air. He closed his palm and then opened it again, showing the six knucklebones to Kyesha with a smile of victory that revealed he was taking the game too seriously.

The remembrance of the prize suddenly cooled his excitement. He looked again at Kyesha and waited for him to speak. Kyesha rose to his feet and seemed to grow in stature, more than ever seeming older than his youthful face suggested. Aleksei stood as well, partly to be less vulnerable, but also from the sense of awe which Kyesha had managed to instil into the moment. Kyesha held out his hand and Aleksei felt compelled to pour into it the knucklebones with which he had so recently claimed victory. Kyesha pocketed them. It was as if they both sensed they would be playing no more.

'Yes, Aleksei Ivanovich, I am a *voordalak*.'

So there it was; from the creature's own mouth, confirmation that, thirteen years on, thirteen paranoid years, Aleksei was finally facing what he feared most. He took a step back, feigning repulsion and surprise, but he had known all day – all week – what he would have to do when this moment came. Now he had only to work out the final tactical details. It was good they had stood up; that would make it easier.

He put his hand to his face and let slip a horrified murmur of 'Oh my God!', then he turned, as if unable to look upon the creature with which he shared that tiny, ancient chapel. It occurred to him, momentarily, that he had been here before. Maks had confirmed with *his* own mouth that he was a French spy, and Aleksei had not believed such a thing could be excused in any way. A few minutes' further conversation would have proved how wrong he was. Did Kyesha not deserve some chance to plead for his life, to explain that which Aleksei could not conceive? Perhaps he did, but practicality screamed against it. Aleksei's best chance was surprise. Even as he turned away from Kyesha he let his mind fill with a hatred that he could not in honesty claim he felt for this particular creature but did for all the other vampires he had met, and for all the misery they had caused. This was for Vadim, for Dmitry and for Maks. Some might say they had already been avenged, but it would be the highest pleasure for Aleksei to settle the score one further time.

He reached out for his sword, knowing that his body blocked Kyesha's view of it. Decapitation was – as Aleksei had discovered for himself – a method that could quickly send a *voordalak* down to meet its hellish creator. In one movement, Aleksei had grasped the sabre and begun to turn, unsheathing it as he raised it to strike. He pictured in his mind Kyesha's precise position, considered his height, the length of his own arm and of his sword, and swung so that the razor-sharp tip would rip out the monster's throat with the same proficiency the vampire itself had used upon every victim it had ever slain. If the stroke did not kill, it would incapacitate sufficiently for Aleksei to move in with the fatal blow.

Aleksei's whole body turned, and the blade sliced through the air. The muscles of his arm tensed, ready to force the steel onwards as it came into contact with the *voordalak*'s flesh. But no resistance came. Aleksei fell forward, off balance as his sword arm carried on, further than expected. The point of the sword clattered into the wall, hacking through the stem of one of the painted flowers that adorned the tile work and splitting the tile in two. The top half peeled away from the wall and fell to the floor, shattering into half a dozen pieces.

Kyesha was gone.

Aleksei whirled round in a circle, but there was nowhere in the tiny chapel for a man to hide. The doorway was closer to Aleksei than it had been to Kyesha, and it was difficult to believe he had slipped through it, but it was the only exit. Aleksei reached inside his greatcoat and brought out the wooden sword, holding it in his left hand while keeping his sabre in his right. He stepped back out into the gallery.

There were two immediate directions in which to turn; to the left would take him back the way they had entered the cathedral. If Kyesha's intent was flight then that would be his most likely course. Instinct told Aleksei to turn the other way. It took him only three steps before he was at the archway that marked the entrance to the Chapel of the Three Patriarchs. He glanced inside, but saw nothing. On the far side of the chapel was another arch, but Aleksei chose to stick with the gallery. From what he could remember, that exit would eventually lead back to the main corridor anyway. He might be mistaken, but with luck, Kyesha would be less familiar with the layout than he was.

The passageway, squeezed between two chapels, narrowed once again. Despite the tightness of the space, Aleksei felt safer. There was no possibility of an attack from any direction but the front. Or, of course, behind. The gallery was a closed loop. Whichever direction Kyesha had gone in, if he moved fast enough he could soon run the entire circle and approach Aleksei from behind. Aleksei glanced over his shoulder, but saw nothing.

He moved forward. There were passageways to his right. One led back to the Chapel of the Three Patriarchs, the other simply out to a window. It was closed. The next archway revealed another chapel. He looked inside, but it was empty. He moved on. A doorway on his left led to the central chapel, the Chapel of the Intercession. Aleksei could see nothing inside. There were three other exits: a small flight of steps that led down to the lower vaults, and two more archways, one directly opposite Aleksei and one to the right. Aleksei glimpsed a movement; something had made its way past the right-hand archway and was coming quickly through the gallery and towards him. He took a few rapid paces backwards, between two of the side chapels. Behind him steps led down to the main entrance. Given the direction he was moving in, Kyesha would have had the option of going there too, via another stairway, or sticking to the gallery. If he had been in the gallery, he would have reached Aleksei by now. Aleksei went down the stairs. There was no sign of anyone. He tried the door. As he had expected, it was locked. It was only the door by which they had come in that he had arranged to be left open.

He ascended the other flight of steps. At the top, the corridor narrowed again, but this time there were chapel entrances on either side of him. He ran forward, turning in a circle as he moved, so that he faced each doorway almost as he passed it. He saw no one. Now he was at the point where he had briefly glimpsed Kyesha. He looked into the central chapel again. The iconostasis glistered even in the dim candlelight. Aleksei moved on. More stairs led down to the door through which they had entered. If Kyesha had headed that way, he would be long gone by now. Aleksei continued, circling the gallery, still anti-clockwise.

He peered through each doorway as he passed. The chapels began to merge into one. In better circumstances, he would have known immediately where he was from the differing decor, but at the moment he could not tell one icon from another. He couldn't even remember which way was north any more.

He poked his head through another archway and saw on the floor the smashed floral pattern of a broken wall tile. He was back where he had started – the Trinity Chapel. He stepped inside and relaxed a little. This chamber had only one entrance, so it was at least defensible. He had no idea whether Kyesha had fled or was still in the building. Perhaps it would be safest to wait till dawn, though that was still hours away. He would be able to fend Kyesha off – if he could stay awake. At least he knew that Kyesha was wary of him. The Oprichniki had had to learn that for themselves. They'd had to learn how to fight him. He wondered if there was anything to be learned from their tactics that might help him to hunt down Kyesha.

He felt a sudden gust of air, but not, as might have been expected, blowing into the chapel, but out of it – as if a window had been opened somewhere in the side of the domed tower above him. He glanced up and discovered where Kyesha had been hiding. The *voordalak*'s arms and legs were stretched out in the shape of a diagonal cross as he fell, as if still being used to brace himself against the sides of the tower. Too late Aleksei remembered the *voordalak*'s uncanny ability to climb even the steepest precipice. Kyesha had not fled sideways when Aleksei attacked him, but upwards.

Aleksei had managed to take only half a step to the side when Kyesha's full weight hit him, throwing him to the floor. His arms splayed outwards and he lost hold of both his weapons. Kyesha scarcely needed to gather himself after landing. His knee had hit Aleksei's chest, winding him. His fist came across Aleksei's jaw in a heavy backhand blow, dissolving his vision into a thousand points of light. Perhaps he would be blessed by unconsciousness before Kyesha's fangs descended upon his throat and took his life in the horrible way he had so often witnessed. But Kyesha had too much self-control for that. As though he had been momentarily dunked under water, Aleksei surfaced back from unconsciousness, instead of plummeting to its depths.

He kicked hard with his right leg, hoping to knock the vampire off him, but Kyesha was ready for it. He rocked slightly to one side with the movement, but then returned, pressing even more weight on to Aleksei's chest.

'You understand nothing, Aleksei Ivanovich,' said Kyesha. His eyes glared down at his victim. His stare was much as any man's would be after winning a fight, a mixture of exhilaration and triumph.

'If you're going to kill me, get on with it,' Aleksei said.

Kyesha raised an eyebrow. Aleksei felt his weight shift, lightening for a moment. It was a bad time for him to drop his guard.

A booted foot flew over Aleksei's face, inches from his nose, and connected firmly with Kyesha's teeth. His head swung back sharply and Aleksei heard an unpleasant cracking sound as his neck was bent to an impossible angle. Blood began to pour from his lips and nose, and he fell to one side.

Aleksei was on his feet in an instant, raising his fists in front of him, for want of any more effective weapon. Kyesha lay against the tiny altar, glaring up at his assailant. Aleksei only needed to glance sideways to see who it was.

'Don't say a word,' he growled.

'About what?' asked Dmitry. He was short of breath, but his voice revealed the smile on his lips.

'About me not needing your help,' said Aleksei, realizing now that it had been Dmitry, not Kyesha, whose figure he had glimpsed in the corridor outside. He glanced over at Kyesha, whose smile seemed to mimic Dmitry's, but whose breathing was slow and relaxed. The *voordalak*'s eyes flicked from father to son, considering them, calculating what his next move should be.

A similar thought was on Dmitry's mind. 'What now?' he asked.

'We kill him,' said Aleksei, with a hint of bile in his voice.

'Papa!'

Aleksei had forgotten that his own view of the situation would be radically different from his son's.

'Do as your father says, Dmitry,' snarled Kyesha from where he sat.

Dmitry ignored him. 'This isn't the kind of Russia we both want,' he continued, addressing Aleksei.

'You don't understand, Dmitry.'

167

'If he's guilty, he'll be punished.'

'Guilty?' asked Aleksei. Could one be 'guilty' of being a *voordalak*?

'Whatever evidence you had to track him down here will be enough for the court. Three murders will see him sent to Siberia for ever. We've done our part.'

It was tempting. Kyesha would never make it to Siberia, of course. The first light of dawn would destroy him, by which time both Aleksei and Dmitry would be safely in their beds, and Dmitry would be spared ever having to confront the knowledge of what Kyesha was. But it was too risky, certainly for whatever poor gaoler they handed him over to. Aleksei would not be able to explain the true danger the captive represented, nor would he be believed if he tried. Kyesha would escape and be more of a threat than ever – both to Aleksei and now to Dmitry. He picked up his two swords and held them ready. Kyesha had to die here and now, and that meant Dmitry had to be told.

But Dmitry had his own plans.

Over on the wall, a coil of rope hung, the slack end of the length that supported the candelabra, tied off on a hook in the wall. Dmitry went across and cut it through with his sword. He held the rope loosely in his left hand and approached Kyesha, holding his sword out in front of him.

'Stand up,' he said. Kyesha obeyed.

'You don't understand this, Mitka,' repeated Aleksei. 'Let me deal with it.' He heard in his own voice the agonized remembrance of friends he had lost.

'He understands,' said Kyesha, with patronizing calmness. 'You mustn't give in to petty vengeance, Aleksei. He's learned that from you.'

Dmitry tossed the rope towards Aleksei, who caught it clumsily with the same hand that held the wooden sword. 'Turn round,' Dmitry said to Kyesha; then to his father, 'Tie him up – I'll make sure he doesn't try anything.'

Kyesha did not turn round. He took half a step forward and

Dmitry raised his sword threateningly. Now it was Kyesha's smile that was patronizing. He reached forward with both hands and grabbed Dmitry's sabre by the blade, grasping it tight and then twisting rapidly, turning his whole body so the sword was raised up over his head and wrenched from Dmitry's grasp.

Dmitry stepped back and shook his stung hands, but Kyesha continued his motion, the sword whipped round in a wide circle, almost grazing the walls on each side of the narrow chapel, and returned to hit Dmitry on the jaw with its hilt, knocking him to the ground.

It took a moment for Aleksei to cast the rope aside and prepare to advance on Kyesha, sabre in his right hand and wooden dagger in his left. It was time enough for Kyesha to toss Dmitry's sword in the air and flip it, so that he was now holding it in the more conventional manner. Aleksei glimpsed the unholy stigmata of blood on the palms of the *voordalak*'s hands where he had gripped the blade, but he understood well enough how quickly they would heal.

They faced each other. Aleksei knew from distant experience how hard it was to fight a vampire with a conventional weapon such as a sword. All the tactics in which he had been trained became meaningless in the face of an opponent who had no fear of the majority of wounds that might be inflicted upon him. Facing a vampire that itself wielded a sword was something new – and seemingly unnecessary – but it might play to Aleksei's advantage, fooling Kyesha into using it and fighting like a man.

Aleksei raised his sword and brought it down towards the side of Kyesha's neck – an attack which even a *voordalak* would have reason to fear. He did not expect the blow to connect, but in raising his sword to parry it, Kyesha would leave the right side of his body exposed. Aleksei's left hand, in it the far more deadly wooden sword, was ready for attack.

But Kyesha did not raise his blade to fend off the assault. Instead, he simply lifted his left arm and absorbed the weight of the blow. It would have broken the bone in a human, and caused horrific pain, but on Kyesha it had no observable effect. Instantly, he counter-attacked with his own blade, aiming not at Aleksei's body, but at the wooden sword. The impact was strong enough both to break it in two and knock it from Aleksei's hand to the floor. Aleksei glanced down and saw that the weapon was useless, broken too close to the hilt to have length enough to penetrate. He took a step back in preparation to continue the uneven fight, but Kyesha did not care to engage him. Instead he fled from the room.

Aleksei dashed to the doorway and looked both ways, but could see nothing. He turned back into the chapel to see Dmitry rising to his feet.

'Are you OK?'

Dmitry nodded, then held his hand to his head. 'It hurts like hell,' he replied, 'but I'll live.' He made for the door. 'Come on,' he said. 'He can't get far with wounds like those.' He followed the gallery round to the right, and signalled to Aleksei to go the other way. Aleksei's instinct was to give up – for the sake of his son and for himself – but waiting in the chapel until they could leave safely at dawn would only delay the confrontation until the following dusk, or the next one, or the next one.

He crept along the gallery in the opposite direction. Dmitry was out of sight in an instant. Once again, Aleksei glanced into each chapel he passed, this time wise enough to look upwards into the domes themselves to see where Kyesha might have secreted himself. He saw nothing. Soon he was level with one of the three archways that led into the central chapel. The only side from which it could not be accessed was the east side, opposite the Trinity Chapel, from where they had just come. Inside he could see nothing, but in the archway on the other side, directly opposite, he caught sight of Dmitry giving a similar inspection and gave him a slight wave. Dmitry nodded that they should continue around the gallery.

Again, Aleksei passed the stairs that led down to Red Square and hoped that Kyesha had chosen to take them, but he himself continued until he approached the third entrance to the central

170

chapel, expecting to see his son arriving at the same point from the opposite direction.

There was no sign of Dmitry. Then there was a cry.

'Papa!'

Aleksei turned and looked into the chapel. Opposite him was the huge iconostasis that filled the entire east wall of the chamber, showing image after image of saints and biblical scenes. In the centre, the Beautiful Gate was closed, as it should be, hiding the altar, which Aleksei had never seen but presumed must be minuscule to fit into the space between the iconostasis and the chapel wall.

To the left of the gate he saw Dmitry. He was pressed up against the iconostasis. In the dim candlelight, Aleksei could see the hilt of the sword that was buried deep into the wooden panels, pinning Dmitry to them, his tightly buttoned coat restraining him, his toes stretching and searching, but unable to quite find the floor. For a moment, Aleksei was reminded of how he had found Vadim's corpse, hung from a nail in the wall of a room of a house not far from here. But this was not the same. Dmitry was alive and, as far as Aleksei could see, unharmed. The sword that prevented his escape had penetrated only his overcoat – not his flesh.

Aleksei stepped into the chapel. He had already checked that Kyesha was not at floor level, and so he lifted his eyes upwards. The tower above the Chapel of the Intercession was the tallest in the cathedral, and was capped not with a dome but with a point-ed tent roof. Aleksei could see nothing of Kyesha, but it would not have been difficult for him to lurk in the shadows.

'He's in there,' said Dmitry. Aleksei looked down and saw his son nodding towards the Beautiful Gate. There was a thud as a booted foot hit wood and the doors swung open, revealing Kyesha leaning casually against the side of the small alcove.

'Best if you don't come any closer, I think, Aleksei,' he said. 'I can't kill you but you do seem to have a strong urge to kill me. It seems your son must be my protection.' The threat was clear. Aleksei stood still in the doorway, opposite Kyesha.

'This is none of his concern,' he said. 'He doesn't even know what you are.'

'Then perhaps he should learn,' said Kyesha, stepping forward, out of the sanctuary. From somewhere deep within him Aleksei felt a sense of relief that that holiest of places was no longer sullied by the *voordalak*'s presence. 'Although you yourself did not recognize my nature the first time you saw me,' continued Kyesha.

'I had an inkling,' he replied. 'It's only taken me a few days to be certain.'

'A few days?' Kyesha expressed both surprise and disdain. 'You still don't remember me, do you, Aleksei Ivanovich?'

'You're not Maks' brother, I know that. He was only a child when he died.'

'What the hell are you two talking about?' interjected Dmitry. He was still incapable of movement, but his weight was taken by his coat under his arms, so he was quite able to breathe and speak.

'I think perhaps a little demonstration would assist you both,' said Kyesha. He glanced around the chapel. Near him was a tall iron stand topped with three candles, none of them lit. Strips of flat, black-painted metal added some decoration. He took hold of one of these and tore it away. The iron was thin, and Aleksei might have been able to achieve the same with his own hands, but only after minutes of twisting and turning the metal.

The jagged, raw edge glistened clean in the candlelight. Kyesha sat down on the stone step in front of the iconostasis and placed his left hand out in front of him, splaying his fingers wide apart against the cold stone. In his right hand, he raised the iron shard above his head and paused. He glanced first at Dmitry, then at Aleksei, smiling as he brought his arm down, and not even looking where it fell.

Dmitry's gasp was just audible above the clang of metal against stone. In front of the iconostasis, Kyesha's little finger lay a few inches from the rest of his hand. His blood had already begun to soak into the stone. Kyesha moved his hand a little, then turned to Aleksei once again.

'One's not enough though, is it, Aleksei?' Aleksei shook his head. Kyesha raised the improvised blade again.

'He's mad!' whispered Dmitry.

Kyesha's arm came down. This time there was no sound but the chime of the metal, like a hammer on an anvil. Two fingers now sat on the step, in full view of the altar through the still open doors of the Beautiful Gate, as though part of some pagan sacrifice from a thousand years before.

Kyesha held up his left hand and showed it to Aleksei, the palm facing towards him. Aleksei raised his own hand in a similar gesture, the three fingers and two stubs an almost perfect match for Kyesha's. Aleksei saw the blood dribbling down across Kyesha's palm, and felt the warmth of his own as if it were flowing down from the stubs of his fingers, even though they had not bled like that for fifteen years.

Kyesha's message to Aleksei was completed, but he still had more to show Dmitry. He stood and took a step towards him. He was close enough for Dmitry to reach out and grab him, but the shock seemed to have calmed Dmitry into inaction. Kyesha held his wounded hand close up to the young man's face, so that the blood dripped down on to his coat. Even though Aleksei knew well what he was about to witness, still he gazed in fascination at the bloody mess Kyesha had inflicted upon himself.

And even as he did so, Kyesha's fingers began to regrow.

CHAPTER IX

DMITRY HAD LONG SINCE GIVEN UP STRUGGLING. HE HAD caught a glimpse of movement in the central chapel and had stepped inside. After that, he'd had but a moment to resist Kyesha's attack. A heavy blow to his chest had lifted him off his feet and propelled him towards the wall. He had seen Kyesha's face in front of him – calm, almost irritated – and seen his own sword raised in Kyesha's right hand, poised to strike. As the blade started to fall, Dmitry had closed his eyes and begun a silent prayer he doubted he would ever finish. He felt the impact of the blow and wondered momentarily why he had experienced no pain, before opening his eyes to realize what had happened.

It was after his father's arrival that events had taken their strangest turn. The conversation between Aleksei and Kyesha about Uncle Maks' dead brother had been confusing enough, but it was Kyesha's act of self-mutilation that caused a coldness to sweep through Dmitry's body, as though his blood had frozen. He felt vomit rising in his throat and forced himself to swallow it back down. He heard a voice speak briefly and suspected it might have been his own.

As the second finger was severed, Dmitry realized what it was that Kyesha was doing – imitating the wounds Aleksei had carried for so long that Dmitry could not remember a time before them. But whatever reason Kyesha might have to mimic Dmitry's father, how could it possibly be so important as to bring about such a deformation? Aleksei's reaction, as far as Dmitry could tell, had been one of realization and distant recognition, as though the matching disfigurements to their hands marked a common membership of some secret society. Was this some perverse evolution of Freemasonry, in which the covert handshakes that marked one member out to another had been abandoned as unsafe – too easily copied by the uninitiated? Had they developed a handshake that could not be so easily reproduced, since it required the hand itself to be a shape no normal man could – would want to – achieve? Aleksei had always said that it was the Turks who had cut off his fingers, as part of a horrendous torture in a Bulgarian gaol, but had that been a subterfuge? Had Aleksei once inflicted those wounds upon himself as part of the same brutal initiation ceremony? It was unthinkable, and yet it was only when Aleksei had witnessed what Kyesha had just done that he seemed at last to understand him.

Kyesha had not lingered in showing Aleksei the sign of their newly created bond. He had turned and begun to approach Dmitry. Dmitry stared, fascinated, at the bloody wounds. He remembered the sensation he had experienced as a boy when examining his father's hand, by then healed – to the extent it ever could be. In his youthful innocence he had felt no sense of revulsion, but now, as an adult, having learned to fear what is abnormal and faced with the sight of mangled bone and sinew through smeared blood, he felt nausea.

But through it, he was still alert enough to wonder why Kyesha was making such a point of showing the wounds to him. They were a message for his father surely, who understood their meaning, where Dmitry could only speculate. Then it dawned on him. Was he too to be initiated that night? Would his own two fingers be joining Kyesha's down there on the altar steps? Pinned as he was against the wall, he would be unable to resist, but his father would protect him – he would never stand by and allow such an act to be perpetrated on his son. Or would he? Freemasons were usually more than keen that their sons should join the fraternity. Aleksei carried his scars with pride – mightn't he want the same for his son? He had learned that the pain was something that could be endured. Didn't the Jewish father happily watch as his baby son was physically marked out as one of the faithful, however cruel the ceremony might seem to outsiders?

But there was a difference between Dmitry and his father. Even when he had them, had Aleksei made any real use of those two fingers on his left hand? Had he spent hours a day practising trills in the bass, so that with those two fingers he had the dexterity and control most men would only dream of possessing with ten? For Aleksei, the loss was an inconvenience, but for Dmitry, it might almost be better to have his tongue cut out.

But Kyesha made no further move to approach Dmitry. He simply stood there, holding his hand up beside him, its three fingers stretched out in a bloody variant of the Polish salute. The stumps of his missing fingers wiggled slightly with involuntary movement; Dmitry had not noticed before, but almost the entire bottom of both fingers, below the second knuckle, remained in place.

No. Dmitry *had* noticed. He'd more than noticed, he'd felt it. As he'd watched the iron plate bury itself right into the third knuckle of Kyesha's fingers, he'd felt in his own hand an echo of what he imagined Kyesha must feel as the blade insinuated itself between the two bones, breaking neither but instead snapping the sinews as it forced them apart. Dmitry glanced down to where the severed fingers lay. It was clear enough, even in the candlelight; all three bones of each finger were there in their entirety. He looked back at Kyesha's hand. It didn't add up. If those fingers could somehow be reattached to the stumps that remained, then the whole hand would be quite out of proportion – the last two fingers stretching out like elongated talons. Dmitry would have spotted the deformity as soon as he set eyes on Kyesha. And besides, Kyesha would also have required a total of four knuckle joints on each finger, since it was now clear to see that two joints still remained attached to his hand.

Dmitry comprehended at last what he was seeing. Kyesha's fingers were regrowing. Each time Dmitry looked there was some slight change, but now he stared continuously, and the miracle – there was no other word for it – played out before his eyes. It was the skeleton that led the way, advancing fractionally ahead of the flesh and skin which wrapped itself along the straight length of the bone. The growth was quite fast, but slowed at the more intricate joints. The little finger was completed first, its tip arcing over the clean white bone to produce a nailless pink dome. Then, the nail emerged, the skin around it receding like a wave slipping back down the beach. The ring finger was almost complete too. Its nail popped out in the same way, and Kyesha flexed his fingers as though to check that everything was working. There were no marks or scars to show what had happened, only the drying blood that spotted his palm – that and the two dead fingers that lay in front of the Beautiful Gate.

Dmitry glanced at Kyesha's face. There was the hint of a smile on it, but still that same suggestion of irritation, that all this was a distraction from what he was really trying to achieve. Kyesha turned back to Aleksei.

'I won't hold this against you, Aleksei Ivanovich,' he said, bending over, without taking his eyes off Aleksei, to pick his now surplus fingers from the step and slip them into his pocket. 'You are exactly the man I expected you to be.' He gave a brief, informal salute, before adding, 'Until tomorrow.'

He turned back to the iconostasis and flung himself upwards towards it. His leap took him not very much higher than Dmitry himself might have managed, but having reached that height he clung to the vertical surface in a way no human could. He gripped the ridges that delineated the various icons and used them to ascend the wooden panels. He was soon at the top, on a small platform where he could comfortably stand. But from there, there was nowhere for him to go. His last words had sounded like a farewell, but his actions did not reflect the notion. Above him now were only the walls of the tented tower, vertical at first, but soon to slope inward, with few variations upon which a climber would find any purchase.

It was no obstacle to Kyesha. He climbed quickly up the vertical, then hung out above them from the inside of the sloping tent without any slackening of pace. How he managed to hold on, Dmitry could not tell.

Aleksei dashed over to his son and pulled out the sword restraining him with a single tug. As Dmitry dropped to the floor, his legs only just reacting in time to keep him upright, they heard the shattering of glass from above and looked to see Kyesha disappearing outside through one of the tower's small windows.

'Quick!' shouted Aleksei. He handed Dmitry his sword and raced out of the chapel. Dmitry followed him through the cathedral's narrow passageways, almost losing sight of him in the darkness. A flight of steps led them down to ground level, to the entrance through which he had stealthily followed Kyesha and his father earlier that evening, and out into Red Square. Aleksei walked backwards away from the building, gazing up at the brightly coloured domes, bland now with only the starlight to illuminate them. 'Go that way,' he snapped, pointing to the right.

Dmitry obeyed, circling the church anti-clockwise as his father went clockwise, in much the same way they had stalked Kyesha along the gallery inside. His eyes never left the towers. At one moment he thought he glimpsed the movement of a figure leaping from one to another, but then it was gone. He was almost at the point where he expected to reencounter his father on the far side of the cathedral when he heard the sound of feet landing on the ground. He looked and saw Kyesha running away to the east – the cover of buildings was closest in that direction.

'Papa!' shouted Dmitry, but even as he did he saw the figure of his father emerging from the other side of the building and dashing across the square in pursuit. Dmitry joined the hunt and was soon only a few paces behind his father, but not long after, Aleksei slowed to a halt, breathing heavily and looking in all directions for any sign of Kyesha.

'He's gone,' said Dmitry.

'He'll be back,' replied his father, panting.

Dmitry paused. He had not had a moment to think since they had been inside Saint Vasiliy's, but now there was only one question on his mind.

'What *is* he?' Dmitry had seen enough to know that this was the correct formulation for the question. Not 'How did he do that?' or even 'Did I really see it?' He had seen it, and what he had seen was beyond his understanding. He had entered the world of folklore – a world his father had always been so keen to reject, and one with which he now seemed intimately acquainted.

Aleksei turned to face his son. His body appeared to straighten and grow a little taller, reminding Dmitry of the father of his youth. He raised his hand and held it to his son's cheek. His lips parted as if about to speak and he seemed to look beyond Dmitry into another world.

But he said nothing. His hand dropped to his side and he walked briskly away. Dmitry trotted to catch him up, but Aleksei was walking at a phenomenal pace. Dmitry almost had to run to keep up with him.

'Papa, tell me!' he insisted, but to no avail. Aleksei said nothing more on the matter that night.

The Clashing Rocks let *Răzbunarea* pass through them un-molested. It was to be expected. Those rocks had not slammed together for millennia, not since Jason had, imitating Noah, let a dove fly between them in advance of his own passage, leaving the channel in future open to all. The passenger wondered if the gods of Greece might have resurrected the custom, just for this one occasion, had they known that *he* was passing between the rocks that night. Perhaps they would have let him pass anyway – those ancient gods had always tended to be less . . . judgemental than their upstart counterparts. Anyway, the gods of Greece were dead, like all gods, and were not amongst those lucky enough for death to be inseparable from rebirth. It was with the gods who could achieve that feat that he felt most kinship, with all the hatred that kinship implied.

Soon the Bosphorus was just a memory, and the ship sailed on into the open waters of the Black Sea. He had not crossed these waters in over a decade, and then his journey had been much more direct. But even he had to bow to affairs of state, he whose own land had been long ago taken from him. That would change soon. Just a few more days' sailing.

Aleksei lay on his back, his mind in turmoil. He felt the warmth of Domnikiia's hand on his chest, but she was not awake. The realization had come to him even as Kyesha's right hand had descended on to his left. The action itself had taken him back fifteen years, to that gaol in Silistria. The Turks had captured seven of them. All appeared to be local men, but they knew that one of them was a Russian spy. Aleksei had been in no mood to reveal that he was that one, but his captors had their own plans for eliciting a confession. They'd worked through the prisoners one by one. Each was taken up to a table, and a rusty meat cleaver fell upon his hand. After seven little fingers had been separated from their owners, there was still no confession. Aleksei knew enough to realize that if he did confess then his ensuing fate would be more horrific than anything he had so far experienced. He might have chosen to relieve the suffering of the other six prisoners, but he cared as little for them as they did for him.

The Turks worked their way through the line again, this time taking the ring finger of each man, but again Aleksei said nothing. Then, as the third fingers went, the confession came. It was a perfect example of the inadequacies of torture. The second man in the line – more a boy than a man – had, bizarrely, waited until he had lost his middle finger before confessing that he was the Russian spy. It was an act of desperation, born out of the false belief that nothing could be worse than the current misery.

But at least it brought some temporary relief. For Aleksei it meant that his left hand would still be of some use. For the boy who had confessed, it would mean further interrogation, the discovery that he was no Russian, and a slow death. The boy seemed to realize this too. He opted to die quickly, vainly attempting to flee the prison yard by climbing a wall, only to receive a bullet to his chest from a Turkish musket. The confusion had been Aleksei's chance to escape, and he had grabbed it. He hadn't stayed to see the boy die, but he hoped that that first bullet had done its work. If it had not, death would eventually come, but only after the resumption of the torture the boy had risked so much to evade.

That had been Aleksei's perception of those events for fifteen years, but now he realized he was quite wrong. The face of that boy, which had been for so long buried inaccessibly at the back of Aleksei's mind, was a face he had seen today. It was Kyesha. He had not aged a jot since that day, and perhaps for many years before it. The fear that had taken him – triggering his blurted confession – had not been a fear of the torture, or for the fate of his fellow prisoners, but the most primal fear that any *voordalak* could experience: the fear of sunlight. The torture session had gone on long into the night, and Aleksei could clearly remember that his escape had taken place as the birds sang to the new day.

The gunshot wound would have been little hindrance to Kyesha. He would have jumped rather than fallen from that high wall beside the gaol and would have hit the ground running. Even if his captors had caught up with him, they would have been no match for a vampire desperate to get under cover before the sun rose. His fingers would have quickly grown back, just as Aleksei and Dmitry had witnessed that evening. There, though, was an oddity. In what he had seen tonight, and years before when dealing with the Oprichniki, the regrowth had been fast – almost instantaneous – but back then it had not. If it had been, the soldiers would surely have noticed that his first finger had returned when they reached for his second.

Perhaps Kyesha had not been a vampire then. But if so, why did he look almost exactly the same age now? If he had not been a *voordalak* when in that gaol, it must have come upon him very

181

soon after; perhaps that very night, encountering another such creature as he fled in terror. That might explain how he had survived the bullet wound, but not how his fingers had grown back. Or was the process whereby a vampire could regrow flesh and bone something that could be applied in retrospect to wounds already suffered?

Aleksei caressed his own hand and chuckled to himself. He had not, as some seemed to think, spent his whole life wishing there were some way to become restored to what he had once been. Even if there were, it would not be worth becoming a vampire. For what shall it profit a man if he shall gain two fingers and lose his own soul?

Kyesha had lost three fingers that night in Silistria, but tonight he had severed only two. The discrepancy mattered little – the point had been made. Nor did it matter whether he had become a *voordalak* before those events or just after. What was more interesting was that tonight he had refrained from killing, up to the point of punctiliousness, even when faced with attack from both Aleksei and Dmitry. This was not, in Aleksei's experience, the normal nature of a *voordalak*, but he was coming to realize that his experience – fourteen of them in all, that he knew of – might prove a poor sample of the breed as a whole.

Domnikiia muttered to herself and turned away from him on to her side. Aleksei turned too and matched the shape of his body to hers. He laid his arm across her and let his hand lie somewhere near to her belly, and he felt her hand gently curl around his. Still she did not wake, the action having become so familiar over the years that she could repeat it without the need for recourse to consciousness. He squeezed her to him.

No, it did not matter what kind of *voordalak* Kyesha was – he would die as they all must die, and if he had reasons for holding himself back in his own defence, then so much easier the task.

It was the seventh and final meeting place. Aleksei had been down this street only twice in the last thirteen years. It was not that he

182

had avoided it, but it led from nowhere to nowhere in terms of the routes he wanted to take through Moscow, and he knew no one who lived in it. It had been almost totally razed by the fires in 1812, and had been in that state when he stood there then, hoping to meet Vadim, fearing he would encounter something else. There had been one visit since then, but the rendezvous on that occasion was not his.

The venue at which they had chosen to meet – chosen before the fires had wreaked their destruction – had been a tavern on the north-west side of the street which had vanished along with everything else. By chance, the rebuilt street also had a tavern, but on the other side and a little further away from Tverskaya Street itself. Aleksei glanced at his watch, and then up and down the street in either direction. It was a quarter past nine and there was still no sign of Kyesha.

'Perhaps he's not coming,' said Dmitry.

Aleksei turned and looked at his son. Everything between them still seemed so normal. Had their conversation earlier that day really taken place? Had Dmitry completely misunderstood what Aleksei had told him? It was impossible. Aleksei tried to recall the exact words he had used. He could not have put it more plainly – and yet it was also impossible that, having learned that the *voordalak* was a real creature, not some inhabiter of dreams, having learned that his own father had done battle with them in his youth, he could remain the same person he had been that morning. But Aleksei had seen the reaction many times before. The turmoil of his own mind at the discovery of the existence of vampires had not manifested itself in any obvious way. He had seen the reactions of Vadim, Maks, Dmitry Fetyukovich and even Domnikiia, and although they had all taken it differently, none of them had been reduced to the jabbering wrecks of humanity such knowledge should surely inspire in any sane person.

Perhaps the strangeness was not the ease with which Dmitry had come to terms with the concept, but the fact that he believed it at all. Dmitry's was the first truly modern generation of Russians, unable to remember the turmoil the French Revolution had brought to Russia, but familiar with the new age that had been ushered in across Europe. But still the old beliefs lurked within his mind, waiting to be given substance. It was not something that was learned – it was in the Russian blood. And how could Dmitry not believe? What he had seen in Saint Vasiliy's the previous night had been beyond any human experience. It had needed an explanation, and the single word – *voordalak* – uttered from his father's lips brought together a belief based both on filial respect and that great mass of Russian folklore. Maks would have pointed out the flaw: vampires may have regrowing fingers, but that does not mean that regrowing fingers necessitate a vampire. His reasoning would have been right, but his conclusion wrong, or at least unhelpfully ambiguous. Maks himself had come to believe in the *voordalak*.

'He'll come,' said Aleksei in response to his son's suggestion. 'There's something he wants.'

'What?'

Aleksei shrugged. 'Let's have a drink.'

They went into the tavern. It hadn't changed much since Aleksei's only previous visit. That had been in 1818. Domnikiia had become happily settled in her shop – truly happy for the first time in her life – and had decided that now was perhaps the time to be reconciled with her estranged family. Her father had thrown her out because she'd slept with one of his customers. Then the distinction between a lover and a customer had dwindled to nothing; at least they had been her own customers. But in 1818, that was all behind her, and she had decided to make amends. She had asked Aleksei to find her mother and father.

Her mother was dead; dead since 1812. At least that was what everyone assumed. She had not been seen after the five weeks of the French occupation. She might have fled, starved, been killed by the invaders or have died in the fires. There was no clue as to which. There was one other possibility – a cause of death of which few were aware – but it would have been an unthinkable coincidence for Domnikiia's mother to have become a victim of the Oprichniki. Even so, Aleksei knew that Domnikiia would want certainty, and so he had told a story of how her mother had been crushed under the walls of a collapsing building ravaged by the conflagration. It was a cruel invention to convey to a daughter, but kinder than allowing her imagination free rein.

News of her father had been more difficult to come by, but eventually Aleksei had found him. His business had evaporated before the war, and his home life had collapsed with the loss of his wife. Aleksei discovered that he spent most of his life slumped against the bar of the tavern near Tverskaya Street. Domnikiia had gone to speak to him, but Aleksei had sat in a corner and kept an eye on them.

Semyon Arkadievich Beketov was a little over fifty, of average height and corpulent build. Greying hair surrounded a large bald patch. His face was bloated, presumably from his continual drinking, and was of a yellow – almost green – complexion. The red slits of his eyes emerged from between his swollen eyelids. Even so, Domnikiia recognized him at once. She had spoken to him, but Aleksei had not been able to make out clearly what was said. He could not even be sure that her father knew who she was. Towards the end of the conversation, he had heard Beketov call her a whore and watched him slide a handful of money across the bar to her – mere copecks. Perhaps he had recognized her and remembered the reason he had thrown her out – perhaps he hadn't, and was genuinely trying to hire her services. Then Beketov had stood and grabbed Domnikiia by the wrist, as if about to drag her to the door. Aleksei was instantly on his feet, but Domnikiia had no trouble freeing herself from the pathetically feeble old man. She hadn't even needed to push him; he had fallen to the floor, unable to maintain his own balance. She had rushed out, and Aleksei had followed.

Domnikiia never told him the details of the conversation, and he didn't really care to hear. He suggested that he continue looking for the rest of the family – her sister and three brothers – but she said she wasn't interested. Three years later he repeated the offer when he told her the news he had heard, that Beketov was dead. He had stumbled out of a public house and under the wheels of a carriage. Domnikiia said she wanted to forget them all, and the topic had never been raised again. Three months after that, Tamara was born.

And this was the first time Aleksei had been back to the street, or to the tavern, since. As they entered, he glanced at the spot at the bar where Domnikiia and her father had spoken. Today, it was occupied by a similar drunk, who somewhere in the city might have a similar family. That was not Aleksei's concern. Kyesha was sitting alone in a corner. He was not to know that this was not the actual tavern of the meeting place arranged in 1812. Whoever he had heard of the meetings from had never been here – the alliance between Oprichnik and Russian had fallen apart long before seven consecutive meetings could be achieved.

In truth it was a surprise to find Kyesha there at all, after the events of the previous night. But then again, Kyesha had proved himself quite capable of resisting the attacks of both Aleksei and his son, so he would feel he had little to fear. That would change – but not tonight. The more logical question was why Aleksei had come. He was the one who had been defeated, so why was Kyesha sitting here, confident that his opponent would come back for more? He knew how well he had set his lure.

Or perhaps he had just come in for a drink. Beside him was a bottle of Bordeaux and three glasses. All were full, including Kyesha's own.

Aleksei and Dmitry sat down.

'I remember you now,' said Aleksei.

'From last night?' asked Kyesha, with a smile that Aleksei had to force himself not to reciprocate.

'From Silistria.'

'Ah!'

'I thought you were either a fool or a hero,' said Aleksei.

'And now?'

'You did what you had to do. I know how much your kind fear the day.' Aleksei knew he had to be careful. There was a purpose for him and Dmitry in tonight's meeting, and that was to prepare the ground for tomorrow. After what had happened in the cathedral, Kyesha would be wary. He had to be lulled. 'I presume you were already a vampire,' he added.

'Oh yes,' said Kyesha. He did not elaborate further.

'So why didn't your fingers grow back then?' demanded Dmitry. It was the right tone – Kyesha wouldn't be fooled by utter acceptance. Aleksei and Dmitry had discussed this very question earlier.

'Regrowth can be repressed temporarily,' replied Kyesha, 'with practice.'

'Why bother?' asked Dmitry.

'A good question. You think like a scientist.'

'And the answer?'

'To survive! History has taught us that, of all the skills that might fend off death for a little while longer, the simplest and most effective is to avoid being recognized for what we are.' He paused for a moment. 'By people such as you.' They were speaking in Russian, and it was clear that his use of the plural form of 'you' was not intended to be polite, merely to encompass a very large plural – the whole of humanity. He was right though. If he had allowed his fingers to regrow before the eyes of the Turks, they would have known precisely how to deal with him.

'I thought *you* were a hero,' said Kyesha after a brief silence, directing his words at Aleksei.

'Me?'

'In Silistria,' continued Kyesha. 'I knew from the start that you were a spy – even before the Janissaries came in to arrest us. I saw you dropping that message out of the window. Obviously I could have escaped when they rounded us up, but I was curious.'

'Curious?'

'I'd heard all those terrible stories about the brutal Turk and his torturous ways – I wanted to see if they were true.'

187

'Wanted to pick up a few tips,' added Dmitry. Aleksei was pleased to hear how quickly his son had understood the vileness of these creatures.

Kyesha chose to ignore the comment. 'I thought the idea of cutting off the fingers one by one was ingenious; the way it incremented the terror, the way that, as the victim became accustomed to the pain, he would become more aware of the permanence of the mutilation. Most of all, I was fascinated by the fact that a single word from you could end it for the rest of us – and yet you said nothing. Were you being brave or callous? Of course now I've learned what you knew then – there's little difference between the two.'

'And so fifteen years later you've tracked me down, just to tell me that?' asked Aleksei.

'Oh, no, no. That's really just a coincidence, but a pleasant one. For years I didn't even know if you'd survived, though I suspected you would have.'

'You did well to remember me.'

'I had my mementos.' It was almost imperceptible, but there was a new darkness, a leering tone to those words. It chilled Aleksei.

'What?' he asked in a whisper.

'I came back the following night,' Kyesha explained. 'Back into the gaol. They hadn't cleared up at all; the table was still stained with blood. And scattered all around, like little pink dog turds, were fingers. Yours were easy to find, long and slender – so much more refined than those of the peasants. You should have been a pianist.' Aleksei glanced sideways towards his son at the mention of the piano. Kyesha misinterpreted him. 'I'm sorry, that was thoughtless. Perhaps you *were* a pianist – until then.'

'Just get on with it,' muttered Aleksei.

'As I say, your fingers were easy to find. If our captors had just looked at our hands rather than hacking at them, they'd instantly have worked out who was the spy. But they didn't, and their loss is . . . your loss. But the gain was mine. I've kept them ever since, as a tribute to bravery.'

'You've kept them?' Aleksei was stunned.

'All these years.'

'But wouldn't they . . . rot?'

'Oh yes,' said Kyesha lightly. 'They're nothing but bones now; six little bones.'

Aleksei's realization came at the same moment that Kyesha threw the six knucklebones on to the table, in the same manner he had done each night they had met. Then he arranged them in two straight lines, and the shape of Aleksei's two missing fingers was plain to see.

Aleksei placed his left hand on the table. He thought of the ballet he had seen less than a week before. Then it was a slipper that had fitted perfectly, but now it was those six small bones. He looked down at his hand, complete for the first time in fifteen years – as complete as it could ever be. The bones lay exactly where they should, as if Aleksei had dipped those two fingers into vitriol and allowed their flesh to dissolve while the rest of his hand remained intact. For a few years after they had first been severed, he had still thought he was able to feel them – if he looked away and flexed his hand, he had been able to sense all five fingers move. It happened rarely these days, but as he looked down at the table he tried to flex them again, tried to take control of the long-decayed muscles that had once encased those bones. He almost expected to see movement, but there was none.

He looked deliberately away and tried again, and this time, just as in the early days, he could observe no difference in sensation in his left hand from that he would have felt in his right. He glanced down again, and almost instantly flung himself backwards, away from the table, knocking his chair to the ground. What he had seen was impossible: his hand complete – truly complete, not just with the two skeletal remnants, but with actual fleshy fingers. He had even seen the nails.

He raised his left hand to his face, holding it in his right, but all was as it should be; a thumb, two fingers and two stumps. He looked back on to the table. There lay two fingers. Yes, they were made of flesh as well as bone, but they were not Aleksei's. They had never been attached to him and had remained on the table as he pulled his hand away. The blood around where they had been cut was dried, but still visible.

Kyesha was smiling. He poured the six small bones of Aleksei's fingers between his hands as he watched their owner's reaction.

'I'm sorry, Aleksei,' he said. 'I didn't realize you'd be so shocked. I just thought it would be a fair exchange: my fingers for yours.'

'You're very kind,' replied Aleksei blankly. He resumed his seat, and attempted to ignore the two lumps of flesh on the table in front of him.

'Not very gracious,' said Kyesha.

'I know how little they mean to you.'

Unlike his father, Dmitry seemed intrigued by Kyesha's gift. He picked up the ring finger, but immediately dropped it back on the table as if it had burned him.

'What is it?' asked Aleksei.

'Feel it! It's not dead.'

Aleksei picked up the finger. Dmitry was right; it was not dead, but neither was it alive – an apt status considering the creature from which it had come. It was warm – around body tempera-ture – with none of the strange, clammy quality that dead flesh exhibited. Moreover, it was flexible, without the stiffness that a dead body-part should have after a day. But there was nothing that more obviously indicated life. It did not move, or resist being bent by Aleksei's own hands. He picked up the other finger and slipped them both into his pocket. Kyesha leaned his head to one side and gave a brief nod of acknowledgement. He let Aleksei's six bones cascade one last time from one hand to the other, and then – mimicking Aleksei's action – returned them to his own pocket.

'I presume this still isn't the reason you contacted me?' said Aleksei.

'Quite right,' said Kyesha. 'But I think it is enough for one evening.' He stood. 'Goodnight, Aleksei Ivanovich, Dmitry

Alekseevich. We shall meet once more in Moscow. I will see you then.'

With that, he was gone.

Aleksei took the two fingers back out of his pocket and began to examine them, but his thoughts were interrupted by Dmitry. 'What do you suppose he meant by "in Moscow"?'

'I imagine he thinks that what he tells me tomorrow will be so fascinating that I'll be tempted away to some other place – somewhere I will be much more vulnerable.'

'But you wouldn't be foolish enough to do that.'

Aleksei looked over to the doorway through which the *voordalak* had so recently departed. 'If I choose to leave Moscow then I shall be able to do so in complete safety, secure in the knowledge that Kyesha will never leave the city.'

'How so?'

'Because tomorrow, Mitka, we'll have help.'

CHAPTER X

ALEKSEI RECOGNIZED CAPTAIN OBUKHOV, WHOM HE'D SPOKEN to at the club near Lubyanka, and a few of the other men who faced him in a small street to the east of Theatre Square. They were all members of the Northern Society, all dressed in civvies, all younger than its average membership, eager to see some action rather than sit around and debate the new order that was to come after the death of the tsar. Dmitry had done the work of recruiting them – in fact, most of the evening's plan had come from him. Aleksei had only made slight modifications, and as he had described each one, he could see the sneer in Dmitry's eyes at the very idea of such caution. But Aleksei knew far better than Dmitry the risks involved, and Dmitry seemed to accept this. Even if he didn't, Aleksei was Dmitry's father, and his superior officer, and something in that mix made Dmitry acquiesce.

The one thing they were in agreement on was the one that would put these young men into the greatest danger. They both knew they could not even think of using the word *voordalak* during any briefing. Many soldiers had in their time willingly followed insane commanders, but there were different strains of insanity; some could raise an army large enough to conquer Europe, others only laughter. Thus they had remained silent on the matter. Even so, it was a cruel mission to be sent in pursuit of a vampire in the belief that it was a man. The simple soldier's faith in the steel of a blade or the lead of a bullet would quickly prove to be his undoing. And there were no rational pretexts that could be devised to insist that a man must be beheaded or stabbed in the heart with a blade of wood. Even men whose grandmothers had not been so well versed – and so forthcoming – in their folklore as Aleksei's would listen to the words 'wooden stake' and hear only '*voordalak*'.

And so Aleksei had altered Dmitry's plan to come up with the safest and surest he could muster. In his final briefing, he emphasized the points he had added to the strategy, afraid that Dmitry might have avoided pressing them home, not out of disobedience, merely youthful over-exuberance.

'Do not approach him,' he said in a low voice as the group huddled round him. 'We know he's extremely dangerous – he's killed six men already.' The body count had mounted during the week. Aleksei had no idea if the blame for all could be laid at Kyesha's feet, nor did he care. Even if the creature had exercised utter self-control for all his time in Moscow, he had managed to live for at least fifteen years as a vampire. The total number of deaths – wherever the bodies lay – must have been far greater. 'But it's not the risk to us I'm concerned about.' Aleksei knew that all these men would only rise to a challenge; he needed a better reason to keep them away from Kyesha. 'We believe he is working with somebody else; someone who rarely goes out into the streets with him but who is the political force behind these murders – perhaps an enemy of Russia, perhaps a member of our own government.' It was ironic that these revolutionaries were such patriots. A foreign invader stirred their passion to just the same extent as did their perceived enemy within. 'Finding the mastermind is far more important than the mere capture of his henchman.'

'But if we capture him we'll make him talk.' It was Obukhov who spoke. 'Ten minutes is all it will take.'

Aleksei felt both amused and sickened. If time had been less precious he would have asked Obukhov how long he thought he himself would last under interrogation. The answer would most likely have been for ever – days, certainly. Perhaps Obukhov could stand torture that long, but then why did he believe that he would be so much better a torturer, and his subject so much less of a man, that the outcome would be any different if the roles were reversed? But a less philosophical response was more appropriate.

'No,' he said. 'There are too many risks. You can't guarantee to capture a man alive – not a man like this – and if you tried you'd be compromised. More than that, we can't be sure he'd talk, and even if he did, ten minutes could be plenty of time for the real enemy to get wind of it and be out of the city. We do this my way, OK?'

Obukhov glanced from side to side at his comrades, to see if he would gain any support from them, but received no encouragement. 'OK,' he said to Aleksei, with some semblance of conviction.

'So we follow him. He has a hideout somewhere in the city. He'll go there once he's finished with me. You track him to wherever he ends up. Then you get word back to me or Lieutenant Danilov.' Aleksei felt a quiet rush of pride as he described his son in this official fashion. 'Work in pairs so one of you can wait while the other brings the message. If he enters a building for a while and leaves again, keep following till his final destination.' And don't take a peek at the bloody mess he's left inside. Aleksei did not give voice to this last thought.

'Why is it that he's meeting you anyway, sir?' Aleksei did not know the name of the man who had asked. It was an astute question.

'I can't tell you. Suffice to say that he believes me to be someone rather different from who I actually am.' A bit of intrigue should keep them quiet. It seemed to stave off any more questions.

'You've all got his description, and you know that, when he speaks to me, I'll give you the signal. He may speak to Lieutenant Danilov, but the plan will be the same. Any questions?'

He looked around them, but no questions came. Despite his

rank, the responsibility of command had not been a frequent feature of Aleksei's career. He'd shouted orders on the battlefield often enough, but usually this was no more than being a link in a chain, not true authority. As a spy, he was most effective alone, or as a member of a team who knew one another to be equals. Tonight, he reminded himself of Vadim, whose attempts at issuing orders had often fallen on the deaf ears of Aleksei and the others. Aleksei was now two years older than Vadim had been when he died, engaged, just as they would be tonight, in a vampire hunt through the streets of Moscow.

Aleksei stepped back from the conspiratorial huddle. 'Let's go then,' he said. He headed down the street, before turning right towards the theatre. Dmitry kept pace with him. The others dispersed in various directions. They knew not to approach the Bolshoi as a mob; they would be easily spotted. Even so, Aleksei could only hope that Kyesha would be too suspicious of him and Dmitry to be on the lookout for so many associates. He hoped also that everyone would stick to his plan. If they did, it would be easy. The news would come that Kyesha had made his way to some address – most likely just before dawn. Aleksei and Dmitry would send the other soldiers away. They would be disappointed not to be in on the arrest, but they wouldn't ask questions. Then it would be a familiar trip down into a darkened cellar. If it could be done with sunlight, that would be better, but he already had a new wooden sword whittled for the occasion.

He smiled as he cast his mind back to earlier that day, as he sat there, carving away at the wood. Domnikiia had been across the room, sewing, aware of what he was planning, but repressing her concerns. Tamara had dashed in and seen the sword. The look on Domnikiia's face expressed both their fears that their daughter would ask what it was for, but in her childish self-interest she had immediately assumed it was a toy for her. 'I don't want a sword,' she had said. 'Swords are for *boys*.' With that, she had raced out again. On a different occasion, Aleksei would have chided her for her rudeness, but instead he and Domnikiia had laughed, a little of the tension between them released. Years earlier, Dmitry had been far happier to receive a wooden sword as a gift from his father. It had only been broken two nights before.

Kyesha had not provided a ticket for tonight's performance as he had the previous week, but Aleksei had had no trouble in purchasing one – or rather two, so that there would be an empty space beside him for Kyesha to sit. Tonight's performance was of *Flore et Zéphire*, a revival of Didelot's production of Bossi's score. Aleksei had already seen it in Petersburg, and while he had enjoyed plenty of ballet in his time, Didelot's over-staged trickery somehow bored him beyond all measure. Artistic appreciation was not, however, the purpose of tonight's visit. Aleksei and Dmitry stood for a while in the square outside the theatre, their eyes darting in all directions in search of Kyesha as the audience made its way between the columns of the theatre's façade to take their seats within.

'I should go in,' said Aleksei.

'You're sure he'll be inside?'

'He was last time.'

'Last time he knew where you'd be sitting.'

Aleksei nodded, but he already had an answer to that. 'Last time, he didn't know what I looked like.' Now it was Dmitry's turn to nod. 'Anyway,' continued Aleksei, 'he's either going to be inside or outside. It's either you or I that will meet him.' And I hope to God it's me, he thought.

'You're certain he'll come.' Dmitry spoke it as a statement, not a question.

'He wants something,' was Aleksei's simple reply.

Aleksei glanced around the square again. To anyone who knew the faces, the whole area screamed out that it was a trap. Even if Aleksei had never seen a single one of them before, he would have felt uneasy. Too many pairs of men, evenly distributed, each in his own way trying to look as if he had a reason for being there. Considering the assumed trade that Kyesha had used to lure some of his victims, he might well guess that there was an embarrassment of competition for him here tonight.

Dmitry took his father's hand. 'Good luck,' he said sincerely, before adding with a smirk, 'Colonel.'

'You too, Lieutenant,' replied Aleksei. Then he turned and went into the theatre.

His seat was again in the stalls, but further back this time, in row nine. As before, he was close to the aisle. He wanted to make it easy for Kyesha to approach him, and just as easy for him to get away. The main plot of the evening would not be unfolding in the theatre. Looking around, he could see three pairs of men he knew to be members of the Northern Society. No – more than that. Three pairs were members of the inner circle which had embarked upon tonight's adventure, but there were almost a dozen other faces Aleksei knew to house the same political point of view. He hoped none of them would interfere with his plans by trying to engage him or his colleagues in any kind of conversation.

The ballet began. Aleksei paid little attention. He glanced around the auditorium. It was almost full. He was pleased to see that the eyes of his comrades were all fixed on him, rather than on the stage. That was an important part of the plan. None of them had seen Kyesha before, and his contact with Aleksei might last only moments. They could not simply follow the man who took the seat next to Aleksei. Kyesha might not sit down – or some innocent, noticing a vacant space, might occupy it instead. It was vital that there be no confusion, and so all knew the pre-arranged sign Aleksei would make to indicate that this was the man. Aleksei clenched his fist in preparation. It was only after he had described the signal he would give that he understood its irony, though he felt sure that some deeper part of his mind, or some mischievous God, had suggested the idea to him in full knowledge of its implications.

The sign was to be a kiss – an inconspicuous kiss to the side of his own forefinger when he was in the presence of the man they should follow. It was not a kiss to the man he would betray, but it

197

amounted to the same. The words of Saint Matthew came to him: 'Now he that betrayed him gave them a sign, saying, whomsoever I shall kiss, that same is he: hold him fast.' And there was another difference. Aleksei's instructions were explicitly not to hold him fast, but to let him go. Even so, Aleksei hoped he would not have to endure the same fate as Judas. The icy cold of winter was his Hell on earth. He did not need to experience that same cold for eternity, down with the traitors in Hell's ninth circle.

Despite having seen it before, Aleksei found the ballet just about incomprehensible. He had, he believed, worked out who was playing Zephyr, the west wind, and who was Flora, the goddess of flowers and spring. Even before he'd entered the theatre he'd questioned why a Greek god should be attempting to seduce a Roman goddess when her Greek equivalent, Chloris, would at least be more likely to speak his language. But looking at the woman who was dancing the part of Flora, he couldn't help but wonder why any god or mortal, Greek or Roman, would want to seduce her, even if she offered him every one of the flowers that she caused to bloom in the spring. It was surprise enough that the rope by which she was all too frequently suspended – an innovation by Didelot in his original production – could hold her in the air long enough for her to fly across the stage and join her lover. Aleksei could only imagine the two, perhaps three, stagehands off in the wings, valiantly straining to keep the nymph aloft.

But he remembered that, just as he was not here to enjoy the ballet, he was equally not here to despise it. He glanced around the auditorium again and then down at the empty seat beside him. It was too late. The seat was no longer empty. On it lay a package, wrapped in paper, with three letters scrawled on its front:

А. И. Д.

Aleksei Ivanovich Danilov. Kyesha had slipped in to deliver it without Aleksei even noticing. Perhaps Kyesha himself had not come at all – he could have asked anyone to place the parcel on the seat. And it could have happened at any time within the last ten minutes. But there was no benefit in speculating. Aleksei grabbed the package and rushed out of the auditorium. The tunnel took him quickly out to the foyer and then he headed straight on, out of the theatre and into the square.

At first, he saw nothing. The square was not bustling, but as busy as one would expect on a Saturday evening. It was only after a few moments that he perceived a consensus of motion amongst a significant fraction of the people. Most walked in their own direction, or stood still, but all around, a number of individuals and often pairs were cutting through the crowd at a run, converging on a point just out of Aleksei's view – around the corner of the Maly Theatre. They were like ants, rushing home and converging on a single entrance to their nest. All were men he had deployed to track Kyesha. He felt a presence at his shoulder and turned. It was one of them – Lieutenant Batenkov, if he remembered correctly.

'We saw him speaking to Lieutenant Danilov, sir,' he said. 'The lieutenant gave the signal.'

'And then?'

'They headed east, over there.'

'Together?'

'Yes, sir.'

'And where's Lieutenant Danilov now?'

'I don't know.'

Aleksei raced down the theatre steps and diagonally across the square. Batenkov ran to keep up with him.

'Did you see what happened next?' asked Aleksei as they hurtled through the crowds.

'No. One of the men must have; he gave a shout. Then everyone started running.'

They crossed the street, dodging the slow-moving carriages, and turned past the Maly Theatre. Quite a crowd had gathered – passers-by as well as the soldiers – but it opened up as Aleksei approached, walking now. Aleksei saw the soles of a pair of boots first, then the body, laid flat on its back, and finally the face, covered in blood. There was only a small wound to the neck, but it had been instantly fatal. More blood oozed around the head in a slowly growing halo, which caused the circling crowd likewise to expand as people stepped back to avoid sullying their boots.

It must have been a wrench for Kyesha to leave so much blood unconsumed, but his motivation that night had not been hunger, but flight. And in that he had succeeded.

CHAPTER XI

'IT'S NOT LIEUTENANT DANILOV, COLONEL.' BATENKOV HAD KNELT down to examine the body.

'I know that,' snapped Aleksei. 'Don't you think I'd recognize my own son?' He stepped forward and looked more closely at the bloody face. It was Obukhov. Aleksei knew he should have sent him home earlier when he had seemed so keen for a fight. He should have sent them all home.

He heard the sound of footsteps trotting down the street and looked up to see Dmitry. Aleksei walked quietly away from the crowd, and Dmitry changed his course to join him. They spoke in low voices.

'I saw him coming out of the theatre,' said Dmitry.

'Did he see you?'

'I thought so, but he didn't come over to me. Had you already spoken to him inside?'

'Later,' said Aleksei. 'Tell me your story first.'

'Well, I went after him, and once I was close, just about where we are now, it was impossible for him to avoid me. I told him where you were.'

'And?'

'He said he knew. He seemed in a hurry to leave, so I gave the signal.' Dmitry repeated the sign. It seemed undetectable to anyone unprepared for it. It wasn't even right to call it a kiss; Dmitry merely touched his curled index finger to his lips, as if in thought. 'He can't have known what it meant, but perhaps he saw one of them react to it. He just turned and ran. Obukhov was further down the street. He threw himself at Kyesha; I didn't quite see what happened, but Kyesha hardly seemed to pause before running on. I tried to follow, but I lost him.'

Aleksei said nothing. The whole plan had been foolhardy. A good, if disobedient soldier was dead and Kyesha was no longer going to trust either him or Dmitry. The worst part was how little concern Aleksei really felt for Obukhov.

'What did he say to you in there?' asked Dmitry.

Aleksei briefly looked up at his son, not understanding the question for a moment. 'Oh, I never spoke to him,' he replied.

'So why did he come here at all?'

Aleksei held up the package he had discovered on the theatre seat. 'To give me this.'

Aleksei's credentials had proved to be almost too impressive when he showed them to the police. His intention had merely been to get them off his back, but the officer had been all too keen to leave Aleksei in charge of the whole investigation. Whether this was the result of deference or indolence, Aleksei could not tell, but it had taken some persuasion before he had finally been able to leave, with the promise that he would make himself available for any further enquiries. Only himself and Batenkov had been there when the gendarmerie arrived. The others – including Dmitry – had followed orders and dispersed. There would be many unanswered questions for the police, but with luck they would remain unanswered.

As he walked back home, Aleksei wondered how long the Moscow police kept records for, and how thorough they were in referring to them. Would they go back all the way to 1812? There would be nothing for them to find during the French occupation itself, but there had been deaths after the city had returned to Russian control, one of which – that of Margarita Kirillovna, Domnikiia's colleague – Aleksei had reported himself. To anyone who cared to look, the similarities between that crime and this would become immediately apparent.

'He got away, didn't he?' Domnikiia spoke within seconds of Aleksei's coming through the door. Even though there was barely enough light to see even his outline, she knew him well enough to perceive his mood. He sat on the bed beside her.

'Yes, he got away.' He didn't mention the death of Obukhov. He hoped her intuition might detect that too, but if it did, she said nothing. She stroked his back.

'Perhaps you've at least scared him away.'

'Perhaps,' said Aleksei. But he had little doubt that Kyesha had been planning to leave Moscow anyway.

'Come to bed,' she said, moving her hand on to his thigh. He looked towards her, just able to make out the glint of her eyes.

'No, there's something I've got to do.' He leaned forward and kissed her, but in the darkness missed her mouth, his lips falling somewhere close to the side of her nose.

'Do me,' she whispered, but he stood up and walked to the door.

'I won't be long,' he said.

In the adjoining room he lit the lamp and sat down at the desk. He laid the parcel down in front of him and slipped on his spectacles. There was no string or other fastening – the crumpled paper had simply been wrapped around the contents. The three letters were the only noticeable marks.

А. И. Д.

He turned the parcel over and pulled the paper gently aside, drawing the lamp closer to see what it was that he had revealed.

It was a book.

A large book, almost the size of a church Bible, but not nearly so thick. It was bound in a pale-brown leather. Aleksei put his fingers out to touch it. It felt extraordinarily delicate, like chamois, but also highly ridged, as though it had not been properly stretched.

203

The leather could be easily deformed and would return to its original shape. It seemed like the work of an amateur. There was nothing written on it. He turned the book over. He had evidently been looking at the back. On the cover were three words:

Nullius in Verba

The ink was a greenish-blue and the style ornate. Both the script and the language were Latin. 'On the words of no one,' was a rough translation. It meant little to Aleksei. He opened the book.

The handwritten text inside also used the Latin alphabet, but not the Latin language. Aleksei was fluent enough in French and Italian to have no trouble reading the script, despite the tight cursive handwriting, but the language itself was neither of those. Nor was it German, of which he had some knowledge. The use of words such as 'the', 'a' and 'is', repeated beyond any necessity, gave it away as English. It was easier to come up with corresponding words in either French or Italian than it was in Russian itself.

Aleksei's understanding of English was woefully poor. He glanced through the book, flicking page after page, but could understand little beyond the structural essentials of the language and the occasional word or phrase that had been lifted wholesale from French or Latin, of which English had so many.

His understanding of the text might have been helped by the fact that much of it was accompanied by hand-drawn illustrations, but with so little knowledge of the language, it was impossible to understand their context. Many of them appeared to be studies of human anatomy, whilst others were less clear, perhaps relating to optics. There were also several tables of numbers, but again, without understanding the text at the top of each column, they offered little enlightenment.

There was one deduction Aleksei felt he could confidently draw. The six characters heading each new section of the book were dates. The formation of two digits, followed by one, two, three or four letters and then another two digits had confused him for a moment, until he had noticed that the letters were limited to a very small set: 'x', 'v' and 'i'. The author was expressing the month in roman numerals. The first entry was dated 9.xii.24 and the last 24.viii.25. Given that the text was English, it was a reasonable assumption that these dates were in the New Style calendar, not the Old. On the other hand, wouldn't even an Englishman, if he was located in Russia, use the local calendar? The difference was only twelve days anyway. After the final date and its corresponding entry, there were several blank pages. This was a work in progress.

The only other thing that could be deduced from the dates was that Kyesha was most likely not the author. If he had been, then why had he kept it in his possession for almost six weeks without writing anything new in it? The final entry was dated a little while before that scrawled message had been left in Aleksei's study in Petersburg. The implication was that Kyesha had acquired the book from its author soon before. It was speculation of course, but it seemed reasonable.

The English text began to dance before his eyes in the dim lamplight. There was nothing more he would be able to discern that night. He wrapped the book back up in the paper and placed it in a drawer of the desk. He took off his spectacles and rubbed the sides of his head above his ears where they had dug in. Maks might have had a greater intellect than Aleksei, but he most certainly had a smaller skull.

Aleksei extinguished the lamp and went back into the bedroom. He undressed quickly and slipped into bed beside Domnikiia, wondering if she was still awake. He ran his fingers down her side, lightly brushing her smooth, cool skin and pushing from his mind the strange texture of the book's covering. When his hand was as far down her leg as he could reach, he ran it back up her body, this time along the inside of her thigh.

She was awake, but she spoke only briefly before rolling over and turning her back on him. 'Some hope,' she said.

The Kerch Strait was not wide; less than five versts across at its narrowest, to use the local measurement. That was a huge gap compared with the Bosphorus, but narrow enough to see the coast on either side from the deck of *Răzbunarea*. The hills sloped steeply upwards on the Crimean shore, the buildings of the town of Kerch itself clinging to them.

Ahead lay the Sea of Azov. This was still the familiar route of thirteen years before, but it would be over much sooner – perhaps in less than a day, according to the captain. Already, they were sailing against the outflow from the river Don, at the other end of the small, isolated stretch of water, but on this occasion, he would not be making the tiresome journey upriver into the heart of Russia. On his next visit, he would make that journey and be hailed as a king, but for now, this outpost of the great empire would suffice. Once they had dropped anchor, then all he needed to do was wait. Others would do the work for him.

A journey taking in all the bookshops of Moscow would be unlikely to yield what Aleksei was looking for. He had never heard of such a thing as a dictionary to assist with translations between English and Russian, and doubted whether anyone else had. Fortunately, he happened to be living under the same roof as one of the greatest bibliophiles in the city, the master of the house himself, Valentin Valentinovich. Not only did he possess an impressive library of his own, but his knowledge of what was in the city's other libraries was unsurpassed.

Aleksei knocked on the door of Valentin Valentinovich's study, and entered when called. He sat down in the chair opposite the desk. After a few cool pleasantries, he asked the most obvious question:

'How's your English, Valentin?' He was ambivalent about the response. If Valentin was able to translate the text directly for him, then it might save hours, or even days, of work. But it would be a bold move to ask anyone for a translation of a text whose contents could reveal anything. On the other hand, perhaps just a summary of the first page might send Aleksei on the right track. He could always claim it was a work of fiction – apparently the principal use for the English language.

'Not a word, I'm afraid,' replied Valentin. 'Why?'

'I have a letter I need to translate.'

'A letter? Why on earth would anyone write to you in English?' He wasn't stupid, and was able to answer his own question almost immediately. 'It's not your letter, is it?'

He stood up from his desk and slammed his hand against the bookshelves. 'This is really too much, Aleksei.' Other men would have shouted, but Valentin Valentinovich spoke as if he had never known true anger. He persisted in using French, even though its popularity had been in decline – certainly amongst men of his class – for a decade. 'I look after your whore, I pretend your bastard is my own, I let you treat my home as though it were a hotel, and now you want to involve me in your . . . your . . . underhand profession.' He spat the word 'underhand' as though it were the foulest profanity he could think of.

Aleksei remained calm. Valentin was speaking with complete accuracy. Tamara was a bastard – the most adorable bastard in the whole wide world. Domnikiia was, or at least had been, a whore – though Aleksei guessed that Valentin was unaware of the literal truth of his words. It was his attitude to espionage that really riled Aleksei. The man thought himself a gentleman, and thought no spy ever could be. It was an insult to so many of Aleksei's friends.

'Shall we go and ask Yelena Vadimovna what she thinks of my profession?' said Aleksei, with a certain sense of pride. It was an obvious enough question for a blackmailer to ask his mark, but in reality it was a three-pronged attack in which blackmail was far from Aleksei's intent; far, but not completely absent.

It was almost possible to see Valentin wilt step by step as each aspect washed over him. The use of Yelena's patronymic, and with it the reminder of her father Vadim, hit him first. Vadim

Fyodorovich had practised that same underhand profession. Yelena loved her father without question. To insult Aleksei for that would be to insult her father, and that would be unwise.

The second problem for Valentin was what Aleksei knew about him. It wasn't much, but for a man as honourable as Valentin, it was monumental. It had been a minor embezzlement, and Valentin had been unaware of it, but he had trusted flattering colleagues who had promised him the rank of Actual State Counsellor in exchange for help in what they assured him was an entirely legal set of transactions. One of them had been siphoning funds to Polish activists, and that's how Aleksei had come across the fraud. He'd looked at the books and found that Valentin was guilty of nothing more than allowing others to use his bank account. He made sure Valentin's name was kept out of the ensuing trial, and even found a way to let him keep half the money. When he revealed what he had done, Valentin had misread him. He'd seen it as an attempt at blackmail and had capitulated in an instant, even though at the time (back in 1818), there was nothing Aleksei had wanted from him. It was that which had precipitated Valentin's move from government into commerce, and from Petersburg to Moscow. Aleksei had stored the incident away, until Domnikiia had fallen pregnant, and then called in the marker. Valentin saw it as coercion, Aleksei as one good deed being repaid with another. It made no practical difference to the outcome.

Of course, it had not been Valentin Valentinovich's decision alone that they should take in Domnikiia and, when she entered the world, Tamara. Yelena Vadimovna had also to be persuaded. On the one hand she would do almost anything for Aleksei, who had been her father's most trusted comrade but, as was the nature of women, she had become somewhat close to Marfa in Petersburg, even though they only knew one another through Aleksei. Thus to support one friend in his hour of need would be to betray another. In the end, Aleksei liked to think that it was Yelena's love for her father that had won the day, but there were other factors. Yelena herself had had a lover when she lived in Petersburg. This had been some while after Rodion's birth, so there was no doubt as to his paternity, and Aleksei could easily understand why an intelligent and vibrant woman like Yelena might seek attention from a man other than Valentin Valentinovich.

But Aleksei had not used his knowledge to blackmail Yelena; he doubted she was even aware he knew. Even so, her guilt made her less willing to judge others. She was unprepared to go to Marfa and reveal Aleksei as unfaithful, not because she feared he would do the same for her, but because she feared God would.

And from that came the third reason why Valentin would do what Aleksei asked, and retreat from the very idea of discussing it with Yelena. Valentin suspected that Aleksei and his wife had at one time been lovers. Thus he both believed she would side with him now and feared that any disagreement between them would result in him being publicly branded a cuckold. It was all fantasy. There had never been any physical relationship between Yelena and Aleksei, just an intense friendship born out of their mutual love for Vadim. But for a man of Valentin's limited imagination, such closeness could have only one explanation. A younger Aleksei would have despised him for ever allowing his wife's lover into the house, but as he had grown to know him, Aleksei had seen something more and more noble in every one of Valentin's actions. It was a desire to do the right thing which Aleksei knew he could never achieve and so did not even attempt. Nor did he attempt to avoid exploiting Valentin's fears when it served his purpose.

It took only moments for all these concepts, or at least his perceptions of them, to mollify Valentin's position. 'I'm sorry, Aleksei,' he said quietly, 'but I'm afraid I can't help you. As I say, I don't speak English.'

'Do you have a dictionary?'

'I'm sure I could find you a copy of Johnson somewhere in the city, or even Webster, but I don't see how that would help you.'

'I meant a bilingual dictionary,' said Aleksei.

'Between English and Russian?' There was greater passion in Valentin's voice at this ridiculous suggestion than there had been in any other part of their conversation. 'I don't think anyone's attempted such a thing.' He paused for a moment in thought, tapping his lips with his pen. 'Wait a minute though . . .' He turned to the bookshelf behind him and brought down a sheaf of papers, clearly not a published work but some notes of his own. 'Yes. Louis Chambaud produced a lexicon of English and French in 1805. That would do you.'

'Absolutely,' agreed Aleksei. 'Do you have a copy?'

'No, no, no. But I know a man who does.'

'Excellent. Tell me his name and I'll go see him.'

Valentin looked at him coldly. 'I think not. There's no need for you even to know the name of the gentleman. I shall ask him for it when I next see him.' He sat down at the desk and resumed his work. Aleksei remained seated. Valentin pretended to ignore him and, much as Aleksei enjoyed the tension that his presence created, he was eager to make use of the dictionary.

'It is rather urgent,' he said unassumingly.

Valentin stood up swiftly and flung his pen down on his desk, or at least began to fling it, but he regained his self-control and by the time the object made contact with the desktop, its movement could be described as no more than a gentle placement.

'Very well, I'll go and see if I can borrow it,' huffed Valentin. 'Wait here.'

The wait was less than half an hour. That would have been time for Valentin to make it some way across the city and back, but Aleksei knew he would not have been able to make a brief call. He would have spent at least ten minutes in polite conversation before putting so direct a question. That put the library from where the dictionary had come very close. Aleksei could easily formulate a list of five likely candidates, with five more who were reasonable possibilities.

In the end, such calculations were unnecessary. A glance inside the front cover as soon as he had returned to the privacy of his rooms revealed an ornate *Ex Libris*, bearing the name of a celebrated prince and government minister whose library (so the best inside information that Aleksei could obtain had it) was more notable for its erotica than for its lexicography.

With so simple an identification of the book's owner in mind, Aleksei turned to the mysterious volume Kyesha had given him the previous night. Had he missed something so utterly obvious? He opened it and looked at the inside. There it was – no decorative bookplate, but the simple, functional name of the author:

Richard L. Cain F.R.S.

It certainly sounded like an English name. The 'F.R.S.', Aleksei presumed, did not signify further initials, but some kind of qualification or decoration. He had no idea of its precise nature.

He set about translating the text. Whilst the dictionary could give him the meaning of words, their formation into sentences was a more difficult issue. He learned as he went. He was immediately reminded of what he had already heard about English – the fact that it was almost totally lacking in inflection. Aleksei knew that in such languages word order took on greater significance. By following roughly the same rules as French, he generally came up with a sensible translation. Even so, the first few sentences took him over an hour. Many others had words that were not listed in the dictionary at all, presumably scientific terms which had not been deemed necessary for general conversation – or perhaps even terms coined since the dictionary had been published. Who could tell? If Richard Cain really was at the cutting edge of science, he might be inventing new words as he went along.

'What's that, Papa?'

He looked up. Tamara had come in. She and Domnikiia had been out most of the day. He could hear Domnikiia's movements in the next room.

'It's a book,' he said, hoisting his daughter up on to his knee.

'Can I read it?'

'You can try.' She was a keen reader already, in French more so than in Russian, though she spoke Russian better. She looked at the book lying open on the desk in front of Aleksei for some time and then frowned.

'It's silly,' she said confidently.

'It's English,' said Aleksei.

She gave a look of concentration and then spoke. 'The king of England is King George IV.'

'Very good.'

'The king of France is King Charles X.'

'Excellent,' he smiled. 'Any more?'

'America does not have a king. It is a republic.' It seemed her long-dead Uncle Maks was having an influence on her. 'A republic is an affront against God,' Tamara added. That sounded less like Maks – or perhaps not; Maks was quite fond of affronting God.

'Who told you that?' he asked.

'Uncle Valentin.'

'And do you believe everything Uncle Valentin tells you?'

Before she could answer, Domnikiia shouted from the other room. 'Toma!' The little girl ran out, leaving Aleksei with a sudden understanding of the Latin phrase on the front of the book. *Nullius in Verba*. On the words of no one. Take nobody's word for it. Certainly not Uncle Valentin's, nor that of any adult. The phrase should be written above the gates of every school in the country.

'Let your father work,' said Domnikiia from outside. A moment later, Aleksei felt her arms around his neck and her chin on his shoulder.

'So this is what it was all for?' she asked. He had told her about the book that morning.

'Seems so. A step along the way, at least.'

'Why couldn't he have just given it to you the first time you met?'

'Or just delivered it to my house in Petersburg,' suggested Aleksei. 'Perhaps he's in league with someone who wants to bring me to Moscow and keep me here. Now who could that be?'

He felt a tight little punch to his shoulderblade. 'Can you decipher it?' she asked.

'I haven't yet. If only Toma would stop pestering me.'

'But she's . . . Oh, I see.' She kissed him on the cheek and he felt her arms uncoil from around him. He heard the door close.

In truth he had made some headway, but he had found nothing that could explain why Kyesha should have wanted him to read the document. It was, as he had suspected, some sort of scientific journal, listing a series of ongoing experiments, many of which were related, to use a term repeated frequently in the text, to 'biology'. It was not a word listed in the dictionary, but Aleksei knew enough Greek to guess its meaning. Many of the experiments were conducted on animals, of a species that was not made clear. Individuals were referred to simply by a number. The image that formed in Aleksei's mind was of rats, but there was nothing concrete to suggest that. Other experiments were of a more chemical nature, many referring to a substance called *lapis lunaris*, which Aleksei this time had to resort to Latin to translate, unenlighteningly, as 'moonstone'.

It was clear that this was simply the latest volume in an ongoing work. The text began abruptly on 9 December the previous year, with a reference to work from the day before. It would be a slow process to translate page by page, though ultimately necessary, but for now it seemed there was a better chance of gaining some clue as to what was really going on by flicking through the book and diving in at random. In doing so, Aleksei stumbled on one further fact. One entry referred to the day of the week. The section was pondering, as well as Aleksei could make out, whether any of the animals changed their behaviour on a weekly cycle. Seemingly they did not, but the text made the comment 'today being Sunday' and therefore placed that entry's date, 8 March 1825, as a Sunday.

Aleksei searched his desk and found an almanac. 8 March was the feast day of Saint Theophylaktos, but more importantly, it was indeed a Sunday. That meant that the book's author was definitely using the Old Style calendar, and probably working in Russia, or at least in the east of Europe.

Aleksei raised his head and rubbed his face with his hands, pushing his spectacles up on to his forehead. It was dark outside. He glanced at the clock. It was half past eight. He'd been sitting there for hours, and he was in danger of missing his appointment – if indeed he had one.

As he passed Tamara's room, he glanced inside. She was in bed. Her mother was singing gently to her. Aleksei could not make out the words. He paused to watch and to listen. It was another twenty minutes before he left the house.

Aleksei had run across the city. As he went, he questioned what he was doing. Kyesha had killed a man the previous night, and had to be well aware that Aleksei had planned the action against him. And yet Aleksei felt no fear. Kyesha had made no move to attack him all week. His ultimate goal had been to deliver the book, and now that was achieved, it seemed even more pointless to do anything to harm Aleksei until he had actually managed to read it.

The greater worry was that Kyesha wouldn't be there. It seemed more than likely – he had said himself on Friday that there would only be one more meeting in Moscow. On the other hand, they hadn't actually met at the theatre the previous night. Aleksei might be taking things too literally, but there was no benefit in ignoring the possibility.

He was only a few minutes late when he arrived at the church. He glanced inside, and inside Menshikov's Tower, but there was no sign of Kyesha. It was raining, and Aleksei didn't feel inclined to wait outside. He returned to the tavern where he had taken Kyesha a week before. There was still no sign of him, but Aleksei ordered vodka and sat down to wait. He was at the same table where they had sat before, where Kyesha had first brought out the bones Aleksei now knew to be his own.

Knew? That was a stretch of faith. Kyesha was, in many ways, like Iuda. Iuda would lie and toy with Aleksei, mixing truth and falsehood, leaving him to doubt any certainty he'd had over either. Even today, Iuda's legacy continued. Aleksei still did not know the truth of what he had seen at Domnikiia's window, all those years before. His joke earlier that evening about her plotting with Kyesha to keep him in Moscow had started as just that, but he had never felt that depth of certainty with Domnikiia that he did with Marfa. He knew it was one of the things that made their relationship so exciting.

But what would have been easier for Kyesha? To sneak back, as he had described, and retrieve Aleksei's fingers, to keep them for a decade and a half, and finally reveal them to their original owner? Or simply to steal a few bones from a peasant's grave and pass them off as Aleksei's own? How could Aleksei tell the difference? Perhaps they were even Kyesha's fingers – he seemed happy enough to harvest them as he thought necessary. Could he have cut them off some months before and waited until, just as the flesh grew back on his own hand, it decayed from those severed fingers and they became no more than dry bones?

Aleksei reached into his pocket. Inside, Kyesha's two fingers still lay where Aleksei had put them. He made sure no one else in the room saw as he drew them out and placed them on the table. They looked and felt just as they had done before, still in that strange state that was both unliving and undead. That was remarkable in itself. It had been three days since Aleksei saw with his own eyes that ragged piece of metal separate those fingers from the body that sustained them. And yet there was not a hint of decay. He raised one to his face, cupping it inside his hand so no one would see, and sniffed it. There was no noticeable odour. It was conceivable that it was still too early, but Aleksei had other ideas.

He had observed putrefaction in the body of more than one vampire in his time. Usually it came on very quickly after death – if the body had not been destroyed anyway, by sunlight or fire. But when he had killed a vampire using a wooden blade to the heart, or by decapitation, the collapse of its bodily integrity had been almost immediate. There had been one exception: a young soldier who had become a vampire only weeks before he met his final end. His decay had been slower and less pronounced. Indeed, as far as Aleksei had been able to tell, the body had decayed, but only to the extent that it would have done if nature had taken her usual course from the point of the soldier's actual death – the moment at which he became a *voordalak*. Ultimately, what Aleksei had seen in front of him had been exactly what he would expect to see in a corpse that had lain in the open, unattended to, for several weeks.

Thus his conclusion was that the state of being a vampire somehow suspended the normal process of decomposition expected in a dead body. In reality, that was all that Kyesha and any of his kin were: lifeless cadavers given the semblance of existence by some foul spirit. That same force which animated the limbs fended off the processes of decay. When it had lost control of the body, nature rapidly reasserted herself.

Those fingers would not decay until Kyesha himself was dead.

Aleksei slammed his fist down on to the table, crushing the little finger beneath it. He smiled to himself, wondering if Kyesha, wherever he might be, could still feel pain in that detached part of his body. The sound of the impact made a few heads turn, but none could see what Aleksei was doing. He ignored them and took a gulp of vodka.

Once again, he placed his hand on the table so that the two fingers lay precisely where his own fingers should have. The skin that had grown over the tops of his shattered knuckles had little feeling in it, but he could see that it was just touching the still-raw ends of Kyesha's fingers. There was no blood in them now, and no healing had taken place, so blood vessels, bones and other structures, of whose nature Aleksei knew little, were clearly visible. It was an anatomist's dream; a body-part that could be studied slowly and over a long period, without ever worrying about losing the sample through decay.

Those two fingers answered another question which Aleksei had asked himself years ago. The Oprichnik Andrei had suffered a similar but far more serious injury than Kyesha. In that case, Andrei had lost an entire arm, severed by a blow from Maks' sword during a desperate fight for self-preservation. Aleksei had seen Andrei not long after with the arm fully restored. The question that had briefly crossed his mind was, if a *voordalak* could grow back a severed arm, could not the arm grow back the body of a *voordalak*? Would such an intersection result in two copies of the original?

It seemed not. There was no sign of a new Kyesha, growing out of his own fingers. Perhaps though, even if they could not grow a body anew, they might be able to reattach themselves to an existing body if the chance arose. For a second time, Aleksei pulled his hand away in revulsion. He had almost felt the sensation of new tendrils growing out of those moribund cylinders of flesh and feeling their way towards his own hand, which lacked what they could so readily provide, making him whole once again – part human, part monster. It was all in his mind, but the thought sickened him. He rammed the fingers back into his pocket and downed more vodka.

He looked up at the clock. It was past eleven. Kyesha would not come tonight.

CHAPTER XII

'*I THINK I KNOW HOW TO HANDLE THE TSAR.*'

Aleksandr smiled to himself as he heard the words in his head, spoken in Clemens von Metternich's refined Austrian accent. It had not been his own ears that had heard Metternich speak, but he knew what had been said. He knew much of what people said.

He gazed out of his study window, across the garden and out to the sea. It was peaceful here in Taganrog, and that gave him the chance to contemplate; not merely to think – though he had done enough quick-thinking in his time – but to look back on how things were, and how they might have been.

They had all presumed to understand him: Metternich, Castlereagh, Bonaparte. The last two were dead, and Bonaparte's fall could be attributed almost entirely to Russia. And Russia was the tsar. That's what Aleksandr's *babushka* had always told him. She, of course, had said 'tsaritsa', but he had chosen to take the more general interpretation of her words – the role, not the individual.

Castlereagh was British, and the British were always more astute in war than in peace. They maintained their own peace by allowing Europe to be at war. Aleksandr had beaten him – beaten Britain – on that. There had been peace now in Europe for ten years, and there was no prospect of it breaking down – all thanks to Aleksandr's Holy Alliance. Metternich had played his role, but only as a broker. To make peace one had to be capable of war, and Austria, even with Metternich as her chancellor, had little strength in that direction when compared with Russia.

For it was war that had proved Aleksandr to be the only man capable of bringing peace. It was Russia that had turned the tide of Bonaparte's domination; Russia that had proved he was not invincible; Russia that had pursued him all the way back to France. Other armies had played their part, Aleksandr would happily concede that, but it was Russia – Aleksandr – that had led the way.

And yet they still belittled him. Years before Metternich had spoken, Aleksandr's friend and advisor Speransky had expressed much the same sentiments. *'Too feeble to reign and too strong to be governed.'* That had been the real reason Speransky had had to go. The most laughable thing was, they thought he would never hear. *Scientia potentia est* – knowledge is itself power. It was another thing Yekaterina had taught him. He had spies everywhere, who could report to him what anyone said – be they enemies or friends, foreigners or compatriots.

But Yekaterina had lacked one thing a truly great leader required – a devotion to God. Sure enough she worshipped Him, acted in His name, but she believed that the Lord was simply a judge within whose rules – at the boundaries of whose rules – she must operate. Aleksandr knew that God did not exist simply to be feared, but to be loved. It was Castlereagh, again overheard by an ear friendly to the tsar, who had noted it, though he meant it as a criticism: *'The tsar's mind has of late taken on a deeply religious tinge.'*

It was an accurate observation – and one in which Aleksandr revelled. He had been mistaken in his youth. He had had a zeal to do right, but it had been misdirected. God's will was not to overthrow the old order – to make serfs into princes – but to protect it; to make serfs prosper as serfs and princes thrive as princes, each knowing his place and doing good for the other. And peace was the foundation for that – an end to 'the destruction that wasteth at noonday', as the psalm put it. Aleksandr had achieved peace in a way his *babushka* never had, and that was what made him greater than she.

But would he yet prove himself to be greater than Tsar Pyotr, his great-great-grandfather? Time would tell – perhaps very little time. He had come to Taganrog to find it out, to face 'the pestilence that walketh in darkness'. And yet he had been in Taganrog now for three weeks, with no sign of how the question was to be answered – with little sign of anything happening at all.

He glanced out to sea again. At least there there was some change. A new sail could be seen on the horizon. She was too small to be a barque – little more really than a large yacht. She was too far to see the name, or even the flag.

It was pleasant to have something to break the smooth horizon, and a single vessel sailing into harbour could do no harm – not to a man who could outsmart Metternich.

Even now, Aleksei felt a thrill as their eyes locked and did not separate for four, five, six seconds. As ever, it was he who looked away first, despite the pleasure he derived from the sensation of his heart beating faster and the flush of blood he felt to his face, and elsewhere. Why did he break away from her gaze? Was it simply out of some sense of gentlemanly etiquette – the idea he had been brought up with since birth that any woman of good breeding would feel ashamed to sense the eyes of a man on her for so prolonged a period of time? Possibly, but Aleksei knew Domnikiia well enough to understand that no such sense of shame would ever cross her mind in those circumstances.

And therein lay the attraction. To stare into Domnikiia's eyes was to see no semblance of resistance, to see no veil of diffidence that said, 'That part of me is not for you,' or even 'You must wait.' Her eyes would yield and allow the gaze of a man to fall upon them almost as though at the same time she had stood up and slipped out of her gown, allowing those same eyes to meander over every curve of her still delectable body.

Not that there was anything wrong with that, had they been in the privacy of their own bedroom, where he would have happily gawped at the reality of her nakedness for minutes on end and yet still returned his attention with inescapable frequency to her eyes.

But they were not shielded by privacy. They were sitting across from each other at a table in a teahouse off Tverskaya Street. Anyone who even glimpsed Domnikiia would instantly see her as the most desirable woman in the room. Anyone who saw Aleksei as he fell into those dark, wide, acquiescent eyes of hers would understand exactly what was going on between them, and might as well be sitting beside their bed as they made love.

As ever, Domnikiia could read his thoughts.

'Do you think they know?' she asked quietly. He glanced back at her. She was sipping her tea, but had not moved her eyes from him.

'Who?' he countered. 'And for that matter, what?'

'All these people.' Her eyes left him only briefly to take in the rest of the clientele. 'And what you're thinking of doing to me.'

'*Planning* on doing to you,' corrected Aleksei.

She raised an eyebrow and sipped more of her tea. 'Do I get a say?' she asked.

It had been Aleksei's idea that they should go out together. They didn't often, in part because Domnikiia hated to leave Tamara, in part because they might be seen together by somebody who knew Marfa. But on this visit to Moscow, he had been so busy with Kyesha, and not with her, that he had looked for an opportunity to make amends. She had displayed no general envy of his time away from her – an occasional comment, perhaps, but as far as he perceived, those were intended more to tease than to rebuke. In that way, and in most others, she was almost perfect, or at least that version of perfection which Aleksei might have come up with if given a blank page to start from: beautiful, witty, irresistibly sensuous and, with all that, as it had turned out, a doting mother. There was just that one niggling cloud on the horizon,

221

which threatened to fill the whole sky: the possibility that the entire thing was founded on a pack of lies.

'Don't you hate me sometimes?' he asked. He had changed the subject, but apparently not her mood.

'Constantly,' she replied. 'Any specific reason you want to focus on?'

'For my absence.'

'I could only hate you for your absence because I love you for your presence.'

'You could love another man who was never absent.'

She paused. 'Lyosha,' she asked. 'Have you made love to any other woman since we met?'

'There's Marfa, obviously,' he mumbled.

'I understand that,' she said. 'That's marriage. But anyone else?'

Embarrassingly, Aleksei had to think. There had been several women in his life over the years, even since he and Marfa had married, but it was a case of going through them in his mind to see if any had been since he had first met Domnikiia – seen her, met her and screwed her, all within the space of about half an hour – back in late 1811.

'You haven't,' she said, before he could reply, 'and believe me, I'd know. But I'm glad you had to think about it, because that's the point.'

'Glad?'

'Absolutely. Ask yourself why you haven't. You never made any promise to me of your undying faith. And even if I found out, I'd probably let you get away with it – a couple of times.'

'Really?' He didn't have the conviction to convey any real interest in the prospect.

'Really. But you wouldn't want to, however much you pretend to, for the sake of God knows who. And why wouldn't you want to?'

'You tell me.'

'Because you know full well she'd be a pathetic disappointment compared with me. Not just in bed – everything about her. You'd get more pleasure by closing your eyes and imagining watching me from half a verst away than you would with her.'

Despite her delightful arrogance, Domnikiia was right, not just about the fact there had been no other women – he'd got through his mental list and verified that – but about the reason. Even in Paris in 1814 and again in 1816 he'd remained faithful, despite the obvious temptations. There were many reasons why a man might be faithful to a woman – because he feared she would leave him if she found out, because he didn't want to hurt her – but Aleksei supposed he was lucky, and perhaps a rarity, in that he knew it simply wouldn't be half as much fun.

'And how do you know all this?' he asked her.

For the first time in several minutes her eyes dropped away from him. Her speech was close to a whisper. 'Because that's how I feel about you.'

She had not needed to look at him, but still another wave of passion – not just physical passion – washed through him. He drank his tea and bit hard on to the glass.

They sat in silence for a few minutes. There was no rush. Yelena Vadimovna was looking after Tamara. They had gone to visit friends near Bogorodsk and would not be back till much later. Aleksei nibbled on a *khvorost*.

'You didn't answer my question,' said Domnikiia.

'You ask so many questions, my dear.'

'You know which one.'

Aleksei honestly didn't, and Domnikiia chose not to pre-varicate.

'Do I get a say?'

'Oh, that,' he said with a smile. 'Of course you do.'

'Good,' she said. 'Then let's go home.'

They cut through sidestreets to find the shortest way back to Arbatskaya. Their conversation was trivial as they teased each other with attempted distractions from what was to come. They walked briskly, but again, each deliberately held the other back a little. Even so, their pace meant they did not hold hands, which proved to be fortunate.

Neither of them saw him as he approached, and he was upon them before either could react in any way.

'Papa!'

Aleksei felt his features freeze for a moment, and then re-form into a smile, which he hoped would be all that Dmitry would perceive.

'Dmitry,' he said. 'I was meaning to come and find you.'

'I've just been at your hotel,' replied Dmitry, but he had quickly stopped paying attention to his father and was looking at Domnikiia.

'Have you met Domnikiia Semyonovna?'

'No, I haven't,' said Dmitry. It was with mixed feelings that Aleksei noted that his son's reaction to Domnikiia was not dissimilar to that of most other men, not least because, as a father, he felt his son should not have eyes for a woman fourteen years older than himself. Domnikiia raised her hand and allowed Dmitry to kiss it.

'Domnikiia Semyonovna is nanny to Yelena and Valentin's little daughter. I just happened to bump into her. Do you remember them?'

'Of course, though I've never seen the daughter. I've meant to call on them since I've been in Moscow.'

There was a formality in both men's manners which Aleksei felt Dmitry must notice as easily as he did. He hoped he would not understand its cause.

'This is Dmitry Alekseevich, my son,' he said to Domnikiia.

Dmitry was taller than his father and, in turn, towered above Domnikiia. She tilted her head upwards and smiled only slightly, but her eyes fixed on his in a way Aleksei found familiar.

'I'm heading back home now,' she said, giving the impression that Aleksei was quite forgotten. 'Perhaps you'd like to accompany me. I'm sure they'd be delighted to see you.' The last sentence seemed almost an afterthought.

'We do really need to talk, Dmitry,' said Aleksei.

Dmitry thought for a moment, his eyes still on Domnikiia, before acquiescing. 'Yes, absolutely. Another time, Domnikiia Semyonovna.'

'I do hope so,' said Domnikiia. She smiled at Aleksei and he gave her a brief nod. She glided away down the street, turning back briefly after a couple of dozen paces to see both men still looking at her. Aleksei suspected it was in Dmitry's direction that her face was turned.

'What a charming woman,' said Dmitry.

'I went to the meeting as usual last night,' said Aleksei, without any acknowledgement of his son's comment. 'Kyesha didn't come.'

'As you expected.' Dmitry's tone was at once deadly serious. 'I spoke to Kirill Antonovich,' he continued. 'The police officer you saw in Theatre Square.'

'Has he discovered anything?'

'No, but he's linking Obukhov's death with the other murders – which now seem to have stopped. Captain Obukhov was the last.'

'It's only been two days,' said Aleksei.

'True, but there was a death almost every night while Kyesha was here. It fits in with his having left.'

'Just one? Never more?' Aleksei had not really been keeping track of the details. The presence of a *voordalak* meant death – what more did there need to be to it? For those other victims, he felt less empathy than he had even with Obukhov.

'Never more, sometimes none at all – unless there are still bodies to be discovered.' Perhaps Kyesha had been restraining himself. In 1812, the Oprichniki had been far less disciplined. Then, though, the city had been in chaos under the occupation, so there was less threat of discovery. And, of course, Aleksei himself had asked them to kill as many French as they possibly could. Even so, it might just be the case that Kyesha was of a different caste of vampire from the Oprichniki, as he seemed to be in other ways.

'What was in the package?' asked Dmitry.

'A book – handwritten. A notebook, really.'

'What does it say?'

'I don't know, it's in English.' Aleksei knew well enough that his son had no more ability in the language than he did.

'I'll ask around, see if I can find a translator,' said Dmitry.

'Someone we can trust.'

Dmitry nodded.

'I'll go to the meeting tonight, just in case,' said Aleksei.

'Where is it?'

'Red Square. We spoke in the Lobnoye Mesto last time.'

'Want me to come?'

'I'll be all right. I'll talk to you about it tomorrow.'

They parted. Dmitry turned north, and Aleksei headed southeast, towards his hotel. At the next junction, having checked Dmitry was out of sight, he turned right and then right again, and was soon once more heading west.

Domnikiia was already naked when Aleksei entered the room. She could not have got there more than five minutes ahead of him, but had not wasted any time. The blankets had been thrown to the side of the bed and she lay centrally on her back, her legs together and her arms by her sides. The long plait of her dark hair curved from behind her head and over her left shoulder, hiding her left nipple and lying across her belly. There was only a small gap of white flesh between it and the matching triangle of hair that nestled between the tops of her thighs. Her eyes were closed, but it was obvious she was not asleep. Aleksei took off his clothes and then ran his finger down her chest, between her breasts.

'Who's that?' she asked, with a smile.

Aleksei threw himself on the bed beside her and pulled her over towards him. She opened her eyes and grinned at him.

'Who did you think it might be?' he asked.

'I met a very charming young man out in the street just now.'

'Man?' It was genuinely an odd word for Aleksei to hear describing his son. 'He's just a boy.'

'I'd make him a man,' giggled Domnikiia. It should have been an uncomfortable conversation, but from her it had a charm that banished all his concerns. He was reminded of how, by way of business, she had slept with Maks. But that had been different; he had been unsure of her then – and sure of Maks. His certainty in Maks had proved misplaced. He had learned to live with his uncertainty of Domnikiia.

'I don't think that would be wise,' he said.

'Afraid you'd lose me to a less wrinkly version of yourself?'

'Afraid I'd lose my son to a lascivious succubus.'

She leaned over him. He felt her breast brush against his chest. 'I'd be offended if I knew what that meant,' she said.

He raised his head so that their noses touched. 'A dirty whore,' he whispered. There had been a time when such a reference to her former profession would have offended her. Now they both revelled in it.

'Well,' she said, 'you'd better keep my attention from straying then, hadn't you?'

He pushed himself up off the bed with his elbow and flipped her on to her back. She looked up at him and he gazed down into her eyes. Still they revealed more of her vulnerability than any of the cool, pale flesh that lay beneath him.

Part of him knew he should be in the next room, working on the translation of the notebook, but the mysteries of a few pages of English offered little temptation in comparison with this Russian enigma, which he had so often unravelled, but which always revealed yet one more conundrum within.

However many times Dmitry visited Red Square, he could never get over the vastness of it. In the past, he'd only come here as a tourist, but since he'd been living in Moscow, although he'd walked through it or close to it almost every day, it had still failed to diminish in its impact. He'd crept into the square through the market stalls between Saint Vasiliy's and the river, arriving at about half past eight; thirty minutes before the appointed time. This was where he had followed his father the previous week, and where he did not now need to follow him, but simply to hide and wait for him to arrive.

He skirted round to the east of the cathedral. Glancing up, he saw that no one had yet repaired the broken glass of the window in the central tower. They might not even have noticed. From there he edged along the side of the square, finally secreting himself amongst the low, wooden shops on the eastern perimeter. He could see the Lobnoye Mesto clearly, though the entrance – a gap cut in its cylindrical wall – was on the opposite side from him. Even so, no one would be able to reach that entrance without him seeing their approach.

By a quarter past nine, there was still no sign of anyone. He – like his father – had doubted whether Kyesha would show up, but he had at least expected Aleksei to. Perhaps he had been delayed. Perhaps Kyesha had intercepted him on his way to the rendezvous and . . . It was unlikely. Aleksei might brag, but Dmitry felt convinced that the stories of his defeats of these creatures, told to him hurriedly since that first revelation inside Saint Vasiliy's, meant that he would not be so easily caught out. And he was right to reason that Kyesha did not seem to be a threat to either of them.

Suddenly, a head popped above the parapet of the Lobnoye Mesto. A figure hoisted itself up on to the wall and then sat there, one leg out straight, the other slightly bent. It was Aleksei. He must have been inside the platform, sitting too low to be seen, even before Dmitry had arrived. There was a brief flash of light, and Dmitry realized that his father was lighting a flame. Only the wide crescent moon illuminated the scene, giving Aleksei an ethereal pallor, but Dmitry could still see the small clay pipe grasped in his hand as he drew deeply on its smoke.

It was unusual for Aleksei to smoke, though not completely unheard of. The reason might be that he couldn't get a drink here in the middle of the square. But on the other hand, Dmitry couldn't help but notice the way his father gazed up at the moon, its rays splintered by the many domes of the cathedral, and observe how contented he looked for once in his life.

It was no surprise. She was a beautiful woman. Domnikiia Semyonovna – that was her name. Dmitry had not known that much before. He'd known she worked for the Lavrovs, but not in what capacity. He wondered if they knew that the nanny to their little daughter was being fucked every night by one of their oldest friends. He doubted it. Anyway, it was their fault for taking a woman like that into the house.

Even so, she had been enchanting – that glint in her eyes. Could Dmitry have mistaken the way she looked at him? He didn't think so. And that was the worst of it. He felt ashamed at any subconscious response he might have given her that could suggest there was any prospect of something happening between them. At her age, she flattered herself. That his father should betray his mother was one thing, but that the woman could even think of betraying Aleksei with his own son was madness.

Dmitry realized he had raised himself to his feet. His father did not appear to have noticed. He stepped back into the shadows and continued to watch. Did it matter that his father was fooling his mother, and was himself being taken for a ride? Until last Thursday – when what he had witnessed inside the cathedral had changed his view of the entire world – it had. But now Dmitry's concerns for Aleksei were far more substantial. And his esteem for his father, which had been at such a low stock for so many years, had risen.

He sat and watched for another hour, during which Aleksei hardly moved, except to take the pipe to and from his lips, and once to refill it. Then, when it was almost half past ten, he dropped back inside the Lobnoye Mesto, and moments later could be seen emerging from it to head north. The shortest route to his hotel was in the opposite direction, but Dmitry had not expected him to go there. He had given up on Kyesha, and Dmitry suspected he was right to. As promised, the *voordalak* had departed the city.

Dmitry waited until his father had disappeared from view, then made his own way home.

Today, Aleksei knew, he must stick to his work. The notebook and dictionary sat in front of him on his desk – the former open, the latter closed. It was early, scarcely nine o'clock, but Tamara had woken them long before. To sleep late was one of the benefits of his other home in Petersburg, but one which he gladly forwent.

He continued his random approach to the text, although he kept notes to make sure he did not go over the same section twice. It was an infuriating procedure. He had uncovered a number of consecutive sections on what the author – Cain – described as 'the healing process', which was a term Aleksei understood well enough, but the details of which made no sense. By Aleksei's translation, one rat (he had settled, for now, on those being the poor creatures in question) that had the most minor of wounds would succumb to them, while another would struggle through and survive the most terrible ordeals. He doubted his own translation, and in many cases hoped he was wrong.

It was when he looked at the text for 22 August, only two days before the final entry, that the tone moved away from the scientific. Before that, there had been a gap of a week without anything being written. Aleksei felt comfortable in his translation of these more mundane matters.

I have contacted APR. He will prevaricate, but he will come. It may take time. I have returned to the peninsula and will wait. Word will be sent when APR departs.

The text then dissolved into another tract of scientific gibberish, which Aleksei shied away from. He moved to the following day's entry.

230

I have looked over APR's residence. It seems humble for him, but regardless of that, Taganrog is not the place to act against him.

Aleksei went back over the word again. There was no possibility of mistranslation, it was mere transliteration. Whatever alphabet was used, the word was the same.

Taganrog
Таганрог

It was the town where the tsar and tsaritsa were spending the winter. The letters APR suddenly made sense as well. Aleksandr Pavlovich Romanov – the tsar himself. Whatever the meaning of the text, it was clear that Cain had some intention to act against the tsar. The words in English could have unknown subtleties, but there was no doubt that something underhand was intended.

Aleksei grabbed the notebook, forgetting about the paper in which he usually wrapped it. He needed help. Dmitry was an obvious choice, but what interest would Dmitry have in the safety of the tsar? Most likely, this book revealed some sort of plot by the Southern Society. No member of the Northern Society was going to act against it. Perhaps they even knew already.

Who in Moscow could Aleksei trust? He couldn't think, but he had to do something. He raced through the house, leaving each door open behind him. In the distance, he heard Valentin Valentinovich shouting at him, but he paid no heed. The next moment he was out on the street. In his mind he ran through the list of generals he knew in the city – men who would trust him, and whom he could trust.

As he stood there in the sunny street, he felt bile rising in his throat. At first he could not account for it, but he understood the cause moments after the sensation came over him. It wasn't fear for the safety of the tsar that brought on that sense of nausea, but a smell – a devastatingly familiar smell, recalled from long ago.

Burning hair. Mould. A scent of decay. He had experienced it only once before, as he stamped down on the wrist of the Oprichnik Pyetr and forced his hand into a beam of sunlight, watching with pleasure as it blistered and burned to nothing, but horrified to see it regrow, as Kyesha's fingers had regrown, before his eyes.

He looked around. The sun was not high but above the buildings and shining bright on this crisp autumn day. Any *voordalak* outside in these conditions would not simply burn, he would be obliterated. There was no sign of any such occurrence, yet still the smell persisted, strengthened.

Suddenly, Aleksei noticed a dampness against his arms, through his shirtsleeves. He was holding the notebook against his chest, with his arms crossed over it. He now pulled them away, and saw that the leather cover of the book had split open, and was curling at the edges, degrading to a yellow pus which blackened as it soaked into the linen of his clothes.

He stepped back inside the house.

'What in Heaven are you doing, Aleksei?' he heard Valentin Valentinovich's voice say behind him. 'What *is* that awful stench?'

'Get back!' shouted Aleksei, raising his hand and again clutching the book to him. He must have given off the aura of some mad starets – a preacher foretelling the end of the world. It did the job. Valentin disappeared back into the house.

Now that he was out of the sunlight, Aleksei looked again at the book. The leather was not completely destroyed; two wide stripes were missing across the front of it, plus most of the top edge of both front and back. The central strip of the front, where the Latin text was written, had been protected by Aleksei's arms.

Even as he watched, and as he had expected, the leather began to repair itself. In parts, it was like a wave riding up a shallow beach in an advancing line which never receded. In other places, a thin tendril of the material would shoot across the cover, like the stem of a climbing plant accelerated a thousand times, and bind to a dangling fragment of leather on the other side. Then those two slivers, reinvigorated by one another, would spread outwards in a thickening band, until, within less than a minute, the cover was as it had always been.

The stench was now no more than a forgotten hint on the breeze.

Aleksei took a step towards the door, holding a corner of the book in front of him. The smell returned, and he saw what he had known he would see. The shadow of the doorframe cut off the sun in a clear line. One small corner of the book was in light, the rest in relative darkness. The corner burned, briefly bursting into flame, and then subsiding as the same noxious fluid as before dribbled from it to the floor emitting its putrid scent. The remainder of the book was unaffected; the same light-brown leather it had been when he first looked at it. The line between what had survived and what had been destroyed was exact – it was the line along which sunlight had been cut off by shadow.

Aleksei stepped inside the hallway again, but he did not need to watch as the wound to the book once again healed over. He had seen all he needed to see.

It explained the strange, delicate texture of the leather that bound the book, so refined it was as if the tanner's salts had never touched it.

It was not leather.

The book was bound in the skin of a vampire; a living vampire.

CHAPTER XIII

ALEKSEI RETURNED TO HIS STUDY. DOMNIKIIA WAS STANDING in the doorway to the bedroom, her hand clasping Tamara's.

'What's happening?' she asked.

Aleksei flicked his eyes towards their daughter, and Domnikiia understood. She led the little girl away. Even before she returned, Aleksei had begun rereading his translation notes. That same sun that had burned the skin that covered the book had shone a new light on the meaning of its contents – it had nothing to do with rats.

'What is it?' said Domnikiia, now alone, closing the door behind her.

'The book,' said Aleksei. 'I understand it now.'

'You understand it?' Domnikiia did not see what he meant.

'Not the detail – but I understand what it's about.'

'Which is?'

'*Voordalaki.*' The single word still held the power to shock Domnikiia, despite what she already knew. She said nothing and he continued. 'This Englishman, Cain, who wrote the book; he's been conducting experiments on vampires – horrible experiments. He cuts them open and watches them regrow.' Fresh understanding was coming to Aleksei even as he spoke. Every bizarre translation of the English suddenly became clear once he had the knowledge of what Cain's victims were.

'So?' said Domnikiia dismissively. 'Let him. He can torture them till doomsday for all I care.'

Aleksei wondered if he could be so callous, even towards a vampire. But that was not the issue. 'It's not torture – it's experimentation. He's trying to find out how they function. The question is, why?'

'The better to kill them.' Again, Domnikiia spoke with a passion she had picked up from Aleksei over the years. 'You've done the same – this Cain's just being a bit more thorough.'

'Perhaps, or perhaps to use them – to make them stronger.' That was the impression Aleksei had got from the notebook, but there was no specific line he could point to that asserted it. It was simply a question of tone – and tone was the hardest thing even for an expert to translate.

'So how will you find out? Translate the rest of the book?'

Aleksei didn't answer her question. 'There's another thing,' he said instead. 'I know where Cain is. He's in Taganrog.'

She looked blankly at him.

'That's where the tsar is,' he explained, his voice dropping unnecessarily to a whisper. It was not common knowledge, and he didn't recall ever having told her.

'More than a coincidence,' she said.

'He's even mentioned in the book. It can't be coincidence.' Aleksei had never discussed with Domnikiia her views on the tsar – not as an institution. She loved him as a distant hero just as almost every other loyal Russian did, but Aleksei had no idea whether she would fall in with or against the members of the Northern Society, or if she would care at all. She had no idea about his own ambivalence.

'So—' She did not have time to finish what she was about to say. Valentin Valentinovich stormed in.

'How dare you make such a scene, Aleksei,' he blustered, still unable to raise his voice to the shout he so evidently wished to produce. Aleksei and Domnikiia both stared at him blankly, unable to think how to respond to his petty complaints in the light of what they had been discussing. 'I should throw you both out of the house right now,' continued Valentin. 'All three of you.'

Aleksei stood, holding the French–English dictionary open in his hands. He slammed it shut just beneath Valentin's nose. The loud clap of air silenced him, and a gust of wind blew his fringe out of place.

'Don't worry, I'm leaving,' said Aleksei. He turned back to the desk and closed the notebook, wrapping it up in the paper in which it had first been delivered. He then tucked both it and the dictionary under his arm and headed for the door. Before leaving, he turned to Valentin Valentinovich. 'But I still have friends in this town – from the highest and lowest echelons – and if I hear from anyone that your daughter and her nanny aren't living in exactly the comfort which they would expect, then I think you know what the consequences will be.'

Valentin looked over at Domnikiia. She appeared confident but not defiant, and Valentin seemed to calm. He turned back and spoke to Aleksei.

'You don't need to say that. Whatever disagreements we may have, they will always have a home here. I gave you my word on that years ago.'

Aleksei felt momentarily embarrassed. He knew he took advantage of Valentin, but knew also it was out of an unnecessary fear – a fear born of his own guilt. Valentin would do as he had promised.

Aleksei gave a curt nod, which he felt conveyed a sense of understanding between them. 'I'll be gone by tomorrow,' he said, turning and walking down the hallway.

Valentin took a few steps towards him and called after him. 'But where are you going?'

'To Taganrog,' Aleksei shouted back.

The mood in the club was sombre, as it had been for the last three days. Dmitry played softly on the piano, sticking mostly with folk songs that were neither too solemn nor too cheery. No one had explicitly reproached him or his father for the death of Obukhov, but the enthusiasm that had greeted him a few days before, when he had first asked if anyone would be interested in a small military venture around Theatre Square, was now replaced by a weary half-acknowledgement. Today, no one had stood by the piano to ask him to perform a favourite tune they could sing along to.

He felt a tap on his shoulder. He looked up from the keyboard to see Lieutenant Batenkov heading away from him across the room. In the doorway stood Aleksei. Dmitry reached them just as Batenkov began talking to his father.

'You're not to blame, Colonel,' he was saying in a quiet tone. 'You warned Obukhov.'

'I shouldn't have picked him in the first place,' replied Aleksei.

'You didn't pick him,' interrupted Dmitry. 'I did.'

'I was in charge,' insisted Aleksei.

'He was a soldier,' said Batenkov. 'Soldiers die, even in peacetime.' He cast his eyes around the room. 'Everyone knows that – whatever they may say.'

Aleksei patted him on the arm and the lieutenant turned away with a brief smile. Dmitry followed his father to a quiet corner, where they sat down to talk.

'I'm leaving Moscow,' announced Aleksei.

'Why?' asked Dmitry.

'I can't say.'

'Is it because of the book?'

Aleksei considered for a fraction of a second, then nodded briefly.

'Do you want me to come with you?' asked Dmitry.

'No, it's best not.'

'But I could help!'

'You'd be court-martialled for desertion.'

Dmitry considered what his father had said. 'What about you?' he asked.

'I have a freer rein. And I know what I'm dealing with.' Aleksei spoke with a whisper that was almost a hiss, avoiding the word *voordalak*. Nevertheless, his meaning was quite clear.

'You know how dangerous they can be,' Dmitry responded.

'Not in this case, I don't think. Kyesha could have killed us both if he'd wanted to. Besides, there are other matters of greater concern – to everyone. I need you here – in the north.' Dmitry looked at his father, his face asking what it was he wanted him to do. 'You know what's going to happen here,' said Aleksei, his eyes flicking around the room and reminding Dmitry of the common cause for which they all fought, 'when the time comes.'

Dmitry let out a gasp. 'Will it be soon?' Aleksei said nothing. 'Is it to do with the book?'

'No. The book – Kyesha – all of it's a distraction from what's really going on. That's why I'll deal with it alone.'

'When are you going?'

'First thing tomorrow.'

'How long will you be?'

'I don't know.'

'Can I see you off?'

'It would be easier if you didn't. I'll try to write. If you return to Petersburg, let your mother know I'm all right.'

Dmitry felt the urge to ask if he should do the same favour for Domnikiia Semyonovna, but he resisted. He could also guess that it was she who would be seeing Aleksei off tomorrow.

He embraced his father, and felt his quick, tight squeeze returned. Then Aleksei left without another word.

Dmitry walked back over to the piano. It was good news on all counts. That Aleksei was out of Moscow would mean that he was away from that woman. Perhaps absence would make him forget her. But what was more exciting was the suggestion that soon the national transformation they had all so long hoped for was close at hand. The moment Dmitry had discovered that his father was a member of the Northern Society, he had forgiven him much. There were still vast distances between them, concerning many subjects, but those could be bridged, with time. Whatever Aleksei

238

had said, the fact that he was at that very moment embarking on a journey in pursuit of a vampire could not be unconnected to the future of Russia itself, though Dmitry could not begin to imagine how. It did not matter. What did was that now, at last, the game was afoot.

The heads of many soldiers in the club looked up and over to the piano in surprise, as Dmitry struck up a jollier tune than he had in many days.

Tamara grinned broadly. She looked from side to side. Two faces smiled back at her: on her right, her mother; to the left, her father.

'And you promise to look after your mother while I'm away?' said Aleksei.

Tamara frowned and then nodded. Her father was usually away. It was only a few days ago that he'd come back. Had he forgotten?

'Where are you going?' she asked.

'To a place called Taganrog,' he said.

'Where's that?'

'On the Sea of Azov.'

Tamara didn't like to ask another question. Her father clearly thought she knew what he was talking about. Mama helped out.

'You remember when we looked at the Black Sea in the Atlas?' she asked. Tamara nodded. 'It's near there.'

'Is that where the Golden Fleece was?' asked Tamara.

'Not far,' said Papa with a smile. It was he who had told her the story of Jason, last time he visited. Mama had shown her some of the places on the map afterwards. But Taganrog and Azov were new to her.

'Taganrog,' she said, listening to the sound of her own voice. 'Who are you going to see there?'

'Papa's going to talk to the tsar,' said her mother. Tamara grinned again. She knew when Mama was making up stories.

'He's not,' she said.

'I'm going to see an Englishman called Mr Cain,' said Papa. Tamara considered. This sounded a little more likely.

'Why?' she asked.

'Go to sleep now, Toma,' said Mama. She leaned over and kissed Tamara on the forehead, then stood up and walked towards the door.

Papa held her hand in his. His two funny fingers felt strange against her palm. He bent forward to kiss her and she felt something cold and a little heavy on her chest. She reached for it. There were two of them, both metal, hanging from chains around Papa's neck. One was plain and silver, but the other had a face on it. It was a man with a beard – younger than Papa. He had kind eyes.

'Who's this?' she asked.

'That's Jesus.'

Tamara was amazed. She stared at her father in awe. 'You met him?' she asked.

Papa laughed. 'No,' he said. 'Nor had whoever painted that.'

'So how did they know what he looks like?'

'They guessed.'

Tamara hesitated. She knew she shouldn't ask for things, but her desire overwhelmed her. 'Can I have it?' she said.

'No,' said her mother quickly from over by the door. She was concerned, almost angry. 'Papa will need that where he's going.'

Aleksei looked over at her as if to disagree, but chose not to.

'I'll bring you back something even better,' he said.

'Promise?' asked Tamara.

'I promise. Now go to sleep. I'll be back again as soon as I can.' He kissed her on the cheek. Before he stood up, he whispered something in her ear.

Tamara watched as her parents walked away, hand in hand, through the open door. On the other side they kissed, and Tamara saw her mother's hand rubbing against her father's chest. Then her father pushed the door shut and they disappeared from view, as darkness filled the room.

Tamara shut her eyes and tried to sleep, but she was puzzled;

not by the way she had seen Mama touch Papa – she had seen that before – but by what her father had whispered to her. Why *should* she ever forget that he loved her?

Tamara felt terribly alone when she woke. She could not remember having had a nightmare, but she had that same feeling that something overwhelmingly dreadful had happened. She remembered that Papa had been about to leave. How long ago had that been? She leapt out of bed and scampered across the room, turning the big brass doorknob with both hands.

Inside her parents' bedroom, the bed was empty. Sheets and blankets lay on the floor in an untidy heap. It was dark outside, but a little starlight spilled through the open curtains, where Mama stood, wearing only her nightdress, her hand resting against the glass. Her plaited hair hung straight and neat down her back.

Tamara went up to the window and looked out. Outside, through the light mist, she saw a man was mounting a horse. It was Papa. She raised her hand to wave, but he wasn't looking. She felt her mother clasp her other hand tightly. Then her father turned and looked up at the window. She waved vigorously, while her mother simply raised one hand and wiggled her fingers very slightly. Papa raised a hand towards her in a similar gesture, but then saw that Tamara was there too. He waved enthusiastically at his daughter, imitating her action, then blew her a kiss. Finally, he blew another to Mama, then he turned his horse and headed away from them, up the street. He didn't look back again, but Mama did not leave the window until he was gone from sight. Tamara stayed with her. She seemed very unhappy.

Finally, Mama stepped away. 'It's a few hours before we need to get up, Toma,' she said. 'Do you want to come to bed and keep me company?'

Tamara turned and nodded, then took one last glance out of the window before jumping on to the bed and snuggling herself inside Mama's waiting arms.

She wondered if her mother had also seen the darkly dressed

241

man who had stepped out from a doorway after Papa had left and walked away in the opposite direction. She decided not to ask. It had been the same man they had both seen a few weeks before, and then, it had seemed to upset Mama. Today, she was sad enough already.

Instead, Tamara gazed out of the window and tried to count the stars.

PART TWO

CHAPTER XIV

TAGANROG WASN'T MUCH TO LOOK AT. NEITHER HAD BEEN many of the other towns Aleksei passed on the way. In total, the journey had taken eight days, part on horseback, part by coach. The final phase had been by horse.

He had never been in this part of the country before. He'd met up with the river Don soon after Tula, and had followed the valley all the way down. It still felt like autumn, but he'd noticed it getting warmer each day. He knew the cold would soon catch up with him again, even so far south. Paris was on about the same latitude as Taganrog, and yet Paris never got nearly so cold in winter. It was a very Russian thing.

His journey down the Don had reminded him of the journey the Oprichniki had taken in the opposite direction in order to 'save' Moscow thirteen years before. Was there a link there? Had they put down roots in the region which somehow connected to the experiments Cain was performing? In the various hostelries he had stayed at along the way, he had asked if anyone remembered the autumn of 1812. Stories had reached Moscow of a plague travelling up the Don, which Aleksei had realized to be the echoes of the revolting feeding habits of *voordalaki*. But as with all such tales, details, even years, became merged. Locals disagreed as to what had happened and when it had happened. More recent outbreaks of pestilence were far more pressing on the memory than what had happened thirteen years before.

And so Aleksei had spent most of his evenings continuing his translation of Cain's writings. It was still difficult, but at least Valentin had not asked for the dictionary back. Much of what Aleksei uncovered was what he already knew, though with a precise, scientific gloss to it. He worried that his prior knowledge might be biasing his translation, forcing it to tell him what he expected it to tell him. But he had no way of avoiding such prejudice.

Several sections discussed what happened when a vampire was injured. Measurements were made concerning the speed of regrowth and the degree to which an individual could resist that regrowth. A table of figures showed how a well-fed *voordalak* could regenerate its flesh far more quickly than one which had been starved. Cain also referred to reported evidence of a *voordalak* who had fended off the regrowth of his missing fingers for four hours in order not to be discovered by humans, and of another who had had an arm hacked off with a sword, and grown it back without the slightest sign of a scar. The first was clearly Kyesha's story. It seemed that Kyesha had been at one time the subject of Cain's experiments. Presumably he had escaped, stealing the notebook and taking it with him. But why had he brought it to Aleksei?

Cain also wrote of the methods by which a vampire could die. There was little new. Fire could kill them, freezing cold could not but would paralyse them, as would starvation and suffocation. Cain had conducted his own experiment with fire – his description of the death of the creature was brutally detached – but of the attempted freezing there was no detail. Aleksei wondered if the winters would be cold enough this far south to conduct such an experiment successfully. His own experience of a *voordalak* being frozen had been much further north.

What seemed to interest Cain most was his investigation of the actual mechanism by which a man could be turned into a vampire. Aleksei was familiar enough with the process, having had it described to him by Iuda back in 1812. Iuda, of course, could not be trusted on any matter, and was not even a vampire, so might not know the truth. However, Cain's studies concurred. The victim had first to have his blood drunk by the vampire and then, close to the moment of his death, had in turn to drink the vampire's blood.

Aleksei had shuddered as he finished translating that section. It was exactly what he had witnessed – believed he had witnessed – at the window of the brothel on Degtyarny Lane, except that, in truth, he had seen Iuda lower his lips on to the woman's neck and pretend to suck the life-giving fluid from her using fangs he did not possess. He had seen the woman lick at the blood that seeped from a self-inflicted wound in Iuda's breast, but it was not vampire's blood. And still today, Aleksei did not know whether that woman had been Margarita or Domnikiia.

Again, Cain's concern was with precise measurement. He was convinced that consumption of the vampire's blood had to occur within a certain time period leading up to the actual moment of death of the victim, but he had been unable to pin down the duration; in some cases it was hours, in others many weeks. Beyond that, the death of the victim did not have to be caused by the original bite of the vampire and subsequent loss of blood. Any cause of death would be effective, as long as blood had been exchanged both ways. In nature, as Cain had put it, the vampire's bite was almost always the cause of death as well, but he had demonstrated that it was not uniquely effective. He went on, somewhat unnecessarily, to list mechanisms of death he had found to work: stabbing, shooting, drowning, poisoning.

Aleksei stopped reading at that point. Evidently Cain was not only using *voordalaki* for his experiments. Humans were involved as well; human, at least, when the experiments began.

That was about as much as Aleksei had discovered by the time he reached Taganrog. There was much he could make neither head nor tail of, and few translations in which he felt entirely confident.

He quickly found a tavern that had rooms available. He had

expected the town to be busy, as social climbers hoping to gain favour at court – and social decliners, desperate to hang on to what slight favour they had left – hovered round the tsar like flies. But Aleksandr's presence had caused remarkably little stir. Aleksei had arrived in time for lunch. The last leg of his journey, from Rostov, had been short – only about seventy versts – and he had set out early. After eating, he wrote letters to Marfa, Dmitry, Domnikiia and Tamara – the last of those he wrote mostly in Russian, with occasional hints in French to help her understand.

Then he set out on a simple quest – an audience with the tsar.

The adopted royal palace was unassuming. It was a low building, with no upper floors. It must have helped in keeping the crowds at bay. Although there was no overt secrecy, few passing the house would have guessed the majesty of the personage dwelling therein. It had a garden and a view of the sea, neither of which Aleksei paid much attention to. There was one piece of comfort he took from seeing the house at last with his own eyes: everything was in order. Whatever Cain was planning against Aleksandr, he had not yet acted.

Aleksei's credentials got him past the guards at the gate and the household staff, but none felt audacious enough to allow him access to the tsar. Instead he was asked to sit in a small anteroom, overlooking the beach, and wait until he could be dealt with by the tsar's personal secretary, Prince Volkonsky. He waited for a quarter of an hour before the door opened and three men entered the room.

Volkonsky was easy to recognize. He was the only one of the three in uniform, but beyond that he had the bearing that only a man raised with the title of prince could carry. He was almost fifty now, and his square face had a benevolence to it which belied his history. Aleksei well knew – though it was not the sort of thing that was ever spoken of publicly – that Volkonsky was one of those who had organized the death of Aleksandr's father, Tsar Pavel I. Just how closely Aleksandr himself had been involved was a matter of wide, if hushed, debate. Few who held him responsible thought less of him for it. The whole empire had benefited. Pavel had been a hopeless monarch. Aleksandr had been a hopeful one, but twenty-four years on, that promise remained to be fulfilled.

'Colonel Danilov?' said Volkonsky somewhat haughtily.

'Yes, Your High Excellency,' said Aleksei, standing.

'You have a message for His Majesty?'

'Yes, sir.' Aleksei felt no sense of awe in the presence of the prince, but he knew his business would be achieved a lot more simply if he appeared to.

Volkonsky held out his hand. 'Give it to me, I'll take it to him.'

'I don't have it written down.'

'Then tell me,' Volkonsky snapped.

'I think the tsar would prefer it if I told him personally,' said Aleksei.

'He would, would he?'

'Just tell him my name, Your High Excellency.'

Volkonsky considered for a moment, but he was by no means a stupid man. It was unlikely that Aleksei would be bluffing about the issue, but if he was, it would only be a short delay before he received his retribution.

'Very well,' said Volkonsky. 'But it may be a while. His Majesty has many matters to attend to.' He strode out through a different door from that by which he had entered, leaving Aleksei alone with the other two men. The shorter of them, a greying man in his fifties or sixties, came over and extended his hand to Aleksei.

'Colonel Danilov,' he said. 'I don't believe I've had the pleasure.' He spoke in French with an undulating accent which Aleksei first took to be English, but then he became less sure. Aleksei took his hand and shook it. 'The name's Wylie,' said the man. 'James Wylie.'

'Dr James Wylie?' asked Aleksei.

'Yes,' said Wylie, with a brief nod.

'It's an honour, sir.' His accent now made sense to Aleksei as

249

Scots, but a Scots that had been smoothed over decades of living in Russia. 'You were a hero to hundreds at Borodino.'

'I did what any surgeon would do,' said Wylie. 'Are you a veteran yourself?'

'I fought under General Uvarov.' It was not a lie, but it did mislead.

'This is Dr Tarasov,' said Wylie, introducing the other man.

'Colonel Danilov,' said Tarasov. The accent to his French was pure Russian.

'I understand you're His Majesty's personal physician these days,' said Aleksei, addressing Wylie.

'We both are,' said Tarasov.

'A man as healthy as His Majesty couldn't be the result of just one pair of medical hands,' added Wylie.

'Tell me, Dr Wylie' – Aleksei instinctively lowered his voice, but not so as to exclude Tarasov – 'do you know of an Englishman about these parts by the name of Cain? Richard Cain?'

Wylie thought for a moment, then shook his head. 'I can't say that I do.' He looked at Tarasov, who shrugged. 'Mind you,' added Wylie, 'people come and go here. There are plenty of ships passing.'

At that moment, Volkonsky returned. 'His Majesty will see you now,' he said, without any hint of annoyance. Aleksei followed him back out through the door. As he passed the window, he glanced out over the sea, but Dr Wylie had been wrong. The water was not teeming with vessels. All Aleksei could see was the sail of one unremarkable yacht, anchored on the horizon.

He went into the tsar's rooms.

CHAPTER XV

THAT SAME FACE.

It was thirteen years since Aleksandr had first seen that face – six weeks since he last had. In between he had grown to regard Colonel Danilov with increasing degrees of trust. But in all that time, the matters over which he and Danilov had confided had been – for want of a better word – temporal. It was only now that he had appeared, without summons, in Taganrog that Aleksandr sensed that the nature of his initial, unearthly vision of Danilov's face would become clear; that the two separate strands of their lives would become entwined into a single cord. Whether that cord would provide mutual strength for them both, or whether one thread would constrict and then strangle the other, he did not know. But if it was the latter, he knew it would be he who tightened his grip first.

'Sit down, Colonel Danilov,' he said. 'You may leave us, Pyotr Mihailovich.'

Volkonsky turned and exited. Aleksandr was confident they would be left in peace. He walked over to the table and poured Aleksei a glass of tea from the silver samovar.

'Are you acquainted with Prince Volkonsky?' he asked, handing over the drink.

'Not until now,' said Aleksei. 'But I fought with his brother-in-law, Sergei Grigorovich, at Silistria.'

Aleksandr noticed, and noted, how he rubbed his left hand,

which lacked the last two fingers, as he spoke, but he chose not to comment upon it. 'Under Prince Bagration?' he asked instead.

Aleksei nodded. 'I was very pleased to meet Dr Wylie at last,' he volunteered, shifting deftly to a different hero of Borodino.

'More so than Prince Volkonsky?' asked Aleksandr. Aleksei nodded cautiously. Aleksandr was not surprised. 'Many old soldiers feel the same. But don't underestimate Pyotr Mihailovich.'

'I won't, Your Majesty,' said Aleksei.

'And what brings you here?' asked Aleksandr, having poured his own tea and sat down again. It was best to play the innocent, for now at least. 'There has been a turn of events concerning our friends in the north, I take it. For good or ill?'

'It's not quite as straightforward as that. I'm here because of a quite different threat . . . possible threat.'

The words chilled Aleksandr, but still he retained his sangfroid. 'I'm not sure what could be greater than half my army preparing to overthrow me.'

'I think "half" is an exaggeration, Your Majesty.' Aleksandr knew very well it was an exaggeration, but even if it had been half a dozen, it still would not lessen the horror of his being turned upon by officers who had sworn allegiance to him – just as their fathers had sworn allegiance to his.

'Do you know any more of what they want?'

Aleksei appeared surprised at the tsar's question, as well he might be. However much he might once have concurred with them, Aleksandr would be a fool to concede to any of their demands. It would be too much of a blow to his authority. Indeed, by laying down any policy, the reformers ensured that it was unlikely ever to be enacted, however much the tsar might agree with it.

'You've read the Green Book?' the colonel asked, although it was a matter they had already discussed.

'Of course. And you know as well as I it's not a true declaration of their intentions – just a veneer to make them appear less bloodthirsty. Don't forget, I've read *Russkaya Pravda* as well, which I think is less intended for public consumption.'

'The best of them share your understanding of the problems,' said Aleksei, 'but not your pessimism as to whether a solution can be found.'

Aleksandr nodded slowly, sadly. Danilov was more fooled than the revolutionaries. Both admired his earlier desire for reform, but it was Danilov who was mistaken to think that his current reticence was born of pragmatism. He had truly changed his mind, and with the best of reasons. 'Do you know how many of them there are – in total?'

The colonel nodded. 'I have a list,' he said.

'Show it to me,' said Aleksandr curtly.

'You'll honour your promise to me?' asked Aleksei. 'That you will not move against them until there is no other way?'

Aleksandr mustered his iciest hauteur. 'It's a brave man who asks a promise of the tsar,' he said. 'It's an ill-mannered one who questions whether he will keep it.' He could have had the list ripped from Danilov's dead fingers, but he was no fool. Dead fingers would no longer be able to steal what the tsar required.

Aleksei slipped his hand into an inside pocket and pulled out a sheaf of folded papers. He handed them to the tsar. Aleksandr scanned through. Most names he knew – and knew would be on the list – but there were still many that angered him; a few that saddened him. It was one close to the beginning that he commented on first.

'We were just talking of Sergei Grigorovich,' he said.

'Yes,' said Aleksei. 'I'm sorry.'

'At least Pyotr Mihailovich is not listed.'

'You thought he would be?' asked Aleksei.

Aleksandr considered. 'I would have let them win if he had been,' he said at length, instantly shocked by his own sentimentality – shocked by the truth of what he said. He looked on through the list. 'I see your name is here, Colonel Danilov.'

The colonel seemed to pause just momentarily, as if tripping over an unseen paving stone, before replying. 'I should hope so. I wouldn't be much use to you if I wasn't a member.'

'Even so – not a pleasant list to be named on, should things not go the way you hope.'

'I'm sure I'll have you to vouch for me, Your Majesty.'

'Oh, absolutely,' said Aleksandr. 'Absolutely.'

'Could we discuss my other business?' asked Aleksei.

Was this the moment? If it was, Aleksandr would be foolish to ignore it. Even so, he felt afraid. He nodded. 'Go ahead.'

Aleksei paused, considering how to start. 'Why did you come here, to Taganrog?'

'Why do you ask?' replied Aleksandr.

'Let's just accept that I did ask.'

It was more the statement of an interrogator to his captive than of a subject to his tsar, though Aleksandr knew he needed a man of such effrontery. But it was still too early to reveal his hand.

'Many reasons,' he replied, 'but chiefly to do with the climate; partly for my own benefit – but mostly for my dear Yelizaveta Alekseevna.'

'The climate? Doesn't the sea here freeze over in November?'

'Later than it does in Petersburg.'

'Why not Greece or Italy?'

Aleksandr longed to confide in someone, but his anger and pride won through. 'I am tsar of all the Russias,' he asserted. 'I may go where I please. And Russia is the place where I should and do wish to go.'

Aleksei nodded. 'Very well,' he said. He clearly did not accept the answer, but accepted it was all he was going to get.

'Is there anything more you need to discuss?' asked Aleksandr. He avoided making it sound like the plea it was. He knew he had to be open with Danilov, but could conceive of no effective way to breach the barrier between monarch and subject.

'Not at the moment, Your Majesty.'

'Then you may go. But don't go far. I may need you.'

That would be better. It was Danilov who had instigated this meeting – he could not be allowed to come away the beneficiary. Next time, Aleksandr would be in charge. The colonel stood and walked to the door, but before exiting, he turned.

'Just one last question, Your Majesty.'

'Yes?'

'Did you ever hear of a man named Cain – Richard Cain? An Englishman.'

The tsar felt a coldness, as though the blood had suddenly vanished from his body, but he pulled an expression of thoughtful puzzlement before replying. 'No. No, I can't say I have. Is it important?'

'I don't know.' With that, Aleksei was gone.

Aleksandr stood and walked over to the window. He gazed out to sea, but still the only thing that broke the shallow curve of the horizon was that one yacht. He heard the door open behind him and feared for a moment that Danilov had returned, but on looking he saw that it was only Volkonsky, who said nothing, waiting first to be spoken to. Aleksandr looked back out across the water.

It was an odd combination of trust and fear that Aleksandr felt for Danilov – and not just Danilov; there were others of his profession who produced the same feeling. The trust was in the absolute sense that such men would neither harm him nor let him be harmed. The fear was in the risk that they would perceive too much; would catch out the tsar in one of his petty misdemeanours. It was the same ambiguity a son might feel towards his father – though not so much in Aleksandr's case. For him, it was a little more like the way he had felt about his grandmother.

It was a comparison he did not want to take too far; the old empress had always been able to catch Aleksandr out in a lie, and he felt that Colonel Danilov shared exactly the same perceptive skills.

Which was unfortunate, because that afternoon Aleksandr had prevaricated with him once and twice told outright lies.

*   *   *

255

It was dark by the time Aleksei returned to his lodgings. He had wandered around the town a little, asked a few questions, but there was not much to be discovered. Cain's book had implied he was not actually resident in Taganrog, but in the 'peninsula'. That could only mean the Crimea, almost four hundred versts away. As Aleksei walked, he had been considering what the tsar had said to him. Aleksandr was a difficult man to fathom. Aleksei had met him perhaps ten times in his life, the first being in 1814, in Paris. On each occasion, he had deliberately tried to reduce the usual formality of such an encounter, and had achieved it to some extent. But the tsar was used to hiding behind the mask of his office, and ultimately could not be browbeaten into revealing information he didn't want to. The tsar always knew best.

Moreover, the tsar was used to filtering every statement he uttered, preparing it for the consumption of advisors, ambassadors and the general public. He delivered the truth with exactly the same lack of conviction with which he did a lie. Aleksei was reminded of Iuda, who had found a way to make his every statement equally valueless. Aleksandr had taken a different approach, but had arrived at a similar result.

Even so, Aleksei was pretty certain the tsar had lied about not knowing Cain.

He asked for a meal to be sent up to his rooms, and then ascended the stairs. His door was on the right. He had only put one foot inside the room when he realized there was someone else in there. Initially the knowledge was instinctive, but he knew that instincts were based on senses, and he quickly honed the source of his intuition down to a smell. It was a familiar smell – the closest thing he could describe it as was raw sheep's kidneys, but even that was a poor comparison. It was a smell he had not noticed the first time he encountered it, or not distinguished, but now, he could associate it with its source.

'Kyesha?' he asked.

'You see almost as well as I do, Aleksei,' said a voice from the darkness, over towards the bed. Aleksei lit the lamp and saw

Kyesha lying there on one side, his chin resting on his fist. Aleksei did not disabuse him of the idea that he had seen him, even if it had been said in jest. He was well aware that the smell was not unique to Kyesha – it was the scent of the *voordalak*. That the *voordalak* in question was Kyesha was an obvious guess.

Aleksei sat down on a chair near the door and fixed his eyes warily on Kyesha, saying nothing.

'You came then,' said the vampire.

'You could have offered a more direct invitation.'

'Would you have responded to that?'

Aleksei considered, then shook his head. He glanced over to the drawer where he had left both the dictionary and Cain's notebook. Kyesha saw his concern. 'Don't worry, it's still there,' he said. 'It makes no sense to me.'

'So how did you know it would bring me here?'

'Richard Cain is a talkative man, at times. He'd told me enough of what was in there.'

'He experimented on you?' asked Aleksei.

Kyesha sat up and unbuttoned his shirt cuff. He rolled up his sleeve to reveal his forearm. 'He . . .' Kyesha interrupted himself with a smile. 'But of course, there are no scars.' He pulled his sleeve back down again. 'One sometimes forgets.'

'You've not been a *voordalak* long then?' said Aleksei.

'Only a few years before we first met. And the word round these parts is "*oopir*".'

It was not a new word to Aleksei. '*Voordalak, oopir*. You all die the same way.' He regretted his harshness immediately. He was filled with the hateful realization that he'd grown to like Kyesha.

'Round here, I'm afraid not. Some die, but many live for years in torment, thanks to Cain.'

'And what have I got to do with it?'

'You will stop him,' said Kyesha confidently.

'Why should I stop a man killing vampires – killing them or torturing them?'

'You will stop him. It's in your nature.'

He seemed sure of what Aleksei would do. He'd certainly managed to predict Aleksei's moves so far – control them even.

'You knew my nature – just from that one night in Silistria.'

'That was a fortunate coincidence. You can imagine my surprise when I heard of the three-fingered man.'

'And you knew it was me?'

'I didn't even know your name, at first. Even then I thought I might be wrong.'

'Wrong?'

'That you were the man I sought – the man who slew eleven vampires in 1812.'

'Hence the questions,' said Aleksei.

'And the code. Only you would know where we were to meet.'

'But why pretend to be Maks' brother?'

'Maksim Sergeivich was the only name I had, to start with. I went to Saratov, to see his family. That led me to you.'

'But where did you get that from in the first place? Why did you choose me?' Aleksei realized his veneer of disdain had dropped – he was fascinated.

'From Cain. It was Cain who spoke of the three-fingered man.'

'And how does he know?'

'I'm not sure, but I know one thing.'

Aleksei sat forward on the edge of his seat, his animosity for Kyesha forgotten, eager to hear more. They were interrupted by a knock at the door. Aleksei raised a finger to his lips to silence Kyesha, hoping the *voordalak* would not remark how similar the gesture was to that which they had used to betray him in Moscow. He opened the door to a narrow crack and looked out.

'Your dinner, sir,' said the boy outside.

'Thanks.' Aleksei opened the door wider and took the tray. On it was a jug of wine, and some sort of pie. He slipped the boy a few copecks and went back into his room.

There was no sign of Kyesha. Above the bed, the curtain flapped in the breeze that blew through the open window. Aleksei put down the tray and climbed on to the bed. He peered out of the window. Just below, clinging impossibly to the wall, was Kyesha.

'What?' hissed Aleksei. Kyesha looked up at him questioningly. 'You were going to say something,' Aleksei persisted.

Kyesha looked below him, judging the distance. Then he turned his face back up to the window.

'Cain fears you,' he said.

A moment later he dropped to the ground and scuttled away. Within seconds, he was out of sight.

CHAPTER XVI

ALEKSEI STRUGGLED WITH THE NOTEBOOK THE WHOLE OF THE following day, but he had made about as much progress as he was going to. He needed the assistance of an English speaker – someone he could trust – and there was only one name that came to mind.

Early on Saturday morning, he returned to the tsar and tsaritsa's humble palace, but asked to see neither of Their Majesties. Dr Wylie greeted him with a smile and a handshake and suggested they walk in the gardens. It was the last place Aleksei wanted to go, considering the nature of the object that he clutched, wrapped in paper, under his arm.

'I don't suppose the tsar has mentioned to you why I'm here,' said Aleksei, once they were away from the house.

'I hope you're not too disappointed to learn that he hasn't mentioned you at all,' replied the doctor. 'Volkonsky told me you're not quite a regular soldier.'

'Ultimately, my job is to protect the tsar.'

'As is the duty of every member of His Majesty's army.'

'The threat may come from *within* the army,' said Aleksei.

Wylie stopped and turned to him. 'I had heard of the possibility,' he said. 'Has the issue become more pressing?'

'Perhaps,' said Aleksei. 'But another matter has arisen; one that I need your help with.'

'Anything relating to His Majesty's health is my concern,' said

Wylie. Aleksei smiled to himself. Wylie could never have conceived of just how radically the tsar's health might be altered.

'I'm calling on your assistance not as a doctor, but as an Englishman.' Aleksei instantly regretted what he had said.

Wylie bristled and pulled himself up to his full height, still shorter than Aleksei. 'Let me assure you, Colonel Danilov, I am no Englishman. I am a Scot.'

'English speaker, then. I need a book translated.'

'A book?'

Aleksei held up the parcel.

'Let me see it,' said Wylie, reaching out his hands.

Suddenly, Aleksei realized the foolhardiness of what he was attempting. If his own translation was only accurate to a fractional degree, then what Wylie read would seem like the ravings of a madman. Either Aleksei would be seen as a dupe for being taken in by such a document, or worse, be believed to have concocted it himself.

And yet the very title of the book itself suggested to Aleksei a course of action. *Nullius in Verba* – take nobody's word for it. Perhaps being out in the garden was a good thing after all.

Aleksei raised his hand to stop Wylie. 'Watch first,' he said. He peeled back one flap of the wrapping paper and turned the skin revealed underneath to the sun. As before, it began to blacken and peel, splitting sideways along a line to reveal the cardboard beneath. The same smell assailed Aleksei's nostrils, and Wylie recoiled in disgust.

'Some form of sulphur?' asked Wylie. 'Or phosphorus?'

Aleksei shook his head, though for all he knew, Wylie could have been correct as to the chemistry. He opened up the flap of his coat and hid the book beneath. 'Look now,' he said. Although the burning had stopped, the fumes concentrated under his coat, making it odious to breathe. Even so, Wylie peered in. Aleksei was not in a position to see, but the astonished look on the doctor's face when he raised his head after a few seconds was enough to tell Aleksei that the skin had re-formed in just the way he had witnessed in Moscow.

'Remarkable,' said Wylie.

'It's nothing compared with what's inside,' said Aleksei.

Wylie glanced up from Cain's notebook and into Aleksei's eyes. The cover had clearly hooked him. The prospect of seeing its contents reeled him in. 'We must go inside,' he said abruptly. His short legs began to move quickly. He was almost halfway across the lawn when Aleksei reached him, having carefully recovered the notebook. 'Not here, I think,' said the doctor as they stepped into the tsar's residence. 'My own lodgings would be more private.'

They walked through the palace and out the other side. Wylie turned left and Aleksei followed. Within a few minutes they were at a lodging house. Wylie went in and led Aleksei up to his room. He closed the curtains, checking for any cracks, and lit a candle.

'Will it be safe here?' he asked.

Aleksei nodded. He laid the book down on the table and removed the paper. Three familiar words stared up at them.

Nullius in Verba

'Ah!' said Wylie. 'Truer words were never spoken.'

'You've seen them before?'

'Of course. It's the motto of the Royal Society.' Aleksei looked blank. 'In London. It's a scientific society.'

'I read it as "Take nobody's word for it,"' said Aleksei.

'That's about right. It's from Horace. "*Nullius addictus iurare in verba magistri.*"' Aleksei tried to translate, but Wylie already knew the meaning. '"I am not bound to believe in the word of any teacher."'

'It's big, is it, this Royal Society?' asked Aleksei.

Wylie looked at him, unbelieving. 'It's the foremost scientific organization in the world.' The doctor caressed the book's binding. 'Do you know what this substance is?' he asked. 'Have you thought of its medical applications?'

'I have an idea – and I don't think it will heal anybody. But judge for yourself; read the book.'

Wylie opened the cover and his eyes fell upon the author's name.

Richard L. Cain F.R.S.

'Aha!' said Wylie. 'The gentleman you asked after yesterday, and a fellow, no less.' Wylie had dropped into English for that one word.

'"Fellow?"' asked Aleksei.

Wylie translated the word into French and then Russian. 'That's what the "F.R.S." stands for,' he explained, 'Fellow of the Royal Society. That makes it more surprising that I've not heard of him.'

'It may not be true,' observed Aleksei.

'Good point. Good point,' agreed Wylie. '*Nullius in Verba*, eh?' He turned his attention to the first full page of text and began to read. His face quickly grew grave. He let out a few exclamations, some in Russian, some in English. He turned the page, but rather than reading, looked up at Aleksei. His face was flushed.

'This is quite extraordinary,' he said. He sat down and mopped his face with a handkerchief. His eyes glanced around the room, before falling on Aleksei again. 'Fiction, of course,' he added. It sounded like a plea.

'You saw what happened to the cover.'

Wylie looked up at Aleksei, then back to the book, weighing the evidence of his eyes against the prudence of his years.

'You must let me read this,' he said. 'It will take time.'

Aleksei considered. He was loath to let the book out of his sight, and yet there was nothing more he could get from it without Wylie's help.

'Very well,' he said at length.

'I'll call on you when I'm done. I presume Volkonsky has your address.'

Aleksei nodded. 'I'll see you soon then.'

'Very,' replied the doctor, shaking his hand.

Aleksei went back out into the street. As he set off home, he glanced up to the window above. Dr Wylie stood there holding the book out in the sunlight. A wisp of smoke rose from it, and Aleksei was sure he perceived that scent of burning hair, even though he was too far away. Wylie rapidly popped his head back inside, taking the book with him.

Had he suspected some trick from Aleksei? Or had he simply been unable to believe so strange an observation? Either way, he must now be convinced. That was all Aleksei needed him to be.

Aleksei sat in his rooms all day Sunday, even missing church. Dr Wylie did not come.

On Monday morning, Aleksei heard feet on the stairs. He leapt upright, then sat back down, feigning nonchalance. He had little reason to suppose that whoever it was was coming to pay a call on him, and moreover, the footsteps were far too heavy to be those of Dr Wylie.

The knock at his door was firm.

'Come,' said Aleksei.

It was Prince Volkonsky.

'His Majesty wishes to see you,' he said, without any preamble, 'at four o'clock this afternoon. Are you available?'

'Absolutely,' said Aleksei. 'I'll be there.'

Volkonsky left without another word. Aleksei stood at his window and watched the prince stride powerfully down the street. He was a bigger man in many ways than his brother-in-law (and distant cousin) Sergei Grigorovich Volkonsky. How would the one, the tsar's right-hand man, react to the treachery of the other, he wondered. He hoped there would never be an occasion to find out. It was still his plan that the whole conspiracy should simply

264

drain away, like rainfall on one of those well-engineered Parisian streets. Once he had dealt with this affair, he would return to trying to effect that hope with new vigour.

What though was the reason for the tsar's summons? He had said he might call on Aleksei, but there had been no indication it would be so soon. Had Wylie spoken to him? It seemed unlikely. To approach an emperor with a story such as that told in Cain's notebook would take planning and caution. Had Wylie simply denounced Aleksei as a lunatic? It did not seem to be in the Scotsman's nature.

He looked at his watch. It was only eleven thirty. Time would tell.

Aleksei arrived at the palace promptly, and was quickly escorted by Volkonsky to the tsar's personal quarters. Aleksandr was alone – there was certainly no sign of Wylie. Even Volkonsky retired after exchanging but a few words.

'Sit down, Colonel Danilov,' said Aleksandr.

Aleksei sat. There was no offer of tea today.

'The last time we spoke,' continued the tsar, 'you asked me why I had come to Taganrog. I'm afraid I did not give you a complete answer.'

Aleksei feigned surprise.

'You're not in a position to patronize me, Colonel,' snapped the tsar, but there was a curl to his lip that Aleksei found infectious. The mood lightened. 'Nor am I in a position to deceive you, it would seem,' he added.

'So, why did you come?'

The tsar handed Aleksei a single sheet of paper, folded once in the middle.

'I don't know how this was delivered to me,' he said. 'I found it on my dresser when I was in Petersburg. Someone must have broken in to deliver it.'

'When?' asked Aleksei.

'July,' said the tsar. 'Read it.'

Aleksei read. The text was in French.

My Dear Aleksandr Pavlovich,

How have you been? Myself, I've had my ups and downs, but I've been patient. You and I are both newcomers to this affair, but I'm sure you know the details of the Romanov Betrayal as well as I do, perhaps better. Betrayal must always be avenged, sooner or later. For you, the day of vengeance is close at hand.

You will be leaving Petersburg soon to winter in a more pleasant climate. Make sure that you do not leave the country. Why not visit the Sea of Azov? My suggestion would be Taganrog, but I will easily find you wherever you choose to stay. Even if you choose not to stay in Russia, I will find you. Or if not I, then the person I represent. I'm sure you understand that it is better to face your fears.

It will take time for you to prepare for your journey, and I imagine that you will want to invent some excuse for your unexpected destination; rather that than have them all hear the truth. I will expect your arrival by the end of September.

Your devoted friend,

Cain

Aleksei read the letter twice, though the second reading was more to allow him to collect his thoughts than to garner any new information. He took only a moment to note that the letter was in the same hand as Cain's notebook, regardless of the differences between French and English. It was no surprise that there was a connection between Cain and Aleksandr, but it shocked him to discover that His Majesty was already fully aware of it.

The tsar was sitting forward in eager expectation of Aleksei's opinion, his head almost imperceptibly tilted to the left. Aleksei was well aware of Aleksandr's deafness but, like everyone else close to His Majesty, he had never made any mention of it.

'And you obeyed,' he said, stating the obvious.

The tsar nodded.

'Why?'

'He gave me no choice.'

'I don't see any overt threats in there,' said Aleksei. 'What's the "Romanov Betrayal"?'

'A family legend.'

'Concerning?'

'I can't say.'

'And this "person" he represents?' asked Aleksei.

'I can't say.'

Aleksei paused for a moment, looking for another angle of attack. This whole encounter was an astonishing breakthrough. He didn't intend to spoil it by pressing in areas that Aleksandr was clearly reluctant to discuss. 'Why do you give the letter any credence?' he asked at last.

'What do you mean?'

'It's so vague. Anyone could have heard of this Romanov Betrayal, or could even have some petty squabble of their own that just happened to bring that phrase to their pen.'

Aleksandr looked pale. 'No one outside the closest of the family knew. The tsaritsa never even told my father – she didn't trust him.'

'The tsaritsa?' asked Aleksei – he hoped the implication of 'Which tsaritsa?' was clear.

'Yekaterina Alekseevna – my grandmother. She told me someone would come.'

'And when did he come?' said Aleksei. 'The first time?'

It was no great insight. The letter implied that Cain and the tsar were not strangers to each other. 'Years ago,' Aleksandr replied.

'Why did you believe him then?'

'He knew all about it. Everything the tsaritsa had told me.'

'And what was that?' asked Aleksei.

The tsar's confidence seemed to return a little. He looked Aleksei in the eye. 'There's no need for you to know.'

Aleksei felt the urge to shout at the man, to grab him by the shoulders and shake into him some sense of his own vulnerability, but the idea of treating the tsar in such a manner was laughable. Again he changed tack.

'Why did you not tell me this the other day?' he asked.

Aleksandr took a deep breath, but then failed to speak.

'To put it another way,' Aleksei continued, 'why have you decided to tell me now? Did Dr Wylie speak to you?'

'Wylie? No, certainly not.' The tsar paused again. 'The reason I called you here was this.' He reached over to his desk and handed Aleksei another sheet of paper. It was more of a note than a letter. The language was again French; the handwriting the same.

'I received it today,' said the tsar.

Aleksandr Pavlovich,

Apologies for my tardiness in contacting you. I was pleased to hear of your prompt arrival in Taganrog, and I thought it only polite to give you a little while to settle down and ensure your wife's comfort.

It is common knowledge that you intend soon to leave Taganrog. Do not worry; that fits completely with our plans. You will be touring the Crimean Peninsula, as would be expected from a visiting monarch. Have you considered taking in the town of Bakhchisaray? It will be advantageous to us all.

Once there, you will know what to do.

Your devoted friend,

C

'Did anyone see who delivered it?' asked Aleksei.

Aleksandr shook his head. 'It was the same as before.'

'And were you planning to go to the Crimea?'

'Of course. Anyone could have known that. Anyone could have guessed.'

'You don't think there's an informant amongst your staff?' asked Aleksei.

'There's no need for one.' It was an interesting answer, which Maks would have appreciated; not reasoning against the conclusion, but against the thought process which arrived at it.

'What do you know of Bakhchisaray?'

'Very little, until today. I've not sat idly since I received that letter.' He reached to his desk for a book, where he had marked a page. He summarized, rather than reading.

'It's in the south of the peninsula, between Sevastopol and Simferopol, on the Churuk Su river. It was the capital of the Crimean Khanate, ruled by the Tatars. We took it over in 1783.'

'Has the Romanov Betrayal got anything to do with the Tatars?'

'No,' said the tsar. 'I can assure you of that much. Do you know of the town?'

'Pushkin has written a poem about it,' said Aleksei.

'Has he? His name did not appear on your little list, I noticed.' Now that Aleksandr had unburdened himself, his manner was once again sharp and precise.

'No,' said Aleksei. If the name had been there, Aleksei would have removed it too. 'Will you go?' he asked.

'I have to.'

'Because of the Romanov Betrayal?'

Aleksandr nodded.

The two men sat in silence. Aleksei considered what the tsar had told him, and what he hadn't. There was far more of the latter than the former, but he could think of no avenues of enquiry which the tsar had not already closed off to him. Eventually he realized the question the tsar wanted him to ask.

'What do you want me to do, Your Majesty?'

'Come with me,' said the tsar.

269

'To Bakhchisaray?'

'And beyond.'

Aleksei read the second letter again. It took only moments. 'He says you'll know what to do once you're there. Do you know now?'

Aleksandr shook his head. 'Perhaps I'll see something.'

'Perhaps he'll intercept you before you even get there.'

The tsar leaned forward with sudden animation. 'Exactly. I mean . . . not necessarily that, but that's the kind of thinking I need. You can think like Cain, outwit him.' *Cain fears you, Kyesha* had said. 'You can protect me.'

There was nothing for Aleksei to consider. 'When do we depart?' he asked.

'Tomorrow,' replied the tsar.

'Utterly incredible.'

Wylie was waiting as Aleksei stepped out of the tsar's study. Aleksei glanced around the anteroom, but saw that they were alone.

'Incredible?' Aleksei replied. 'So you don't believe it?'

'I wouldn't have done – had it not been for what you showed me.'

'Even so . . .'

'Don't argue against your own case, Colonel Danilov,' said Wylie. 'That strange leather was enough to convince *you* of the book's veracity.'

Aleksei hesitated. Neither Wylie's premise nor his conclusion was true. Aleksei knew little of the validity of the notebook's contents, since he had made so little headway in them. But whatever the book revealed, he had seen far more evidence of the existence of living vampires than a mere trick with a self-repairing bookbinding. He chose to focus on the former point rather than the latter.

'You forget, Doctor, the reason I gave you the book,' he said. 'I cannot read your language.'

Wylie smiled. 'Then I shall have the pleasure of witnessing your astonishment as I translate it for you.'

'You've read it all?'

'Not in detail, but the sections I have studied already are quite fascinating.' Wylie suddenly straightened his posture and spoke more loudly. 'I trust you will be joining us on our travels to the Crimea, Colonel.'

It was a tone of voice that Aleksei had heard before, on the lips of many an amateur spy. He did not need to look round to know that someone else had entered the room.

'I certainly shall be,' he said, his demeanour unchanged. He saw a fleeting look of concern cross Wylie's face, revealing the suspicion that he had not cottoned on to what was happening, but Aleksei was simply playing the game better. 'I hope we'll have time to speak more as we travel.'

'Absolutely,' said Wylie.

Aleksei gave him a brief nod of goodbye and turned to leave. 'Prince Volkonsky,' he said, as an acknowledgement of the new entrant to the room, whose face he could now see.

'Danilov,' came the reply, but beyond that, Volkonsky was too interested in talking to Wylie to say any more.

Aleksei made a quiet exit and headed for his lodgings. It was only a few minutes' walk through the dark streets of Taganrog, and he scarcely thought about where he was going. He felt a sense of excitement, with which he was familiar, but which he would never have associated with the prospect of learning the contents of a mere book. It was akin to the feeling he got every time he approached Moscow after weeks or months of absence – the anticipation of knowing Domnikiia's body once again. He would not mention the comparison to her. Anyway, it would be a long time before he saw her again. He would be learning the contents of Cain's book well before that.

'What have you discovered, Aleksei Ivanovich?'

Kyesha learned quickly. That evening, he approached Aleksei from downwind. The first Aleksei knew of his presence was a

271

voice, whispering in the darkness just before he arrived at his rooms. He started and then turned. Kyesha's face was close. Aleksei wondered how he could have missed that unmistakable smell in the past. He had known for some time what his first question to Kyesha would be.

'What do you know of the Romanov Betrayal?' he asked.

'Only a little more than I care.'

'Don't piss me around,' said Aleksei.

'I've heard Cain use the phrase occasionally. I never understood it.'

'Is Cain his real name?'

In the darkness, Aleksei saw Kyesha shrug in a disturbingly human manner.

'Is he even English?'

'He could be. I don't have an ear for the accent. His French and Russian are both near perfect.'

'I've seen a letter from him,' said Aleksei. He would make no mention of the letter's recipient. He doubted if Kyesha would be interested. Aleksei's concern might be the safety of the tsar, but Kyesha's only interest was in vengeance against Cain.

'And?'

'What do you know about Bakhchisaray?'

'He mentions it in the letter?' asked Kyesha.

Aleksei nodded.

'And you're going there?'

'That's the plan.'

'From there, he'll take you to Chufut Kalye,' said Kyesha.

'"Take" us?'

'He'll find a way.'

'And what is Chufut Kalye?'

Kyesha said nothing. He was looking over Aleksei's shoulder. A man was walking past on the other side of the road – a serf by the looks of him. As he turned back, Aleksei felt sure he glimpsed Kyesha licking his lips.

He grabbed Kyesha by the arm. 'We can't talk here,' he said, leading the *voordalak* down the street. When the serf was out of sight, Aleksei repeated his question. 'What's Chufut Kalye?'

'Did you ever hear of a sect of Jews known as the Karaites?' Kyesha asked.

Aleksei had heard the name, but little more. 'Go on,' he said.

'Some of them claim they're one of the lost tribes of Israel, others that they're descended from Khazars, but it's all really just to shake off the blame for murdering Christ.'

'I'm not really interested in the theology,' said Aleksei, though it surprised him that Kyesha should be.

'Well, they used to be all over the Crimea. There are fewer now. Chufut Kalye was their citadel. It's an old fortress – partly built, partly burrowed. There's a handful of them still live there.'

'How far is it from Bakhchisaray?'

'A few versts. It's a bit of a climb.'

'And what will happen when we get there?' asked Aleksei.

'I'm not a fortune teller.'

'You must have some idea.'

Kyesha stopped walking and turned to Aleksei. 'Do you really want me to tell you what I think's going to happen?'

'Tell me.'

'It's very simple,' Kyesha informed him. 'You will kill Richard Cain.'

Aleksandr heard the coachman call to his horses, and the carriage began to rattle along the road. He leaned out of the coach window and looked back. Volkonsky stood there, watching his departure. Aleksandr was sorry to leave him behind, but he was concerned for the tsaritsa, and though she had her doctors with her, she needed a man of sterner temperament to make sure she did nothing to risk her health. The tsaritsa herself had not felt well enough to come out and say farewell, but she had watched from a window.

Though he might miss Volkonsky, Aleksandr still had with him sufficient aides. Baron Diebich sat opposite him in his carriage. Somewhere else in the train, a few coaches behind, was Colonel

Salomka. And, of course, he had his own doctors with him; Wylie and Tarasov were back there somewhere too.

The excursion was planned to last just seventeen days. The original idea had been for longer, but Yelizaveta had insisted he should not be away for so many weeks. It was certainly important for them to get back to Taganrog before the weather really turned on its path towards winter.

In the end, what did it matter if he planned to be away for seventeen days or seventeen years? On the tenth day they would arrive at Bakhchisaray. He did not know if he would ever leave.

He looked further down the short line of carriages and wagons that accompanied him. Behind them, a few of the party rode on horseback. It was difficult to pick out individual figures, but one was clear.

Aleksandr sat back down inside the carriage. He knew that he must face what was ahead of him, but he also knew that, in Aleksei Ivanovich Danilov, he had an ally.

Răzbunarea weighed anchor. Its course was back, west, along the northern coast of the Sea of Azov, but keeping well away from the shore. It was not even certain that there was any need to track Aleksandr Pavlovich; what had to be done might just as well be achieved at a distance. But on the other hand, proximity would lead to flexibility. There was still much that could go wrong, despite the assurances he had been given.

They would sail to Sevastopol, or thereabouts. The royal party was travelling by land, and so their paths would diverge even before *Răzbunarea* left the Sea of Azov. It was a pity that Bakhchisaray wasn't closer to the coast, but otherwise it was a well-chosen location. The cargo could not, of course, be carried through so populous a city as Sevastopol, but a slight diversion to an appropriate, secluded cove would make it easy to take on board.

There had been rumours – rumours which had crossed Europe, though no human would have noticed – about what else was going on in Bakhchisaray, but they were of little concern to the passenger of *Răzbunarea*. When this was all over, perhaps he would take revenge on behalf of his entire race, but for now he had more pressing needs.

And even before the ship took on its cargo, there was one essential task that its passenger had to perform. It would take concentration and fortitude, and for that he would require rest, even though there were still days to prepare. Rest now would make him ready.

He lay back and listened to the creaking of the ship around him. It was pleasant to be surrounded by wood, but the wooden hull was not so comforting as the tighter wooden walls that now entombed him as he rested. He reached out and pulled the lid over him, sensing it above him, inches from his face. Now all was dark. He slept.

CHAPTER XVII

'LORD JESUS CHRIST, HAVE MERCY UPON ME, A SINNER.'
Their two voices spoke in unison, but the starets kept his low, allowing the kneeling tsaritsa to dominate as they spoke the Prayer of the Heart.

'Why have you come here?' he asked.

The tsaritsa looked up, and the starets could see fear in her eyes.

'It's my husband,' she said.

'Has he been unfaithful?'

'No.' The starets raised an eyebrow. 'Yes,' the tsaritsa acknowledged, 'but not recently, and that's not what I'm concerned about.'

'Then what is your concern?'

'Father,' she moaned, 'I'm afraid for his soul!'

'We should all fear for our souls,' he said softly, 'but prayer will be our salvation.'

'There are some acts that are beyond salvation.'

The starets paused, wondering what the tsaritsa could know of her husband. 'Acts?' he asked.

'Acts which cannot be repented.'

He spoke the word that she seemed afraid to utter. 'Suicide?'

She nodded. 'Yes.' Her response was scarcely voiced, but in the stone-walled cell of the monastery, it filled the air.

'Why do you think he contemplates that?' The starets

deliberately avoided repetition of the term she had been so keen to leave unuttered.

'He talks as though he anticipates his own death.'

'That does not mean death will come by his own hand.'

'But if not, how can he know?'

'His anticipation may not be correct.' He wondered whether such words would be comforting. It was not reason that drove the woman's grief. But she seemed to understand.

'He believes it to be. And he accepts it.'

'We must all accept death eventually,' said the starets.

'And embrace it?'

'Are you sure you're not seeing things in him that are not really there?'

'How can I know?' Her voice was despairing.

'We must pray for you.'

'And for him.'

'For both of you.' The starets placed his hands on the tsaritsa's head and muttered a prayer in Old Slavonic that she was unlikely to understand. Then she stood.

'May I come to you again?' she asked.

'Perhaps it is better if I come to you.'

She nodded meekly. 'When?'

The starets searched for the most reassuring answer. 'When the Lord's work needs doing,' he said. It seemed to satisfy her.

Aleksei had not appreciated how tiresome a royal tour could be. Much of the landscape they passed through had been of enormous beauty, and the towns and cities so different from what anyone from the north of the country was used to, that he would truly have enjoyed the journey if he had been able to travel at his own pace. But the place of a tsar, it seemed, was not with his land but with his people. Everywhere they stopped he would spend time in conversation with local dignitaries or merchants, as if his authority as tsar somehow rested on their approval. Perhaps he was more sympathetic to the democratic ideas of the Northern

Society than he claimed. He had certainly held some truck with them in his youth. Aleksei could have wandered off on his own, and was tempted to, secure in the knowledge that there would be no danger until Bakhchisaray. But that was an obvious ploy; an invitation to a location could easily be a trap that would be sprung en route there. Kyesha had thought that the ultimate destination was in fact beyond Bakhchisaray, but there was no benefit to be drawn in relying on that. Aleksei was never close beside the tsar, but was never beyond his summoning.

They had stopped before they had ever really got going at Mariupol, a little way down the coast from Taganrog, and Aleksandr had talked to a group of Mennonites – Germanic, protestant pacifists; hardly representatives of the Russian outlook on life. After that they had visited Berdyansk, and the tsar was once again welcomed by the local populace.

At last they passed along the narrow isthmus at Perekop and entered the Crimean Peninsula itself. From a military perspective, it was a frightening terrain. The isthmus was perhaps only eight versts across at its narrowest, and the land beyond was flat and without cover. It felt like they were riding into a trap. But Aleksei knew the trap would not be sprung here. A narrow strip of land such as Perekop would be ideal to contain an army, but a single man, be he a peasant or a tsar, would need closer attention.

From there they went on to Simferopol, where the first signs of a magnificent landscape began to appear. Many Russians, certainly those from Moscow or Petersburg, could pass their whole life without ever seeing a mountain. To the east, the Urals were too far from civilization to attract much interest. Aleksei had heard that the Caucasus mountains were impressive, but he had never seen them. He was luckier than most of his countrymen to have travelled west on the march towards Paris and to have seen the Alps, though only looking up from their foothills, and before that the Carpathians, when fighting on the Danube. But it had all been many years ago, and Aleksei had become used to the vast, flat steppe of his homeland. Much of the Crimea was the same, but suddenly now the mountains rose out of it, and as the tsar's party carried on further south, they rose even higher.

As the roads became steeper, Aleksandr chose to travel on horseback rather than by carriage. In view of the terrain, it was a sensible move, but it did nothing to assist his personal safety. And when the tsar travelled by horse, so must the rest of his entourage. Their guides led them through a broad pass in a range of peaks that stretched out unendingly to the east and west, and at last the Black Sea lay before them. Plunging down towards it, the mountains were at their steepest, at some places descending as cliffs directly into the water, at others leaving a narrow strip of level ground between themselves and the waves. At each such point, human habitation was in evidence.

One of these locations was their next stop, Gurzuf, not far from Yalta, where Aleksei suspected from the cleanliness of the town and the self-satisfaction of the local governor, Count Vorontsov, that the latter had recently made a supreme effort to achieve the former, or had instructed others to.

There they also met a man who had at once aroused Aleksei's suspicion: Count Vorontsov's personal physician – an Englishman by the name of Robert Lee. It was unfair to suspect every Englishman on the peninsula, but it would be foolish to ignore the link. Dr Lee was first introduced to the tsar by way of the demonstration of a miraculous new cure for swamp fever – which was prevalent in the area – administered to a local tatar chief. The results were effective and almost instantaneous, and Lee was invited to dine with the royal party.

Dr Lee revealed that the principal ingredient of his tonic was a substance he called 'sulphate of quinine', which was extracted from a South American tree known as the cinchona. Both Wylie and Tarasov were fascinated to learn more of this; it appeared that their isolation in Russia had prevented them from keeping up to speed with medical progress in the West. Aleksei was also intrigued. 'Quinine' had been a term that occurred more than once in Cain's notes, though through lack of familiarity with the word, he had not been able to translate those sections. He glanced over at Wylie, but the doctor showed no reaction.

The conversation then moved on to the subject of homeopathy – not a word that Aleksei recalled seeing in Cain's book. Much of the detail was lost on Aleksei, but it appeared that Wylie was a proponent of the concept, while Lee was not. However, it was Count Vorontsov, rather than his physician, who seemed to pursue the issue with the greater passion.

'Like cures like,' insisted Wylie. This apparently had been the claim of homeopathy's inventor, a German called Hahnemann.

'So if I were to stab you through the heart,' asked the count, 'bringing about your death, would a second stab wound restore you to life?'

Before Wylie could respond, Colonel Salomka had interjected. 'There is a peasant myth in these parts concerning a creature called an *oopir*.' He had chortled as he spoke, but Aleksei had instantly paid attention. He glanced again at Wylie, but still saw no response. There was no reason the Scot should be familiar with the local term. 'As with many of these creatures,' continued Salomka, 'the *oopir* must be killed by stabbing through the heart with a stake of hawthorn. But here's the thing' – he sniggered again – 'you mustn't stab it a second time, or it will come back to life. Maybe that's where Herr Hahnemann got his ideas from.'

Most around the table laughed. The tsar did not, perhaps out of respect for the views of Wylie. Nor did Wylie himself. That might have been out of pique at being mocked, but Aleksei noticed that this time it was Wylie's eyes that were on him, looking for a reaction.

A moment later, Wylie resumed the defence of his pet subject. 'That's why Dr Hahnemann promulgates the use of only the most dilute quantities of his medicines,' he said.

'So more of a scratch than a stab?' suggested Salomka.

'As an analogy, yes,' said Wylie, choosing simply to ignore the attempts at humour from around the table.

'But what about the diseases we get around here?' asked

Vorontsov. 'Inflammation of the brain? Or the bowel? Or fever? Would one thousandth of a grain of that sulphate of quinine Dr Lee showed us working today have done the trick, eh? What do you think, Lee?'

'In my experience, a large dose will always arrest the fevers almost instantaneously,' replied the doctor calmly. 'I have tried with smaller doses, as have others, and the results are ineffectual.'

Aleksei said little. His instinctive view on homeopathy was to note that doctors charged their patients by the hour, but paid for their medicines by the grain. But he was prepared to listen to the two experts. As an individual, he trusted Wylie more, but Lee appeared to be the more rigorous scientist. Again, that had echoes of Cain. Could they be one and the same man?

At one point, Dr Tarasov posed a somewhat less controversial question. 'Doesn't the term "homeopathic" originally relate to a form of black magic?'

'It still does,' muttered Lee, but before Wylie could rise to his bait, Vorontsov answered the question more fully.

'It does indeed. Traditionally there are three types of magic: homeopathic, sympathetic and contagious.' He glanced at the surprised expressions around the table and chose to explain himself. 'All nonsense, of course, but some of the Tatars still believe it, so it's worth understanding.'

'And what's the distinction?' asked Tarasov.

'Homeopathic is imitation. The tribe want to catch a deer, so they put on a sort of play in which they catch a deer – the creature itself is played by one of their own. The next day, if the magic works, life imitates art and all eat heartily. Sympathetic is similar, but the object of the magic is represented by some kind of doll or effigy. You stab the doll, and the person it represents falls ill.'

'And contagious?' It was the tsar who asked.

'Contagious magic is where you take something *from* the victim's body – hair or nail clippings often – and through them, the witch can control the person from which they came.'

'So watch out next time you go to the barber,' said Lee.

281

'Often a severed body-part may be used,' continued Vorontsov, 'a finger or a toe.'

Aleksei's thumb ran over the stumps on his left hand. There had been no magic, but Kyesha had used the remains of his severed fingers to control him, to bring him down here as an agent of revenge. Lost in his own thoughts, he scarcely listened to the rest of the count's explanation, his ears only pricking when he heard the final word.

'Or it can be a bodily fluid, such as semen – or, very often, blood.'

After the cigars had been handed out, Aleksei managed to isolate Lee and sound him out.

'You argue your points well,' he said as an opener. 'I can imagine you speaking in front of the Royal Society.' It was taking a chance to speak so glibly about an organization of which he knew little.

'Well, thank you, Colonel,' replied the doctor. 'Sadly, I have not yet had the honour of speaking there, but when I return to London, I hope to make my mark.'

'You'll be acquainted with a compatriot of yours who's also been working in these parts. A gentleman by the name of Cain – a fellow of the Society, I believe.'

'Richard Cain is here – in the Crimea?' exclaimed Lee. Both Dr Wylie and the tsar looked over towards them, presumably not just at the raised voice.

'So I believe. You know him?'

'I've read his work – a brilliant man. Perhaps a little too enthusiastic as a vivisectionist, but sometimes there are prices that must be paid.'

Count Vorontsov joined them, and the conversation moved on. Aleksei's best guess was that Lee was what he seemed to be. For a start, he could see no motivation in one man leading a double life as both Cain and Lee. Russia was not short of British émigrés, particularly doctors, as Wylie exemplified. But if Lee was to be trusted, then it meant that Cain was a real person; an Englishman, a scientist and Fellow of the Royal Society. On the other hand, it might just be a case of stolen identity; some imposter writing the name in the notebook and using it to sign the letters in the safe assumption that the real Richard L. Cain was never likely to set foot across the English Channel.

'An interesting correlation with the notebook, don't you think, Colonel?' It was Wylie who spoke to him. Vorontsov and Lee were now talking to Diebich.

'The quinine you mean?' asked Aleksei.

'That too, but I was referring to the story of the *oopir*.' Aleksei looked at him quizzically. 'Utter nonsense that a second stabbing would resurrect it, I'm sure you'll agree,' continued Wylie.

'I would assume so,' said Aleksei. He could not recall ever having stabbed a *voordalak* twice, though on one occasion he had attacked with so jagged a piece of wood that it was impossible to say how many times the creature's heart had been pierced.

'I know so,' said Wylie, interrupting his thoughts.

'How?' asked Aleksei, making no attempt to disguise his astonishment.

'It's in Cain's book,' said the doctor grimly. 'Cain heard that story and decided to investigate it. He repeated the experiment on three separate occasions. Without exception, the creatures remained dead.'

It struck Aleksei for the first time what a profoundly useful thing Cain's notebook might prove to be. So many times he had relied on folklore, on his grandmother's dark tales of fabulous beasts, to inform him of how he might deal with these creatures. Cain turned superstition into science, and with it brought certainty. Aleksei realized he had been wooed by Kyesha, who by his very nature must take the side of his kin. But in the ultimate analysis, was Cain doing good or ill? As with all learning, it was not the knowledge itself that could be classified as good or evil, but how it was utilized.

Now was the first real chance that Aleksei had had to discuss the notebook with Wylie. There were a thousand questions he wanted to ask. The one he started with was of a very general nature. 'You've read it all now?'

'I have,' replied Wylie. 'And with every word I have become more and more astounded. If you hadn't shown me the effect of light on the creature's skin – I can only assume that is what the binding is made from – I would have taken the whole thing as some perverted joke. The words on the cover are almost a warning – tattooed, I believe, by the way.'

'Tattooed?'

'On to the living skin of the vampire before it was flayed.'

Aleksei felt his stomach tighten. 'My God!' he muttered.

'This Richard Cain is a strange man indeed.'

'I suspected briefly that he and Dr Lee might be one and the same; both English, both scientists.'

'It's not *that* bloody difficult for you people, is it?' said Wylie, with a mocking snarl.

'What?'

'Robert Lee is not English. He's as Scottish as I am.'

After that the party travelled on to Baidar and then Sevastopol. In Aleksei's opinion, the tsar overworked himself, visiting fortresses, hospitals and dockyards and even inspecting the Black Sea Fleet. On the other hand, they were closing in on Bakhchisaray – filling his day would make the time go faster, or at least not allow his mind time to dwell on what was to come. Close to Balaklava, he rode out ten versts on horseback to pray at the monastery of Saint George. Aleksei was reminded of the statue back in Petersburg, of Aleksandr's great-great-grandfather, Pyotr, styled – as Aleksei saw it – after Saint George. Perhaps those associations Aleksei had made with the symbol of the serpent beneath his feet were beginning to come true. The tsar could know nothing of those connections, but somehow he instinctively took comfort from that famous, dragon-slaying saint.

'And before you even think about it,' Dr Wylie had said to him after Colonel Salomka had mentioned the monastery to which the tsar was riding, '*my* country's patron saint is Saint Andrew. Saint George is the saint of the English.'

Aleksei had smiled, but he hadn't known either country's saint. Cain was English, and was – in his own, very modern way – fighting the monsters that threatened humanity. Probably a coincidence, but again Aleksei wondered whose side he would take when, and if, he finally met Richard Cain.

The following day, after more exhausting engagements, the tsar decided once again to travel by carriage, where he slept on the final leg of his journey to Bakhchisaray. They arrived late in the afternoon. Even at that hour, Aleksandr continued to do his duty. He visited the ancient palace of the Crimean Khanate, the baths and, finally, the mosque. The mufti led a service of prayers for the tsar's long life, which Aleksandr himself attended, politically standing behind a screen so that he would not be seen supporting a religion other than that of his nation.

When they left the mosque, darkness was drawing in. Here they were at last in Bakhchisaray, and the time of the *voordalak* was at hand. Aleksei would have to be wary. Fortunately, the tsar returned directly to his lodgings and went to his room. Wylie reported that His Majesty was feeling a little unwell, but it was only to be expected after the exertions of the past few days.

Aleksei asked one of the locals in the tavern where they were staying about Chufut Kalye. He didn't say much, but pointed along the road to the east. They were just on the foothills of the mountains that guarded the peninsula's southern coast, but already the steep limestone cliffs formed a twisting canyon along which it was impossible to see very far, certainly not to the citadel that Kyesha had foretold they would visit.

But the dying rays of the sun did highlight something in the rocks much closer to Bakhchisaray, overlooking the palace itself. It was a natural formation, created by centuries of rain and wind, but Aleksei could not help but see a human face looking over where the tsar slept – a giant skull formed of stone.

Aleksei's thoughts turned once again to Golgotha.

It was an uncomfortable and unaccustomed sensation. The dark figure, wrapped in an overcoat against the cold wind, stood on the very prow of *Răzbunarea* and, though his eyes were tight shut, stared out across the water and over the land.

Usually, there was some sense of response; just as when an officer commanded a foot soldier, he would hear the occasional 'Yes, sir!', so it was normal to sense some response from the mind into which his will was being applied. It was not necessary to feel that response, any more than it was necessary for the officer to hear the soldier – he knew full well, in a disciplined army, that the orders would be obeyed – but even so, it gave comfort.

But with this half-breed there was nothing. Tonight, he was . . . Beethoven. He smiled at the analogy. What he had to achieve was akin to playing the piano whilst being deaf to the sound produced when his fingers pressed the keys – worse than that, he could not even feel the keys with his fingertips. And yet he knew what to do with his fingers. The movements were practised, repeated a thousand times before. He had no need to feel the keys or hear the resonance of the strings to know that what his will had directed would come to pass. The officer had no need to look through his spyglass and observe the hundreds that lay dead as the consequence of his command.

Confirmation would come, but it would not be immediate. Beethoven could turn and see, if not hear, the applause of the crowd. His own ovation would come in the form of a cart, with a single, oblong packing case as its load, racing down from the mountains and across the steppe to where *Răzbunarea* waited.

He formed his entire will around two simple words:

Chufut Kalye

* * *

Aleksandr awoke with a desperate intake of breath. His bed felt steady beneath him. He had been on a boat, but he was on dry land again now. There had been a conversation, but it had been one-sided. Aleksandr had heard the man clearly, but whenever he replied, his words had fallen on deaf ears.

It had been a dream. It had taken Aleksandr a few moments of wakefulness to realize that, but now it was clear. And as that clarity descended, so the details of the dream faded. He had been standing on the deck of a ship – or perhaps not even on it. Beneath his feet he had seen the waves lapping against the hull of the vessel. He had been level with the deck, but floating out above the sea.

He had instantly recognized the tall figure with its full eyebrows and thick moustache, contrasting with a smooth, domed forehead much like Aleksandr's own. And yet though he knew the man, he could not place him. Perhaps it was a family friend who had visited often in Aleksandr's childhood, but whom he had not seen for many years.

The man had been telling him to go somewhere. He had spoken it very clearly, but now Aleksandr had forgotten. He remembered repeatedly saying, 'Yes,' or 'I understand,' or 'I will,' but still the demand was repeated. Aleksandr had been willing to go there, eager to go there, but however much he had insisted, he had not been heard. Now he was still eager to make that journey, but he could not recall where.

The dream had ended, as dreams often do – Aleksandr's dreams, anyway – with him falling. Whatever force of will it was that had suspended him above the waves was suddenly broken, and his stomach had flown upwards as his body descended. He had reached out and grabbed the wooden rail of the boat, clinging on to it for a few vital moments as the sea spray dashed against his feet. The man to whom he had been speaking did not act to save him. His own hand was inches from Aleksandr's, steadying him against the rocking of the boat, but he did not move a single muscle to aid the tsar.

Then Aleksandr's fingers had begun to slip and he had fallen backwards, his arms flailing, into the waters beneath him. In

287

his last seconds, he had had the strangest, most incongruous perception. As he had fallen ever downwards towards a watery oblivion he had been pursued; pursued by a dragon – a golden dragon, with eyes of deepest emerald, and a protruding, forked, red tongue that flickered at Aleksandr as the waves consumed him.

Then he had awoken, and the one aspect of the dream he knew with terrible certainty he had to remember eluded him. He stared into the darkness for an unmeasured period of time, and realized that sleep would be his salvation. Sleep would recover the memory and abate the terror.

And so it did, but sleep took many hours to come.

A rush of air awoke Aleksei. He hadn't intended to sleep, but it was inescapable. Before he could even open his eyes, he was further roused by a shout.

'Diebich!'

The tsar was in his nightclothes, turning his head around like a strutting cockerel in search of his chief of staff. He seemed not even to notice Aleksei, sprawled uncomfortably in the chair.

'Diebich!' he bellowed again.

The baron emerged from his room across the hall. He was pulling on his tunic, but still wearing – and displaying – his longjohns. Evidently, the first call had inspired him to dress before meeting his master, the second had convinced him not to.

'Diebich, we shall be visiting Chufut Kalye today,' said Aleksandr.

'Chufut Kalye, Your Majesty?'

'Yes. You know where it is.'

'Certainly,' said Diebich, becoming more alert.

'Arrange it then.'

'Yes, Your Majesty,' then, 'Why, Your Majesty?'

'Why?' asked Aleksandr, with an indignation which Aleksei perceived as affected, but perhaps Diebich did not. 'Because I am your tsar.'

288

Aleksandr turned back to his room and noticed Aleksei for the first time. It was unspoken, but the same question – 'Why?' – was on Aleksei's mind too. Aleksandr must have guessed, for he averted his eyes and hurried on into his room.

They left Bakhchisaray on horseback, under the gaze of the great stone skull. The route was flat for the first few versts as it headed out of town, but then the path began to steepen. The road – if it could be called such – hugged the hillside on its right, with the valley sloping away to the left. Beyond that, on the other side of the valley, another precipice rose, equally unassailable. While the land remained relatively flat, gypsy encampments were scattered, displaying horrendous poverty. Aleksei wondered whether the tsar might stop to learn more about them, but he seemed too intent on his goal even to glance to one side. Most of the remainder of the party were pleased to bypass such squalor and head onward into the narrowing gorge.

Aleksei kept his neck craned upwards, searching the tops of the hills that overshadowed them. Though steep, they were still largely wooded until close to the very top, where they became craggy and vertical. There, little plant life could take root. There were plenty of caves in view, but none seemed inhabited. The soldier in Aleksei felt fearful of the whole terrain. They were trapped on either side, with no open ground behind them for more than a verst and perhaps worse in front. For anyone looking down on them they were easy targets.

Suddenly, Colonel Salomka shouted and pointed over to the left, to the tops of the cliffs on the other side of the valley. There, through the trees, they caught their first glimpse of the citadel. It was still distant, but the straight edges of manmade structures could be seen to merge with nature's more graceful curves. They continued up the slope and the trees began to thin, affording them ever better views of their objective.

As they came to the head of the valley, the path turned across it, almost doubling back on itself, and they found themselves at the foot of the final slope leading up to Chufut Kalye. The soil was too thin now, it seemed, for trees, and coarse grass covered the ground up to the cliffs, interspersed with a few bushes. Here they were forced to dismount to make the rest of the way on foot. The entrance was a natural gap in the cliff, which had then been reinforced – effectively replacing the cliff – by a stone wall, in which only a small doorway allowed access. As far as Aleksei could see on either side, there was no other breach in the cliffside. If the heavy door was closed, then no creature without wings could reach the plateau beyond.

Through the doorway, a short path took them above the level of the wall and into the city itself. All were surprised by the degree of civilization. The Karaites who lived there were comfortable and well organized – a contrast to the gypsies they had passed below. The people – or at least the men; the women appeared bound to stay indoors – greeted the tsar with curiosity and some affection. Their customs might be strange, but Aleksei could see no immediate threat to Aleksandr. He certainly felt more comfortable than he had in the valley below. The greatest reason for this was that it was the middle of the day. The citadel was the highest point for miles around – nothing cast a shadow on it. And so, whatever it was that might make some move against the tsar, it would be of this world.

The Karaite chief took tea with Aleksandr and then introduced him to his wives and children. The women were all beautiful, but Aleksei was disturbed by how pale they looked – almost bloodless. Was it some Jewish law that kept the women indoors, or was there a greater need to protect them from the sun? A city of human men and vampire wives? It seemed impossible. Aleksei sniffed the air. He noticed nothing of that smell that he had learned to recognize in Kyesha, and which he hoped would be shared by any like him.

The tsar was further impressed by the school which he was shown. He was told that all the children in the city attended. He commented on his wish that every child in Russia could go to school, but Aleksei remembered that the tsar had been making wishes like that ever since he had come to power. Nothing had come of them.

The citadel itself was partly built from stone blocks, but also constructed from existing caves, which had been further carved into shape by the hand of man. There could be little said against them, except perhaps that high on the hilltop and with the windows unglazed, the draughts might be discomforting. The tsar was informed that the earliest occupation, in natural caves with little human modification, dated back over two millennia. Those parts of the city were mostly unoccupied now, but Aleksandr expressed an interest in seeing them, and so some of the party – Aleksei, Wylie, Salomka and a couple of locals to act as guides – accompanied him as he left the populated heart of the city to view its wilder environs.

They soon reached the other side of the plateau, and Aleksei gazed down into a gorge even less hospitable than the one through which they had ascended. Again there was a steep cliff, perhaps three or four times his own height, dropping away beneath his feet before transforming abruptly into a slope of at least forty-five degrees. There were fewer trees than on the other side, and Aleksei could see no pathways. Across the valley, broader than the one they had come through, a similar slope led up to a similar plateau – though Aleksei could see fewer signs of caves. Far to the west he could just make out a collection of houses. He could not quite get his bearings, but it was not Bakhchisaray, or at least not the part they had come from. An outlying farm, perhaps.

The area they had come to was rocky, and the caves represented an earlier stage in the development of their inhabitants. Some still showed the neat edges that indicated human modification, but many appeared entirely as God had created them, with His usual disdain for anything so mundane as a straight line. Though they may not have been built by men, they had certainly been inhabited by them. The party went a little way down into one of them and discovered the walls covered with scratched writing and drawings. The local who went with them said that these went back to the Middle Ages, and Aleksei saw no reason to doubt it. Beyond, the tunnel continued onwards into darkness. No one was tempted to go too far in and so they returned to the surface.

'We should go soon, Your Majesty,' said Colonel Salomka.

'Yes, yes,' said Aleksandr. 'Just one last look at the view.'

Aleksei went over to Dr Wylie as the tsar took a few paces towards the steep valley slope. There had been no danger so far – nothing of any note at all – and yet he would be glad when they were back down from this ancient place. Even if they left now, they would not be back in safety for a few more hours, and Aleksei could not help but remember Kyesha's certainty that it would be here that something happened.

'A reminder of home,' said Wylie.

Aleksei looked away from the tsar to see what the doctor was referring to. He had plucked out the dried, dead stem of a thistle that had grown amongst the grasses and shrubs that managed to find sustenance on the rocky terrain.

'A sorry specimen,' continued the doctor, 'but it's pleasant to see Scotland's flower thriving so far from home.'

'This place must be even more impressive in spring,' commented Aleksei.

'Indeed,' replied Wylie, but he evidently had something else on his mind. 'You know, it occurs to me that we're making something of an assumption that your man Cain is English. He's an English speaker, for sure, but he could be Scottish, Irish – even American.'

'Can't you tell from the name itself?'

'Not really, though I'm no expert. Even if we could trace—'

'Your Majesty!' The shout came from Colonel Salomka. He repeated it seconds later. 'Your Majesty!'

Aleksei and Wylie looked around, but there was no sign of the tsar anywhere near where he had been standing moments before. They rushed over to the spot and looked down towards the valley floor, but there was nothing to be seen. It would have been impossible for them to miss him in that vast, smooth expanse if he had fallen, or even if anyone had taken him. And yet there was nowhere else for him to have gone. He could not possibly have walked or been taken back across the hilltop without one of them noticing, unless with the assistance of some magical invisibility. Aleksei doubted it. A more realistic possibility had occurred to him.

He lay flat on his stomach and pulled his body forwards, to lean out over the cliff top as far as he dared. He quickly saw what he was looking for. The smooth, vertical limestone was pockmarked with the mouths of caves – dozens of them along its length. There were three or four that Aleksei could almost reach out and touch.

In a moment he was up on his feet, looking around him. Just to the right of where he stood – of where the tsar had been standing – lay a cleft in the rock just wide enough for him to climb down a little way. It was precarious, but he was soon out on the very face of the cliff. A narrow ridge ran horizontally, allowing access to any one of the nearby cave mouths. The tsar could have been dragged into any one of them.

'He's in the caves,' shouted Aleksei up to the two men on the precipice above him.

'What?' asked Salomka.

'Just get help,' said Wylie. 'We need a search party.'

Salomka ran off in the direction of the city.

'We've no time,' said Aleksei, eyeing the cave entrances and wondering which to choose. Then a thought occurred to him; a ridiculous long-shot, but the only chance they had. 'Wylie,' he shouted. 'Do you have the book with you? Cain's notebook.'

'I do indeed; it's in here,' replied the doctor, indicating the knapsack he carried over his shoulder.

'Get it out. Expose it to the light.'

'What? Why?' Even as he questioned Aleksei's instructions, he carried them out, unshouldering the bag and bringing out the book, still wrapped in the paper that bore Aleksei's initials.

'Do it,' said Aleksei. 'Now.'

The doctor opened up the paper, and Aleksei saw smoke rising from the book. He couldn't smell the foul odour of decay, but he saw Wylie blench at it.

And there was something else.

As the skin began to blister and burn under the rays of the sun, a distant, tortured scream echoed from one of the cave mouths in the cliffside, just to Aleksei's right. There was a broken exhaustion to the sound, and yet it was still powerful enough to carry from deep within the caves. Wylie clearly heard it too.

'Cover it,' shouted Aleksei.

Wylie did so, and the scream died away almost instantly. They waited a few moments.

'And again,' said Aleksei. Wylie revealed the book's cover to the sun once more, and the howl issued forth from the same cave; louder this time, but even more weary. Wylie quickly drew the paper back over, and Aleksei felt a sense of relief as the sound faded.

'You know what that means?' said Aleksei. The doctor didn't reply, even though he must surely have comprehended. Aleksei spelled it out. 'It's in there; the *voordalak* from which that skin came; still living – still feeling the pain, even though the skin is no longer attached.' He remembered slamming his fist down on those severed fingers, and knew now that Kyesha must have felt that pain, wherever in the world he might have been.

'It must be,' whispered Wylie.

'And wherever that creature is,' continued Aleksei, 'so is Cain. And so's the tsar. I'm going in there.'

'You'll never find them,' said Wylie. 'The cave system is immense.'

'Keep exposing the skin,' explained Aleksei. 'Every half-minute, just briefly, then let it regrow. I can follow the sound to its source.'

Wylie looked down at him, horrified, but nodded in agreement. Aleksei gave him a brief wave goodbye and then slipped into the cave entrance. It was just big enough for him to stand upright. He walked a few paces over the rocky floor, and then reached into his own knapsack. Inside, he had a couple of candles. He lit one and held it up, searching for the path ahead.

From somewhere in front of him, that same scream echoed again, amplified by the close stone walls. It died away quickly. Dr Wylie was doing as he had been asked.

CHAPTER XVIII

THE TUNNEL DIVIDED SEVERAL TIMES ALONG THE WAY, BUT AT each junction Aleksei had only to stop and wait for a few moments until, on the hilltop above him, Wylie once again let sunlight fall upon the skin of the creature that lay imprisoned ahead, and the sound of its wailing would guide him along the correct path. As far as he could tell, he was heading a little south of west, back towards the centre of the citadel itself, and would soon be beneath it, but the incline was steep and he knew he had descended deep under the ground.

Before he had gone very far he realized that, though he had a means of finding his way into the labyrinth, there would be no similar siren voice calling him out. Mostly it would be easy – simply by taking the uphill path he would be able to retrace his steps – but at those few junctions where he felt he might be confused, he drew his knife and marked the rock with an indication of the direction he should go. He hoped he would be able to find the marks again, especially if he was leaving in a hurry.

He'd been going for about ten minutes – using the half-minute regularity of the screams as a clock – when he first noticed the smell; the *voordalak* smell. It wasn't quite the same as the scent of Kyesha, and far stronger – there were many vampires ahead. He had never noticed when he had first dealt with the Oprichniki, but it must have been there. The smell of death that had permeated Moscow at the time would have done much to disguise it. Soon, he noticed that the caves were becoming lighter – not with sunlight, but from lamps and candles. He blew out his own candle and slipped it back into his bag. Now he had both hands free. In each he carried a sword; one of steel, the other of wood; one for Cain, the other for his victims. He had a pistol too, hidden inside his jacket, but the solid feel of a sword in each hand gave him a far greater sense of protection.

Ahead of him, around a corner, he could see the edge of the bright, glimmering circle that indicated there was a lamp hung from the wall. Another scream came, but it was still too distant to be coming from that next chamber.

Aleksei turned the corner. The tunnel widened; a portion to the side was fenced off with an iron grille. There was a heavy lock on the door. It was like a prison cell. An unnecessary simile – it *was* a prison cell. Aleksei took a step towards it and looked inside. It was empty. There had been little work done to the natural shape of the cave in order to adapt it to its new purpose. The stone walls were still rough and jagged. At the far end, where the space tapered to nothing, sat a wooden bowl. It held nothing, but its bloodstained sides gave a clue as to its usual contents. He took a step closer to see if there was anything more of note in there, his face almost brushing against the bars. Another scream came from further ahead, as Wylie once again inflicted his necessary torture.

There was a rush of movement from inside the cell. Aleksei did not see where the creature had come from, but its face was instantly close to his and its fangs were bared. A hand reached through the bars and pressed against the back of Aleksei's skull, dragging him inwards. Aleksei struggled to pull away, and in no time he was free. The creature was weak – starved. It retreated into the cell and crouched in the middle, looking sullen. It was a sad vestige of a human being but still – in the way that every *voordalak* did – it appeared human. A man who had been starved in the same way would have gone into the same decline. The clothes on the creature's body were dirty rags. Its limbs were as thin as sticks and its lips and gums had receded, revealing the only physical feature that did distinguish it from a human – its fangs. A healthy *voordalak* would have been able to hide these behind a charismatic smile and pass itself off amongst mortal men, but this creature had not enough flesh on its lips to bring them together and cover its mouth.

It – Aleksei knew he should think of it as a he, as he would still have considered any other vampire, but the word just did not fit – eyed Aleksei for a few moments and then slunk back towards the cave wall, lying against it with its arms pressed into the crevices. It did not completely vanish, but Aleksei had the benefit of having seen it move there. That must have been how it had hidden when Aleksei first arrived, camouflaged against the stone walls that somehow in the dark matched its sallow complexion. Aleksei had seen that same skill of disguise years before.

He moved on. The tunnel bent round to the right. Again he heard the metronomic scream. The passageway opened out into another small cave. This time there were no bars; the creature was manacled against the wall, suspended by its arms but with its feet also pinioned so it couldn't kick out. The iron of its shackles was twice as thick as would be used to restrain a man; clearly Cain – like Aleksei – was aware of the *voordalak*'s superhuman strength. This specimen appeared well fed. It raised its head from where it had lolled against its chest and fixed its eyes on Aleksei. Behind them shone the intelligence that Aleksei knew could reside in any vampire, and also the malevolence. It looked as though it might speak, but said nothing.

On the wall beside the *voordalak*, at the level of its chest, was a small patch of light, brighter than the candle-lit surroundings. Aleksei traced its source and saw, high on the other side of the cave, a tiny hole through which sunlight was shining. Though they were deep beneath Chufut Kalye, Aleksei realized that he had walked far enough to now be close to the inside of the cliff face itself. Cain would need a source of sunlight to conduct some of the experiments he described, and these caves – situated where

298

they were – would provide the perfect balance of light and darkness. Like a desirable garden, the cliff faced south, and would get the maximum of each day's sunlight.

He looked back at the chained vampire. On the stone wall a number of lines had been chalked. They started on one side of the naked torso, passed behind it and emerged the other side. At the end of each one there was writing. Aleksei peered closer, careful to keep out of range of any slight movement the *voordalak* might be able to achieve. It was a list of dates. Each of the chalked lines that crossed the vampire's body was labelled with one. The dab of sunlight Aleksei had noticed lay exactly on the line with that day's date – 30 October.

It suddenly became clear to Aleksei what was going on. This was a sundial, one that told the date as well as the time. As autumn progressed into winter, the sun would fall lower and lower on the horizon, and the beam would move up the wall. But within each day, the spot of light would move from west to east, following the chalked line for that day, and cutting across the *voordalak*'s body. There were no scars, but that did nothing to remit the pain that would have been inflicted as each day the sun took – what? – five hours to cross that part of the sky, slowly burning the vampire's chest or stomach as it went. It would heal, only for the torture to resume, as sure as day follows night, the following morning.

It reminded Aleksei of a trick he himself had once played to escape a vampire – and a man posing as a vampire. It had involved a beam of light shining through the shuttered window of a house in Moscow, traversing the room as the day progressed and threatening to trap them in a corner. In that instance, they had fled, but for this creature, flight was impossible. Even so, Aleksei shuddered as he perceived how closely his own thinking had run to that of Cain.

He glanced again at the vampire's face. Still it looked at him but did not speak. Above its head something else had been chalked. Aleksei took a step closer, still wary, but desperate to see what

299

was written. The text was in the Latin alphabet, but the name was the same in almost any language. It was a sick joke:

Prometheus

The saddest thing was that Aleksei understood it: Prometheus the Titan, punished by Zeus by being chained to a rock where every day a vulture would fly down and peck out his liver, only for it to regrow each night, ready for the bird to return and feed the next day. Once again, it appeared that his mind and Cain's were cut from similar cloth.

Ahead of him the screaming continued. Aleksei wished he could somehow get Wylie to stop, to communicate to him that he no longer needed that siren guidance. But Wylie could not know, and would not risk leaving Aleksei alone in the silent darkness of the caves before he was certain he had found his way through. Aleksei would have dearly loved it if, like Jason, he had Orpheus to drown out the sound with his lyre, or like Odysseus's crew, he had beeswax to cram in his ears.

The next cave was again divided into cells – two of them this time. In the first a *voordalak* sat alone. It too wore rags, and appeared emaciated. Only bars, not stone, separated it from the next cell, and so it could communicate with its neighbour, if it so desired. It did not do so. It did not even look up as Aleksei passed. The other cell had two occupants – a male and a female *voordalak*. Aleksei had never encountered a female vampire before, but had no reason to suppose that such a creature did not exist. These two were completely naked, and huddled together with unexpected affection at the back of the cave. The female's hair was long and unkempt and covered most of her shame.

Aleksei noticed on the floor of both these cells remnants of fruit and vegetables – a rotten potato here, an olive pit there. It seemed Cain was trying to discover whether vampires could survive on a diet less rich in human blood. A noble goal, but would not the creatures have tried it years ago if it had been possible?

300

He walked on. The tunnel narrowed and then widened again. He was reminded of the dark passageways between the chapels in Saint Vasiliy's. Ahead of him he saw an armchair, made of red leather. It seemed quite incongruous. Beside it was a table, and on the table, a book. As Aleksei moved closer he noticed the image of the chair wobble a little, and realized that he was in fact looking at a reflection. The actual chair was still out of his sight, behind a bulge in the rock face. A huge mirror – it must have cost thousands of roubles – was fixed along the far side of the cave. Aleksei could only guess at how it could have been brought down through the tunnels in one piece.

'Can you see me?' said a voice.

Aleksei whirled round, feeling that the sound had come from behind him, but there was no one there. He looked in every direction but still there was no one. The source could only be in the section of the cave Aleksei could not see; and yet the mirror revealed all of that to him. His grandmother's stories immediately came back to him. Of all of them, this was the most absurd; even to a man like Aleksei, who had believed in the solid reality of the *voordalak* for thirteen years, yet could not conceive how the idea that their image was not reflected in a glass was true.

But as he peered round into the cave, he saw that the chair was not empty. In it sat a woman – a very beautiful woman. Her hair was blonde and she looked like she was in her mid-twenties, though what her real age was Aleksei could not guess. She wore an exquisite gown of velvet and silk, golden, with lace at the neck and cuffs. He eyes were of a scintillating blue, but they betrayed no movement. At first, Aleksei suspected she was blind.

'Can you see me?' she said again, not moving her gaze from straight out in front of her.

'I can't see you in the mirror, but I can see you in the flesh,' he told her.

She stood and turned, and as her eyes fell on him Aleksei realized she was not blind, she had simply been too intently

301

focussed on what she saw in the mirror in front of her to look away.

'What do I look like?' she asked. Aleksei took a deep breath and was about to describe her when she asked a slightly different question. 'Am I beautiful?'

'Yes,' said Aleksei, without the need to prevaricate.

'Still?' she said. Aleksei couldn't provide an answer. 'They call me Raisa Styepanovna,' she said. 'And you?'

'Aleksei Ivanovich.'

She walked towards him, holding out her hand. 'You are a strikingly handsome man, Aleksei Ivanovich,' she said.

The introduction was so natural that Aleksei almost bent down to kiss her hand before he remembered that she was a vampire. He need not have worried. While she was still two steps away from him her head jerked suddenly backwards and she came to an abrupt halt. Her hands went up to her neck and Aleksei saw for the first time the iron band around it that constrained her. It was narrow and could almost be taken for a choker. It even added to her allure. From it, a heavy metal chain, now taut, stretched out behind her to where it was attached to an iron ring fixed to the cave floor.

Aleksei looked to the mirror again. Still there was no sign of Raisa Styepanovna in its image, nor of her beautiful dress, nor even of the chain stretching out behind her. Aleksei saw his own reflection, and those of the chair, a table and a book, but between them, where this beautiful lady stood, all that could be seen was the bare rock wall behind her. Of all the strange phenomena that surrounded the *voordalak*, this seemed the one that most needed the intervention of a discerning god, to intercept those rays of light that carried images of the *voordalak*, her clothes, or anything related to her, but to allow through the more mundane objects that anyone would expect to see.

Another scream came from along the tunnel. Raisa pressed her lips together tightly, and her eye held back a tear. 'Will it never stop?' she said. 'He does it only to torment me.'

302

'I'm not sure he can be blamed for his agony,' said Aleksei.

'But the man who causes it can.' Aleksei presumed she was referring to Cain, and chose not to disabuse her. 'Hasn't he done enough to me?'

'Compared to some that I've seen,' said Aleksei, 'you appear to be living in relative comfort.'

'Hah!' she snapped. 'He told me I would be beautiful for ever – that's why I allowed myself to succumb to one of these dreadful creatures.'

'Your beauty has endured.'

'Yes, but at what cost?'

She stood staring into the mirror, her gaze met only by empty space. 'How do I know that I am beautiful?' she asked, her voice on the edge of hysteria.

He left her to her sorrow and carried on down the tunnel. The scream came again, and this time Aleksei knew it was close, just around the next corner. He gripped the handles of his two swords firmly and stepped through the rock archway. Beyond, he found much that he had seen before. Another natural cell, separated from the tunnel by heavy iron bars. The *voordalak* inside had been given a chair to sit on. This one did not look underfed. It was wearing very little, just torn undergarments, with nothing to cover its top half. And the top half of its body was the strangest thing so far. It was covered in tattoos; some simple lettering, others ornate decorations. Aleksei tried to read some of the text and saw that it was nauseatingly mundane. Along the left side of its belly, parallel with its bottom rib, was a phrase in English simple enough for even Aleksei to understand.

Volume VII

How long would it be before Cain was harvesting that for the covering of his latest book?

The *voordalak* flung its head back and uttered a terrible howl

303

into the air. Dr Wylie was remaining true to his word. Within seconds, it fell silent again. Its head dropped back down and it didn't even see that it was no longer alone.

'I'm sorry,' muttered Aleksei through the bars.

The vampire looked up. It peered at him as though it saw the shapes that formed his body, but could not associate them with any concept it recognized.

'Sorry?' it asked. In appearance, it was in its late twenties; a chubby round face was topped with a blob of dirty, curly blond hair.

'Your pain. It's my fault.'

'It's his fault,' spat the *voordalak*, and flicked his eyes further down the corridor along which Aleksei had been heading.

'Cain?' asked Aleksei. The *voordalak* nodded. 'Is there anything I can do?' Aleksei almost laughed as he heard the question on his own lips.

'Could you give me some water?' It pointed behind Aleksei. He turned to see a full pail and a ladle.

'You drink water?' considered Aleksei; again, it sounded too much like the sort of question Cain might ask. The creature replied, shaking its head.

'No, but it eases the pain. Here' – he indicated the left side of his back – 'this is where the skin came from; one piece, at least.' Aleksei looked where he was shown, but, as was to be expected, there was no scar.

Aleksei turned to fetch the bucket. Even as he did so, another scream shook the cave. He put both his swords into his right hand and then carried the water over with his left, placing the pail on the ground beside the bars, within easy reach from inside. Then he dipped the ladle in and passed it, handle first, to the *voordalak*, knowing he should be wary, but allowing his humanity to overcome his caution.

The vampire reached out and then stopped, staring down at the ladle, or something near to it. It briefly glanced into Aleksei's eyes and then back to what had captured its attention. 'The three-fingered man,' it murmured quietly, almost to itself, staring at Aleksei's left hand.

'You expected me?'

The *voordalak* gritted its teeth in agony, but did not scream out loud. It grabbed the ladle and threw the water over its back, breathing heavily. The water did not hiss or evaporate; there was no heat in the creature's body, only the sensation of it. The true heat was up above them, out in the sun. But the water appeared to alleviate the pain.

'No one expects you, least of all Cain,' it said. 'He pretends you are a myth, but he talks of you.'

'What does he say?'

'Enough for us to know,' said the *voordalak*.

'To know what?'

'That he fears you.'

Aleksandr could not clearly recall the reason he had come here. He had been standing atop the cliffs at Chufut Kalye, gazing down at the valley. He had sensed a presence standing beside him and known it was the figure he had seen in his dream, standing on the prow of the boat, ordering him to come to this place. He had dared not look up into the man's eyes, but it had been unnecessary. The figure had taken him by the hand and led him forward. He felt the cold metal of the gold dragon ring against the flesh of his fingers, even though he knew it had no more substance than the man himself. It had seemed such a simple idea, to take a step forward, to fall and fall and fall down, tumbling over the rocky ground, his spirit coming to rest long before his lifeless body did the same. But that was not where the figure had led him. Instead, they had climbed down a narrow crevice to a ledge on the cliff below.

There Cain had been waiting, aged since their last encounter, in 1812, but unmistakable. The dark figure with the dragon ring had vanished, along with his influence over the tsar, but now there was a far more concrete reason to follow Cain deep into the caves; he carried a pistol. Eventually they had found themselves here, wherever here might be. Along the route Aleksandr had seen no one. His main concern had been to remember the way out – in the hope he'd get the chance to leave.

It was, to be blunt, a cave – but a well-appointed cave. There was a carpet, chairs, tables and a desk; even a clavichord, sitting in the corner, its lid open. All around were items of scientific equipment – smoked glass and polished brass – whose purpose the tsar could not fathom. Curtains and tapestries hung from the walls around, giving a slightly greater sense of it being a room, but they did not cover all the rocky surfaces and so the reminders of Cain's troglodyte existence were never far away.

'You're wise to have come,' said Cain, speaking in French. He had already put down his gun. He wafted his hand towards a chair, indicating that Aleksandr should sit. The chair was wooden, with no cushion. Its high back was intricately carved. It looked medieval. The tsar sat down.

Suddenly, the air was pierced by a howling scream, which came from a doorway to Aleksandr's right. It was not the route they had come by. Cain gave a tight, apologetic smile. He walked over and closed the door, then drew a heavy red-velvet curtain across it. He returned to face the tsar.

'I don't think I really had a choice,' said Aleksandr in response to his earlier comment.

'The choice was offered, but your great-great-grandfather made the decision for you – for all of his heirs.'

'I'm not sure a man can be bound by the promises of his ancestors.'

'You admit Pyotr made a promise then?'

'I'm told that's what your master believes.'

Cain flashed Aleksandr the briefest look of anger, which mellowed into a smile. 'I think the word "employer" more aptly describes our relationship.'

'Just like an Englishman to go into service,' said the tsar, in English. He wondered for a moment whether it might be dangerous to taunt Cain, but discovered in himself no sense of fear. Whatever plan Cain was to execute had been set in place over generations – human generations – and was unlikely to be affected by anything Aleksandr might say now.

'I'd forgotten how excellent your English was,' said Cain, continuing in the same tongue. He changed the subject. 'Would you care for a drink?' He went over to a dresser, atop which were several decanters. It should have been incongruous against the rough stone wall, but somehow the furniture and the decor, after an initial surprise, seemed quite appropriate for their surroundings.

'No, thank you,' said the tsar. As he spoke, he thought he heard the scream again, muffled through the heavy oak door – but he might have imagined it.

Cain turned back to him with a look of disappointment. 'Oh, come now, Aleksandr Pavlovich. Do you think I'm going to poison you? Look!' He pointed to a cabinet on the other side of the cave. 'I have swords and guns. If I wanted to harm you, I wouldn't need to be so subtle as to use poison. Claret?' Aleksandr remained silent. Cain lifted the top from a decanter and poured two glasses. 'You see?' he said, raising one of them to his lips. He took a swig and sucked the wine through his teeth to aerate it. 'It does me no harm.' He walked over to the tsar and placed the wine on the broad arm of his chair.

'Why doesn't your employer come and see me himself?' asked Aleksandr.

Cain nodded towards a grandfather clock that stood behind his desk. It was still mid-afternoon. 'It's not a good time of day for him. But he has made himself known to you; otherwise, why would you be here?'

Aleksandr thought of the dark figure of his dreams and visions, and again of today, when he had been tempted from the cliff top.

'That was the same man that Pyotr met?' Aleksandr asked, though he had no doubt of the truth of it.

'One hundred and thirteen years ago.'

'It's a long time to hold a grudge.' Aleksandr sipped from his glass without thinking, but realized he had little to fear from it. Cain's argument made sense. Besides, it was an exceptionally good wine.

'He has little else to amuse him,' said Cain, slipping a strand of his blond hair behind his ear. 'But it's more than that. If he simply sought revenge then, as you suggest, it would hardly be fair to take it out on Pyotr's descendants. And he would have had ample opportunity to do so before now.'

'So what does he want?'

'He wants what is owed to him. What your great-great-grandfather promised him.'

'That's still not my concern,' said Aleksandr. He took another sip of claret.

'It is when you have in your possession that which is not rightfully yours. That which was promised to my employer and which you have presumed to inherit.'

'And what would that be? I've inherited a lot of things, from many people.' Again, Aleksandr heard the muffled scream outside.

'What Pyotr Alekseevich Romanov promised seemed worth less then than it does now. Yet still he chose the path of betrayal. You must make amends.'

'Tell me then, what is it he wants?' Aleksandr drank again. Now the wine had begun to taste sour – metallic. He feared he already knew the nature of the claim against him.

Cain explained in a single word.

'Russia.'

Aleksei had left the *voordalak* whose skin had provided the binding for Cain's notebook and carried on through the tunnels. There were no more cells or chains, though Aleksei knew he had taken but one path out of the many that penetrated the hillside. There could be a dozen others, each with its own set of miserable, filthy victims. Even from the little he had read of Cain's book, Aleksei understood that the number of experiments being carried out would need more subjects than these few wretches.

Behind him, he no longer heard the sound of screams. With the same regularity, they had been replaced by short, self-controlled gasps, which still conveyed quite persuasively the pain the creature must have been experiencing. The water was evidently bringing some relief – or perhaps the hope Aleksei had seen in its eyes at the arrival of the three-fingered man had made it braver.

The tunnel ended abruptly in a large wooden door. Here, the passageway, though still largely a natural phenomenon, had been dug out so that the door fitted snugly. It would have suited any nobleman's house in Moscow or Petersburg. On the stone of the cave wall above it, more writing had been chalked. The handwriting was similar to that of the word 'Prometheus' earlier. It was most likely Cain's – any slight differences from the book could be explained by the difficulties of writing on rock.

Again, the alphabet was Latin, not Cyrillic, but the language this time was Italian.

Lasciate ogni speranza, voi ch'intrate.

It was an archaic form of the language, somewhat different from that spoken today. In fact, Aleksei could date it very specifically, to the first quarter of the fourteenth century, for the same reason that he did not have to struggle with the translation. It was Dante – *Inferno*; the words written above the gate of Hell.

Abandon every hope, you who enter.

Given the Hell that Aleksei had just walked through, he wondered what greater horrors could possibly lie ahead. He put his ear to the door. He could just hear the sounds of speech, but could discern no distinct words.

He turned the handle and pushed against the door. It moved smoothly and silently – well engineered considering its unconventional housing. Behind it, there was darkness. The voices were clearer now. They were speaking English, but even so Aleksei could recognize one of them as being that of the tsar.

He pushed the door further and realized that the lack of light was down to the curtain that covered the doorway. Looking to its edge, he saw a glimmer of illumination seeping through – artificial, to his best guess, rather than sunlight. He made sure he didn't push the door so far open as to disturb the cloth, and slipped through the narrow gap, closing it behind him. He listened for a while to their conversation, but only occasional words – names, mostly – made sense to him. 'Romanov' was repeated several times, and he heard 'Paul', which he knew to be the English equivalent of 'Pavel'.

There were only two voices to be heard – that of Aleksandr and one other, which Aleksei could only presume belonged to Cain. If those were the only people in the room beyond, then Aleksei felt safe. It would be two against one, and surprise would be on his side. He peeked around the edge of the curtain.

Aleksandr was sitting in a wooden chair with his back to Aleksei. Only the top of his head was visible, slightly tilted as he listened, and his hand, which rested on the arm of the chair and clutched a glass of red wine. Even so, it was unmistakably the tsar. There was no sign of Cain, but Aleksei could still hear his voice. He took a sidestep to get a better view of the room. It looked as though a duke had lost his mansion and been forced to live in a cave. The furnishing was opulent. A chandelier hung from the roof of the cavern, suspended by a long rope. Its owner had made himself comfortable.

Cain stood with his back to the tsar, his hands placed firmly on his desk and his head bent low, hanging from his shoulders. He spoke a few words in English, then raised his head. His blond

310

hair covered his neck, and dangled over the collar of his jacket. He reached forward and picked something up. Aleksei saw it was a knife. Cain spoke again, this time in French.

'And now, Aleksandr Pavlovich, I think we have waited long enough.'

He began to turn, holding the knife as if preparing to stab, though he still had several paces to cover to reach the tsar. The knife itself was terrifyingly familiar.

Aleksei ran from behind the curtain and shouted, 'Your Majesty!' Even as he did so, he recognized a tone in Cain's voice of which there had been only a suspicion when he had been speaking in English.

Cain turned and caught sight of Aleksei. Despite the look of surprise on his face and the years that had passed, the tall physique, untidy blond hair and distant grey eyes made him unmistakable.

It was a face Aleksei had last seen as he thrust it beneath the icy surface of the river Berezina, the face of a man who should not have survived, who should have died a cold, choking death by Aleksei's own hand, thirteen years before. It was a man more degenerate and corrupt than any *voordalak*.

It was Iuda.

CHAPTER XIX

'LYOSHA!'

His voice was full of warmth and the happiness of reunion as he drooled over each syllable of the name, but Aleksei had seen and noted that brief flicker of surprise in Iuda's eyes before he had time to regain his composure. The three-fingered man had arrived, and Iuda was afraid.

'An unexpected pleasure,' he continued. 'What am I saying? An unexpected *delight*.'

'Even less expected for me, I think,' said Aleksei.

'True, true. But don't blame yourself. I was quite convinced you had me. It was pure luck that I managed to . . . wriggle free.' He stroked his head, as if feeling for the gap where those few strands of hair had been ripped out to remain coiled around Aleksei's fingers. He turned and placed the knife back on the desk. Its parallel double blades had, years before, allowed Iuda to inflict injuries that mimicked the bite of a *voordalak*, at a time when Iuda had been trying to pass himself off as such a creature. But Aleksei realized it could not be the knife Iuda had been using then – that had vanished for ever beneath the surface of the Berezina, as its owner should have. It would have been easy enough for him to have made another.

'And how is Mademoiselle Dominique?' asked Iuda. Aleksei had not thought of Domnikiia by the French version of her name for many years, but it was the only way Iuda had known her.

'Thrown over for some newer beauty fresh from the cradle, no doubt.'

Aleksei said nothing, but either Iuda knew already, or could read his expression, or his mind.

'Not yet then,' said Iuda with a smile. Aleksei tried to keep Tamara from his thoughts, for fear that Iuda could indeed read them, but the beautiful red-headed girl rushed into his consciousness. Iuda made no comment, and Aleksei dismissed his paranoia.

'Are you all right, Your Majesty?' he said, turning to the tsar.

Aleksandr stood up. He looked pale and shocked. He nodded thoughtfully to himself. 'Yes, yes, Colonel. I'm very well.' He seemed to grow more confident of it as he spoke. 'You know this man?'

'I'm afraid so,' said Aleksei.

'Some friends of mine and I helped Aleksei to save your country back in 1812,' said Iuda airily. 'Then he turned against us. I was the only survivor.' His tone didn't waver.

The tsar looked over at Aleksei, who gave a slight shake of his head. Nothing that Iuda had said was false, but it would take too long to explain what had really happened.

'I think you should leave, Your Majesty. They're looking for you. You know the way out?'

The tsar nodded. 'I think I can remember it,' he said.

Another scream echoed from the tunnel down which Aleksei had come. Evidently the tattooed *voordalak* had lost the battle to master its pain.

'And tell Dr Wylie he can stop now,' Aleksei added. The tsar looked questioningly. 'He'll understand,' said Aleksei.

Aleksandr walked across the cavern and exited by another doorway. Aleksei was pleased – he did not want the tsar to have to pass by what he had seen. There could be equal horrors down that path too, but if so, Aleksandr would at least already have seen them. It was a risk to let him go unaccompanied, but Aleksei had business to attend to with Iuda alone.

'So, is Cain your real name?' he asked, sitting where the tsar had been. He rested his elbows on the arms of the chair, but still his two swords were ready to strike, and he felt the pistol nestling in his tunic.

'It's a name many know me by.' Iuda leaned back against his desk.

'In England?'

Iuda nodded. 'Yes. I am the real Richard Llywelyn Cain, to the extent that such a person exists.'

'But it's not the name you were born with – simply one you chose to use when dealing with the Romanovs.'

Iuda looked at Aleksei, seemingly trying to judge how much he knew. In reality, Aleksei had no idea what had been going on between the tsar and his captor, but anything that might make Iuda wary could be helpful.

'I am known by *many* names.' He looked at Aleksei pointedly as he stressed the word 'many'. 'But of them all, you know, I think Iuda is my favourite.' He sighed. 'Happy memories.'

'I should have seen the link,' said Aleksei.

'Cain and Iuda? An Old Testament murderer and a New Testament traitor? I suppose there's a connection, but I can't take all the credit. The name Iuda was chosen for me.' He looked away, pondering the question.

'I think I preferred Iuda,' said Aleksei, 'the man, not the name. I presume you are still a man?'

'And not a vampire? As we discussed some years ago, I'm not sure I really see the benefits of such an existence. Though if I did, I would have no qualms about changing my . . . lifestyle. But I'm scarcely older than you, Lyosha; not yet fifty. One day, perhaps, it will be a better state in which to exist, though I have my doubts. When faced with death, I may see things differently, but I have plenty of time before I need to consider how I'm going to deal with my own mortality.'

'Prove it.' Aleksei had long ago learned that Iuda lied with much the same frequency as he spoke. If he were in fact a *voordalak*, and Aleksei judged him to be human, the consequences might prove fatal.

'That I'm not a vampire? How?'

Aleksei looked back at Iuda, then held out the two swords in his hands – one wooden, one steel. 'These should discriminate,' he said.

Iuda swallowed with mocking exaggeration. 'I don't think we need to go that far,' he said. He turned slightly and picked up the knife with which he had been menacing the tsar. Its two blades were sharp. He held his left hand upright, its palm facing towards Aleksei, and moved the knife towards it. For a moment Aleksei thought he was going to witness a repeat of Kyesha's demonstration in Saint Vasiliy's – but in that instance the intent had been to demonstrate that Kyesha *was* a vampire.

Iuda's performance was somewhat more restrained; a tiny scratch, just along the outside of his palm. The blood ran down his wrist and disappeared beneath his cuff.

'"If you prick us, do we not bleed?"' said Iuda. 'We certainly don't heal, as they do.'

Aleksei shook his head. 'Not good enough, I'm afraid. I know a *voordalak* can hold off regrowth if need be. I've read your book, remember?'

Iuda raised both his eyebrows, then smiled benevolently. Damn it! thought Aleksei. Iuda hadn't known he had the book.

'So that's where it got to,' said Iuda. 'But you're right; it's a poor proof.' He put his hand to his lips to clean the blood. It was an ordinary enough action, but it seemed deliberately intended to cast further doubt into Aleksei's mind. Iuda walked over to a high bookcase he had somehow assembled there, deep underground. A ladder lay against it, allowing access to the upper shelves. Iuda climbed the ladder but ignored the books, instead reaching out for a cord that stretched out up to the cavern's ceiling. He tugged at it and above the shelves a curtain was pulled back, allowing Aleksei to see the sky.

'You see,' said Iuda as he descended, 'we're actually very

315

close to the cliff here. As you can imagine, I need light for my experiments.' He climbed down and walked across the room to where the beam of sunlight that had been let in hit the floor. He stood in its rays and held his arms open, smiling up at the sky as if basking in the sun's warmth. The patch of light was wide enough that even his outstretched fingertips did not escape it on either side. If Iuda had been a vampire, he could not have stood there for even a fraction of a second and lived.

'Very well,' said Aleksei. 'Now tell me, what is all this – all this experimentation? And what's it got to do with the tsar?'

'Nothing at all,' said Iuda, almost bemused by the suggestion that it should. 'In my dealings with Aleksandr Pavlovich I am acting merely as an intermediary; as a representative of an old friend. In terms of my discoveries – I have you to thank for that.'

'Me?'

'You inspired me.' He walked out of the sunlight and over to a huge tapestry that covered one of the cavern walls, becoming the foreground to a scene of unicorns and demure maidens. 'You remember when we met in that house in Moscow, when you pulled down the boards over the window and trapped us in the corner of the room?'

'I remember,' said Aleksei. 'Are you saying that's what gave you the idea for "Prometheus" back there?'

'Yes,' replied Iuda, his enthusiasm breaking into his voice, 'but more than that. You inspired me to learn. Don't you remember? You asked so many questions – questions I found myself unable to answer. About how they die – how they breed. I'm not a man who likes to be floored.'

'And so you decided to find out?'

'They are wonderful creatures in many ways – dangerous. Can you imagine how powerful that danger would be if it could be directed?'

'That was Dmitry Fetyukovich's idea when he first brought you to Russia. It didn't work.'

'Really?' replied Iuda. He seemed more nervous than in the past. Perhaps that was a trick of Aleksei's memory, though he doubted it. Every detail of Iuda's persona had stayed with him over the years, engraved on his heart. 'I would suppose that it didn't work for Dmitry because I knew better than he how to direct the behaviour of the brutes,' continued Iuda. 'But not all vampires are brutes, and so one must learn their subtleties.'

Of course, the anxiety that Aleksei perceived in Iuda might still be an artefact of the passing years, not a result of Aleksei's fading memory, but of the ageing process in Iuda himself. What had he gone through since they had last met? Aleksei's instinct was to imagine for him a life of success after perverted success, but the reality could have been very different.

'Now I know their strengths and weaknesses.' Iuda was still speaking, but Aleksei was scarcely listening to his words. Even so, he noticed that the tone was becoming more confident. Was he bluffing now, to cover his unease? Or had the bluff been in the earlier mood?

'The knowledge of their weaknesses protects me from them – makes me almost free to walk amongst them, taking a few sensible precautions. But to know only how they are weak would be of little benefit if I did not also know how they are strong.'

Iuda's voice began to rise with a controlled anger that Aleksei found chillingly familiar.

'That knowledge gives me a far greater power,' he continued. 'It is an understanding of their strengths that makes them, in my hands, an invincible weapon . . . a weapon against anyone who would dare to threaten me!'

As he spoke he reached up and grabbed the edge of the tapestry, pulling it aside. It easily came loose from its fixings and fell to the floor. Behind it was revealed another set of cages, with *voordalaki* within. Aleksei could not see how he operated the mechanism, but in an instant Iuda had unlocked the barred iron gates. There were four of the monsters, and they at first appeared confused, but Iuda shouted directions at them and they turned to face

317

Aleksei. Meanwhile, Iuda crossed to the other side of the room and pulled aside another curtain. Behind that were three more of the creatures, which he released in a similar manner.

'If only I'd known you were coming, Lyosha,' said Iuda, 'I would have had more time. I would have taken such pleasure in chatting with you.' He looked at Aleksei and to all the world seemed sincere in what he was saying. 'But the fact that you let Aleksandr Pavlovich go really does cause problems for me, and I don't have time to deal with you in a more interesting manner. I'm truly sorry.'

Aleksei backed away as the seven *voordalaki* approached him. Converging from either side, they had already cut him off from both the door he had come in by and that by which the tsar had left. The only possibility of safety lay in the patch of light in which Iuda had stood earlier, and that would only protect him until nightfall. Moreover, it would not protect him from Iuda. He had already noticed the pistols in the cabinet against the wall. Iuda would not even have to come within reach of his sword to get rid of him – or wound him and leave him to his fate.

'I will give you one small consolation, however,' continued Iuda. 'When you were attempting to kill me, there was one question on your mind; a question which I was happy to answer, but over which you found yourself quite unable to trust me.'

Though it was already thumping in fear, Aleksei's heart beat a little faster still. That mistrust had been deliberately kindled by Iuda himself, so that Aleksei could never believe what he said and hence never know the answer. And yet now, at the moment of Aleksei's death, perhaps he would tell the truth. What would be the point of lying? Aleksei knew Iuda did not need there to be a point, but still he listened eagerly.

'You saw me at the window with a woman,' said Iuda, 'but you have never been sure who that woman was. At one time you believed it to be Dominique; at another Margarita. You require the truth and now there is no point me keeping it from you. At the moment of your death, you will receive enlightenment. The

318

woman you saw me with was . . .' He grinned and scratched his head. 'Who was it now? Oh yes. It . . .'

'Look!'

The shout, in Russian, came from one of the vampires on Aleksei's left. It pointed out towards him; towards his hand. Aleksei realized in an instant what had caught its attention. He transferred the wooden sword over to his right hand and stood calmly upright, his left palm facing out towards the *voordalaki*.

'The three-fingered man,' murmured one of the creatures.

'What?' asked Iuda, almost laughing. Whatever myths about Aleksei had spread amongst the vampires had not been shared with their master. They hesitated, some stepping back – none moving forward. 'He's just a man. Devour him!'

'A three-fingered man,' said Aleksei. 'Do you fear Cain?' he asked, addressing the vampires. None spoke, but it was obvious they didn't obey him out of love. 'And whom does he fear?' Aleksei asked. He again held up his left hand, swinging it from side to side so that all could see his deformity.

The vampire that had first noticed his fingers turned towards Iuda. Iuda took a step back and the creature advanced, along with two of its comrades. Iuda glanced around. It was difficult to see what power it was he had over them, except perhaps the power of his reputation, and his overblown self-confidence. It was the same authority that Louis XVI had held over France – a bubble of credulity on the part of both the oppressor and the oppressed that could for years allow one to hold sway over the other, and yet which could be burst as soon as enough of them, on either side, saw it for what it was. Perhaps it had only been one brief comment that had revealed to Iuda's captives his fear of Aleksei, even if he had not mentioned him by name. Perhaps the fear itself had not even been real in Iuda – a self-deprecating joke. It did not matter; they believed in that fear, and the presence of the three-fingered man, a myth made real, transformed that belief into certainty.

And once the concept of Iuda's fear became real for his victims, it became just as real for him. It showed itself in his eyes. He

319

stood his ground for a moment, hoping to reverse a tide that he must have succeeded in turning many times before, but quickly understood that, on this occasion, he would fail. He turned and leapt into the cone of sunlight he had basked in earlier. The vampires approached, surrounding him, but not daring to come into contact with the sun's rays. They had forgotten Aleksei for the moment. He walked over, closer to Iuda, but staying back from the circle of *voordalaki*. Iuda crouched, turning from side to side, trying to face an enemy which came from all directions. In his hand he held the knife that was so familiar to Aleksei, with two parallel blades separated by the width of two fingers, razor sharp on the bottom and serrated on the top. It would do him little good against the creatures that now faced him.

'Clinging on to life for just a little longer?' said Aleksei. 'It'll be dark soon; then what will you do?'

'Please, Lyosha,' said Iuda. 'Call them off.'

Several of the vampires looked towards Aleksei expectantly, as if waiting for him to give them such an order, as if they would obey him if he did. Such was the authority of the three-fingered man. But Aleksei had no plans to give any such command.

'They'll turn on you too,' shouted Iuda to him. 'You can't trust them – you know that.'

'I think I can trust them to deal with you. And by then I'll be long gone.'

Suddenly, one of the *voordalaki* screamed. Aleksei smelled the foul, familiar smell of burning vampire flesh. The creature had dared to step up close to Iuda, but as it screamed it fell back. Aleksei looked at Iuda and saw that in his hands he was holding a small looking-glass. He had reflected the sun's rays on to the face of one vampire, and now he was directing them at another. The beam caught Aleksei's eyes, but it was triflingly weak – enough, though, for the *voordalaki*. They began to step back. Wary glances were exchanged between them. One took a step forward, and Iuda flashed the mirror towards it and smoke erupted from its cheek. It screamed and fell away.

'Back to your cells, now,' said Iuda. His voice was calm and firm, like a shepherd talking to his dogs. Whatever tortures he had used to train them – and this trick with the mirror could only be a small part of it – had broken their wills sufficiently that some of them now began to obey, returning awkwardly to the cages from which he had released them. Soon it would be just man against man – Iuda and Aleksei. It was a fight Aleksei felt comfortable he could still win, but he would be a fool to yield such an advantage.

'Oh, for Heaven's sake!' he shouted, marching over towards Iuda. He brought the flat of his blade down sharply on Iuda's hand. The mirror flew to the ground and shattered, its fragments cascading across the stone floor before coming to rest. Iuda snatched back his hand and rubbed it. Aleksei wondered why he had chosen not to use the edge of his sword and sever the man's hand – it seemed no less brutal than leaving him to be devoured by his former prisoners, as Aleksei assuredly intended to do.

It was a simple enough action to break the mirror, but one that would have been impossible for any of the vampires. The fact that it was done by Aleksei – the three-fingered man – might have added something to their bravura as well. Once more they advanced on their former master.

'You're going to have to stick around, I think, Lyosha,' said Iuda. 'To keep an eye on things. I can easily control *this* lot.'

Aleksei noticed the unusual stress in what Iuda had said. '*This* lot?' he queried.

'All of them,' replied Iuda quickly; too quickly. It would make sense that the vampires Iuda left in here – the ones he had felt assured enough of to release and set on to Aleksei – would be the ones he had made most subservient to his will. But they could not all be like that. The more assertive ones – the more dangerous ones – he would keep separately, locked in a separate cell, or manacled to a wall. Aleksei headed for Iuda's desk and began searching it.

'What are you doing?' said Iuda. His fear revealed he had some inkling of what Aleksei had worked out.

'Looking for your keys,' said Aleksei.

'You won't find anything there.'

But Aleksei already had, in one of the drawers: a bunch of five different-sized keys on a large iron ring. They looked medieval compared with the keys of modern locks, but they evidently did their job. He snatched them up and headed back to the door he had come in by.

'No, Aleksei!' shouted Iuda after him, but Aleksei was already gone.

He came first to the tattooed monster with which he had spoken. It was sitting down again, but looked up when it heard Aleksei approach.

'The pain has stopped,' it said.

'Good,' replied Aleksei, but though the word was intended for the *voordalak*, the sentiment behind it was relief that the tsar must have spoken to Wylie – and that meant the tsar was safe.

Aleksei tried one of the keys in the lock, but it didn't work. 'Do you know which one it is?' he asked.

'No,' said the vampire, shaking its head. Then it leapt to its feet with sudden realization. 'You're freeing me?'

'I'm freeing all of you,' he said, moving on to the second key. It was bizarre to hear himself saying it. How many *voordalaki* were there down here? He had seen over a dozen, but there would be more in other caves. Once they had taken their revenge on Iuda – Cain, as they knew him – then they would be free to revert to their normal way of living; living off the blood and flesh of humans. Did he really care? Not enough. They deserved some chance of retribution, but after that they would fend for themselves. If they attacked humans, then humans would destroy them – so it had been through the centuries. Aleksei himself would gladly assist in their extermination, but not today.

The third key did the trick. The door swung open. The vampire stood there, considering its freedom, wary of it and perhaps of Aleksei too.

'They've got Cain cornered in there,' said Aleksei. 'But they're afraid of him.'

'We were all afraid of him, but not now.' The creature ran out of its cage. Aleksei instinctively took a step back, but it didn't seem to notice. 'We'll need more help,' it said.

They carried on down the corridor and soon came to where Aleksei had encountered Raisa Styepanovna. She was sitting in her chair, reading. Aleksei glanced into the mirror again, but saw only the empty cave and its incongruous furnishings. Of the woman whose beauty was so obvious when he looked at her directly, there was nothing. He ran over to her, lifting up her hair to find the fetter around her neck.

'Sir!' she exclaimed shrilly. 'You presume too much.'

Aleksei had already found the small lock. There was only one key in the bunch that could possibly fit it, and she was free in moments. Aleksei rushed on, now with two vampires in tow. He opened the cages of the three *voordalaki* that had been fed on vegetables, but they seemed even more fearful now that the gates were open than they had been before. Aleksei had no time to convince them of their good fortune.

He could do nothing for 'Prometheus'. There were no locks on his manacles. They had been forged as single rings of metal. They must have been hammered into shape after his wrists had been slipped inside them.

'There's no time,' said Aleksei.

'We'll do what we can later,' the tattooed vampire told him.

Lastly, they came to the cell of the creature that had attacked him – that had camouflaged itself so effectively against the wall. Aleksei was wary to go near.

The *voordalak* whose screams had led Aleksei down into this pit in the first place spoke. 'We'll deal with it,' it said. 'There are many others of us down here. I'll release them all. Cain will not escape.'

Aleksei looked at the creature. It was absurd to trust a vampire, but if they were not to be trusted then it would be foolhardy to stay. Their hatred of Iuda seemed genuine enough, and that would make their actions over the next few hours pleasingly predictable.

Aleksei nodded. 'Thank you,' he said, then turned and ran back up the tunnel which he had descended scarcely an hour before.

'Thank you!' he heard called from behind him, but he did not stop to look back. He didn't stop to check the tiny scratch marks he'd left to guide his way out; instinct told him the correct path.

Only when he saw the light of day streaming in through the end of the tunnel and finally made it outside – pressing himself against the cliff face to avoid falling from the narrow ledge – did he stop, and take in huge, grateful lungfuls of the cool, fresh Crimean air.

CHAPTER XX

THE ROYAL PARTY HAD LEFT THE CITADEL BY THE TIME ALEKSEI returned to it. It was the right thing to do – Wylie might have been tempted to stay and wait for Aleksei to emerge from the caves, but his duty was to ensure that the tsar got safely away.

They were almost halfway back to Bakhchisaray when Aleksei caught up with them. They had stopped and dismounted at the Uspensky Monastery, which they had passed by on the way up to Chufut Kalye. The previous day the tsar had attended a Mohammedan ceremony in the khan's palace. Earlier today he had been taking tea with Jews, and now he was going to visit an Orthodox chapel. It was not a reflection of the make-up of his nation as a whole, but the Crimea had had too many masters over the years to settle upon any one god.

The most remarkable thing Aleksei observed was the dutiful calmness with which Aleksandr was continuing his activities. He asked the usual, polite questions of the priests and the monks, and showed great interest in the architecture. Like so much in the area, the monastery was built into natural caves in the rockface. For a moment, Aleksei feared there might be some subterranean path back to Iuda's lair, but it was unlikely. They were on the other side of the valley from Chufut Kalye, and any tunnel would have had to go around it, or underneath it. It was at that moment that the tsar first caught sight of Aleksei, across the open courtyard.

Only a raised eyebrow indicated he had any recollection of the events they had both witnessed that day.

Wylie caught up with him as they were all treated to an impromptu lecture on the history of the building from one of the older priests.

'You're all right then, I see,' he said.

'Nothing broken,' said Aleksei.

'You can imagine my relief when His Majesty returned.'

'How is he?'

'He seems perfectly well; a little distracted perhaps. He won't tell me anything of what happened.'

'Did he explain his absence?' asked Aleksei.

'He just said he'd gone exploring and complained that Colonel Salomka had panicked.'

'I suppose he wasn't down there for very long.'

'You met Cain?' asked the doctor.

Aleksei nodded.

'What happened?'

'Some of his experiments got a little out of hand.'

'You mean . . . ?' gasped Wylie.

The priest had taken them to a long flight of steps that led up to the chapel itself. He had begun to ascend. Aleksandr was just behind him, followed by Tarasov and Salomka. Aleksei and Wylie were next.

'I don't think Richard Cain will be making any more presentations to the Royal Society. Even so, I'd very much like for us all to be off these damned mountains before nightfall.'

'Of course,' said Wylie. 'Did His Majesty witness any of this?'

'No, I sent him away almost . . .'

In front of them, Tarasov and Salomka suddenly rushed forward. The priest turned back to see what the commotion was. Aleksandr had collapsed. Tarasov loosened his collar and Wylie dashed forward with a bottle of sal volatile, which he waved under the tsar's nose. Aleksei felt his own approach was a little more practical. From his pocket he fetched a small flask of brandy, from which the tsar took a grateful sip. The whole incident was over in moments, and the tsar was back on his feet before any but those in the closest proximity to him could even notice what had happened.

'I really must apologize, gentlemen,' he said, continuing his climb of the stairs, but stopping almost immediately to catch his breath. 'I have overstretched myself a little.'

Wylie glanced at Aleksei. 'A delayed shock, you think?'

'It's only to be expected.' Aleksei thought for a moment. 'Perhaps it will do us a favour – persuade the tsar to return sooner.'

'Let's hope,' said the Scotsman.

But as the others moved on, Aleksei paused for a moment, standing on the steps at the point where Aleksandr had fainted. Just ahead of him, at the top of the stairway, was a small gatehouse, and to the left of the gate he saw what Aleksandr must also have seen. It was a ubiquitous sight in Moscow, but it was not uncommon elsewhere in Russia either. Only recently, Aleksei had been considering its echoes in a statue in Petersburg. But this was the first time he had suspected that the image might mean to Tsar Aleksandr something akin to what it meant to Aleksei himself.

It was an icon; an icon of a saint on horseback driving a spear into the mouth of a monster. An icon of Saint George and the dragon.

After his collapse, the tsar most certainly did appear to take a more cursory interest in the sights before him. After the monastery they directly began their journey back to Bakhchisaray, with only a few farewell waves to the local people hindering them in any way.

Once they were back down in the river valley that would lead them to the town, Aleksei and Wylie rode side by side in discussion. Aleksei briefly described what had happened. He did not mention his previous meeting with Cain, under a different name. Wylie shared Aleksei's ambivalence as to how the problem had been resolved. In the end he concurred with Aleksei's decision

– or at least said he did. For him, hatred of the *voordalak* was not as entrenched as it was in Aleksei, but neither had he seen for himself the piteous specimens in those caves. So though he might have weighed the two sides of the argument differently, in the end he came to the same conclusion. What was most important, they both agreed, was that it was Cain who had been the main threat to the tsar and that he was a threat no longer. Aleksei felt more relaxed than he had riding out along the same road that morning.

As might be expected from a man of science, Wylie showed a keen interest in what Iuda had been trying to discover, if not in his methods. When Aleksei mentioned Raisa Styepanovna and her absent reflection, Wylie began to describe one of the experiments from the notebook.

'As you said,' he explained to Aleksei, 'it seems very selective in terms of what can be seen and what cannot. Why can't you see their clothes, for example? And in the end you're right, an intelligent selection is being made – the interesting question is, by whom?'

'How do you mean?'

'Well, Cain's thought is – was – that it's the mind of the viewer that blocks out the image of the vampire. So you *do* actually see the creature, in terms of the light falling into your eyes, but your brain blots it out. For what reason, he couldn't tell. The point is, the viewer's brain isn't going to be so stupid as to just remove the vampire and leave its clothes standing there empty, or indeed the chain stretching out in the case you described. The brain is trying to protect the viewer in some way, so it presents a coherent picture of the scene – sans vampire.'

'But how could he test that?' asked Aleksei.

'Well, first he thought he'd do it by having people who didn't know that the creature they were seeing was a vampire look at one in a mirror. If they didn't know it was a vampire, then why should the brain block it out?'

'And the result?'

'Didn't make any odds. If the viewer was a human or a vampire, informed or uninformed, they still saw nothing.'

'Concept disproved then,' said Aleksei.

'Well, Cain was a bit more meticulous than that. It could be that the information that they're looking at a vampire is communicated to them by some means other than their prior knowledge.'

'Smell perhaps?'

'A possibility, though Cain didn't get that far. What he did do was sheer, unadulterated genius.' To Aleksei's distaste, Wylie didn't even attempt to hide the admiration in his voice. 'He got hold of a children's toy, a *diable-en-boîte* – a jack-in-the-box we call it in English. You know the sort of thing – you wind it up and then, after a random period of time, a little man pops out and scares the children. The point is though, it's random. Even if you know it's going to pop out, you can't predict when.'

'I know what you mean,' confirmed Aleksei.

'So,' continued Wylie, 'he puts the box on a shelf and then lets the viewer – himself in the early experiments, but others later – look at the scene through a mirror. Then the vampire, your lady Raisa Styepanovna, I suppose, walks in and stands in front of the *diable-en-boîte*. The viewer then describes what they see – of course they don't see the vampire, they just see the shelf behind with the box on it. Finally Raisa walks away to reveal whether the devil has popped out of the box.'

'So?'

'Well, if the viewer had no idea that box was a *diable-en-boîte*, then universally they never saw it pop open. They looked in the mirror and just saw a box on a shelf. When the vampire walked away, they were surprised when the box suddenly appeared open – most believed it had popped open at that instant. On the other hand, those who did know the box might potentially pop open did sometimes see it do so. But they were wrong just about 50 per cent of the time. Some saw it open when it didn't, some didn't when it did. Some got it right. And it doesn't matter if the viewer is a human or another vampire.'

'I still don't see what that proves,' said Aleksei.

'It proves Cain's theory. The viewer couldn't see the box at all, because the vampire was in the way. So their mind had to re-create the scene behind the vampire from what it remembered before she came in. Thus, if they didn't know the box could pop open, it just stayed closed the whole time. If they did know, then they subconsciously made a guess as to when it opened, and persuaded themselves that that was what they had seen. And of course, half the time, the guess was wrong.'

Aleksei tried to get his head round the idea. Occasionally he thought he had grasped it, but then it eluded him. 'I'll have to think about that a little,' he confessed. For now, despite that three-word Latin motto, he would take Dr Wylie's word for it. He had seen Raisa Styepanovna, and her beautiful dress, and the iron ring around her throat and the chain stretching back from it in the mirror, but he had convinced himself he hadn't.

'The book!' he exclaimed, suddenly remembering. Wylie turned and looked at him. 'When I went back,' Aleksei continued, 'when I looked in the mirror, her book was on the table. But when I looked at her, she was reading it.'

'So your mind,' explained Wylie, 'didn't make the book invisible, or leave it dangling in mid-air, but put it in the sensible place – on the table.'

'Cain was a very clever man.' Aleksei had to catch himself – he'd almost said 'Iuda'.

'He was about to move on to experiments with silver salts, but then the book ends.'

'Silver?'

'*Lapis lunaris*, that sort of thing,' said Wylie, as if Aleksei would understand such things beyond recognizing the name. 'They react to light. I'm not sure what he was planning. The big question in my view is how does the viewer know they're looking at a vampire even if they haven't been told? Your idea of smell is an interesting one. And why does it only happen in mirrors? Why aren't vampires just invisible all the time?'

'You're not thinking of picking up where Cain left off, are you?' asked Aleksei grimly.

'It might be tempting,' mused Wylie, 'but I suspect I might have you to answer to if I did. And I wouldn't want to end up like *him*.' He nodded back the way they had come as he spoke.

Aleksei glanced over his shoulder, and then ahead of them to where the sun, though not yet setting, was low in the west. It would no longer be shining through that hole in the rocks and giving Iuda his cosy shell of protection. And without that protection, there would be nothing to stop the entire horde of *voordalaki* from having their first decent meal in years. He wished he could have been there to see it.

*   *   *

> '"*Princess, I know the fault not thine*
> *That Giray loves thee, oh! then hear*
> *A suppliant wretch, nor spurn her prayer!*
> *Throughout the harem none but thou*
> *Could rival beauties such as mine*
> *Nor make him violate his vow;*
> *Yet, Princess! in thy bosom cold*
> *The heart to mine left thus forlorn,*
> *The love I feel cannot be told,*
> *For passion, Princess, was I born.*
> *Yield me, Giray then; with these tresses*
> *Oft have his wandering fingers played,*
> *My lips still glow with his caresses,*
> *Snatched as he sighed, and swore, and prayed,*
> *Oaths broken now so often plighted!*
> *Hearts mingled once now disunited!*"'

Aleksei recognized the words as soon as he heard them. It was Pushkin – *The Fountain at Bakhchisaray*, published just the previous year. It was apt in more ways than one. The first was the most obvious; that even as he heard the words, Aleksei was sitting in a courtyard, enjoying the fading warmth of the autumn twilight, sipping at a local vodka of which he planned to take home with him at least a bottle and listening to the trickle of the very Fountain of Tears that had inspired Pushkin when he had visited the town.

But more than that, the subject of the poem itself could not help but suggest comparisons to Aleksei's own life. Zarema, the former favourite of the Khan Giray, had crept into the bedchamber of his new love, the captured Polish princess Maria. Zarema was begging Maria to reject Giray, in the hope that once his love for this new beauty had proved to be a passing fancy, he would return once again to Zarema.

Would Marfa, if she knew, creep into Domnikiia's room and beg her to abandon Aleksei, in the hope that he would return to her? Was Marfa Zarema, Domnikiia Maria and Aleksei himself Giray? The comparison broke down on many points. Marfa knew nothing of Domnikiia, nor had she lost Aleksei's love. And where would Marfa's new love, Vasya, fit into the analogy? But the biggest difference was that, though Maria did not love Giray, Domnikiia did love Aleksei. For her to abandon him would not be some casual act of indifference, but a dagger to her heart.

At least, so Aleksei hoped. Again today Iuda had taunted Aleksei, offering to tell the truth about Domnikiia. Aleksei had been tempted to listen, but would still have believed what he wanted to believe. And now Iuda was dead – truly dead, and more aptly than by having been drowned in a freezing river. He had died at the hands – at the tearing claws and ripping teeth – of creatures that in 1812 he had tried to emulate and in 1825 had tried to subjugate. But now he was no more. The tsar was safe, and Aleksei felt at peace.

But it was not only the words of Pushkin's poem that Aleksei had recognized. The voice that spoke them, from somewhere out of the shadows to his left, was also unmistakably familiar.

Kyesha stepped into view.

'You're alive,' he said, 'so I presume Cain is dead.'

332

'Maybe not yet,' said Aleksei. 'It depends on just how merciful your friends are feeling.'

'You left him to them?'

Aleksei nodded.

'Then I doubt they'll have finished with him just yet – though they will be hungry. He may have inadvertently saved himself a little suffering when he starved us.'

'Can you tell me the full story now?' asked Aleksei.

'I'm not sure that's wise. Now Cain is dead, surely we are enemies again.'

Aleksei thought about it. His plan in Moscow had been to kill Kyesha, simply for the reason that he was a *voordalak*. Kyesha had led him to Iuda, but that didn't change what Kyesha was. But Aleksei was in no mood for killing.

'Tomorrow, perhaps,' he said. 'We can remain allies for today. He was Iuda, when I first knew him.'

'I didn't know that. All I learned was from conversations we had, early on.'

'Early on?'

'To begin with, he posed as a vampire,' said Kyesha.

'He's done that before.'

'He recruited many of us quite willingly. We helped him assemble everything that you saw up there in the caves. It was a huge task – but he had money as well as our labour.'

'And then the experiments started?'

'At first it was all voluntary. A lot of what he did was pain-free; investigating reflections, sleeping patterns, religious imagery. Then he asked for volunteers for experiments that involved a greater degree of physical intervention. Many agreed; there was no risk of permanent damage and some saw it as a badge of honour to be able to withstand the pain. All of us thought that, ultimately, knowledge of our own nature would make us stronger.

'But then, imperceptibly, a division began to emerge between us. Cain – Iuda – orchestrated it, though none of us was ever aware explicitly. There were those who carried out the experiments, and those who actually *were* the experiments. Guards and prisoners, Cain called it, but only much later on. I was lucky – I suppose – to be one of the guards. But when there were only a few of us left, and we began to realize what had happened, he rounded us all up and locked us away too. He has the place rigged with various ways for letting in light.'

'I saw,' said Aleksei.

'Of course, we thought it would have the same effect on him as on us. It was only too late we discovered he was human. By then we couldn't do anything about it. That was six years ago.'

'But you escaped.'

'Earlier this year. He made a mistake. He had me chained up by the wrists, and in a cave where daylight could get in. Each day it would burn me, and each day I'd recover. I don't know what he learned from it. Much of what he did was just to terrorize – to keep us to heel.'

'He's doing much the same thing again now,' said Aleksei.

'With one major difference, I suspect. He made the chain too long – gave me that little bit of freedom, and I grabbed at it. One morning, when the sun first crept into the cave, I clenched my fists and thrust them into the light. You saw me cut off my own fingers, but that was nothing. I stood there as my hands dissolved into a stinking mess that seeped on to the floor. Oh, I knew they'd regrow, but I still felt every scintilla of pain that you would if you thrust your hands into a fire and held them there until they shrivelled to nothing.'

Aleksei looked at his own hands as Kyesha spoke. It was a horrible concept.

'In the end though,' continued Kyesha, 'I was free. The manacles just slipped off. I ran and hid somewhere deep in the caves, whimpering in agony. It took two days for my hands to grow back. You've seen how quickly it can happen, at least for my fingers, but that was when I was healthy and well fed. When you're starving, the whole thing slows down – sometimes even stops completely. That's another thing Cain discovered.'

'And how did you get hold of Cain's notebook?'

'Raisa Styepanovna helped me with that.'

'I met her,' said Aleksei.

'You did? A beautiful woman. It was I who actually turned her into one of us, though it was Cain that persuaded her. Thankfully, when she realized the awfulness of what had been done to her, it was him, not me, that she blamed. We are close, as any vampire is to the one that created it; as any child is to its parent. For instance, I can tell you with absolute certainty that she is still alive.'

'Really? Where?'

'That much, I don't know. Some can develop the bond to a very precise extent, but it takes much practice.'

'So how did she help you?' asked Aleksei.

'She told me where he kept the notebook – just the one he was working on; the others were locked away. Plus some other documents.'

'What other documents?'

'How do you think I knew where your meetings were, and the codes for them? But we knew you were the only person who could defeat Cain – at least, that's what *he* thought.'

'But you said you didn't know my name.'

'No, but Cain had said a lot about Maksim Sergeivich Lukin, and particularly about his death in Desna. He said you blamed yourself for it.'

'Yet he still never told you who I was?'

'You were just the three-fingered man. And the only clue about Maks was that he came from Saratov. So once I was free, I went there. His mother was dead, but I found one of his sisters. She told me about their poor little brother Innokyentii Sergeivich, and when I mentioned a man with three fingers, she told me all about you.'

'And that's when you came to Petersburg?'

'Yes, but from what Cain said, you weren't likely to treat me any differently from how you had all those other vampires. Hence the somewhat long-winded introduction.'

335

'You realize you've helped to save the tsar's life,' said Aleksei.

'Do I get a medal?'

'You get to live.'

'Perhaps a good point to say goodbye,' said Kyesha.

'What will you do now?'

'Meet up with some of my friends that you've freed. I thought I would have heard from them by now.'

Aleksei didn't ask how Kyesha expected to be contacted by them. 'Probably having too much fun with Iuda.'

'Probably.' He held out his hand but Aleksei did not take it. 'I will try to make sure our paths never cross again. Really.'

With that, he disappeared into the shadows.

CHAPTER XXI

FROM BAKHCHISARAY THE PARTY HEADED BACK FOR TAGANROG, but with no greater haste than it had travelled out. Aleksei had not had an opportunity to speak to the tsar about what had happened in Chufut Kalye. Wylie had attempted to do so, but Aleksandr had been prepared to tell him nothing.

The day after they left Bakhchisaray they were back at the Perekop isthmus, in the town of Perekop itself. The tsar made a tour of the local hospital, accompanied by both Drs Wylie and Tarasov. After they came back, Wylie spoke to Aleksei with some concern.

'His Majesty suddenly shows a great interest in malaria,' he said.

'Is that unusual?' asked Aleksei. 'It's his duty to take an interest in whatever his subjects are interested in. He was in a hospital and in the south. It's a common enough disease round here.'

'Yes, but in these situations, the duty of the tsar is to ask simple questions and nod politely at the answers. Today he's been suggesting that malaria is a disease of the blood, for Heaven's sake! The doctors could scarcely contain their laughter. Even you must know it's borne in the foul air that comes from the swamps round here.'

Like most soldiers – especially those who'd fought south of the Danube – Aleksei was familiar with the disease, and the tricks for avoiding catching it, though it was still a lottery; one in which

Aleksei so far had been a winner. However, Aleksandr's mistake didn't seem too concerning to him.

'So, he got it wrong,' said Aleksei. 'Probably heard it off some quack and thought he'd show off his knowledge. Maybe Dr Lee said something to him.'

'Dr Lee is an acknowledged expert on the subject,' said Wylie, with some indignation.

'I'm sorry, but I don't see why it's such a concern.'

'Because of the mention of *blood*. There is a disease – if I may call it that – which we know full well is carried in the blood; one with which the tsar has recently come into close contact.'

'And from which he is suffering no symptoms. Believe me, I would know.' Even as he spoke, Aleksei wondered if he was being overconfident.

'I'm not suggesting he is, but I think he may be *concerned* that he is. Did you hear any of what he and Cain were discussing?'

'They were speaking English most of the time. The only thing I heard in French suggested that Cain was about to kill His Majesty. That's when I intervened.'

'So before that, Cain could have said something that put this idea into the tsar's head.'

Aleksei shrugged. 'Possibly, but I think it will be out of his head again pretty soon. He's not one to perceive illness where there's nothing there, is he?'

'Quite the reverse, I would say,' replied Wylie. 'Even so, I shall mention my fears to Tarasov.'

'Will he believe you?'

'I won't convey to him the unusual facts we know unless it is absolutely necessary. But if it does prove necessary, I think I'll find it just as easy to convince him as you did me; and by the same method.'

Aleksei considered for a moment whether to protest at the cruelty of this approach now that they understood the physical pain that would be caused to the *voordalak* who had donated his skin in the book's manufacture, but he realized that that was not the true nature of his objection. What he really didn't like was the way control of events was suddenly being taken out of his hands. *He* was the expert on vampires, and if consultation were needed with a second doctor, then *he* should seek it.

But he knew his place. The man he was talking to was personal physician to the tsar. It was a more influential role than that of some secret policeman, however much he might have assisted His Majesty.

And what did he care? If the tsar believed himself to be a chicken, a chimpanzee or a Chinaman, it would be a problem for Russia, but not one that was Aleksei's responsibility. If he thought himself to be a *voordalak* then, again, it was nothing to do with Aleksei. Aleksei's duty lay in dealing with the monsters of reality, not of the mind. And there his duty had been fulfilled.

Aleksei saw for himself the tsar's preoccupation a few days later. They had quit the Crimea and were now only a few days from Taganrog. The party had stopped for lunch and all of its more senior members – colonels included – were sitting at the same table. It was Aleksandr himself who raised the issue.

'You recall that demonstration of the effectiveness of quinine that Dr Lee showed us,' he said, addressing his words to Wylie.

'I recall it,' replied the doctor, though Aleksei suspected a note of caution concerning the subject that the tsar might be turning to.

'Well, I have heard that one of the limitations of the substance is that it tastes so foul. Patients simply will not drink it.'

'It's not exactly foul, Your Majesty, merely bitter. The flavour can be disguised, but even on its own it is not unpalatable.'

'I find that very hard to believe,' responded the tsar. 'Let's find out. Do you have any?'

Wylie exchanged a glance with Tarasov, and the latter left the table and went out of the room. Aleksei watched him out of the window, going through one of the bags strapped to the back of his carriage. He returned moments later carrying a jar containing a white powder. The tsar opened it up and, having licked his finger, dabbed it in and put a little of the substance on his tongue.

He pulled a grimace, like some child who had encountered a new and harsh flavour – obviously exaggerated – and all round the table laughed. After he had flamboyantly recovered himself, he spoke to Tarasov.

'You and Wylie certainly don't go out of your way to spoil patients with pleasant-tasting medicines.'

Again there was laughter at the table and when it subsided the conversation moved on elsewhere, but Aleksei noticed – as he suspected did both Wylie and Tarasov – that the tsar never returned the jar of quinine.

Aleksei had grown a little saddle-sore after two weeks on the road. There was a spare coach, which on the way out had been packed with provisions that had now dwindled to almost nothing, and so he chose to journey on in there for a little while. He had quickly found it to be, if anything, less comfortable than riding on horseback. On these uneven roads, at least a horse had the ability to pick its way between the potholes.

It was early evening before they changed horses. Soon after they had stopped, Aleksei's slumbers were interrupted as first Wylie and then Tarasov clambered into the carriage.

'Look at this,' said Tarasov. He held out what appeared to be the jar of quinine.

'So His Majesty returned it to you,' replied Aleksei. 'Good.'

'But look how much is missing,' insisted Tarasov. 'He's taken five or six doses.'

'Is that dangerous?'

'Probably not,' said Wylie, still with the same urgency that his colleague had conveyed. 'If he's got any sense he'll have kept them for later use rather than take them all together. The point is his state of mind.'

'You still think he believes he . . .' Aleksei glanced at Tarasov '. . . has malaria?'

'Don't worry,' said Wylie. 'I've explained everything to Dr Tarasov.'

'Even so,' persisted Aleksei, 'it could just be malaria.'

'It could,' replied Wylie, 'except for this.' He took out the notebook he had been carrying under his arm. He glanced at Tarasov, who pulled down the blinds on his side of the carriage. Aleksei did the same on the other side. It was probably dark enough for the skin not to be damaged, but privacy was also an issue. Wylie unwrapped the paper and flicked through the book, quickly finding the page he wanted. He held it open under Aleksei's nose.

'Look,' he said. 'Look at that.'

Aleksei shrugged, reminding Wylie of his lack of understanding of English.

'Oh, I'm sorry,' said Wylie. 'I'll summarize for you. It's a section describing how this affliction – vampirism, if you will – may be transmitted from one individual to another. Apparently blood must be exchanged, each consuming the other's, and then death must follow within a certain time period for the full transformation to take place. Otherwise the effect of the blood expires.'

'That much I worked out for myself,' said Aleksei, not mentioning that he also knew it from experience. 'Cain couldn't determine what that period was though.'

'No, but he does say this: "Perhaps unsurprisingly, this period can be substantially shortened if the subject of the potential induction" – that's the word he uses for it throughout – "if the subject of the potential induction consumes a standard dose of quinine at regular intervals during this period. I would conjecture that the effect works by the same mechanism as does the similar action of quinine on malaria, but I have not yet considered how to verify this."'

Wylie looked at Aleksei, and the latter could not help but accept that there might be some connection.

'You haven't shown His Majesty this, have you?' he asked.

'No, but I'm wondering if Cain might not have told him the

same information – or if he might have got it from elsewhere. He clearly knows more than he's saying.'

'It's been four days since he was with Cain,' said Aleksei. 'You'd think he might have acted sooner.'

'Perhaps he did,' said Tarasov. 'There was another bottle missing from my case. I noticed it a couple of days ago, but I didn't make the connection until now.'

'But it's inconceivable,' said Wylie, 'that he would actually imbibe any of the blood of these monstrous creatures.'

'He drank some wine!' said Aleksei in an excited whisper. 'Cain must have given it to him.'

'You think the blood could have been in that?'

'It's possible, but as you say, that's only half the story. He would have had to have been bitten by a vampire – and Cain was threatening to kill him with a knife. That doesn't fit with what you've got there.'

'True enough,' said Wylie. 'And I've read the whole thing cover to cover. There may, of course, be something in earlier volumes. And I've given His Majesty a cursory examination since his return; there is no sign of any physical wound.'

'Anyway,' added Aleksei, 'the tsar's safe now. Cain is dead and no longer a threat. If His Majesty has been taking quinine, all the better. If not, the blood will eventually leave him anyway.'

Wylie was about to reply, but was silenced by the sound of a horse riding past at high speed. The three men glanced at one another in concern. It was Aleksei who looked out to see what was happening.

Aleksandr tried to sleep. He still felt unwell, but he was certain the worst had passed. If it had been Tarasov's drug or simply time taking its course, he did not know. Soon they would be on the move again, within two days they would be back at Taganrog, and he would be with Yelizaveta Alekseevna once again.

But the danger had not passed for good. Cain had been only a servant, and his master – his employer, as he had taken such pains to put it – could recruit other servants to do his bidding. Time was not on Aleksandr's side.

There was a knock at his carriage door.

'Yes?' he said.

'Dispatches, Your Majesty,' shouted Diebich's voice.

Aleksandr opened the door and stepped down from the carriage. It was always wise to accept dispatches from the rider in person. The officers who brought them often rode alone over many versts, never to see the face of the dignitary for whom they were carrying such vital documents. For a middle-ranking officer to carry dispatches to the tsar, only in the end to hand them over to one of his aides, did not make a good story to tell his grandchildren. To see His Majesty in person would cheer him no end – and might make him travel a little faster on his next mission.

The fellow was a major. Aleksandr asked his name.

'Maskov, Your Majesty. They told me at Taganrog that you'd be returning soon, but I thought it best to try to intercept you.'

'Well done, Major Maskov,' said Aleksandr, glancing at the various papers. 'Some of these are most urgent. You'll be returning with us, I take it?'

'Yes, Your Majesty.' The major shifted his stance uncomfortably. He'd obviously been in the saddle for many hours.

'Can I offer you a place in one of the carriages? You must be exhausted.'

'That's all right, Your Majesty. I wouldn't want to put anybody out.'

'He can use mine.' It was Colonel Danilov who spoke. Aleksandr turned to see that he had emerged from his carriage, along with Wylie and Tarasov. 'I prefer to ride.'

'Thank you, Danilov. That's agreed then,' said the tsar. He began to climb back into his carriage. Ahead he noticed that the final horse had been harnessed to the carriage at the head of the train. 'I think we're about to be off,' he announced. 'Maskov, I'll deliver you my responses to these in the morning.'

'Thank you, Your Majesty.'

Aleksandr closed the carriage door and sat down. Within seconds he felt the wheels begin to turn. He closed his eyes, but the road beneath was too bumpy. He would have dearly loved the blessing of sleep.

On these roads, a carriage was not much more comfortable than a horse. Major Maskov could well understand Colonel Danilov's eagerness to give up his seat for a junior officer and in other circumstances would have attempted to resist the offer. But this evening he was tired enough that even if he had been on a horse he might have fallen asleep, and thence fallen down on to the road. Dangerous, possibly, but the potential embarrassment, in front of His Majesty the tsar, was of far greater concern.

Maskov was eager to please the tsar, as would be anyone in his position. It was not just the fact that, if the tsar noticed him, it might bring him favour. A soldier who sought promotion would do better to flatter his immediate superiors than one who stood so far above him in the pecking order that he would not even remember Major Maskov in a couple of days. Far more important was that Maskov loved the tsar. It was a realization he had come to back in 1812, on a parade, the first time he had seen Aleksandr in the flesh. He had heard others speak of their love for their leader, but he had thought they were speaking figuratively, of a love for their country that was embodied in the tsar. But one look at that glorious, golden-haired young man had made him think differently. It was not a sexual love – Maskov's wife and nine children back in Petersburg testified to that – it was almost akin to the love that a monk or a priest felt for God.

Many officers who had felt like Maskov – perhaps not as strongly – had come back from Paris disillusioned, but Maskov had been wounded at Borodino, and had never been to Paris. Today he still regarded Aleksandr in the same way so many had back in 1812. Now his view was in a declining minority, but he knew that he was right and they were wrong. The words 'Well done, Major Maskov,' as they issued from the tsar's lips, had confirmed that to him. How could one so lofty, who still paid so much courtesy to the humblest of his minions, be anything but a great man? Maskov would follow him to the ends of the earth; he would obey any order the tsar cared to issue; would happily die for him.

Major Maskov began to doze, and visions of a battlefield appeared before his eyes. Aleksandr was seated on a white steed with Maskov, now a field marshal, mounted beside him. The sound of a cannon blast ripped the air and Maskov turned to see a cannonball bouncing across the field towards them. He launched himself from his horse and flew through the air in front of his tsar, catching the blow of the cannonball full in his chest as it splintered his ribcage into a dozen bloody fragments. But as he fell to the floor, life ebbing agonizingly from him, he felt Aleksandr's strong arms cradling him and heard the cherished words, 'Thank you, Maskov. You saved me.'

Now he was at a banquet, in a privileged position opposite Aleksandr. The tsar was about to drink, but Maskov knew with inescapable certainty that the goblet was poisoned. He reached out and grabbed it from the tsar's hand, taking down the tainted wine in a single gulp and seeing white smoky vapour rise from his own lips as it seared his throat and corroded his body from within. Now he lay in his coffin as it was lowered slowly into the earth. He knew that he was dead, but he was happy to be dead as he looked up and saw Aleksandr at the head of the mourners, an expression of benevolent wisdom on his face and a tear in his eye. Shovelfuls of earth cascaded on to him, entombing him for ever, but even in death he smiled, hearing through the dirt and soil the muffled words, 'Thank you, Maskov. You saved me.'

Major Maskov awoke with a start. He was not alone. He had not noticed the carriage come to a halt at any time, but somehow a passenger had got on board. He was stood on the seat opposite, with his back to Maskov, dragging down a bag from the rack above.

'What the devil?' muttered Maskov, still half asleep, his hand reaching for his sword.

The figure turned and jumped down to the floor of the carriage. At that very moment the carriage rocked sideways, its wheel bouncing over a large stone. The intruder landed badly, falling to one side and banging his shoulder against the door. Maskov was now on his feet, his sword drawn and at the man's throat. He glanced back over to the seat and saw that there were already several bags on it, opened, their contents strewn about.

'What do you think you're doing, looking through Colonel Danilov's things?'

'What do you think *you're* doing, sleeping in Colonel Danilov's carriage?'

'I'm the one with the sword,' explained Maskov, 'and so I'm the one who gets to ask the questions.'

The intruder looked at him ruefully, and seemed to accept his status. 'He has something which belongs to me.'

'I find that very unlikely.' Maskov knew very little about Colonel Danilov – it had been a presumption that these were his bags – but it did well with this sort of vagabond to give a clear impression of authority. 'How did you get on board?'

'When you changed horses. I climbed on the back.'

'And then planned to do your dirty work and be off while I was still asleep?'

'No, I intended to kill you. I hope to get round to it.'

Maskov snorted. 'Fine words. Now tell me, what was it amongst Colonel Danilov's things that you were so interested in?'

'It's in there.' The man nodded to one of the bags open on the seat. Maskov glanced into it. There was nothing but clothes. He poked around with his left hand, still keeping his sword pointed at his prisoner. At the bottom of the case he found a bottle of vodka. It was full.

'There's nothing there,' he said.

'May I?' asked the intruder, making to stand up. Maskov decided to let him. He kept his sword close as the man delved

346

into the case. As he watched, it occurred to him to wonder why, if what he was looking for was in one of the cases he had already searched, the thief had left it there and gone to search in other cases. But it was too late.

The man turned. From somewhere, he had produced a knife. His right forearm knocked Maskov's sword aside and the knife in his left hand slashed across the major's chest. But Maskov was no greenhorn. He stepped back just half a pace and the blade sliced through the air, missing his flesh and not even catching his clothes.

At that same moment though, the carriage jolted again, and Maskov's deft movement became an uncontrolled lurch. His back slammed against the carriage door, which, loosened by the earlier impact, swung open. He braced himself against the doorway and managed to regain his balance, but in doing so, lost the grip on his sword. It fell out of the coach and bounced on its hilt, then its tip and then its hilt again, before finally coming to rest by the roadside.

Maskov's attacker had closed on him. He slashed out with the knife again, aiming for Maskov's fingers where they clutched the doorframe. Maskov snatched his arm away briefly and regained his grip only a hand's width further up. The knife sliced into the wooden frame, scarcely missing his fingers. It was a game they could go on playing time after time; one that Maskov had only to lose once for him to be sent tumbling towards the road that hurtled past below him. But at least his luck might hold until someone saw what was happening.

The game, however, was not to be played like that. The intruder smiled to himself, as if reading Maskov's thoughts. Then he lifted his hands, gripping the luggage racks on either side of the coach and raising himself into the air.

Two heavy, booted feet slammed into Maskov's chest. He tried to maintain his grip, but the fingers of his left hand yielded. Without their support, his right hand could do nothing. He erupted from the carriage, turning to his left as he fell, gaining a better view of the road that sped both across his path and towards him. And yet the final thought to occupy his mind before his skull was dashed against the stony ground was not to consider his wife, his children or his prospects in the life eternal, but to worry that when the tsar stepped from his carriage and looked down on his lifeless corpse, Major Maskov would be wearing a muddy uniform.

CHAPTER XXII

MASKOV WAS NOT DEAD. THAT WAS DR TARASOV'S PRO-
nouncement and, standing a little further away, Wylie
could only defer to his opinion. The whole train had
pulled up quickly when the alarm was raised, and it had only
been a short run back to where the body lay.

'Is there anything you can do?' asked the tsar.

'It looks grave,' said Tarasov. Again, Wylie could only concur.
There was blood all over the major's face, and a concave impression in his skull, just in front of the right temple. But he was
breathing, albeit in shallow, desperate gasps.

'I put him in your care, Doctor,' said Aleksandr. 'Do whatever
you can.'

'What happened?' asked Baron Diebich.

'I was in the carriage behind him,' explained the tsar.
'My coachman and I both saw him fall. We called for them to
stop.'

'We hit a huge hole in the road,' explained the driver of Maskov's
coach. 'It must have been full of mud or clay – I didn't see it. It
knocked him clean out of the door.'

'Unlikely.' The voice belonged to Colonel Danilov, who had
only just arrived at the scene.

'It looks like it to me,' said Wylie, but a glance at the colonel
reminded him not to take what he said lightly. 'What's that?' he
asked, pointing at what Danilov had in his hand.

'It's Maskov's sword,' he replied. 'I found it back there; a long way back.'

Wylie instantly grasped the implication. Maskov had had reason to unsheathe his sword, and had lost possession of it some moments before he himself fell from the carriage.

Aleksei, Tarasov, Wylie and Diebich together lifted Maskov and manhandled him back into the coach, laying him on the floor between the two rows of seats. Aleksandr stood back, looking on with a mixture of concern and unease. Soon they had him in the coach, and Tarasov clambered in after.

'It looks like the impact knocked down all the luggage too,' he said, looking around at the mess inside. Danilov merely glanced at the chaos into which his own luggage had been hurled. He seemed more concerned with a minute inspection of the carriage's doorframe.

Then the tsar spoke. 'Let's be on our way.' Then he turned to the driver of Maskov's coach, 'And for God's sake, man, drive more carefully.' The coachman bowed his head in acknowledgement, happy to accept the unwarranted rebuke rather than face greater punishment.

Wylie made his way back to his own carriage and was about to remount when he felt a hand on his arm. It was Danilov.

'I'm going back,' he said.

'Back?' asked Wylie.

'To Chufut Kalye.'

Wylie felt his own cheeks whiten at the implication. 'But why?'

'That was no accident.'

'You can't be certain.'

'I saw a man,' said Danilov sternly. 'Running from the other side of the carriage. You were all distracted by Maskov.'

'A bandit,' asserted Wylie. 'That's no reason to go back.'

'He was searching my bags – searching for the book. Do you still have it?'

Wylie reached into the carriage and picked up the notebook,

350

still wrapped in paper, from where he had left it on the seat. 'It's here,' he said. 'It's safe.'

Danilov took it from him, somewhat brusquely, and put it into his knapsack. 'I'll be back as quickly as I can,' he said, and then turned, heading down the road, to where his horse was waiting.

'It's a wild goose chase!' shouted Wylie after him, but he knew in his heart that Colonel Danilov was not a man to pursue shadows. A whip cracked, and he saw that Maskov's coach was about to start moving. He held his hand out to stop it for a moment and went to the door. Inside, Tarasov was leaning over Maskov's unconscious body, listening to his shallow breathing. He turned to Wylie and shook his head grimly.

But that was not the information Dr Wylie was here to obtain. Instead, he looked at the frame of the door, at the same spot which Danilov had found so fascinating – fascinating enough to send him all the way back to the citadel of Chufut Kalye.

It wasn't much, but it was certainly new and clean enough that it could be connected with what had happened to Maskov. The wood had been cut away by a jagged knife. There were two notches, side by side, about the width of two fingers apart. The only thing of note about them was their alignment. They were perfectly parallel.

It would be their last night before getting back to Taganrog. Aleksandr could not tell if he felt better or worse. He had now consumed all the quinine that he had taken from Tarasov. It tasted foul. He had exaggerated it at lunch the other day, but it was still not pleasant. How could he know if his current frailty wasn't due to the cure itself, rather than to the affliction he hoped it was addressing?

Orekhov was not a large town, but they had all been able to find accommodation. Beds were usually made available for the tsar and the whole of his retinue. If need be, lesser guests would be turfed out, awake or asleep, to make room. They would be happy to make such a sacrifice for their sovereign. And if they weren't happy – well, then they hardly merited the comfort of a soft bed.

Tonight the man most in need of comfort was Maskov. Seeing him lying there on the muddy road, Aleksandr had felt a deep sympathy for him, of a kind that had not touched his heart for many years. Even so, he was no fool; he could see there was little hope for the major. But Tarasov would do his best, even if his prognosis was rose-tinted.

There was one thing the tsar himself could do for the man – not save his life, but at least give some slight purpose to it. He picked up the wad of dispatches. Regardless of Maskov, they would take Aleksandr's mind off other matters. He sat down in front of the warming fire, wrapped in a robe. There was nothing of enormous interest in them. Despite what had happened at Chufut Kalye, his concern was the issue of potential revolution. Maskov had brought reports from many of the tsar's sources in Petersburg, but none of them was as close to events as Colonel Danilov. Rationally, he would feel safer if Danilov were back in the capital, where he could feel at first hand the mood in the barracks. In his heart, it felt comfortable to have the colonel in his presence.

There was a knock at the door. Aleksandr glanced at the clock on the mantelpiece above the fire. It was just after midnight. It could only be bad news. He called out, and Dr Tarasov entered. Aleksandr could see Baron Diebich hovering in the background. He rose to his feet, perhaps faster than he had intended. He felt a moment of dizziness, but asked the question that seemed suddenly more urgent than any.

'How is Maskov?'

Tarasov hesitated for a moment, but the tsar was not a man who needed to be shielded from bad news. 'Dead, Your Majesty. His skull was split. I think he was probably dead when we got here.'

'What a tragedy,' replied the tsar. 'I so pity the poor man.' Aleksandr hoped it did not sound like a platitude. So much that he said was taken to be such, perhaps rightly. Aleksandr turned away from the doctor, afraid to show his face. He heard the door close as Tarasov left.

Aleksandr returned to his chair, dropping the dispatches to the floor beside him. There were so many other things he had wanted to say about Maskov, but none of them would sound sincere. What he really wanted to know was what in Heaven the Lord could have intended for Maskov. Why kill him in such an inconsequential manner? Could he not have died at home, bathed in the love of his family? There was nothing in the dispatches that was worth sacrificing a life to deliver – nor had Maskov died in attempting to deliver them; it had come later. It made God seem cruel, but Aleksandr knew enough to understand that, if he believed that, it was a fault in his own nature, not in the Lord's. It was a fault that would take time to rectify – time and seclusion.

He felt a sudden pain in his stomach, a burning that spread out to his arms and legs. This was worse than anything he had experienced before, though each time the pattern was the same. Sometimes it began in his stomach, sometimes – he suspected – in his heart. He stood painfully and turned out the lamp on the table.

It was dark now, but he knew the way to the bed. He lay down, and the agony began to recede. His breathing slowed and he felt the sweat on his skin cool. The pain was not gone, but it was tolerable once again. Aleksandr knew it would return. Deep in that cave beneath Chufut Kalye, Cain had told him so.

Aleksandr opened his eyes. His body ached, but he could tell that the shaking he now felt was not caused by the convulsions of his own body, but by the coach itself. They were travelling more slowly now, partly out of consideration for the tsar's delicate condition, but also with regard to the awful accident that had killed Major Maskov. They had buried him quietly in a cemetery in Orekhov, not very far from where he had fallen. The heavy local clay had been hard for the men to dig through. Aleksandr

353

had begun a letter to his family, but had not been able to finish it before the fever had overcome him.

Aleksandr still felt cold, although he was sweating. They had piled blankets and furs over him, but it did little to help. His greatest fillip was that soon the journey would be over and they would be back in Taganrog, though he would hate for Yelizaveta to see him like this. He forced himself to sit up and look out of the window.

The view outside was very familiar. They were closer to home than he had imagined, though it was easy to lose sense of time as he slipped between consciousness and an unconsciousness that was sometimes sleep and sometimes a thing far deeper and more disturbing. They were already in the outskirts of Taganrog. He recognized some of the buildings, especially the churches. It would be less than a quarter of an hour now before they were home.

The coach turned on to the coastal road that ran along the length of the town, and Aleksandr immediately felt more comfortable. It was not as familiar a place as Petersburg, but it brought to him the same sense of contentment, with few of the pressures. Little had changed. Perhaps, if he thought carefully about it, he could notice that the leaves on the trees, golden when he left, had mostly fallen to the ground. It had been a gradual process, and one he had observed all through his journey. Even that one yacht was still anchored out to sea. He really should send someone over to see if its passengers were people of any note.

The ship had, he observed, moved a little since he had last seen it – of that he was sure, despite the numbness that seemed to grip his memory. It was unlikely there would be need for so small an adjustment to its position. Perhaps it too had made a sojourn that had coincided with the tsar's own. Where might it have been, he wondered.

It did not matter. The carriage clattered to a halt and the door opened, revealing the kind but concerned face of Prince Volkonsky. Aleksandr forced himself to his feet and stepped down from the carriage, ignoring Volkonsky's proffered arm for fear of showing weakness. In front and behind, the other carriages were disgorging their occupants, and he could see Wylie, Tarasov, Diebich and others stretching their limbs and appearing happy to be somewhere that was a little more like home. But turning his head anxiously from side to side, he confirmed that the one man he most desperately wanted to speak to was not with them. Colonel Danilov was nowhere to be seen.

CHAPTER XXIII

ALONE AND ON HORSEBACK, IT ONLY TOOK ALEKSEI FIVE DAYS
to get back to Chufut Kalye. It was mid-afternoon when
he finally made it to the cliff top. He noticed the weather
cooling all through his journey back and, although there was still
no snow, the place felt wintry. He saw groups of Karaite men
talking in the streets, but he didn't make contact with them. If a
host of vampires had suddenly escaped the cave system beneath
them, then the neighbours of those men might well have become
an immediate source of nourishment. Aleksei didn't feel inclined
to stand there and look into their eyes if that had been the case.
He made his way to the rocky hilltop from where he had first
entered Iuda's lair, over a week before. He scrambled down to the
cave mouth and peeked inside.

It was not what he had expected – certainly not what he had
seen the last time he was here. The tunnel was impassable. The
roof had collapsed, and rocks filled the way. He could see a few
small gaps, but none that would be enough for him to get through.
He could possibly dig his way in, but he had no idea how deep
the cave-in went. He traversed the hillside and found two other
tunnels, similarly blocked. Others seemed passable, but it was a
superficial appearance. One had caved in just a little further into
the hillside, whereas two more were undisturbed but led nowhere,
terminating naturally without ever connecting to the underground
labyrinth Aleksei had explored.

It was all very contrived; only those tunnels which might have led deeper had collapsed – those that had never led anywhere were spared. These were not the results of some random earth-quake. The question was, had the vampires, once they had fled their former prison, caused this collapse so as to bury all memory of what they had endured there? Or had the tunnel roofs given way with the *voordalaki* still inside, and now unable to escape?

Aleksei climbed back up to the rocky plane above. There was one way of finding out, though it was not guaranteed. He sat on a boulder and opened up his knapsack. Inside was the book. Aleksei's initials were still there on the paper in which Kyesha had wrapped it before giving it to him in Moscow. It seemed like years ago. He folded a corner of the paper to one side, and the skin once again began to smoulder in the sunlight. He listened carefully. The wind was blowing strongly, and it was difficult to differenti-ate the sound of a scream from its whistling between the rocks.

He went over to the edge of the cliff, just above the tunnel he had gone down on his first visit, and pulled the paper aside again. This time he was sure he heard nothing. He got on to his hands and knees to be closer to the cave mouth, but still there was only silence. He knew, though, that there was more than one tunnel that led down to those cells, and any one of the openings around there could be an entrance.

He walked back towards the middle of the rocky plain. He was surrounded by caves now, the mixture of natural and artificial he had seen here before. He prepared to open up the book again, but he didn't need to. From somewhere nearby, he heard a muffled cry. He looked around, trying to work out where the sound had come from, and it came again. It sounded almost like words rather than a holler of pain, but if it was, he could not make them out.

He ran in the direction from which he thought he'd heard the sound come. An outcrop of rocks stood up higher than the ground around them, by more than a man's height. Aleksei skirted round them and saw that they were in fact the housing to the entrance of a large cave, shaped like a gaping mouth. There had been a

357

rockfall here too. Aleksei could only guess that this collapse was as recent as all the others.

Again the shout came.

'I'm here! I'm in here!'

Now it sounded close. It was definitely ahead of him; somewhere in, or behind, the jumble of boulders that filled the passageway. He scrambled down the short slope and began hefting the stones to one side. Some of the larger ones were immovable, but it did not matter too much; they were wedged at odd angles, leaving sizeable gaps in between. Aleksei tugged away at the rockfall, working opposite the point at which the voice called to him. He now clearly recognized it to be the tattooed *voordalak*.

It was almost twenty minutes before he caught his first glimpse of the creature, no more than a view of its eyes through a gap between two boulders, but it gave him new vigour. He saw one large stone towards the base of the pile that he thought he would be able to shift, and which, if he did, would free up a number of others. He put his hands around the rock, feeling for any crevice that might give him purchase, and knowing that his left hand would never grip it as strongly as his right. Then he pressed down against the ground with his feet, the muscles of his face and neck straining as he tried to pull the rock away.

At last it came, and as it did, Aleksei fell backwards. He didn't see, but heard the rumble of collapsing stones as those around the rock he had pulled out cascaded in to take its place. He felt a sharp pain to his ankle and looked up to see it pinned under one large rock and several smaller ones. He sat up and tried to push it away, both with his hands and by moving his trapped leg. It was painful, but he quickly freed himself. He stood up and put weight on the injured ankle. He lifted it from the ground again almost immediately, wincing. He didn't think it was broken, but it would take a few days before he could walk on it again without pain. He turned back to his work, and let out a gasp.

Aleksei's efforts had revealed the tattooed skin with which he was familiar, but the figure of the *voordalak* to which it belonged was hard to discern. It had not occurred to Aleksei that being crushed was not one of the ways in which a vampire could die. Had this creature been human, it would not have survived its ordeal. An enormous weight of rocks had fallen on it – most were still there. Its head was trapped, as was one of its legs; the other was out of Aleksei's sight, still buried in the mass of rocks behind, and must have been bent back at the most extraordinary angle. Another huge boulder pinned its chest to the ground, and moved up and down only slightly as the creature breathed. But its arms were now freed, and it began to use them to pick away the rocks that covered it. Even in its degenerate state, it was stronger than Aleksei, and cast aside rocks with a single arm that it would have taken a block and tackle for men to move.

'Thank you,' it said.

Aleksei hopped back up the slope, a little way away from the cave mouth, ostensibly to find a comfortable place to sit, but also wary now that the *voordalak* was almost free. It certainly needed no more of his assistance. It had freed its legs, and indeed every part of its body but for the head. It kicked out hard with both feet, sending a ripple through its body like an eel flicking its way through the water. Its body tugged against its head and popped it out of the grip of the rocks. It would have been agony for a human – probably fatal. It may have been agony for the vampire too, but it was expedient and would not kill it.

Now that Aleksei could see the creature's entire body, he realized what a sorry state it was in. *Voordalaki*, he knew, healed quickly, and this one had had many days to recover from the initial damage done to it by the rocks pounding into its body. But the healing process had not been free to take its natural course, and had done its best within the strictures the fallen rocks forced upon it. The body had healed in much the same way that a limb set at the wrong angle will heal – rebuilt, but not in the form in which it had been originally created.

The creature's left hand was relatively normal, but its right was bent back at the wrist, almost to a right angle. When it moved its fingers, the bones within its palm pushed forward and caused the skin to rise and fall in sympathy. One leg was shorter than it should have been, between the knee and the ankle, while the other – the one that had been bent back under the rocks, curved out in a huge bow. It must have been broken in over twenty places. The remarkable outcome was that the creature was able to stand with its feet side by side, but it left a gap so wide a child would have been able to climb through its legs.

Its chest was utterly concave, like a mixing bowl from a kitchen. Bone and flesh had not always re-formed in the correct order, and in places ribs could be seen erupting from the skin then submerging back under inches later. The skin itself was very thin, particularly on the left-hand side, and Aleksei could see the slight motion of a beating heart beneath it. Another huge dent was visible in the side of its head, almost reaching the eye. Aleksei was reminded of Major Maskov's wound.

'Aren't you in pain?' asked Aleksei.

'Less than I was a moment ago, but I don't think it's going to get any better than this.'

'Perhaps if . . . if your bones were broken again, they'd have a chance to heal more freely.' Aleksei had not really considered the concept, and had spoken in some sense out of politeness, but the *voordalak* took on his suggestion.

It placed its right hand on a large, flat rock and then raised a smaller stone in the other, smashing it down on its upturned fingers. It made a slight grunt as the stone impacted, but the sound was drowned by a horrible crunching as its finger bones were smashed. It lifted its hand and shook it vigorously, as a man would on trapping his fingers in a door. At first Aleksei could see the crushed bones wobbling loosely, but even as he looked they stiffened and the hand opened like a flower to reveal itself once again in its proper form – or close enough.

The *voordalak* inspected its new hand, looking first at the back, then the front.

'Thank you, again,' it said. 'Though I'll leave the rest for later.'

It sat on a rock and looked at Aleksei. It was still just inside the cave. The sun had not yet set, and it would not dare venture further out.

'What happened?' asked Aleksei.

'Cain,' it replied simply.

'I thought you had him at your mercy.'

'That was your mistake – and ours. He had assistance.'

Aleksei was surprised, though he knew he should not have been. Iuda would have been a fool not to have someone watching his back. 'Where were they hiding?' he asked.

'Hiding?' The creature laughed humourlessly. 'There was no need to hide. You saw for yourself.' Aleksei said nothing, nor did he understand. 'One of our own number – Raisa Styepanovna.'

'Her? But she hated him as much as the rest of you.'

'It seems not. Somehow he had persuaded her that he would find a way of letting her see herself in a mirror. Perhaps he can – though God knows what she'll see. She'd been on his side all along.'

'What did she do?'

'Once I'd released everyone, we all converged on the main chamber, where you'd left Cain surrounded. He was trying to talk the creatures in there into going back to their cells. They were weak-willed, and he might have done it, but the rest of us were not so easy to assuage. We stood there watching him, saying nothing, except me. All I did was read out the time from the clock, every five minutes, counting the remainder of his life before the sun set and he lost its protection.

'None of us noticed that Raisa Styepanovna had made her way over to his desk – and why should we care about it if we had? But suddenly she pulled on some rope or lever, and the whole room was flooded with sunlight – not even flooded, it was cleverer than that. There were wide corridors of light that surrounded pools of shadow. Only a few of us were caught so quickly as to be killed, most recoiled into the shade, just where Cain wanted us. Raisa had opened a whole set of curtains that let in sunlight in the exact

361

pattern required – the point at which she stood remained safely unilluminated. Cain must have planned for the eventuality long before.'

'It relied on Raisa Styepanovna – he was lucky she was there to save him.' Even as he spoke, Aleksei realized how Iuda had tricked him into releasing the other prisoners, safe in the knowledge that one of them would be his rescuer.

'Perhaps,' said the vampire, 'but even if she had not been there he would have found a way. It was less than ten paces to his desk. He might have made it and released the mechanism himself before we got to him.'

Another realization hit Aleksei as he listened. This was not the only part Raisa Styepanovna had played in recent events. Kyesha had told him it was she who had revealed the location of Iuda's notebook, and the other information he had needed to contact Aleksei. Perhaps Kyesha's entire escape had been contrived, and with only one purpose – to bring Aleksei to Chufut Kalye.

'What happened then?' he asked.

'Cain and Raisa discussed what to do. They were considering whether they would be able to round us all up and put us back in our cells, but they decided it would be impossible. Cain said it was time to move on. He lit a taper and disappeared with it down one of the tunnels. She stayed behind, taunting us, telling us that hers was the last beauty we would ever look upon. Cain soon returned. He picked up his notebooks and some other bits and pieces, and they left together. It was difficult for her to pick her way through, always keeping in the shadows. She caught her hand once and let out a scream as the skin burned, but it was nothing. I've had worse from you reading that damned book.'

Aleksei couldn't help but smile at the creature's stoicism, but he didn't interrupt the story.

'They headed off down the tunnel and we waited. Some were unconcerned, saying it would be dark soon, but others knew Cain better. There was a fear that he somehow had worked out a way of flooding the entire cavern with light, but it seemed unlikely.

Even if he had, there were plenty of places we could have sheltered until sunset. But that wasn't his plan. As soon as I heard the first explosion, I realized what he was up to. I knew there wasn't much time. I ran for all I was worth in the direction they'd gone, dodging the light as much as I could, but it was impossible to avoid it completely. I felt the burns, but they didn't slow me – it's something I'm used to.

'I was only just out of the main chamber when the roof behind me collapsed. There were several routes out, but some of them were blocked already. Again, he'd had it all planned – gunpowder packed into crevices in the rock, primed to entomb us and let him walk free, should the need arise. I came up this way. I didn't know what I was going to do. It was still light outside, so it was either be entombed or burned. In the end, the choice was made for me. There was an explosion above my head and down came the roof, and that's where I've been for – however long it is.'

'Ten days,' said Aleksei.

'It seemed longer.'

'What about Raisa? Wouldn't she be in the same boat as you – unable to escape into the sunlight?'

'Who knows? What would Cain care, anyway? If she was lucky there was some bit of cave she could shelter in until dark. If not – you won't find any remains.'

'You reckon it's completely sealed?'

'If that's what Cain intended, then he'll have achieved it. There were only five routes in and out, plus those gaps where the light came in from the cliff. It wouldn't take much gunpowder. Some of it was shored up anyway. It wasn't safe at first. We helped him build it!'

'I know,' said Aleksei, recalling what Kyesha had told him. 'So what will happen to the others? Can't they dig their way out?'

'If they were going to, they should have done it by now. They'll grow weaker every day. There's not much food supply in there.'

'Not much? What do you mean?' Aleksei was aware that his

mind was working slowly, but even as he realized the only possible implication of what the *voordalak* had said, it was spelled out for him.

'We weren't just vampires in those cells. He had to feed us. I think there were seven humans in all. You saw three of them. Didn't you *know?*'

Aleksei jumped to his feet, ignoring the pain in his ankle. His hands covered his face and he felt cold. He'd seen them there, two men and a woman. That was why they'd had vegetables to eat – not as an experiment to see what nourishment a *voordalak* could survive on, but to provide a food supply for the subjects of Iuda's other experiments. And the man and the woman had been together. Did Iuda see them as breeding stock – not themselves to feed to those creatures, but to provide future generations that could be? Now, entombed, there would not be food enough for the humans to last more than a few weeks. There would be no prospect of their producing children to follow them in their fate. But those few weeks that drew their lives to a close would be indescribably vile. And Aleksei had seen them – opened their cage with the intent of letting them out, but with the effect of letting their tormentors in.

He turned away and vomited, spasms racking his body as he came to understand what he had done. He had been lulled, by Kyesha's charm, by his own pity for each *voordalak* he had seen suffering some monstrous fate, and by Iuda's guile. He had made the mistake of judging any of them by human standards. Kyesha could smile and smile and be a villain. The imprisoned *voordalaki* could suffer what they had and still it would not make up for the very first meal they ever took in their altered existence. And Iuda? Iuda had played him for a *prostak*, just like he always did. Iuda had summoned him down to the Crimea, and Aleksei had trotted there with willing obedience. What Iuda's ultimate intent might be was as yet unclear, but for the moment it would be enough for him simply to toy with Aleksei.

There was nothing left for Aleksei's stomach to yield. He turned back to the *voordalak* that still lurked in the shadows of the cave. The sun had not yet set, but the moon was already visible – almost full – in the east. Aleksei had not killed one of these creatures for many years, but before the night was out, he would. But there was much to be learned before that.

'And when those seven have given all they can, your kin will starve to death anyway,' he said. 'Pointless, don't you think?'

'They may starve,' the *voordalak* replied, 'but they won't die. They will weaken, become unable to move, unable to speak. If they conserve their energy, they may last a little longer. Eventually they'll become insensible to what's going on around them, perhaps indistinguishable to you from a rigid corpse. But dead? No. It is not a pleasant fate.'

'One which you all willingly chose,' muttered Aleksei.

'True. And few do not learn to regret it.'

'Do you regret it?' asked Aleksei, clambering sideways across the slope before sitting back down. He felt the comforting hardness of his wooden sword, hidden under his greatcoat, as it pressed into his armpit.

'Half an hour ago, I think I did. Now, I do not.'

The urge to kill rose in Aleksei, and he decided it was time to draw the conversation to a close. He asked the question head on.

'What did Cain have in store for Tsar Aleksandr?'

'To make him into one of us.' It was said with a simple coldness.

'There was the blood of a vampire in that wine?'

'That was the rumour, but who other than Cain would know the truth?'

'And how would it work?' asked Aleksei. 'Even if Aleksandr had drunk the wine, he was never bitten by a vampire. Doesn't that have to happen first?'

The *voordalak* nodded thoughtfully. 'I have always believed so,' he said. 'But there was one thing that Cain said in explanation of that.'

'Which was?'

'"It's in the blood."' The creature shrugged its shoulders as it spoke.

'"It's in the blood"?' Aleksei's question accurately revealed his lack of understanding.

'That's what he said.'

'*Already* in the blood?' asked Aleksei. 'Is that what he meant?'

'I can only tell you what he said. You must trust me on that.' He smiled, much as Aleksei might have sneered, at the idea of trust between them. 'We're like Androcles and the lion, you and I,' he said, as if changing the subject.

'I take it I'm Androcles,' replied Aleksei. He doubted he would get more on the matter that interested him.

'Exactly. And I am the beast towards whom you showed not fear, but mercy. The thorn in my paw was enslavement. You freed me of it. I should show you eternal gratitude.'

Aleksei considered. Theirs was a version of the tale that had never been told. Androcles finally faced the lion at the Roman games. Would it remember the benevolence shown it, and spare the gladiator, or revert to its animal state, and devour him? In no variant of the story had it been Androcles who saw the error of his ways, who realized that a lion cannot change its true nature, and that though it might spare the life of one man to whom it owed a debt, it would still prey on every other creature whose path it crossed and devour them without mercy. Aleksei would be the wise Androcles, who before the cheering crowd plunged his sword between the beast's shoulderblades, ignoring the look of betrayal in its face and thinking only of the lives it had taken and the lives it would have taken if not stopped.

He reached beneath his coat and felt the handle of the wooden sword. The creature was weak and hungry; now was the time to strike.

'And I do feel grateful,' said the *voordalak*. Aleksei wondered if it had guessed his reasoning and was about to beg for mercy. 'But I prefer a story from Aesop to that of Androcles.' It stood and took a few paces towards Aleksei. The sun had now set, and there was no restriction on its movements. 'You know the one, about the scorpion who begs a ride across a river on a frog's back. The frog is afraid the scorpion will sting it, but the scorpion explains it would be a fool to do so, because it would drown too. And so they set off across the river, and of course the scorpion stings the frog and the frog begins to sink. And as they both face death the frog gasps, "Why? Why did you sting me when it means your own death?" The scorpion – itself drowning – makes a simple reply. "I'm a scorpion; it's my nature."'

'I know the story,' replied Aleksei, tensing himself for action.

'Well,' said the tattooed *voordalak*, '*I* am a vampire. And I'm hungry.' It looked almost sad as it spoke. 'It's *my* nature.'

As the creature spoke, it launched itself at Aleksei. He was ready for it, and yet still he was too slow. He was getting old. He felt its weight push him backwards, and his head banged against the stony ground behind him. His hand was still inside his coat – as though he had become a portrait of Napoleon – grasping the sword but pinned there by his attacker's weight. He felt the strange shape of the creature's body pressed against his – the arcing leg, the hollow chest – but none of those deformities served to hinder it. Its teeth had suffered no malformation. Its mouth gaped wide open as its eyes gazed lasciviously at Aleksei's throat.

Aleksei grunted as the wind was knocked out of him, but the creature chose to hear the sound as a question.

'You ask why after what I've already told you? Well, why not? And there's one thing you've forgotten, three-fingered man; we're already across the river.'

Its hand descended and pushed Aleksei's head to one side, stretching his neck in readiness. All Aleksei could see was the monster's heart pumping faster, its blood blue through a thin membrane of skin which its deformed regrowth had created. He felt its hands squeeze tighter as its fangs descended, and saw the heart beat faster still. Despite everything that whirled through his mind, he tried to concentrate, to ensure that in death his thoughts were only of the things he loved. He saw in front of him a happy scene. He was at its centre. Cradled in his left arm was Tamara, too big to be held like that now, but still happy to be picked up by her father. On his right stood Domnikiia, her hand on his chest and her beaming smile directed towards the child they both loved; had together created.

The image was ripped in two, and Aleksei felt the weight pressing down on him relax. The *voordalak* had turned its head to see what attacked it, but it was too late. The heart stopped beating and the skin through which it had been visible was ruptured. Aleksei saw the tip of a wooden blade, much like his own, disappear back into the body above him with a slurp that faded in an instant as the creature's flesh began to desiccate in a way with which Aleksei was entirely familiar and wished he had had the chance to see more often over the past weeks. He closed his eyes and mouth to stop the powdered decay of the vampire's body from in any way infiltrating his. He listened for the sound of tumbling ashes to cease, but his consciousness was instead assailed by a voice that was inescapably recognizable.

'That story's not from Aesop.'

Aleksei opened his eyes. It was Iuda. The wooden stake he had used was cast on the ground beside him. Now he had in one hand his familiar double-bladed knife, and in the other a pistol. The latter was aimed at Aleksei's head.

'Why didn't you let him kill me?' asked Aleksei.

'Why should I?'

'You were happy enough for me to be torn apart by creatures like that last time we met.'

Iuda smiled and glanced away from Aleksei, as if embarrassed. 'Yes, well, you did rather take me by surprise that time, Lyosha, I have to admit. It was you or me, and I think we can both guess which one I'd choose. In this case, it was you or him. I think the decision is almost as obvious.'

Aleksei was more interested in the idea of Iuda being surprised than in his self-serving attempts at flattery. 'You made sure Kyesha would have enough to tempt me here . . . how can you not have been expecting me?'

'Aleksei Ivanovich, I really don't know what you are talking about. Now lie down and hold your hands out behind you.' He waggled the gun in Aleksei's direction with enough menace to induce his compliance. He placed his booted foot on Aleksei's back before tucking the pistol under his elbow and bringing from his pocket a length of rope. 'As far as I knew, you were happily ensconced in Moscow screwing that whore of whom you seem so fond.' He slipped a loop of the rope over Aleksei's proffered wrists. 'Sorry, nanny – must keep with the times.' He jerked the rope tight.

'Don't take me for a fool, Iuda,' said Aleksei, ignoring the comments about Domnikiia. 'I know that it was Raisa Styepanovna who told Kyesha where to find your notebook.' The real relief was that Iuda had made no mention of Tamara.

'Kyesha?' asked Iuda, looping another coil of rope around Aleksei's wrists and tying it tight, before pulling on it to bring him to his feet. 'Stand up, would you?'

'The vampire who stole your notebook.'

'Oh – him! You know, Aleksei, I think you're about the only person I've met in this godforsaken backwater who can manage to live his life passing himself off under just one name.' He dragged Aleksei along by the rope, forcing him to walk backwards. 'Did I say Aleksei? I meant Lyosha – though I think I've just ruined my own point.'

'Whatever his name, you know who I mean.' The rough cord cut into Aleksei's wrists. He saw little point in resisting Iuda's movement.

'I do. I do. But let me assure you, his theft of my notebook was quite a surprise. And you say Raisa Styepanovna helped him? There's a woman who's not to be trusted, if ever there was one.'

'And I'm supposed to believe that?' The rope was made of long, coarse strands, unlike anything Aleksei was familiar with. He suspected it might be horsehair.

369

'No, no. I'd much prefer it if you were to believe I planned the whole thing and lured you here. I'm happy you think I'm up to it. The problem is, it all makes me look quite the fool when you interrupt just at my moment of triumph over Aleksandr Pavlovich. Sit down.'

They had reached the edge of a patch of bushes and a few small trees. Aleksei sat with his back to a tree trunk, as Iuda indicated.

'And how were you to triumph over His Majesty?' asked Aleksei.

'Clever stuff, Lyosha, but let me assure you, on this occasion, you are going to live. Therefore I am not going to reveal my plans to you, safe in the knowledge that you will take them to the grave. Let go of your bag.'

Aleksei's bag had been tucked under his bound arms as they walked across the hilltop. He still had just enough movement to drop it on to the ground beside him.

'Why don't you just kill me?' he asked.

'I take it,' said Iuda, picking up the stray end of the rope and taking it with him around the tree, 'that that is a question rather than a plea, and so I shall answer it with another. Why should I kill you?'

'Why else did you go to such effort to tempt me here?' Aleksei felt the rope tight across his chest as Iuda came out from behind the tree and began another lap.

'Believe me, Lyosha, none of that was my doing.' He emerged again and went over to Aleksei's knapsack. 'If I had wanted you to get hold of my notebook, why do you think I've subsequently been making so much effort to get it back? Why do you think I killed that gentleman who happened to be travelling in your carriage? Why do you think I then followed you back here? Why do you think I'm now doing this?'

He reached into Aleksei's bag and pulled out the notebook. It looked different somehow.

'Oh, dear!' said Iuda, with an air of disappointment. He

blew on the cover of the book and a cloud of dust scurried in Aleksei's direction, only to be quickly dispersed in the air. The fine *voordalak*-skin binding of the book was no more. All that remained was dull, grey card. Iuda glanced back in the direction of the cave mouth, where he had so recently reduced one of his former prisoners to a similar state of desiccation. 'I *knew* there was a reason I'd kept that one alive,' he said.

He opened up the book and pored over its contents, occasionally nodding as he was reminded of some vital point. It was a full five minutes before he looked back up from it and spoke to Aleksei.

'Do you believe me now?' he asked. 'This evening, I admit, I was expecting you. More than that – I'd followed you. But I have no reason to kill you.'

'Do you need a reason?'

He smiled, as if caught out for being excessively modest. 'Perhaps not, but I also have a reason not to.'

'Which is?'

'There is something I want you to find out – and I'd hate you to go to your grave without ever discovering it.'

'So tell me now,' said Aleksei, unsure why he should be attempting to hasten his own death.

'I'm afraid you'd never believe me,' said Iuda, mournfully. 'That is my curse. But for now, I have the two things I require.'

'*Two* things?' said Aleksei.

'These notes,' said Iuda, holding up the battered notebook, 'and this head start.'

He turned and ran into the darkness. Within moments, he had disappeared from view.

CHAPTER XXIV

MUCH AS HE DESIRED IT, ALEKSANDR KNEW HE COULD NOT shun the responsibilities of his position any longer. Across the room from him sat Volkonsky, and with him, two less familiar faces: Baron Frederiks, the military commander in Taganrog, and Colonel Nikolayev, who was in charge of the troop of Don Cossacks which guarded the tsar's residence. He had hoped that Danilov would be here too, but he'd been away for almost a week. Dr Wylie said he was due back soon, but the tsar could wait no longer.

'And when do you plan to reach Petersburg, Baron?' he asked.

'A little over a month from now, Your Majesty; certainly before the end of the year.'

Aleksandr squeezed his lower lip and considered what might come to pass in that space of time.

'I can easily find a courier,' added the baron, 'if your despatches are more urgent.'

'No,' said the tsar firmly. 'Certainty is more important than speed. I need them to go with a man I can trust.'

'You can certainly trust *me*, Your Majesty.'

'And me,' added Colonel Nikolayev.

'You will ensure that Baron Frederiks completes his journey safely?' asked the tsar.

'I would die rather than fail in my duty,' said Nikolayev.

'There shouldn't be any need for that,' said Aleksandr. He had hardly heard what the colonel had said. He examined the packages in front of him. There were five of them, mostly addressed to various ministers and generals who worked in the capital. It was the envelope on the top of the pile that was of most importance to him. He handed the other four over to Frederiks.

'These are to be opened immediately upon receipt,' he said.

'Yes, Your Majesty,' replied the baron.

Aleksandr held the final envelope in his hands. He looked at the name on the front, written in his own handwriting:

Nikolai Pavlovich

'This is for my brother,' he said with sudden resolution, passing it to the baron. He had thought of addressing it to 'Kolya', and of signing it 'Sasha'. Those were the names they had always called each other by, face to face, but today it didn't seem appropriate. 'But remember, he is only to open it in the event of my death.'

'I might as well burn it now, and save the trouble,' said Frederiks.

'I don't recall suggesting that it was to be opened in the near future, Baron,' said Aleksandr icily. 'But my brother *is* nineteen years my junior, so the time will come.' He knew as he spoke that the time might come sooner than any of them thought. 'Now is there anything more?' he asked.

There was a general shaking of heads. The tsar rose to his feet and the others followed suit. Soon he was left alone. He raised his hands to his face and fell back into a chair, sucking in lungfuls of air. The shaking returned; he had managed to contain it throughout the meeting, but the effort had exhausted him. Now it took him over completely.

At least he had done what needed to be done. That letter to Nikolai explained everything – well, not everything, but enough. Even so, there was something else he had meant to include with the papers; something he couldn't remember. It concerned Colonel Danilov; a commendation perhaps? Aleksandr could not recall.

Another spasm of pain racked his body. He struggled out of the chair and tugged on the bell cord. The effort exhausted him and he collapsed into the chair, with but one thought on his mind: Wylie would be here soon – Wylie would help.

The coach rattled to a halt and the door opened. The starets climbed up inside. The tsaritsa sat alone. Her face was veiled, but she was easy to recognize. The starets had sent a note asking her to meet him here. He had known she would not fail to attend. She feared for her husband – and in that fear she would do anything to save him.

'Father, how did you know?' she asked as soon as the carriage had begun moving again.

He raised a finger to silence her. 'First, we pray,' he said.

They spoke in unison, as they had done before. 'Lord Jesus Christ, have mercy upon me, a sinner.'

There was a moment's silence after the prayer was finished, but Yelizaveta Alekseevna could not contain herself for long. 'You said it in your letter – how did you know my husband was ill?'

Should he claim to have heard it from above, the starets wondered. He decided against it. It might add sway to his authority, but a simpler answer would be more effective.

'Who could not know?' he replied. 'This is a small town and he is the tsar. Even my ears are not immune to rumour.'

'But you said you could help.'

'It is not only I who can help – prayer is available to all of us.'

He could not see her face, but the way her head dropped revealed her disappointment. She had been hoping for something a little more temporal.

'Your letter suggested . . .' She could not finish her sentence.

'There are certainly other things that can be done,' said the starets, 'but none will have any effect unless we open our hearts to God and ask that He ensures their success. Can you do that?'

The tsaritsa nodded. 'You know I can. I must.'

The starets paused for a moment. The approach he was about to suggest was outside what would be considered his realm. 'There are preparations that can be administered – blessed by the Lord – that can be of great efficacy.'

'Medicines? My husband has two doctors with him day and night. There can be little they have not tried.'

'They are like all men of science – they place too much reliance on what they have observed and too little on what they have been told. Who was it that created your husband's body?'

'I . . . I don't understand.'

'Who created all our bodies?' The starets's voice was raised.

'The Lord God,' whispered Yelizaveta.

'And so whom would you most trust to care for them – a man who has studied for a few decades, or the Lord, who knows everything?'

'The Lord,' she said.

'It is your faith in the Lord that will heal your husband. The remedy I give you will merely be a conduit for that faith.'

'May I take it?' Her voice was eager, as was to be expected.

'I do not have it with me. Such a treatment takes time to prepare.'

'Perhaps Dr Tarasov already has some. Do you have a name for it?'

'No!' said the starets firmly. 'Doctors are proud of their learning – too proud. It makes them jealous of the greater knowledge of others. They would never allow it.'

'I will not tell them,' she said.

'Good. It will not take me long to prepare it. I will contact you again when I have.'

'Thank you, Father.'

'Now stop the coach, if you please.'

She banged on the carriage ceiling with the tip of her cane, and their rocking motion came to a halt. As the starets was about to climb down, she reached forward, grabbing his hand and bringing it to her lips to kiss. He let her hold it there for a few moments before pulling it gently away.

'You have great faith, my child,' he said. 'Your husband will thank you.'

He stepped out of the coach and closed the door, watching it rattle off into the distance before turning and continuing on his way.

It was a thing of beauty. Aleksandr had never really noticed before – he had thought of it as just a tool – but some craftsman had poured his soul into its creation. The handle was of nacre. It shone warmly in the early morning light, the band of gold around its middle glinting as it caught the sun. The handle was capped with more gold, shaped into the form of a helmet, its plume intricately carved, to no practical purpose. The base of the handle, again wrapped in gold, was where the blade was pivoted. The blade itself was exquisite. It was steel, but shone almost as brightly as the gold leaf embossed into its side. It had been well cared for – not by Aleksandr himself, but by Anisimov, his valet. The gold leaf was patterned with curlicues, but again they were mere decoration – perhaps even a distraction.

It was the edge of the blade itself that fascinated Aleksandr the most. He had used it – or one like it – every day since he had first become a man, but he had never stopped to consider it until now. It was a marvel how something so straight, so narrow, could be so unutterably sharp. A saw was serrated to make it cut more effectively, as were many blades, but a razor was different. Its acuteness lay in its simplicity. He rested his thumb against the edge of the blade, with only the slightest force. He could feel it pressing against his skin, but that did not convey to him how it really felt. With any other item, to feel was to caress, to run one's fingers over the object and experience not just one static sample of its texture but to feel how it moved, how it interacted with the skin.

But with a razor, that could never be. If he moved his thumb just slightly, one way or the other, then his skin would not sense its texture, but be ripped through by it. It was King Midas, never

376

to touch but that it destroyed what it touched. He pressed a little harder with his thumb, daring himself to draw blood, though the very idea of it repelled him. He moved his thumb away, holding the razor once again by the handle, and began to sharpen it against the strop.

His face was already lathered. He raised the edge to his cheek and scraped it slowly downwards, revealing a swathe of smooth, pale skin. He flicked the razor and a mound of lather landed in the sink. He returned it to his face and repeated the action again and again until his cheeks were clear. Then he raised his head and began to shave his neck, starting on the left and moving round to the right.

He took a sharp intake of breath as the blade curved round the tip of his chin. He looked at himself in the mirror. There it was, beneath his lower lip, a smudge of red that grew into a droplet as his heart continued in its task of pumping, unaware that it was forcing the blood so vital to it out of the tsar's body. The droplet became too large to support itself and plunged downwards. Aleksandr would have sworn he heard it as it splashed on to the porcelain of the sink and splattered in a hundred directions. He looked down, gazing at his own blood. Another drop dripped from his chin and into the bowl.

He felt a knot in his stomach, a revulsion at the sight of blood – his own blood – that he had never felt before. But the feeling quickly changed. It was still located in his stomach, but the sensation was now one of hunger. He licked his lips and stared down at the red droplets that glistened against the white porcelain. He reached out with his finger to scoop one up, but then stopped as he noticed his own reflection gazing back at him, tinted with red. His bald forehead was familiar, but he looked old – as old as he felt. He frowned and touched his upper lip with his fingers. There was nothing there, but in his reflection, he could clearly see a long moustache of dark, iron grey.

The nausea returned and the room around him began to swirl.

His eyes flicked open suddenly. It was morning and – though he could not see it – the sun was high. Now should be the hour of his deepest slumber, but the passenger of *Răzbunarea* felt awake and vibrant. The sides and lid of the coffin squeezed in tight around him, but it did not matter. He did not need to rise in order to enjoy the experience – it was not his experience anyway, but a stolen one, taken from a mind linked, however weakly, to his own.

Within moments, the sensation faded. The pain to his chin was inconsequential. The blood was of more interest, but he was old, and perhaps becoming jaded. Blood was commonplace.

What was of significance was that he had experienced anything at all. Until then, there had been nothing. When he had urged the tsar, from the prow of *Răzbunarea*, to visit Chufut Kalye, he had sensed no response. When he had imagined himself above the caves, guiding Aleksandr down into them, he had had only his imagination to see that what he had asked had been done.

But now, with the blood that was already in Aleksandr, and with the shock of the blood that had left his body, a connection had been made. It had not lasted long, but that would come. Aleksandr was alive, and that could only heighten the resistance of his mind. Soon things would be different.

Aleksei arrived at the palace in the midst of uproar. He saw the back of Tarasov's heel as it disappeared in the direction of the tsar's rooms. Volkonsky was in close pursuit. Aleksei joined the chase and soon found himself in Aleksandr's bedchamber. There was a small crowd gathered around the washstand, and Tarasov pushed his way through. Aleksei stepped into the gap and saw for the first time what had attracted so much attention.

The tsar lay on his back on the floor. His head was being cradled by his valet, Anisimov. There was blood on the tsar's chin, but it was no more than a smear; blood loss was certainly not the cause of his collapse.

'What happened?' demanded Volkonsky.

'His Majesty cut himself whilst shaving,' said Anisimov, almost whimpering. 'He fainted. I didn't catch him in time.'

'Did he hit his head?' asked Tarasov.

'I don't think so,' replied Anisimov. 'Not hard.'

Dr Stoffregen – the tsaritsa's personal physician – arrived and knelt down beside the prostrate figure. He looked over the tsar briefly, then began to rub eau de cologne into his forehead and temples.

'Too late. Too late,' moaned a voice quietly in Aleksei's ear. It was Wylie. The sight of his patient in so weakened a condition had sent him into a panic.

'Get him on to the bed,' shouted Aleksei. The command had some effect, and those around him began to lift the tsar off the floor.

At that moment, the tsaritsa arrived. Aleksei had scarcely seen her move from her own rooms since arriving in Taganrog. Stoffregen immediately stepped away from Aleksandr and went to her side. Fortunately, there were enough others around to take the tsar's weight, and soon they had him on the bed.

'Stand back! Let him breathe!' ordered Tarasov. The crowd moved away from the bed. The tsar groaned and threw his head from side to side. Then he became calmer, and his eyes flickered half open. The tsaritsa went to him. Tarasov and Wylie stood in quiet discussion. First Aleksei then Volkonsky joined them.

'What can you do for him?' asked Volkonsky.

'I would suggest leeches,' said Tarasov.

'You want to let his blood?' asked Aleksei, aghast.

'It's a standard medical practice.'

Volkonsky nodded. 'I'll ask him,' he said. He went over to the bed and bent down to speak in the tsar's ear.

'Send them to the devil!' Aleksandr's answer was loud and forthright. He stared over at Wylie and Tarasov as he rejected their advice, but within seconds the effort was too much, and his head fell back on the pillow.

'What he needs is a spiritual physician,' said the tsaritsa.

'I think what he also needs is a little peace and quiet,' said Volkonsky softly and out of the tsaritsa's earshot, although the remark was not directed at her. It was sound advice. The room began to clear, leaving only Tarasov, Stoffregen and Yelizaveta inside.

'Cain is not dead,' announced Aleksei. It was more than an hour since he had arrived back at Taganrog, and the first opportunity he had had to speak to the two doctors alone.

'What?' gasped Wylie. 'How do you know?'

Aleksei told them the story, or what they needed to know of it, from his return to Chufut Kalye up to Iuda's departure, though he avoided ever using that name.

'But you escaped,' commented Tarasov, stating the obvious.

'Cain wanted me to escape,' stated Aleksei bitterly. 'He said that he wanted a head start, and that's what he meant. I was released at dawn, giving him a little over twelve hours' lead on me. He wants to ensure that I witness his victory.'

'Released?' said Tarasov. 'So he had an accomplice?'

Aleksei glanced over at Wylie and saw a knowing smile on the Scotsman's face. 'I don't think he needed one, did he?'

'Did he mention it in his notebook?' asked Aleksei.

'Not specifically,' replied Wylie, 'but he did speculate on the endless uses to which the by-products of a vampire's body might be put.'

'By-products?' said Tarasov. 'Like the skin on the book, you mean?'

'Or the hair on the head. I'm right, am I not, Colonel Danilov?'

'Entirely,' said Aleksei, quietly impressed at Wylie's perspicacity. 'The rope was made from the hair of a *voordalak*. At dawn, when the sun hit it, it just burned away.' He held out his hands, palms up, and showed them the charred skin where the rope had been in contact with his wrists. It still itched.

'And where do you think Cain is now?' asked Tarasov.

Aleksei looked around, almost fearing that his answer would be even more literal than he meant it to be. 'Here,' he said simply.

'In Taganrog? But why?'

'Because of the Romanov Betrayal.'

'And what is that?'

'That's something that only His Majesty can tell us.'

'And will he?' demanded Wylie.

'He'll have to,' replied Aleksei, 'eventually.'

'He's asked for a priest.'

Tarasov looked ashen as he spoke. It was a little after five the following morning, and few of them had got much sleep.

'Is it as bad as that?' asked Volkonsky.

'He seems to think so.'

'I'll go fetch Father Fyodotov,' said Diebich, who had been waiting outside the tsar's room with the rest of them. He marched out swiftly.

'I don't understand it,' whispered Aleksei to Wylie, who sat beside him. 'There's been no sign of Cain, but still the tsar's condition worsens.'

'Perhaps whatever Cain gave him in the cave was enough,' suggested Wylie.

'Then why did Cain need his book? There was something more he planned to do. He's not done it, and yet still Aleksandr is dying.'

Wylie looked at him harshly. It was not something that any of them wanted to hear uttered out loud. 'It may be that that is precisely Cain's concern,' he said. 'The death of His Majesty – a true, Christian death – might not suit his plans at all.'

Aleksei said no more. Wylie was right. In some ways the tsar's death would be a blessing for all – not least for Aleksandr himself – but Aleksei prayed they could find another way.

The monastery was not far, and Baron Diebich returned with the priest within half an hour. A small crowd followed him into the tsar's room, and he began by saying a blessing. Aleksandr opened his eyes and smiled at the sight of the priest, and when the blessing was over, he spoke weakly.

'Thank you for coming, Father Fyodotov. I wish to confess. I ask you to hear me – not as an emperor, but as an ordinary man. Please do it quickly. I am ready for the sacrament.'

The others departed, leaving the tsar and the priest alone together.

The act of confession took almost an hour. When Fyodotov emerged, his face was sallow. Volkonsky slipped in immediately to speak with the tsar. The rest of them looked at the priest. His face was paler even than Aleksandr's own had been. His eyes scanned the ground as he walked out of the building, afraid to look up and make contact with those of anyone else. At the door, Aleksei caught his arm and spoke to him.

'What did His Majesty say?' It was a question born of instinctive concern, but one that no priest could ever answer.

Fyodotov's eyes flicked up and looked into Aleksei's. In them Aleksei saw a fear that he had seen in few soldiers – never before in a priest. The eyes scanned his face, as if in search of – begging for – responses to the sort of question a priest might normally be expected to answer, not ask.

'I can't tell you,' he whispered. 'I can't.'

The first time he said it, it was the normal reply of a holy man observing the sanctity of the confession. The second, it was the purest expression of fear.

CHAPTER XXV

VOLKONSKY EMERGED FROM THE TSAR'S ROOM ALMOST immediately.

'He wants to speak to you – alone,' he said. All eyes turned to follow the direction in which the prince was looking; all except Aleksei's. His eyes had no need to move. Volkonsky was staring straight at him.

'Me?' he said.

'He says he wants to tell you about Cain.'

Aleksei glanced around the room, nodding at both Tarasov and Wylie to indicate that they should come too. All three approached the door, Aleksei in front. Volkonsky stood in the way.

'He said just you.'

Aleksei nodded briefly, and Volkonsky let him in, stepping back across the doorway in case his word was not enough to keep the two doctors at bay.

Aleksandr lay in bed, propped up on a mound of pillows, smiling benevolently. Strange though the comparison seemed, he might easily have been mistaken for someone's grandmother – and yet now more than ever Aleksei could think of no one more suited to rule their nation.

'You've had dealings with *voordalaki* before, haven't you?' said the tsar. His voice was barely more than a murmur, but its clarity was absolute.

Aleksei nodded.

'It seems we've both been keeping things from one another,' continued Aleksandr.

'I've kept nothing from your physicians,' said Aleksei. Then he realized that now, only absolute honesty would do. 'Almost nothing,' he added.

'Then bring them in.'

Aleksei went back to the door and opened it, beckoning to Tarasov and Wylie. Volkonsky looked over to his master for confirmation, and got it. The door closed behind the two doctors, and the three men sat beside their tsar; Wylie on his left, Aleksei and Tarasov on his right.

'Do you remember your grandmother, Colonel Danilov?' Aleksandr asked.

Images came rushing back to Aleksei of the old, decrepit house and the old, decrepit woman whom as a child – even though he had laughed at her – he had loved more than anyone in the world except his parents. As he'd grown up, his cynicism over her silly, hand-me-down stories had overtaken the kinder feelings he should always have held for her. As he'd grown old, he'd learned that much of what she had said was true – even though in her mind truth had meant merely belief – and had learned to love her once again. It was she who had first told him of the *voordalak*, but even before he had read the words, he had understood the meaning of *Nullius in Verba* and had had to wait until he saw such creatures for himself before accepting what she had told him. If he had accepted what she had said from the outset, perhaps God would not have felt obliged to provide him with proof.

A cold, clammy hand squeezed his, awakening him from his reverie. 'Do you, Colonel?' asked Aleksandr, clutching his hand.

Aleksei nodded.

'My grandmother was an empress,' explained the tsar, 'the greatest empress Russia ever had.' He paused for a moment, in thought. 'The greatest leader. All over the world, they think it. The English call her Catherine the Great; *La Grande* in France.

Yekaterina Alekseevna she was officially. I just called her *babushka*, though not often to her face.'

The tsar smiled, lost in similar memories to those that had washed over Aleksei moments before, but he stepped out of them more quickly.

'She raised me to be tsar,' he continued. 'She knew my father would succeed her, but she could see he wasn't right for it. Even so, they didn't need to . . . I could have stopped them. Perhaps Papa was lucky; *babushka* never told him of the Romanov Betrayal.'

Aleksei glanced at Wylie and Tarasov. They were both staring intently at the tsar. There were tears in Wylie's eyes. It was hard to comprehend that such depth of affection could come from a foreigner, but perhaps the affection itself proved that the once Scottish doctor was now no such thing.

'I bet your grandmother told you stories, Danilov.'

Aleksei nodded and squeezed the tsar's hand. Wylie's emotion was infectious, and Aleksei doubted he would be able to speak.

'And I bet you didn't believe them, did you?'

A shake of the head this time.

'Well, that's where we differ.' The tsar spoke with a little more gusto now. 'Or, I suspect, where our grandmothers differed. No one with any sense would disbelieve what Yekaterina told them. Do you know what she told me?'

'No,' whispered Aleksei, though the tsar had already told him some of it – but it was obvious there was more.

'She wasn't a Romanov, you see,' explained Aleksandr. 'Not by blood. But in her belly she was. That's why they told her everything – all the family did. Someone had to know, and she was the strongest any of them had ever met. So she learned the story of Pyotr, her husband's grandfather, my great-great-grandfather. Pyotr the Great they called him. Pyotr the Sly was what she said.

'He travelled all over the place did Pyotr. And on his travels he met the strangest of men. One of them became a close friend – travelled with him up north, to the swamplands on the Gulf of Finland. This friend told Pyotr he should found a city there, but Pyotr said it was impossible. The friend brought in engineers from his own country, and somehow – through sheer, brute force, they managed to drain part of the swamp. And that's where Pyotr built his fortress. He named it after two saints, one of whom shared his own name – the Peter and Paul Fortress. It's still there, more than a hundred years on – right at the centre of Petersburg.

'After that, the rest of the city was easy to build – easier. Pyotr's own men began to take on a greater share of the work, following the techniques that had been begun for them. I say men, but Pyotr may not have thought of them as such. They were serfs, but they were still freer than the workers they took over from.

'And as you know, within nine years, the city was built, or built enough for Pyotr to declare it as the new capital. And Pyotr asked his friend what he could give him in exchange for his help.

'"Half the city," came the reply.

'Pyotr laughed. Such audacity was unusual. "The city is the new capital," he said. "The city *is* Russia. I cannot give you half Russia."

'"For what would you give me half of Russia?" asked the friend. Pyotr didn't reply, and so was presented with another question. "What is it that you most desire?"

'When my grandmother first told me this story,' said Aleksandr, breaking from his narrative, she asked me to guess what Pyotr's answer was. Of course, I got it wrong, but every subsequent time she told it, she asked me again, and I'd still get it wrong, deliberately. I'd answer "Power!" or "Wealth!" or "Victory!", but *babushka* would smile and shake her head.'

'And what *did* Pyotr answer?' asked Tarasov. Aleksei scowled at him for breaking into the tsar's recollections, but Aleksandr did not notice, and was happy to answer the question.

'Pyotr replied, "Enlightenment." It was all he had ever wanted – to know.

'"That I can give you," said the man. "But it is worth more than half of Russia."

'"I will not give all of Russia," Pyotr said.

386

'"No, but you can give me your soul."'

'Pyotr did not blink at the concept. His response was far more practical. "How?" he asked.

'His friend explained. He was what we would call a *voordalak*. An undead creature. He told Pyotr of how, when he, centuries before, had become a *voordalak*, he had briefly known the mind of every other such creature on the planet. This was not a blessing that was shared by them all, but one which he would endow on Pyotr – in exchange for half his nation.'

'What was the name of this *voordalak*?' asked Aleksei, though the answer was already forming itself on his lips. Aleksandr looked at Aleksei perceptively, detecting the foreknowledge that the question implied.

'He told Pyotr the name in his own language, then translated it into French, and then Russian. Its meaning was "the Son of the Dragon".'

'Drakonovich?' whispered Tarasov.

'So you might think,' explained the tsar, 'but the creature chose to formulate his Russian name in a slightly different manner. He chose . . .'

'Zmyeevich,' interrupted Aleksei. His voice was full of hatred.

'Zmyeevich – that's right,' said Aleksandr, without surprise at Aleksei's knowledge.

'How did you know?' asked Wylie.

'We met,' answered Aleksei.

'When?' said Wylie.

The tsar interrupted them before a reply could come.

'1812,' he said.

Aleksei was astonished. 'How did *you* know?'

'Because I saw you,' said the tsar, simply. 'But I'm getting ahead of myself. We are speaking of 1712, not 1812. According to my grandmother, Pyotr expressed no doubts as to the existence of such a creature as the *voordalak*. He asked merely how he could become one.

'Zmyeevich explained that the process was simple. First, he

would drink Pyotr's blood. He would drink deeply. It would be enough to kill Pyotr, but not immediately. Then, Pyotr need only drink a little of the blood of the *voordalak*, but it would be enough to ensure that he did not die, but lived for ever as another such creature. Then they two could rule Russia together – and for ever.'

'It's just like in Cain's book,' hissed Wylie. 'You knew all along.'

Aleksandr laid his head back on his pillow for a few moments. Telling the story was a strain for him, and he needed the strength to continue.

'Pyotr asked for three days to prepare himself,' he continued.

'He agreed?' asked Aleksei, aghast.

'He asked for three days to prepare himself,' the tsar repeated. 'Then he met Zmyeevich where they had arranged, just before midnight, in the place we now know as Senate Square. Zmyeevich was there, waiting. Pyotr knelt down in front of him, by the very bank of the Neva, which they together had tamed, and ripped open his shirt, exposing his flesh to the *voordalak*. The fangs descended and Pyotr felt Zmyeevich's lips close around his throat as his teeth penetrated his skin. It was, he later told, an ecstatic sensation, to feel the very blood being drained from one's body, but Zmyeevich did not go too far. What he drank would kill a man, but the man would still have the chance of – in a quite perverted sense – salvation.

'"Now, give me your sword," Zmyeevich said. Pyotr unsheathed it and handed it, hilt first, to the *voordalak*. Zmyeevich took it, and with its tip inscribed a cut across his own breast, from which blood began to ooze.'

Aleksei hung his head and shut his eyes tightly. The image was far, far too familiar; not a memory of Zmyeevich and Pyotr but one much more recent and, for Aleksei, indescribably more poignant – an image of Iuda and . . . God knew whom. But even by closing his eyes, Aleksei could not shut out the tsar's story.

'"Drink!" instructed Zmyeevich. Pyotr looked up at the

voordalak, and his mind became filled with understanding. He knew all that Zmyeevich knew – and Zmyeevich was centuries old. He gazed at the blood which ran in a thin line down the creature's chest. He desired to taste it, though he knew that that desire came not from himself, but from whatever had passed into him when the vampire had drunk his blood. He might share Zmyeevich's knowledge, but he had also to share his tastes.

'Pyotr stood back up on his feet, his eyes fixed on the bloody wound in front of him. He felt weak from his own loss of blood, and he knew that to consume a single drop of Zmyeevich's would make him strong again, make him strong for ever, make him immortal. All he had to do was to bend forward and suckle.

'But he did not. Instead, he looked Zmyeevich in the eye. "You imagine that I would want to become a thing like you?" he hissed. Then at a signal from him, Pyotr's personal guard revealed themselves. They grabbed Zmyeevich. He was strong, but there were a dozen of them, and they wrestled him to the ground. Pyotr stepped forward and, with what little strength he had, placed his foot on the monster's chest.

'"I have beaten you, Zmyeevich. Russia has beaten you. We have taken everything we could from you, and given you nothing in return."

'"You have betrayed me," replied Zmyeevich, with a snarl. "I helped to build your city. I gave you knowledge. Without me you would be nothing."

'"You took as much as you gave," said Tsar Pyotr. "Do you think I didn't know what you are – you and all those you brought with you? Do you think that I didn't observe that as your kind grew fat, good Russians would vanish in the night? You came to feed, not to help. Don't forget; I know your mind. You would not have shared Russia. You have tried to rule me and thereby rule my country. You would probably have succeeded. But instead you will die."

'Pyotr raised his hand to his brow. He felt faint. He knew he must end it quickly. He held out his hand to the commander of the troop – a Colonel Brodsky – who placed in it a stake made of hawthorn. He raised it, preparing to strike, but did not have the strength. He handed it back to Brodsky. "You do it," he said.

'It was a momentary distraction, but enough for Zmyeevich to exert his huge strength and throw off his captors. Blows from his bare hands were enough to kill two of them, snapping their necks like dry sticks. He ran towards the Neva and then turned back to Pyotr.

'"It was your choice, Romanov," he shouted. "To live or to die. You are dead now – dead since I took the blood from you. To live, you only had to drink my blood in exchange, but you refused. You feel unwell. Your heart beats weakly – it has little to pump, too little even to sustain itself. Soon you will die and you will die knowing this: I have your blood – Romanov blood. That cannot be undone. You have completed the first part of the transaction, but rejected the second, but it is not only you who can accept. I shall ask them all, in each generation, and one day, one of them will accept, and then, Romanov, Russia shall be mine."

'"Kill him!" shouted Pyotr, though he had barely the strength to make a sound. The soldiers ran across to Zmyeevich, but he was ready for them. He leapt into the Neva. The moment he jumped was the moment Pyotr lost consciousness. Zmyeevich must have been a strong swimmer. No trace of him was ever found.'

'But Pyotr lived!' said Aleksei. 'For another thirteen years.'

'He certainly did,' said Aleksandr. 'Pyotr was far more cunning than anyone gave him credit for. Do you know what he'd been doing in those three days he had asked Zmyeevich to wait? He had been eating: rare beef, venison, liver – *kishka* especially. Anything to build up the blood. He'd known he was taking a risk, that Zmyeevich might still take enough blood to kill him, but Pyotr was always a gambler. They took him straight to his bed, and he was there for almost three weeks. They fed him on the same sorts of things. He had no appetite, but he knew he must do it to live. Before long, he was as healthy as he had ever been.'

'But why go to all that risk?' asked Wylie.

'For the enlightenment that Zmyeevich had promised him. He claimed that in those few moments, as the monster fed on him, he could see the whole world. He saw the future of Russia – an illustrious future. The knowledge faded quickly, but he remembered a little of it, enough to make his country a great one. Perhaps if he had completed the process it would have stayed for ever – but at what cost? Later in his life, he occasionally saw images in his mind that he knew must come from Zmyeevich – as do I. I saw you through his eyes, Aleksei Ivanovich, briefly, when he met you in 1812. Though why you were with him, I still do not know. Perhaps one day you will tell me.'

'And did he call on the other generations of Romanovs?' asked Wylie.

Aleksandr shook his head. 'Not all. Or perhaps he did, but they kept it to themselves if so. He certainly visited my grandfather, Pyotr III. Convinced him too.'

'To become a vampire?' asked Wylie, astounded.

'That's what Yekaterina told me – and that's why she overthrew him, though she had plenty of other reasons. But she wasn't a Romanov, you see, so she was . . . immune. When Zmyeevich came back to take his prize, he learned that the tsar was dead. Yekaterina was waiting to confront him. He knew he wouldn't get anywhere while *she* was alive, but he had time to wait. He was not confined to a single generation.'

'But hang on,' interrupted Tarasov. 'You – and your grandfather – are descended from Pyotr by his daughter Anna Pyetrovna.' The tsar nodded. 'But she was born in 1708, before any of this happened. How could this . . . infection be carried to you by her?'

'It's not an infection,' explained Aleksandr. 'Zmyeevich took Pyotr's blood, not the other way round. Pyotr's blood was Romanov blood, as was Anna Pyetrovna's – as is mine. It doesn't matter if it was taken before or after she was conceived.'

'Contagious magic,' muttered Tarasov.

The tsar nodded. 'That would seem to be the term for it.'

391

'Yekaterina told you all this?' asked Aleksei.

'Some of it. Cain told me more. He was quite keen that I understood what was to happen to me. He claims to understand much more of it than Zmyeevich.'

'I bet he does,' said Aleksei.

'So what happened – in the cave with Cain?' asked Wylie.

'He had a vial of Zmyeevich's blood. He offered it to me. All I had to do was drink it. Then death for me would not be an ending, but a transformation. I would rise again, a new creature, wiser, stronger, more powerful than I had ever been before. I would live for ever.'

'Just as Zmyeevich promised your great-great-grandfather,' said Aleksei.

'Yes, but *babushka* had warned me. I would get all those things, but I would become completely subservient to Zmyeevich. Russia would still be mine, but I would be his. Cain confirmed it. They were going to take me away, back to Zmyeevich's country, but then I'd return and rule Russia. Someone would eventually understand that all wasn't right, but by then, Zmyeevich hoped, it would be too late; he would have taken his grip on power.'

'And when you refused, that was when he decided to kill you,' said Aleksei. 'I must have arrived just in time.'

'Oh, no,' said Aleksandr. 'My refusal meant nothing to him. He told me I had no say in the matter.'

'But I thought a man could only become a vampire willingly.'

'That's what Zmyeevich thought – and why he waited so long. Cain believed it at first, but he wasn't going to be fool enough to take Zmyeevich's word. He experimented. It turns out the victim does have to be willing – and that in this case, he was.'

'You were happy to become a *voordalak*?' gasped Aleksei.

'No,' said Aleksandr. 'The free will does not come in drinking the vampire's blood. It comes in allowing one's own blood to be drunk. Pyotr did that quite happily, and his acquiescence is – apparently – good enough for all of us.'

'Not quite all of you, I think,' said Wylie, with half a smile.

'What do you mean?' asked the tsar.

'Something in Cain's notebook,' explained the doctor. 'I didn't understand it at the time, but now it makes more sense. It said something like, "In each generation, the blood can exert its influence on only one sibling. Whichever is first touched, the others become free." Once Zmyeevich exerted his power over you, he lost any chance of doing the same to your brothers or sisters.'

'My brothers, safe?' said the tsar joyously, despite his weakness, and sitting up a little. 'Konstantin, Nikolai, Mihail – all of them?'

'So it would seem,' said Aleksei, 'though I wonder how Cain knew.'

'He didn't write that down,' said Wylie.

'He didn't shy from experimenting on humans,' said Aleksei. 'Why not an entire family?' He tried to force the image from his mind as he spoke.

'He's been planning this for a long time,' said Aleksandr. 'Not as long as Zmyeevich, obviously, but this isn't the first time I've encountered him. That was during the Patriotic War.'

'In 1812?' Aleksei failed to hide his astonishment.

The tsar nodded. 'At the very time of Bonaparte's occupation of Moscow. I was in the capital. He came and offered me much the same arrangement. Back then, he thought I needed to be in agreement, but on the other hand, our country was in direst need. He said Bonaparte would be no match for Zmyeevich and me if we stood together. He even claimed that Zmyeevich was already working to liberate Moscow from the French yoke.'

Aleksei glanced at the other two men, but realized that no one in the room but himself could know what had really happened in Moscow. It was a surprise to him that Iuda had been to Petersburg in that time, but it was perfectly reasonable. Aleksei had spent most of the five weeks of Bonaparte's occupation of the old capital hiding in Yuryev-Polsky. He had assumed that Iuda had remained in Moscow, but why should he have? There would have been plenty of time for him to travel to Petersburg, spend several

393

days there, and return. His visit to Aleksandr would have taken only a fraction of that time. But all that was history. Aleksei's concerns now were for the present, and for the tsar.

'You're safe now,' he said. 'Neither Cain nor Zmyeevich will get to you while we're here.'

'Safe?' wailed the tsar. 'How can I ever be safe? Even in death I can seek no protection.'

'Don't say such things, Your Majesty,' said Tarasov.

'Believe me, I would gladly ask you to kill me now if it would free me of this curse, but it will not. To die would be to bring about all that Zmyeevich desires.'

'What do you mean?'

'I have drunk his blood,' said Aleksandr, his lips articulating precisely, though only the slightest of sounds escaped his throat.

'What?' exclaimed Tarasov, but it was just as Aleksei had suspected.

'At Chufut Kalye – he gave me wine. I didn't think. I didn't understand – not then. I just drank it. When Cain offered me Zmyeevich's blood, he was toying with me. I had already drunk it. It's in me. The blood has been exchanged both ways, and there is only one further step before I come to be like him.'

'One step?'

'I must die. You're right, Aleksei Ivanovich, Cain was about to kill me when you interrupted us, but it was no act of petty vengeance. The blood had been exchanged – that is the purpose of the vampire's bite, but death itself does not have to be caused by that bite. He wanted to stab me, but I could be poisoned, fall ill. I could have been like that poor fellow Maskov and fallen from my carriage. Cowards die many times before their deaths, but I must truly be afraid to die, for when death comes it will bring for me so awful a resurrection that I cannot bear even to think of it.'

'You're not going to die,' said Wylie, though the sorrow in his voice would have done little to convince Aleksandr of his confidence in the statement.

'I think the blood I drank may be poison anyway – or perhaps Cain added something to it. I have felt ill since that day. I've been taking quinine in the hope of curing myself, but I feel no better. Cain likened my contamination to malaria, and I reasoned that a similar ailment might respond to the same cure, but who knows? It may even have made things worse.'

'What can we do?' asked Tarasov. He did not appear to have any expectation of an answer.

The tsar tightened his grip on Aleksei's hand. 'When I die, Colonel Danilov will know what to do. He must be to me as Colonel Brodsky was to my great-great-grandfather.'

'Your Majesty, there would be no greater pleasure for me than to kill Zmyeevich, but he could be anywhere in the world. I would have to . . .' Aleksei knew this was not what Aleksandr meant, even before the tsar interrupted him.

'Pyotr wasn't sure whether his plan would succeed. He couldn't know whether, once Zmyeevich had drunk his blood, he might find irresistible the urge to do likewise. So Brodsky brought the wooden stake; he had been given two alternative sets of instructions for what to do with it. He was lucky Pyotr had such strength of will. I fear you may not be so fortunate, Aleksei.'

The two doctors stared at Aleksei, dumbfounded. Aleksei himself said nothing, but in his heart he made a silent promise. He would allow no mawkish sentiment to sway him, and his love for his tsar would drive his hand. He prayed it would not come to pass, but he knew that if it did one day become necessary, he would do his duty by his tsar.

CHAPTER XXVI

ALEKSANDR OPENED HIS EYES. HE FELT AS THOUGH HE HAD slept for an eternity. He looked around him. All was familiar. He was in his bed, in his room, in his palace, in Taganrog. A memory returned to him. He had spoken to Danilov, Wylie and Tarasov and told them all he knew. He should have done it earlier. He should have told Danilov the first time he set eyes on him – in the flesh. But when General Barclay introduced them, it had been two years since he had seen that image of the colonel, viewed through Zmyeevich's eyes. His fears over Zmyeevich and Cain had then long since faded, washed away in the jubilation of Bonaparte's defeat. It had all seemed unreal, and he had convinced himself his recognition of Danilov was a coincidence. And even if it had been him in the vision, did that make him friend, or foe?

Still, Aleksandr really should have told all to Danilov back at the Nevsky Monastery, as he set out for Taganrog after that first letter from Cain. It had been thirteen years since Cain had spoken to him. Aleksandr hoped he had given up, at least for this generation. But in that time, Danilov had proved himself to be a brave and loyal officer, and Aleksandr had been able to dismiss any doubts over the nature of his relationship with Zmyeevich. But even in Petersburg, Aleksandr had found it difficult to truly appreciate the danger that might come from Cain. It was all too fantastical – a terror by night. The greater danger came from the plotters amongst his own men, and so he had been happier to leave

Danilov in the capital, close to where that danger lay. Even so, he had been glad to see him when he first arrived in Taganrog.

Not that the threat from the Northern – or Southern – Society had diminished. He might still fall prey to one of their assassins. Now the consequences would be worse. His death now carried with it a far greater dread. Perhaps though, it would not be so bad for Russia. If his death – whatever his subsequent fate – marked the beginning of a new dynasty, one that was not touched by Romanov blood, might that not save his country from this curse? Beyond that, if Russia became – God forbid – a republic, it would end Zmyeevich's hopes for ever.

But no. It was not for one man, even a tsar, to toy with the succession to the Russian throne as ordained by God Himself. Aleksandr would die and his brother would take his place; a brother who, so Wylie had said, would remain untainted by this plague of the blood. He had asked Danilov to carry out the task. Danilov had seen these creatures; he would not fail. But whatever the outcome, Aleksandr was glad to have unburdened himself to those three. He felt better.

He really did feel better. He raised his arms from the bed and looked at them. They were still pale, but they did not glisten with sweat as they had done before – and most importantly, they did not shake. He felt his forehead; it was cool. His stomach didn't tug at him as though desperate for freedom. In fact, he felt hungry. It was a wonderful sensation, having for so many days been unable to tolerate even the smell of any but the most insubstantial foods.

He threw the bedclothes aside and was about to stand, but a voice interrupted him.

'Whatever are you doing?'

It was his beloved wife, Yelizaveta. She was seated a little way from the bed.

'How long have you been there?' he asked in surprise.

'Since dawn,' she said.

'What time is it now?'

'Almost eleven.'

'On what day?'

'Tuesday,' she said. 'You've been asleep for a day and a half.'

He swung his legs over the side of the bed and attempted to stand. That was not such a wise idea. He ached all over, but that was still no bad thing. The aching was an aftereffect; a reminder of what had been, not a warning of what was to come. It was best to stay in bed for now though.

'Anisimov!' he bellowed. The sound was louder than he had expected. His voice was returning too.

His valet's head appeared around the door. 'Anisimov,' said the tsar, 'open up the shutters. And then go fetch Dr Wylie. And Tarasov. And Danilov.'

Anisimov followed his master's instructions in the order they were given. The autumn sunlight flooded in through the window, and the valet left to summon the three men. Yelizaveta came over to the bed, and Aleksandr clasped her hand.

'How utterly beautiful it all is,' he exclaimed, gazing at the sunlight pouring in.

The two doctors and the colonel arrived presently. Yelizaveta was perceptive enough to leave the men alone. 'I must write to my mother and tell her how much better you are,' was her proffered excuse.

Wylie and Tarasov poked, prodded and examined Aleksandr in ways with which he was all too familiar. Danilov stood back throughout, leaning against the door. The doctors then moved aside and discussed their patient in undertones. They beckoned Danilov over and the conversation continued in the same vein. At length, they turned to face the tsar.

'Am I better?' he asked.

'You have no symptoms.' It was Wylie who responded.

'So I'm better.'

'You are as you were before your visit to Chufut Kalye.'

'Before I drank the blood of a *voordalak*, you mean?' said the tsar, irritated by the doctor's equivocation.

'If your ailments were as a result of . . . what you drank,' said Tarasov, 'then it would seem that the effect has passed.'

'For Heaven's sake,' said Aleksandr, slamming his arms down on the bed and immediately regretting it. 'Danilov, will *you* speak plainly?'

'I'll speak honestly,' said Aleksei. It seemed to Aleksandr a quibbling distinction, but the colonel made his meaning very clear. 'We have no idea what we're talking about,' he explained. 'The good doctors here know about the disorders of men – but your affliction does not fit well into that category. I have encountered vampires, but every one of their victims I have ever seen has either become such a creature himself, or has died and become their prey. I have never met anyone in the limbo in which you find yourself.'

'Take a guess,' replied the tsar.

'We think Zmyeevich's blood has left your body,' said Aleksei.

'Cain's book said that such a purification might take weeks, even months,' explained Wylie.

'But Your Majesty's use of quinine may have precipitated matters,' added Tarasov.

'So I am not at risk of becoming . . . like Zmyeevich.' The three men glanced at one another like naughty schoolboys. 'Well?' Aleksandr insisted.

'If you were to die now, we believe you would die a normal death,' said Danilov. 'Your corpse would putrefy and rot like any other.'

Aleksandr blanched slightly at the words, then stifled a giggle, then laughed out loud. 'Was ever a man so pleased to learn of his own mortality?' he said.

'Who knows?' said Aleksei, returning the tsar's smile. 'Ask a priest.'

'I did,' said the tsar. 'I asked Father Fyodotov. He was no help at all, which is why I called on the three of you.'

The two doctors both expressed their congratulations on

Aleksandr's recovery, as did Danilov, but the colonel watched the tsar throughout with an eye of concern that was unnerving.

'Can I get up now and go about my business?' Aleksandr asked.

'Not yet, I think, Your Majesty,' said Wylie, striding over to the bed to ensure that Aleksandr did not attempt to get out. 'Your body is weakened from fighting its assailant. It has been victorious, but now it needs rest.'

'Oh, very well,' said the tsar. He felt he had the energy to go out and run all the way along the perimeter of the town, but he knew the sensation wouldn't last. 'Send Volkonsky in, would you?'

Wylie nodded, and the three men turned to leave.

'And thank you,' said Aleksandr. 'All of you.'

'It must be by his death,' said Wylie. They were the same words Aleksei had heard uttered months before, and then, as now, their object had been the tsar, but on this occasion they were motivated by an affection that would not have been dreamed of in Prince Obolensky's house in Petersburg. Aleksei was pleased Wylie's train of thought was following his own.

They had gone down to the beach, where they felt assured of speaking in privacy. Volkonsky had been summoned to the tsar's presence, as requested. It was a good thing that, for now, he would not hear their conversation, much as they might need his complicity, when the time came.

'The question,' replied Aleksei, 'is *when* he dies.'

'A long time from now, I should hope,' said Tarasov.

'I think we need a more precise reply than simply "sooner" or "later".'

'When he is free of Zmyeevich's blood, you mean,' said Wylie.

'But he *is* free of it,' said Tarasov. 'I know it's guesswork, but we're all agreed.'

'And that's why Cain is coming for him,' Aleksei pointed out.

'He knows that any dose of Zmyeevich's blood will wear off eventually. He needs to re-administer it.'

'But why risk coming here?' asked Wylie. 'He could gain access to His Majesty at any time – back in Petersburg even – and slip the blood into his food or drink.'

'That's true,' said Aleksei, 'but I think Cain will act here and soon.'

'Why?'

'For two reasons. The first is simply that that was what he implied when we spoke in Chufut Kalye.' Aleksei knew that Iuda could lie just as easily as he could tell the truth, but that did not mean he always lied. If he did, then predicting him would be child's play.

'And the second?'

'The second,' replied Aleksei, 'is that he is afraid the tsar will die.'

'Afraid?' asked Tarasov.

'Desperately. His Majesty can only die once. If that happens when he is free of Zmyeevich's blood then all is lost for Cain – and Zmyeevich.'

'And so he'll try to get His Majesty to drink more,' concluded Tarasov.

'Exactly,' said Aleksei. 'And then kill him – as quickly as possible.'

'But the influence of the blood lasts for weeks,' said Tarasov. 'We've seen that. Cain would have no need to rush.'

'He can't take the risk. Cain hasn't observed the state of the tsar's health. And anyway, how do we know that the period during which the outward symptoms manifest themselves has any correlation with susceptibility to becoming a vampire?'

'We can make a good guess,' said Tarasov.

'We can,' said Aleksei. 'But that's not a chance Cain can take. If you ask me, his biggest fear right now is that Aleksandr is so weakened by what he's suffered he may die anyway.'

'So what can we do?' asked Tarasov.

Aleksei hesitated. What he had in mind would be more readily accepted by the tsar himself than by his two loyal doctors. But he knew it could not be executed without them. His reply, when it came, was soldierly.

'We do what the enemy least wants us to do.'

'How?' asked Tarasov.

'We make sure Cain's greatest fear becomes a reality.'

Aleksandr reclined on his bed. It was now a day since his recovery. That, at least, was how he saw it, though his doctors seemed less confident. Should they not at least have faith in their own remedies? Perhaps they knew more than they were telling. He certainly did not yet feel well enough to get up, but he felt no worse than yesterday. Better? It was hard to judge. Time would tell.

There was a knock at the door.

'Come,' he boomed. There, that proved it. His voice was quite recovered. He had attempted only to raise his voice a fraction above the normal level, but he could not disguise its strength.

Volkonsky entered. 'Are you able to receive visitors, Your Majesty?'

'Visitors?' Aleksandr found himself almost excited at the prospect. 'Who?'

'Drs Wylie and Tarasov. And Colonel Danilov.'

Aleksandr tutted. 'Oh, they're hardly visitors, are they?' he said petulantly. 'Never mind. Send them in. Send them in.'

Volkonsky left. Aleksandr was not entirely sure he wanted to see Danilov, Wylie and Tarasov. They were all intelligent gentlemen – cleverer than he was, he knew that. And so what he'd managed to piece together over the preceding day would surely have occurred to them much more quickly – particularly if they had been working together. Perhaps, with luck, their minds had got beyond the point which his had reached, and found some alternative to his own dark conclusion, some hidden door in the woodwork that would allow him a quick exit from reality. God knew he had sought one.

But his reasoning seemed utterly sound. When he had first told all to Wylie, Tarasov and Danilov, he had told them of his terror of death; not the terror most men have – that fear of the unknown that latches on to every tiny doubt they might have about the goodness of God and the cleanliness of their own record – but a concrete, confident fear that his death would mean his rebirth as a creature that had spewed forth from Hell. If he had died then, his fate would have been inescapable. It had seemed inescapable for all time. He had prayed. 'Let this cup pass from me,' had almost been his words to the Lord, but he understood that they would be blasphemous. At the same time he knew that even to have thought them was for God to have heard them. The blasphemy could not be undone.

And yet, it seemed, God had indeed answered his prayers. The cup, or at least the fever, had passed from him. Wylie and Tarasov might feign ignorance, but Aleksandr had known in his very bones that he had recovered. That the vigour of his blood – Romanov blood – had been powerful enough to defeat that which had invaded him. It had taken both time and torment, but in the end he had won.

But the Lord had only taken one cup from his lips so that He might offer him another chalice – one that contained a venom far less appetizing, and yet far less foul. Aleksandr might have lived to fight another day, but if he did fight another day, there was every chance he would lose. He was forty-seven years old. His *babushka* had survived to sixty-seven. He might well do better. And yet every day of that life he would run the risk of dying – dying with the blood of Zmyeevich, freshly introduced, inside his body. There was only one solution – to die when he was certain that his blood was pure. And that time could only be now.

Colonel Danilov entered first, then Dr Tarasov, and finally Dr Wylie. Each looked upon the tsar with his own brand of affection and his own veneer of pity. But, to a man, their faces were grave. They were clever men; the tsar knew that. It was flattering to have his conclusion endorsed by such minds as theirs.

Aleksei breathed deeply as he left the tsar's bedchamber. Prince Volkonsky had been hovering outside. He looked at Aleksei enquiringly. Aleksei shook his head briefly and the prince's face fell. Baron Diebich looked from Volkonsky to Aleksei and back. There could be no mistaking the news.

Wylie and Tarasov came out of the room a moment later. Their faces showed the same gloom as Aleksei's.

'Is there no hope?' asked Volkonsky.

'There is only hope,' replied Wylie.

'He seemed so much better,' said Diebich, as if the assertion would change things.

'A flicker of life,' Wylie told him. 'I have witnessed it in more than one case. The will of the patient can be strong enough to overcome all symptoms, but only briefly.'

'How long does he have?' asked Volkonsky.

'Days – perhaps hours.'

'The poor tsaritsa,' muttered Diebich.

'He has asked to speak with you,' said Tarasov, addressing Volkonsky. Diebich half rose to his feet, but Tarasov raised a hand to him. 'Only the prince, I'm afraid, Baron – for the time being.'

Diebich nodded and pressed his lips together hard. Volkonsky went into the tsar's room. Aleksei took another deep breath. There were still matters to be discussed with the doctors. Diebich was slumped mournfully in a chair beside his master's door. Aleksei glanced at first Tarasov and then Wylie, nodding towards the door that led out to the garden, before heading through it.

Neither of the doctors was cut out to be a spy. They appreciated the fundamentals – that if three men intended to meet for a private conversation, then it was wise for them not all to head off to it at the same time – but the execution of their seemingly casual departures from the house was excessively theatrical, and the timing of the separation between their exits too precise. It did not matter. No one would be concerned that three of the tsar's staff were talking at this time – however much they might be curious about the role of an interloper such as Aleksei. In their grief, no one in the house would be up to observing anything much.

'You think His Majesty will be able to convince Volkonsky?' asked Aleksei.

'He has to,' said Tarasov. 'The prince is far too sharp not to spot what's going on – and to stop it. He has to know that what we are planning is, ultimately, in the tsar's best interests.'

'And His Majesty is the only person who can convince Volkonsky of that,' added Wylie.

'The prince will think he's delirious,' said Aleksei. 'We should have stayed to add the weight of our voices.'

'If Volkonsky wants our opinions, he will seek them,' insisted Tarasov. 'Those two have known each other a long time – in the end, Volkonsky will obey. And the tsar is not going to tell him everything.'

'I suppose you're right,' conceded Aleksei. 'But we do need Volkonsky. Security is vital.'

'You're sure Cain will come?' asked Wylie.

'He must. There's nothing he can do once His Majesty is dead, and so he will try to find a way to administer a further dose of Zmyeevich's blood. Then – if I were him – I'd also make sure of the tsar's death. It would be foolish to leave anything to chance.'

'We should be grateful you're not him,' said Wylie.

'Are we really certain that the effects of the first taste of the blood have passed?' asked Tarasov.

'We can't know for sure,' said Aleksei, 'but I'm convinced Cain thinks they are. That is why he will come.'

'And we'll be ready for him,' said Tarasov.

'You two will be attending the tsar,' replied Aleksei. 'Volkonsky will arrange a guard around the palace. I'll make sure he puts me in charge of them.'

'From all we've seen, Cain's a dangerous man.'

'That's why they'll have orders to kill,' said Aleksei. That, and other, more personal reasons.

'If only we could do more,' said Wylie.

'You can do the most important thing of all,' insisted Aleksei. 'You must both make sure that His Majesty eats and drinks nothing in the hours leading up to his death – otherwise everything else we do will be a waste of time.'

Aleksei walked away from them briskly and strode back towards the house. He had seen that Volkonsky was beckoning to him.

The tsaritsa was more desperate than the starets had ever seen her. She had heard from Father Fyodotov – and other gossips in the royal household – how grave her husband's condition was. Fyodotov seemed to know more, but his lips were closed by the seal of confession. The starets wondered how much Aleksandr had told him.

She had come to the monastery again to speak to him – at his summons, though he felt certain she would have sought him out anyway.

'He is dying, Father,' she said after they had recited the Prayer of the Heart.

'Has he made his confession?' It was better for the starets not to reveal the conversations he had had with Fyodotov.

'Yes. And then it seemed he had got better, but it was only a passing rally. He might die within hours, the doctors say.'

The starets leaned forward. This was surprising news. 'As soon as that?' he asked.

'I should be with him, Father. But you are my only hope.'

'Jesus Christ is the hope of the world,' said the starets. 'I am merely His representative on Earth.'

'Please, Father – there is so little time. Do you have the remedy you promised me?'

The starets might have taken time to lecture the tsaritsa on the virtue of patience, but from what she had said, he knew that time was now pressing. For the tsar to die now would be intolerable. He slipped his hand into his robe and brought out a small vial.

He handed it to the tsaritsa. She took it from him and grasped it to her chest. A flood of hope ran across her face, and yet still she doubted.

'So little?' she said.

'So little your faith?' he replied. 'That is all that is needed.'

She nodded and looked down at the thick, dark liquid that clung to the glass sides of the bottle.

'Should I mix it with his food?' she asked.

'With food, or with drink – but only after the food has been cooked. Or it can be given to him directly, if he will take it.'

'Why shouldn't he?'

'His doctors will try to prevent you giving it to him, and in his state, he may be swayed by them. You must be determined.'

'I will be.'

She remained kneeling, staring at the floor of the stone cell in the monastery, awaiting her dismissal. He did not delay her.

'Go now, my child,' he said. 'I will pray for you both.'

The tsaritsa thanked him, then rose to her feet and left quickly. The starets stood and went to the doorless archway that formed the entrance to his cell. He watched her as she left, clearly battling against her own ill health simply to make it to this appointment, which she believed would save her husband.

She was mistaken; Iuda knew that full well as he pulled the starets' robe off over his head. He had more work to do that night, and beneath the habit he was almost dressed for his next task. The other monks might remark on his disappearance, but they had always seen him as a nomad – a starets who occasionally used their home as a place of quiet contemplation. There were many like him.

The military were by nature far more suspicious. To have passed himself off as a soldier for any length of time would have required forged papers and – to get close to the tsar – at least one personal recommendation. But the acquisition of the lieutenant's uniform whose tunic he was now buttoning up had been a much simpler affair – taken from a drunken soldier whose half-hearted resistance had provided little entertainment. The others might miss him, but they would not find his body for another few days, at the very least.

Iuda straightened his new collar and noticed that his fingers felt wet. He looked at them and saw blood still damp on the uniform. It did not matter – his plans would be carried out before anyone had the chance to inspect him.

He took one final glance around the cell. Stone walls, of one kind or another, had become quite familiar to him over the last few years, but no more. He hurried out into the night.

CHAPTER XXVII

IT WAS ALMOST MIDNIGHT. WEDNESDAY WOULD SOON BE THURSDAY, and Thursday, 19 November 1825 was the day that Tsar Aleksandr I would die. Aleksei had not discussed with Wylie or Tarasov the exact hour, but all agreed it would be before noon. Aleksei felt happier not to know.

Volkonsky had been content to place the guard under Aleksei's orders – a mixture of regular troops close to the palace and Colonel Nikolayev's Cossacks covering a wider perimeter. Volkonsky himself wanted to stay by Aleksandr's side, along with the tsaritsa, Wylie, Tarasov, Diebich and several others. Aleksei would spend most of the night at the tsar's door, much as he would have loved to ride once again with the *Kazaki*. But that was where Iuda would be heading, whatever direction he might come from, and so Aleksei would be in the best place to intercept him. He considered standing guard inside the bedchamber itself, but it would be an insult to the tsaritsa – and all those who loved Aleksandr – to see Iuda exterminated over the very bed upon which the object of their love lay dying. More than that, Aleksei felt uncharacteristically disinclined to be present at the death of a man whom he held in such esteem.

He had made one tour of the palace grounds already. He wished he had known the men better – he did not recognize many of their faces, let alone know their names. But Volkonsky vouched for them, and they vouched for each other. There was one concern;

a Lieutenant Morev had not reported for duty. The view of most of his comrades was that he was a drunk and they were better off without him, but it was still a cause for apprehension. He asked to be informed the moment the man was seen.

It was distasteful even to attempt to think in the way that Iuda did, but Aleksei knew that his foe rarely did anything without forethought, and so it was a necessary unpleasantness. Though they might remark on the absence of a lieutenant, there would be less note taken of his return. Who was to say that in the meantime he might not have been recruited to Iuda's cause? Recruited by induction, to use Iuda's own word. He would have to be willing, but a young drunken soldier might easily be persuaded. Iuda would also need the assistance of a *voordalak* to carry out such a plan. But – who knew? – Zmyeevich himself might be nearby, awaiting his henchman's success. And then there was always the beautiful Raisa Styepanovna. If she were assisting Iuda, then the processes of persuading the young lieutenant to accept his rebirth as a vampire might have been very simple indeed. But if the soldier did return, Aleksei would be waiting, and if he was no longer human, Aleksei would know.

He leaned against the wall, beside the door to the tsar's room, and listened. He heard no sound from within. He tried to picture the scene inside, but he remained glad that he was not a part of it. It would be a long night for him, standing guard outside, but for those who sat in tears beside Aleksandr's bed, it would be an eternity.

Aleksandr looked at the figures around him and smiled. So many of those he loved were here. Most important of all was Yelizaveta. She would be devastated by his death – but how much more would she suffer to learn of the alternative? He knew that if Cain and Zmyeevich succeeded in their plan to make him a *voordalak*, then he would have no vestige of the affection he had once held for his wife. She would not know it, but she would be happier for him to die.

His greatest regret was that he would never see his brothers again – his sisters too, though none of those living had remained in Russia still. But he would have dearly loved to say goodbye to Konstantin, Nikolai and Mihail. He and Konstantin had grown up side by side – there was only two years between them – but he still sometimes looked upon Nikolai and Mihail as children. He had been eighteen when Nikolai was born. All three of them were fine men. He might have preferred to have had children of his own, but Aleksandr had no qualms about the succession passing to his brother.

It would not, however, be his brother Konstantin. Few in Russia knew it, but Konstantin did not want to become tsar. It was the wisest opinion he had ever expressed, and one which Aleksandr shared. Konstantin was too much like their father. Aleksandr had begun his reign by removing an unsuitable tsar from power; he was not going to end it by bequeathing his throne to another. Nikolai would make a far better ruler – better not just than Konstantin would be, but better than Aleksandr had been. The reason, at least in part, was obvious. Nikolai had been less than six months old when Yekaterina died. He had never been touched by her influence. Aleksandr loved his *babushka*, but he knew that she had ruined him.

It was already morning, as far as he could guess. The shutters were closed, but light was just beginning to seep through. He had drifted between sleep and wakefulness throughout the night. These, he knew, were precious hours, the last he would spend with Yelizaveta Alekseevna.

The door opened. Aleksandr started, wondering who it might be, but it was only one of the maids. She carried a tray. On it was a bowl of broth, and beside it some bread. She placed it on the table next to the bed.

'I'll do it,' said Yelizaveta, reaching over for the bowl. She held it under Aleksandr's nose.

'Drink, my darling,' she said.

Aleksandr would have dearly loved to accept. It was not out

of hunger – though he was hungry – but simply to allow his wife the feeling of having done something to help. But Danilov, Wylie and Tarasov had drilled him thoroughly. Their concern was his – the prospect of his eternal damnation. A small slip now could ruin everything. He glanced over at Wylie, but it was only for confirmation of what he already knew. The side-to-side movement of the doctor's head was minimal, but Aleksandr understood it. He feigned a violent coughing fit and pushed his wife's hand away.

She returned the soup to the tray. 'Perhaps later,' she said, and Aleksandr nodded through his seizure.

'You may go,' said Diebich to the maid. The girl hurried out, frightened by what she had seen in the tsar. Aleksandr lay back on his pillow and tried to rest. As his eyelids lowered, he noticed Volkonsky leaving the room, almost as if in pursuit of the maid.

'You were instructed to bring no food or drink.'

Aleksei immediately recognized the voice as Volkonsky's. It came through the window. Aleksei had been taking another tour of the grounds. It was light now, and he was satisfied no *voordalak* would attempt to gain admission to the tsar, but there was still the possibility of human attack – and Iuda was most definitely human.

Aleksei looked inside. The prince was talking to a girl – one of the maids; Aleksei couldn't remember her name. They were just outside the kitchen. He went in through the kitchen door, and was with them in seconds.

'He told me you had asked for it, sir, for His Majesty.' The girl was almost in tears. All in the palace – the staff as much as anyone else – were living on the ragged edge of their emotions, but to be interrogated by Volkonsky, however benevolent his motivation, must have been an ordeal.

'I?' thundered Volkonsky.

'Asked for what?' said Aleksei. His tone was lighter than the prince's, though it had the same sense of urgency.

412

'She brought His Majesty soup,' Volkonsky explained. 'Says some officer gave her the instruction.'

'A lieutenant,' said the maid.

'Lieutenant Morev?' asked Aleksei.

'No, sir. I know Lieutenant Morev,' she said. 'We all do. I didn't recognize this one.'

'And he told you to fetch soup for His Majesty.'

'That's right – well, no. He had the soup; he'd brought it from the kitchen. He gave it to me and told me to take it in.'

'What did he look like?'

'Tall, sir. About your age. Blond hair – needed cutting.'

Aleksei rubbed his hand across his mouth.

'Cain?' asked Volkonsky.

Aleksei nodded. 'Did he drink any of it?' he asked.

Volkonsky and the girl replied together, both in the negative.

'Where is it now?'

'It's still there,' said Volkonsky.

'Well, get back and make sure he doesn't touch it.' If the prince objected to taking orders from a mere colonel, it wasn't reflected in the speed of his departure. 'Which way did he go?' said Aleksei, turning back to the maid.

'Back into the kitchen,' she replied, pointing.

'How long ago?'

'Five minutes.'

Aleksei ran into the kitchen. The same air of gloom hung over the staff in there as it did in the rest of the house.

'A lieutenant came through here,' said Aleksei. 'Tall. Blond. Which way did he go?'

The head chef pointed to the back door.

'He just wanted something to eat,' said a voice.

'I thought I saw him heading for the beach,' added another, more helpfully.

Aleksei ran outside and looked around him. 'Heading for the beach' covered a multitude of directions from a house situated so close to the sea. Aleksei guessed that Iuda would veer more to the

413

east, avoiding going back past the tsar's bedroom windows, from which he might be recognized.

'Who goes there?' came a shout. A young *ryadovoy* emerged from the bushes, his bayonet aimed at Aleksei's belly. 'I'm sorry, Colonel,' he said, as soon as he recognized Aleksei.

'Doing your job,' said Aleksei curtly. 'Did a lieutenant come by? Blond?'

'Yes, sir.'

'And where did he go?'

'That way, down the coast road.'

Aleksei was already running. The boy was lucky not to have attempted to stop Iuda. If he had, it was unlikely he would be alive now. Within seconds, Aleksei came across someone who hadn't been so fortunate. This one he recognized – a captain by the name of Lishin. He also recognized the wound to his neck, two jagged, parallel lesions separated by the width of two fingers. It was the signature of Iuda's favourite weapon.

But in killing, Iuda had made a mistake. He'd dumped the body off the road and on the beach. Footprints – the round, tiptoe-like indentations of a man running – led away across the sand. Aleksei chased after them. He constantly felt he was about to fall over as the soft surface beneath his feet collapsed with every step, but still he ran as fast as he could.

At last he saw his quarry. Iuda had his back to him, intent on his task of dragging a dinghy down towards the sea. Destabilizing though it might be, the sand brought the blessing of making Aleksei's approach silent. When he was only a few paces away, he launched himself, feet first, at Iuda's back. With the run-up he had had, his feet landed with tremendous force, smashing Iuda's ribs against the side of the boat. Aleksei felt confident he had managed to break something.

Aleksei was on his feet in moments, but Iuda lay on his side on the ground, clutching his chest and moaning. Aleksei pressed his boot against Iuda's shoulder and rolled him on to his back.

'Not enough of a head start over me this time,' he said.

'It would seem not.' Iuda's voice croaked with pain.

'Where were you off to, I wonder,' said Aleksei. 'You couldn't have been going very far in that.' He glanced out to sea. That yacht – which had been there every day while he had been in Taganrog – stood on the horizon, as if waiting. 'Over there, perhaps?'

Iuda rolled slightly on to one side, as if trying to look where Aleksei was pointing, but in an instant he flung himself back the other way, and Aleksei felt a sharp pain in his calf. His sword was in his hand in an instant; its tip at Iuda's throat. He could see the double-knife in his hand, with fresh blood on it; Aleksei's own, mixing with Lishin's. The wound to his leg stung, but he doubted it was serious.

He jerked his head to one side and pressed the blade a little harder against Iuda's skin. Iuda threw the knife away from him. It rolled half a dozen times before coming to rest in the sand.

'I take it my plan failed,' said Iuda.

'Which plan?' Aleksei never understood his reason for asking it. Perhaps some subconscious voice, thinking faster than he ever could, had suggested it to him. Perhaps that voice came from outside of him. Perhaps he was just trying to be sarcastic. The reason did not matter – the result did.

Iuda considered for a fragment of a second before answering. 'The poisoned-soup plan.' Aleksei scarcely listened to the answer; the delay had told him everything. Iuda had needed to think about it, which meant there was more than one answer – more than one plan.

Aleksei turned and began to run back to the palace. The pain in his ankle from the rockfall at Chufut Kalye was beginning to hurt, but he ignored it. Ultimately, Iuda had chosen the right answer – the plan Aleksei did know about. It was obvious enough; the soup had been handed over by a man in a lieutenant's uniform, and Iuda, lying there in the sand, still wore that uniform. If he'd answered differently, he'd have told Aleksei even more, but he had told him enough. Iuda had at least one more line of attack, and Aleksei had to get back to the tsar and prevent that attack from coming to fruition. He had had to abandon Iuda, but it was a worthwhile sacrifice to save the tsar.

Damn it! Why hadn't he just killed Iuda? A single thrust of his sword would have done it. Somewhere inside Aleksei there were the remnants of an absurd sense of chivalry. You have a man as your prisoner – it would be ungentlemanly to kill him. He was a fool, but it was too late to turn back now. Iuda would be gone already, and there was no time to be wasted if Aleksandr was to be rescued. He didn't even turn his head. There would be nothing to see, and it risked unbalancing him as he ran across the sand.

He had to consider what Iuda's other plan might have been. Surely it could not succeed. There were three men around the tsar's bed who knew he should consume nothing – not to mention the tsar himself. Iuda had described the other plan as the 'poisoned-soup plan'. How precise had he meant those words to be? It had not been the 'blood in the soup' plan, but Aleksei would bet there was Zmyeevich's blood in there too. Iuda had to improve on his previous attempt – he had to ensure that death came to Aleksandr within moments of him consuming the blood. A cocktail of blood and poison would serve his purpose – and also block off the one possible escape route the tsar had: to survive a few more weeks and wait once again until the influence of Zmyeevich's blood left his body.

Aleksei was on the road now, and able to run faster, though his own exhaustion compensated for any advantage. Ten years ago, he would have covered the ground more quickly – but ten years ago, he might not have been wise enough to guess what Iuda was up to. He arrived at the house with aching lungs, but still he dashed on through towards the tsar's room. Outside it stood Diebich. His face was disconsolate, but it was impossible for Aleksei to tell whether this was in anticipation or consequence of the dread event, nor was there time to ask. He opened the door to Aleksandr's room.

*   *   *

416

'Drink, my darling. Drink.' It was a voice Aleksandr trusted. He was still drifting between sleep and wakefulness, but he had listened to the conversations around him.

'The end is close.' It had been Wylie who said that. He was a good doctor, and a good friend. There were many men in Russia like him – from all walks of life. It was not simply their skill or their kindness that was remarkable, but the fact they had chosen to make Russia their home. It was easy for a native to love his country – he had no choice. But that someone like Wylie should adopt Russia as his homeland said a lot about the man – and the country.

'Might we be alone?' His wife's voice.

'We must stay by his side.' Volkonsky. They went back to before Aleksandr was tsar. Pyotr Mihailovich had helped make him tsar. There was no matter upon which they did not trust each other.

'Some privacy, please!' Yelizaveta Alekseevna again.

No one else had spoken. Aleksandr had strained to open his eyes and seen that many around him had taken a step back from the bed. Volkonsky looked fixedly out of the window; Wylie and Tarasov were in feigned conversation.

'Please drink.' The tsaritsa's lips were close to his ear. He felt her warm breath. Her fingers rested upon his cheek and her palm cupped his chin. There was something cold there too – glass. She was pressing a bottle against his lips. 'It will cure you,' she said.

Aleksandr knew that he was beyond cure, but he was thirsty. He smelled wine; good, red wine. His doctors had refused him any drink, but for the little water they carefully rationed to him. He understood why they were doing it – he had agreed, but this might be his last ever chance to taste a fine French vintage. And it came from his wife, of all people. She would never harm him.

And besides, there was another figure in the room – tall and dressed in dark clothes. Aleksandr could not see his face, but he was sure he recognized him. On his finger was a ring in the shape of a dragon, with emerald eyes and a red, forking tongue. Aleksandr did not know how he had entered, but if the others in the room had been aware of his presence, they would have cowered in terror. His deep, grinding voice was compelling as it spoke.

'Drink! Drink! Drink!'

Aleksandr parted his lips slightly and his wife began to tip the bottle.

Aleksei strode across the room and swung his open palm at the tsaritsa's hand. The tips of his fingers caught Aleksandr's cheek, but it did not matter. What mattered was that the vial in her hand was flung from the tsar's lips and on to the bed. Huge gobbets of the thick, crimson liquid inside spilled out, sitting as perfect, hemispherical domes upon the sheet for a few seconds before slackening and oozing their way into the linen as wide, red stains.

What the hell had they all been thinking, wondered Aleksei. Tarasov, Wylie – even Volkonsky – all looking away like wise monkeys. Were they all in league with Iuda? Possessed by Zmyeevich? No – they were simply fools, persuaded by a woman's love. Now that the spell was broken, they rushed over to Aleksandr.

'How dare you?' hissed Yelizaveta Alekseevna.

'How dare I?' replied Aleksei, his voice quiet, but unshakably firm. 'I would not condemn His Majesty's very soul.'

'How could the gift of a holy man condemn his soul?' asked the tsaritsa.

Aleksei calmed. She seemed sincere.

'A holy man?'

'A starets, from the monastery.'

Had she been fooled? It was impossible to tell. It seemed likely she was quite ignorant of the horror she had almost perpetrated, but that could be a façade; Iuda had wiles that could persuade the most faithful of wives.

'A starets? Tall and blond, with grey eyes, I imagine.'

She nodded. 'Yes,' she said in a whisper.

'That was no medicine,' said Aleksei.

418

She looked up at him. She had not moved since he had struck the vial from her hand. She knelt on the floor, arms stretched out across the bed and across her husband's pale, limp body. 'It could not have made things worse,' she said bitterly.

Aleksei wondered if he should reply. He could find no words that would help her. The decision of whether to speak was taken from him. Dr Wylie had approached the tsar's bed and been examining him. He raised his hand and Aleksei obeyed the gesture with silence.

The tsar's breathing was shallow. His eyes were closed and his skin showed a pallor worse than Aleksei had ever seen, but there was no sheen of sweat to it. The tsaritsa knelt up and Volkonsky stepped in closer. Aleksei took a step backwards. It was not his place to intrude on this moment.

Aleksandr's eyes opened slowly, flickering like the shaking fingers of an old man as he tried to gain a final glimpse of the things he loved. His frail hand reached for the table beside him, feeling its way, and his fingers found the crucifix that lay there. He lifted it and turned his head so that he might glimpse it. Now he lay back, exhausted from the effort, letting the figure of Christ fall back on to the tabletop. His eyes remained open, gazing at the woman who had stood beside him, and a smile formed on his lips.

He breathed in deeply, then released a sigh of unutterable contentment. Then he breathed in no more.

Wylie took a step towards him and examined him briefly. The tsaritsa looked up into the doctor's face, but saw in his eyes no hint of solace. She released a sob, but then became silent. Wylie raised his hand towards the tsar's face, but Yelizaveta saw what he was doing and reached out herself. The doctor withdrew his hand and the tsaritsa touched her late husband's face, gently closing his eyelids. Wylie stood and faced the room before making his announcement.

'The great monarch has stepped into eternity,' he said.

CHAPTER XXVIII

IUDA WAS TERRIFIED. IT WAS A NEW AND REVOLTING SENSATION. He enjoyed the feeling of fear – more in others, admittedly, but also in himself. Fear focused the mind, precipitated action, punished failure, but above all it forced Iuda to flee from it. It forced him to the extremes of his abilities – mental and physical. There was no other emotion that could so powerfully drive him to achieve what most would regard as impossible.

But terror was different. Terror was to sit in the dank hold of a ship, in the presence of a creature so dangerous even Iuda would hesitate before deceiving him, and to wait for events to unfold. That was the worst of it – it was out of his hands. Not like a stone rolled down a hill, which gathers momentum, dislocates more stones to join it in its descent, ever accelerating in a noisy cascade until they crash upon some innocent in a terrible, but predictable landslide. This was like a coin thrown in the air; a coin he had weighted, but whose landing still had no certainty. The die was cast.

'Look again.'

He reached out and took the spyglass from the hand that offered it, wincing at the pain in his cracked ribs. His eye dwelt on the ornate ring rather than looking up at the face of its owner. The tail of the gold dragon curled around his finger and the red, forked tongue seemed to flick out, reaching for Iuda. The emerald eyes were almost as compelling as those Iuda was so conscientiously trying to avoid.

He walked over and pulled back the shutters on the porthole. In the distance, he could see the Taganrog shoreline and the tsar's palace. He had been aboard *Răzbunarea* before, several times – to plan, to discuss, to gloat over events which had not yet come to pass – but this time there was nothing to be decided, except perhaps his own fate. And his fate was bound to the fate of the tsar. He glanced across the hold before raising the spyglass to his eye. Zmyeevich had retreated into the shadows, wary of even the small patch of sunlight Iuda had allowed to enter. Perhaps, if it came to it, Iuda would be able to flee. The steps were not too far away, and outside the daylight was bright. It was a cool autumn day in human terms, but for Zmyeevich, it would mean an instant, burning death. But Iuda would still have to get as far as those steps – and Zmyeevich could move with enormous speed. The open porthole might help, but Iuda did not rate his own chances.

He looked more closely at the palace. The flag still flew above it – three horizontal stripes of white, blue and red. He did not need to look for long. He collapsed the spyglass and closed the shutters, turning to Zmyeevich with a shake of his head.

'He lives?' asked Zmyeevich.

'It seems so. Do you feel nothing?'

Zmyeevich closed his eyes and breathed deeply. After a moment, he opened them. 'No,' he said, 'nothing.'

'Would it be instantaneous?'

'It has always been in the past, but I'm sure you must have conducted some . . . experiment to determine that.'

Iuda chose not to comment. Zmyeevich had benefited hugely from what Iuda had discovered, but he still gave the impression that the experiments upon his fellow creatures disgusted him. It was another reason he should be feared.

'Your influence over him was real enough.'

'I have drunk his blood – his family's blood. That gives him some insight into my mind. Sometimes that insight may influence his actions – influence him, perhaps, to drink what he knows he should not. But the connection is weak and capricious compared to what it will be once he has drunk my blood and succumbed to death. And until then, I cannot know his mind. I do not know it now.'

'Things would have been easier if Danilov hadn't been here,' said Iuda. He had not conveyed to Zmyeevich the information that he had had the opportunity to deal with Lyosha and had not taken it. Beyond Iuda's own motivations, it was useful for him to be alive simply as someone to shoulder the blame.

'Captain Danilov – a colonel now, you tell me – appeared to be the most resourceful of them all on the brief occasion that we met; though it seems he is a little prone to sentimentality.'

The last phrase struck Iuda as odd. It matched his own assessment of Lyosha, but he could think of nothing he had told Zmyeevich that might give him that impression. He was about to claim the colonel was lucky, but it would weaken his position. 'He's certainly caused us problems,' he said instead. 'But you can afford to be patient – he won't live for ever.'

'You think we have failed in this generation then?'

'Aleksandr still lives,' said Iuda, 'so there is still hope.'

'Danilov has a child, does he not?'

'A son.'

'Perhaps he will thwart me next time.'

'I think not,' said Iuda.

He opened the shutters and looked through the spyglass once again, letting out the minutest of gasps at what he saw.

'The flag of death is flying?' asked Zmyeevich.

Iuda nodded. The tricolour above the palace had been lowered to half mast to make way for the invisible flag that superstition maintained had been raised there by Death itself. He closed up the spyglass and stepped away from the porthole. This time he did not close the shutters.

'I feel nothing,' said Zmyeevich.

Iuda's sense of defeat was not overwhelming. Aleksandr was dead and had died free of Zmyeevich's blood. It was a disappointment, but he suspected he would not have benefited greatly from Zmyeevich's power over Russia. He doubted whether the vampire shared his stoicism, and suddenly felt his terror increase a thousandfold. The dark presence in the room with him seemed to smoulder with wrath. 'You're sure?' he asked.

'I would know,' said Zmyeevich firmly. He strode across the hold towards the door, passing within inches of the beam of light that entered through the open porthole, but not touching it. 'I felt, for example, as if it was my own skin that was burning.'

Iuda flicked his eyes around the room, searching for any route of escape, but he saw none. Zmyeevich stood between him and the door. The porthole was far too small. 'Burning?' he asked, trying to give himself time to think. 'When?'

'I felt before as you tattooed me; as you flayed the skin from me,' continued Zmyeevich.

'I see,' said Iuda, now understanding. He slipped his hand inside his coat.

'I saw, as well as felt,' said Zmyeevich. 'Saw through the eyes of a vampire which *I* created; a vampire which you enslaved, which you abused. He was my offspring.'

'You've benefited from what I've learned.'

Zmyeevich nodded, his face thoughtful. 'True enough,' he said. 'Though what you learned from *him*, I cannot guess. I also learned your tricks.'

Zmyeevich took two long, brisk strides across the room. Iuda moved at the same moment, towards the light of the porthole. The mirror he had taken from his pocket was now in his hand. But Zmyeevich was quicker. This time he made no diversion, walking directly through the sun's rays, his cheek burning briefly as it passed through, but he did not flinch. He stood between Iuda and the porthole.

'For example,' he said, 'I have learned that a mirror is of no use without a source of light.'

423

Iuda could see he had been outmanoeuvred. If he could have reflected the sunlight into Zmyeevich's face, he might have fended him off, but he had no chance of getting near the porthole. He cast the mirror aside and heard it smash against the wall.

'I can still be of help to you,' he said. He was surprised how calm his voice sounded.

'Why did our plans for Aleksandr fail?' asked Zmyeevich. Iuda was strangely reminded of his father, his patronizing voice asking some question of mathematics or history that his young son should easily have been able to answer, but failed to.

'Because of Danilov.' The word 'sir' almost tumbled from his lips in pursuit.

'I saw Danilov too,' said Zmyeevich, 'through my offspring's eyes, when he returned to Chufut Kalye. We were on the verge of tasting his blood. And then nothing. The child of my blood died. The last image his eyes saw' – Zmyeevich's own eyes blazed as he spoke – 'was you.'

'That was necessary,' said Iuda.

'Perhaps, but you let Danilov live. That was unforgivable.'

Iuda opened his mouth, but had no words to speak. Zmyeevich stepped forward. His foetid breath invaded Iuda's nostrils, and only fear prevented him from throwing up. Zmyeevich placed a hand on his shoulder and the other under his chin.

'I would not sully my lips with your blood,' he said.

Iuda felt the grip around his chin tighten. A click somewhere in his neck told him that his vertebrae were moving apart. His skull was filled with a squeaking sound, like a cork being removed from a bottle. He knew that Zmyeevich had sufficient strength to rip his head from his shoulders in an instant, but to kill him quickly would have been unnecessarily merciful. It was an error, though. Zmyeevich had not learned all Iuda's tricks.

Iuda's hand searched for the side pocket of his coat. He had no weapon, and even if he had had, Zmyeevich was too close for him to strike. But then his hand closed around cold glass. He had found what he was looking for. Still, he would have to be lucky. He raised his hand and then flung it forward.

The vial flew through the air across the ship's hold, spinning top over tail, but the stopper did not come out. The dark liquid within remained constrained by its glass walls. Iuda's aim had been true. The porthole was not large, but large enough. The vial disappeared through it and into the open air beyond.

From deep within his chest, Zmyeevich's scream filled the room, and his grip instantly relaxed. Iuda did not wait. He raced to the door, only glimpsing what he left behind. Zmyeevich stood still, his eyes shot with blood, his whole body shaking as if under the strain of some tremendous weight as he tried to resist the agony that surged through his veins.

Iuda had little time. The vial of Zmyeevich's blood would have burst into flame as soon as it was hit by the sun's rays. It would soon burn to nothing, and then the searing pain in the blood in Zmyeevich's own body would recede. Iuda threw himself through the door and up the stairs to the deck, rejoicing in the sensation of the sun on his back. The ship's crew stood in bemused horror at the sound of their master's screams, but they did not go to his aid. Neither did they attempt to hinder Iuda's escape.

He climbed down into the dinghy and rowed away, parallel to the coast, not towards it. He had no plans to come ashore anywhere near Taganrog.

It was dark now. It had been almost twelve hours since Wylie had announced the death of Tsar Aleksandr I. Almost twelve hours that Tsar Konstantin I had reigned, though he did not know it. It would take a week for news to reach him in Warsaw; about the same to reach Petersburg. Taganrog knew already. The flag above the palace would have told them, and gossip spread rapidly.

The palace had died its own death since that morning. Yelizaveta had composed herself and quietly retired to her rooms. The guards had been stood down; there was no one to guard. Wylie and Tarasov had no one to make well. The staff sat idly in their quarters. There was only one less soul to tend to in the house than there had been when all awoke that morning, and yet the reason for anyone to be there had gone.

Aleksei noticed it now as he returned more than when he had left. It had not been a long trip, but a necessary one – just to Orekhov and back. He had to go by carriage, which slowed him down, but he had driven himself, so there had been no questions.

When he got back to Taganrog, he had called immediately at Wylie's lodgings. Both doctors were there. The three went together to the imperial palace. Tarasov uneasily eyed the heavy burden that Wylie and Aleksei carried between them.

Volkonsky let them in through a side door. His face was grim. He knew what they had to do, but he had chosen not to participate. It was to the good – someone had to wait outside Aleksandr's bedroom. They arrived at the door. Aleksei felt the urge to knock, and almost laughed at himself.

'This is going to be the worst part,' he said to Wylie.

'I'm a doctor,' came the reply, 'a field surgeon. I've operated on men who've screamed in agony as I worked. I don't think I'm going to have any qualms over whatever must be done to a dead body.'

'The worst part is the pain we're causing the tsaritsa,' said Tarasov. Wylie nodded.

Aleksei opened the door. It was dark inside. Only the moonlight, leaking through the closed shutters, cast any light, picking out on the bed Aleksandr's familiar, still profile.

The three men went inside, closing the door behind them.

CHAPTER XXIX

TAGANROG WAS JUST VISIBLE, A FEW VERSTS AWAY TO THE SOUTH-west, its lights shining through the early twilight. In the other direction the road led to . . . who knew where? It was an adventure – the first ever adventure in the life of a man who, since the instant of his birth, almost forty-eight years before, had spent each moment of his existence under the minutest scrutiny. Freedom was terrifying to him, but so, so exciting. To make his own way in life, to plan his day, merely to be ignored as he walked down a street – all those were joys too familiar for others to appreciate.

He looked down from his horse at the four men who had made it possible: Volkonsky, Wylie, Tarasov and Danilov – two soldiers and two doctors. They had killed him, and they had resurrected him. And it had taken them less than a day. It was terrible to say goodbye, not because of who they were or what they had done – though there was that too – but because this was the final good-bye, the final cut that separated him from the life he had known.

'I so wish we could have told Yelizaveta Alekseevna,' said Aleksandr.

'She would have wished to come with you,' replied Volkonsky.

'I would have dearly loved that,' Aleksandr answered, 'but in the end, *she* would not have. Even if her mind had grown accustomed to the privations of our new life, her body never would have.'

'She is a frail woman, Your Majesty,' said Tarasov.

Aleksandr nodded, then frowned. 'I'm not "Your Majesty" any more,' he pointed out. 'That burden has passed on.'

'So what should we call you – Aleksandr Pavlovich?'

Aleksandr smiled. 'For the next few minutes, yes,' he said, 'though it's not the name I will be keeping.'

'Where will you go?' asked Aleksei.

'I don't know. And if I did, I would – as with my new name – keep it to myself. Only Volkonsky will know these things; it's much safer for all that way.' He looked down at the four mournful faces in front of him. 'This is worse than when I was dying!' he exclaimed.

There was laughter all round.

'You would have made a fine actor, Your . . . Aleksandr,' said Wylie.

'There was no acting involved. Whatever it was that Tarasov gave me had me halfway to death already.'

'It was laudanum,' explained Tarasov. 'I'm not even sure its effects will have worn off sufficiently for you to be riding yet.'

'He has to leave today,' said Aleksei. 'Someone might see him.'

'I don't think anyone's going to recognize him looking like that,' said Volkonsky.

Aleksandr put his hand to his face. There was stubble on his chin that would soon grow into the full beard that would be essential if he was going to pull this off. The sides of his cheeks felt the cold of the wind where his sideboards had been shaved. For now, that – plus the application of a little grime – was all that could be done to change his facial appearance. It was his clothing that would fool most people. He wasn't exactly dressed like a peasant, but he no longer looked like a city dweller. His clothes were practical – comfortable, even. There was no sash across his chest, no epaulettes on his shoulders or cockade on his hat, and these were the things by which he was recognized as tsar, not by his face, which few outside Petersburg or Moscow would know. At least, that was what he had been assured.

'I hope you're as much a master of disguise as you claim to be, Aleksei Ivanovich,' he said.

'And what was the one vital thing I did say?' Aleksei asked with a laugh, his Russian countering Aleksandr's instinctive French.

Aleksandr repeated his question, switching to his people's language. It felt a little uncomfortable on his tongue, as it always had done, but he would get used to it.

'That's better,' said Aleksei.

'Will Major Maskov's body really pass for mine?' asked Aleksandr. He looked at Wylie as he spoke. It was a strange repetition that the doctor should be involved in falsifying the deaths of two successive tsars. Not that Pavel's death had been a falsehood, merely the declaration of its cause. They had never spoken of it, and Aleksandr would not change that now.

'His body was remarkably well preserved, thanks to the nature of the soil,' said Wylie, his eyes seeming to guess Aleksandr's thoughts. 'The fact that his death occurred earlier than yours will scarcely be noticed – and the embalming process distorts the features. By the time the body gets to Petersburg, I doubt anyone will want to examine it too closely.'

Aleksandr swallowed hard at the thought. 'You must ensure that his family is well cared for, Volkonsky.'

The prince nodded.

'And what of Cain and Zmyeevich?'

'I think we've convinced them,' said Aleksei. 'No one saw Cain return after he rowed out to that yacht – and the yacht itself left within hours of your "death".'

'But if they should become suspicious . . .'

'In a few years, you'll be of no use to them,' said Volkonsky. 'Once the new tsar has established himself, you'll be . . . forgotten.'

'Charming.'

'I mean,' explained the prince, 'that few would believe a man who returned to the capital and claimed to be the late tsar; fewer still would let him retake the reins of power.'

'What about those False Dmitrys?'

'That was in a different time,' said Volkonsky.

'Zmyeevich wouldn't run the risk,' added Aleksei.

'So the Romanovs are safe,' said Aleksandr, 'until the next generation; then what of my poor nephew?'

'I'll see that he remains safe,' said Volkonsky.

'You'll tell him?'

'If it proves necessary. And if Zmyeevich or his emissary returns I can call on Colonel Danilov's experience.'

'It'll be a pleasure,' said the colonel.

'You must go,' said Volkonsky.

Aleksandr turned and looked to the east. A thin orange line was just appearing on the horizon where the sun rose. He had never felt so alone. The whole thing felt like madness to him now, and yet was this not the moment he had yearned for since – when? – his father's death? Regardless of Cain and Zmyeevich, he had always dreamed, sometimes planned, how he would one day be free. It was far, far too late to turn back.

'Yes,' he said with a sigh, 'I must.'

He reached out his hand, and each of the four men kissed it in turn.

'I will forget none of you,' he said, and turned his horse into the sun.

He did not look back; he would have seen nothing through the tears in his eyes. They were the tears of a newborn, thrust into a world he did not understand and would have to learn. For his entire life he had been a virtual god – destined first to rule and then, by betraying his own father, becoming ruler of this beautiful country. Then that life had ended, and he had spent a day in death. Now he was reborn.

First a god, and then a corpse, but as of today he was all he had ever wanted to be. Today he was a man.

All four of them got very drunk that evening, sitting in Volkonsky's rooms. They started on vodka, but then Wylie brought out a bottle of whisky, which was something Aleksei had never tried. He liked it.

'I don't think I can bring myself to let them bury Maskov amongst the tsars,' said Volkonsky. 'It's not right for either family.'

'I'm sure you'll work something out,' said Aleksei.

'We have a lot to work out,' said Wylie. 'There will be many in Petersburg who ask questions.'

'Make sure our stories hang together, you mean?' asked Tarasov.

Wylie nodded.

'You keep a journal, don't you?' said Volkonsky, addressing Wylie.

'Of sorts.'

'I do too,' said Tarasov.

'We'll go through those,' said Volkonsky. 'Make sure there's nothing in them that doesn't fit our version of the story.'

'What about other people's recollections?' asked Wylie.

'It's only you three that know about any of this, really,' said Volkonsky. 'Until His Majesty spoke to me, I suspected nothing – beyond his illness.' He breathed deeply. 'It's been a long two days.'

'I'd rather you kept me out of this,' said Aleksei.

'You refuse to help?' Volkonsky was astounded, as well he might be.

'Not at all. I mean, keep my name out of your journals.'

'Why?' asked Tarasov.

'Because I have no good reason to be here. If people see my name – particularly people who know what I do for a living – they'll start to wonder. What was a spy doing hovering around the tsar's deathbed?'

'The others here will remember you,' said Wylie.

'Maybe, but just as another soldier. I doubt there's many here can even remember my name.'

'I'd be prepared to bet the tsaritsa remembers it was you who

431

knocked that bottle out of her hand,' said Volkonsky. All of them joined in his laughter. 'But I see your point,' he continued, when it had subsided.

'I'll leave tomorrow,' said Aleksei.

'So soon?' said Wylie, refilling Aleksei's glass.

'Makes me easier to forget.'

'None of us here will forget you, Colonel,' said Volkonsky, raising his glass to him. 'Nor will His Majesty,' he added more quietly.

'I think you mean Aleksandr Pavlovich,' said Wylie.

There was another round of laughter, which faded into silence. Aleksei was suddenly reminded of another occasion when he had sat drinking with three friends – many occasions. When had been the last? In Moscow, in 1812, just before they had set out west with the Oprichniki. Everything had changed after that – after Dmitry, Vadim and Maks had died. It was odd, but from somewhere Aleksei had the sense of having been in the presence of Maks very recently – or of someone like him. It was not one of these three, but then who? It did not take him long to work through the list of people in whose company he had been of late. For an awful moment, he thought it might be Kyesha, but it was not.

It was Aleksandr Pavlovich. Yes, he was old, spoilt and jaded, but just that morning he had rode away from all he had with more of a sense of curiosity than dread – or at least a reasonable balance of the two. That was the sort of thing Maks would have done, had he lived.

'You'll remain in contact with him?' Wylie asked. 'In his new life?'

'He'll send me word under his new name of where he is,' said Volkonsky. 'I'll send him money, and whatever else he needs.'

'He had quite enough gold packed into those saddlebags,' observed Tarasov.

'He may need it,' said Volkonsky. 'Could any of us learn to live like he plans to?'

'So what is his name going to be?' asked Wylie.

'I'm sworn not to tell,' said Volkonsky. 'Suffice it to say that Aleksandr I is no more.'

'To the new tsar, then,' said Aleksei, holding his glass up high. 'To Konstantin I.'

Four glasses clashed together, and four voices spoke as one. 'Konstantin I!'

Aleksei had only a little more packing to do in preparation for his departure, and he chose to leave it until the following morning. He was just pulling off his boots when he noticed a new item amongst his possessions, sitting on top of his saddlebags. It was a letter. He went over and picked it up.

А. И. Д.

The handwriting was familiar, as was the text itself. He ripped it open, but even before he read the signature, he knew that it was from Kyesha.

Dear Aleksei Ivanovich,

You must have discovered by now, as have I, that your attempt to destroy Cain in Chufut Kalye was unsuccessful. I do not blame you for it. You left the task to my kindred, and that seemed as appropriate to me as it must have done to them. The failure to achieve what all of us so desired is theirs, not yours.

I have no doubt that should you encounter Cain again you will set aside the poetry of vengeance in favour of the certainty of a steel blade or a lead bullet. And yet even in that, I carry in my heart the hope that of the two of us, it is not you who next encounters him. It is only fitting that it should be a creature such as I that ultimately brings an end to his life.

433

Indeed, you will be pleased to learn, I have already chanced upon some clues that may lead me to where he is currently hiding, planning, I believe, to recommence the experimentation to which your actions so effectively put an end. With luck, I will be upon him within days. As to the ending of our encounter, I am sure you will one day learn its outcome, one way or another.

I hesitate to say farewell under a name I once used in order to deceive you, but it is the only one by which you know me and is one which, I hope more than know, you regard as that of a friend.

With the greatest admiration, three-fingered man,

Innokyentii Sergeivich Lukin

Aleksei folded the letter and slipped it into his pocket. It was a good thing that Kyesha planned to pursue Iuda, because Aleksei himself most certainly did not, not for now, whatever the fate of the Romanovs might be. As to whether he would succeed – it was possible. One day, Iuda had to die. One day, his luck would run out. Perhaps it would be to Kyesha that the luck would flow.

But Aleksei could not help but remember another letter he had received years ago, from Dmitry Fetyukovich. Dmitry had, like Kyesha, discovered some clue as to the location of Iuda and set off in pursuit, urging Aleksei to follow. Aleksei had done so, and found Dmitry dead, and Iuda free. From Kyesha there had been no such entreaty, and Aleksei was not going to pretend there had been. His path was north, to his home – to his homes. It would be a long journey, but tomorrow it would begin.

He looked at the clock. Tomorrow was today. He went to bed.

Only Wylie rose to say farewell to Aleksei. They had agreed on that the previous night. It was all part of Aleksei's plan that his involvement not be too clearly remembered. An early farewell from the late tsar's personal secretary and his two physicians would raise eyebrows.

'I almost wish I'd never met you, Aleksei,' said the doctor.

'This would have happened, even if I hadn't come.'

'I know. And far worse. You're a brave man.'

'Quite a compliment, from an Englishman.'

Wylie raised an eyebrow, then smiled. 'Are you heading straight back to Petersburg?'

'Moscow first, but only for a short while.' Aleksei did not explain the real reason for his haste. The Northern Society had spoken of assassination, but they had also considered a spontaneous uprising, if Aleksandr were to die of other causes. In saving one Romanov, he might have ended the whole dynasty. And that would end the threat from Zmyeevich. Perhaps it was a worthwhile price.

Wylie shivered and hugged himself. 'It's turning cold,' he said.

'It'll get colder as I head north.'

'I'd better not keep you.'

Wylie held out his hand. Aleksei took it, then embraced the doctor.

'Goodbye, Aleksei.'

'Goodbye . . . James.' The sound of the first letter was strange on his tongue.

Aleksei mounted his horse and headed away. He turned and gave one final wave to Wylie, then accelerated to a canter. His departure seemed far easier than Aleksandr's had been the previous morning as he headed off with a new name into a new life.

Aleksei knew what that name was now. Volkonsky had taken him aside the previous night and told him, afraid that the knowledge was too vital to be possessed by just one man. There was nothing remarkable about it:

Fyodor Kuzmich.

Aleksei wondered if he would ever meet a man going by that name. He hoped so.

As he rode north, he felt the cold begin to penetrate him, but it was of no concern. He thrust from his mind thoughts of what had happened in Taganrog and the Crimea – even in Moscow with Kyesha. He turned his mind instead to what was ahead of him – Domnikiia and Tamara, only a few days away. The cold did not matter, however much he hated the winter. It could never be winter where they were.

It even began to snow – a light, fine snow that did not settle – but Aleksei did not mind. If it was snowing here, then it would be snowing in Moscow, and Domnikiia and Tamara would feel it too. The snow was therefore beautiful. He let the tiny white flecks embrace him, as though they were a blanket of stars.

PART THREE

CHAPTER XXX

THERE HAD ONLY BEEN THREE LETTERS FROM PAPA. THEY'D all been in Russian, but Mama had helped Tamara to read them. Papa did it deliberately, she knew, to make her learn. It was nicer – even if it was harder – to read his words in Russian, because that was the language he normally spoke to her. It was only recently she had understood that French and Russian were separate. Her parents had laughed when she mixed the two, but not in a nasty way. She still did it now sometimes, but not nearly so much.

Papa had also sent letters to Mama, but Mama had not let Tamara read those. Instead she had read bits of them out to her. It was obvious that Papa had very important business with the tsar. She hadn't believed Papa at first when he said who he was going to see, but now she was convinced. Even so, she wished the tsar would hurry up and let Papa come home. He'd been gone almost two months. He would be concerned to know how much taller she had grown – he always commented on that.

'He's there again,' said Mama. Tamara looked up. Her mother was standing at the window, peeking through the curtains. The words had not been addressed to her; Mama had been talking to herself. She did that a lot, particularly when Papa wasn't here.

'*Who*'s there?' asked Tamara.

Domnikiia looked down at her. There was a frown on her face, but it changed into a smile, which Tamara returned.

'Will you be a good girl and stay here?' she asked. Tamara nodded. Her mother began putting on her coat, buttoning it rapidly down the front. 'I won't be long,' she said. She kissed Tamara on the forehead and departed.

The little girl waited for a few moments, then trotted over to the window. She lifted the heavy curtain up over her head and disappeared behind it to gaze down on the street below. Even in the twilight, the whiteness gleamed everywhere. It had begun to snow a couple of weeks earlier, and by now it had settled. Wherever Tamara and her mother went was covered with it. She remembered having seen snow before, but could not specifically remember it arriving like it had this year.

Tamara decided that she loved the winter, whatever Papa might think of it. He'd said in his letters how much warmer it was in Taganrog; perhaps that was why he was taking so long to come home.

There was a man standing outside in the snow. He didn't seem to be doing anything, just standing there. It was the same man who had been there before – the man who had stood and watched Papa leave. Perhaps that meant that Papa would be returning soon. She hoped so.

Another figure walked out into the snowy street, emerging from somewhere below where Tamara stood, and heading out to join the first. This was someone she recognized. It was Mama.

Dmitry wondered if there was really much point to what he was doing. He could tolerate the cold and the snow blowing in his face, but that didn't mean that he was actually achieving anything. Essentially, he wanted to irritate her – to scare her – though what either of those might accomplish, he wasn't sure. And if he scared her then he might scare the innocent little girl who her trusting parents had placed in her care.

But the monotony allowed his mind to empty, and allowed the music to swell. It was still strange and beautiful, and if only a fraction would stick, he would be a happy man. More than

440

that, he would be a genius. Perhaps it was ambition like this that had persuaded God to prevent him ever remembering any of it. Perhaps God was just delaying the moment. Dmitry could wait.

He looked across the street. Someone was coming. The music faded as his attention was drawn. It was Domnikiia Semyonovna. He had been in no doubt that she was aware of being watched; now it seemed she had decided to do something about it. It was all to the good. Perhaps now he could really scare her off.

'Just who the hell do you think you . . .' Her voice tailed off as she approached him. Evidently she'd had no idea that it was Aleksei's son who was watching her. 'Oh,' she said. She pulled down her fur-lined hood so that he could see her face. She tried to smile, but failed. Her mood seemed to have changed from anger to annoyance. 'Your father asked you to keep an eye on us, I suppose.'

Dmitry looked at her blankly, then began to understand. The arrogance of the woman was appalling. Did she really believe that she held such a place in her father's heart that he would ask his own son – his *wife's* son – to look out for her safety while he was away? And did she really believe Dmitry would do it, even if he had been asked? Who did she think she was?

'I beg your pardon?' he asked, almost spitting the words. 'You think I'm here to make sure you're all right? Why should my father give a fuck about that?'

Domnikiia looked at him. There was none of the flirtation he had seen in her eyes when they had met in the street not so many months before. She looked confused – surprised too. She scanned his face as if trying to determine if this was some kind of joke. She decided quickly. She turned and walked back towards the house.

'You're not the only one, you know,' Dmitry shouted after her. As far as he knew, she was, but there was little else he could think of that might rile her. It had some effect. She stopped still, then turned slowly and walked back towards him.

'Dmitry Alekseevich,' she said softly. 'There's no reason for us to be enemies.'

There was nothing suggestive in the tone with which she had spoken, but he chose to make her think he had taken it that way.

'You're insatiable,' he said, attempting to convey disgust.

She smiled, as if at some comment that he had not heard. 'When it comes to your father, yes I am. He loves you very much, you know.'

It was evident she was not going to rise to his bait. 'Possibly – but it seems questionable whether he loves his wife.'

'So who are you angry with?' she asked. 'Me or Aleksei?'

'He loved her before he met you – loved us both. But not every whore that sleeps with a soldier during a war tries to dig her claws in.'

Her eyebrows dipped in the middle as she frowned. Dmitry could not help but note that it made her look even more attractive, but he was not so distracted by it to not also observe her surprise that he knew so much about her past.

'Oh, yes,' he said. 'I know all about how you found him. Whereabouts was it – that brothel? Near here? How many soldiers did you get through in a night? And did you manage more or less once the French got here?'

Now she seemed genuinely puzzled – not surprisingly. 'But you were . . . five. How could you know?' Still there was no anger though.

'Your other former clients don't hold you in quite the same esteem as my father does,' he lied. 'There's still stories going round Moscow about Mademoiselle Dominique. You were a fool to give it up – if you did.'

'I can't change my past,' she said.

'You could change the present,' said Dmitry. 'Leave him.' It certainly wasn't something he had come here planning to say – he'd had no plan.

'For you?' Her smile mocked him.

'If that would get you away from him.' He meant it – he thought – as a joke, but it fell flat.

'How noble,' she said.

442

'I'm sure there are plenty of others you could turn to. You'd only be losing – what – one night a week?'

'And Aleksei would go running back to your mother – the happy family once again?'

'There's nothing wrong with my family!'

'No,' she said. 'No, I don't think there is. He's certainly raised you well enough.'

'What would you know?'

She shrugged. 'Does Marfa Mihailovna know?'

Dmitry clenched his jaw at the sound of his mother's name on the whore's lips. 'Don't bring her into this,' he said coldly.

'I've brought no one into it.' There was anger in her voice now. 'You're the one who's come to my home; who's spied on me; who waited till his father was away so that I'd be undefended. Why couldn't you leave me well alone?'

It was an anger he'd been waiting for, one that allowed him to release his own wrath. He'd hated this woman for years, silently brooding, unable to mention it to his mother – certainly not to his father – sharing it with the only true friend he had in the world. And now she was here, in front of him, and she dared accuse him; accuse him of destroying his family, of being a spy, a coward.

He raised his hand and brought it across her face. She was fast, bringing up her own arm to fend him off. Even then it must have hurt her arm – but at least it saved her looks. How typical of the woman.

'Would your father do that?' she asked. She had lost her anger, and had never showed fear. Dmitry lowered his hand. He had no idea of the answer to her question. He tried to place Aleksei in his situation, but he could not make him carry out any action. The worst of it was, *she* seemed to be pretty confident about how his father would behave.

This time he grabbed her wrist with his left hand before lashing his right across her cheek. Her head jerked to one side. She looked up at him, raising her hand to her face and touching the wound. She winced as her fingers made contact, but there were no tears

443

in her eyes. She looked at her fingertips and saw the blood Dmitry could already see on her lips.

Then she said something that made no sense to him at all.

'How very like your namesake.'

She turned and headed back into the house.

Dmitry looked back up at the window. The little red-headed girl was standing there looking down on them. Dmitry smiled to himself. With any luck she would tell her parents what she had witnessed, and then they'd have no choice but to fire her nanny.

The chapel of the Winter Palace, in the heart of St Petersburg, was at present as royal a location as any in Russia. Every member of the royal family who could reach it had come to attend a mass that had but one objective – to pray for the life of the one member of that family who beyond all others they wished could be there: His Majesty Tsar Aleksandr I.

Grand Duke Nikolai opened his eyes and, still with his head bowed, glanced around. As family gatherings went, it was not the greatest of turn-outs. The dowager empress, Maria Fyodorovna, was there. It would be a tragedy for her to hear of the death of her eldest son. She was sixty-six years old now, and had lived as a widow for twenty-four of them, as long – inescapably – as her son had reigned. Nikolai was the only one of her sons that was present. Grand Duke Konstantin, the tsarevich, was in Warsaw. It was his duty; he was viceroy, in practice if not in name. But Nikolai suspected it was more than duty that called him there. He shied away from Russia, and from his responsibilities there. He was not suited to take the crown – he was too like their father.

Grand Duke Mihail – youngest of the four sons – was at least returning from that same city, as far as Nikolai understood, but would not arrive for many days. A number of the dowager empress's grandchildren were there, including his own son, Aleksandr – just seven years old. He felt a surge of pride at the thought the boy would one day be tsar.

He glanced over towards his mother again. Her eyes were

closed and she was deep in prayer. He asked himself the question he had gone over again and again. Did she know the role her own son had played in the death of her husband? Nikolai had not been aware of it for very many years, and even now he could not be sure how much Aleksandr had been told. It was men like Volkonsky who were to blame. Nikolai would never trust him, however he might smile at him when they met. He'd been four at the time of his father's death – and scarcely a man when he first heard the rumours of what had really happened. Initially he had been shocked, but the more he spoke to those who had been close to power at the time, the more he appreciated how unsuitable Pavel had been for his role. But was that a good enough reason for him to die? Could a tsar not . . . retire?

No, it was ridiculous. He was thinking like his elder brother. More than once Aleksandr had expressed the same wish. But it was a foolish idea. It was not what the Lord had ordained, nor what the people would want. The serfs could not retire and live in their dotage by the sea; what would they think if their tsar could do so? And yet that was effectively what his other brother, Konstantin, had engineered, with Aleksandr's connivance. He had wed beneath him, and by thus entering into a morganatic marriage, he had voided his right to be tsar, and so the throne would pass to Nikolai, and one day to his son.

Nikolai did not fear the responsibility, but the circumstances of the transition would be difficult. Few outside the inner circle of the royal family knew what arrangements had been made. It would be all very well for Nikolai to declare himself tsar, but until Konstantin returned to Petersburg, there would be those who believed that Nikolai was trying to usurp his brother. Perhaps Nikolai should delay; acclaim Konstantin as tsar and then, once they were together, announce the true succession. The more he considered it, the better an option it seemed.

But he was writing his brother's obituary. There was still hope – more than hope – and also confusion. Two days ago – on the evening of 25 November – a courier had arrived from Taganrog with the news that Aleksandr had died six days before. But the following day a letter had arrived from the tsaritsa, full of optimism that Aleksandr was over the worst. Nikolai suspected that people were clutching at straws, but there was nothing else to clutch at. Two masses had been organized for today; this small one for family and the highest nobility, and another for high-ranking civil servants and officers at the Nevsky Monastery. The Lord would be in no doubt as to the will of the Russian people, but the Lord might have His own plans.

The contemplation was broken by the tiniest of sounds; a knock at the chapel door. All heads turned in that direction. A face peeped around the door. Nikolai recognized it; it was his mother's valet. Even across the chapel, Nikolai could see the sorrow on the man's face. He had to make sure that it was not the dowager empress who received the news. He rose to his feet and strode across the room.

The valet displayed his relief that it was the grand duke who had come to the door. Once in the anteroom adjoining the chapel, Nikolai could see that it was still dark outside. He guessed it was no later than eight thirty in the morning. Waiting there was Count Miloradovich, governor-general of Petersburg. His face told the story even more clearly than had the valet's.

The news was succinct and irrefutable. Nikolai listened calmly and understood.

His brother Aleksandr Pavlovich was no more.

His son, Aleksandr Nikolayevich, was tsarevich.

He, Nikolai Pavlovich, was tsar.

That was for Russia, but for him, there was only one item of significance: his brother, Aleksandr – Sasha – the man who had headed the family since Nikolai was four, was dead.

CHAPTER XXXI

IT WAS AN ODD SOUND; A THUD, BUT BROAD AND QUIET, FILLING the room but not deafening Tamara. She looked up. Mama was standing at the window, as she did for so much of the time these days. The man who had hit her had not returned. It had been almost a week. Tamara hoped they would never see him again.

But she knew it was not that man that Mama was looking for; she was looking for Papa. She had glanced out of the window, from time to time, every day since he had left, but it had not obsessed her. It was only since the news that the tsar was dead that Mama had leaned her hand against the window and looked out almost every spare moment she had.

Tamara knew she should be sad about the death of the tsar, but she had never met him. Mama Yelena and Valentin seemed to be very sad. Tamara could usually tell when people were pretending to be sad, and she'd suspected this might be the case with Yelena and Valentin, but once she'd seen them, she knew she was wrong. Rodion wasn't quite so sad, but everyone else who came to the house was.

Only Mama seemed to share Tamara's lack of concern about the tsar. She was worried about Papa. Tamara remembered that Papa had said he was going to Taganrog, and that was a place that everyone was talking about as where the tsar had been when he'd died. Mama had shown it to her again on the map, and she'd

447

tried to remember where it was. It didn't look very far away, but Petersburg looked even closer, and that was where Papa spent most of his time; it was still difficult for him to visit them from there.

The sound had come from Mama throwing her hand against the window. Tamara couldn't think why she would be trying to break it, but it looked as though she had simply forgotten it was there and was trying to reach through it.

Her mother turned to her. Tamara had never seen such a wide smile on her face.

'He's here!' she said.

She had smiled so widely it had hurt her. She put her hand up to her face, where the man had hit her. It had almost healed, but now it had started to bleed again, but only slightly. Mama went over to the dressing table and started to powder her face. When she turned back to Tamara, there was no sign of the cut.

'Papa's back,' she said.

Tamara wasn't stupid. She'd guessed that before her mother had said anything, but the excitement of it was only just beginning to affect her. Her mother knelt down in front of her and held both her hands.

'Now you remember what you promised, Toma,' she said. Tamara was fairly sure what it was her mother was talking about, but she didn't nod, in case she was mistaken. 'You won't tell Papa about the man outside, will you? You promise?'

Tamara nodded. 'I promise,' she said.

'Stay here.' With that, Mama ran from the room. She didn't put her coat on this time. Tamara went to the window and looked out again.

There were quite a number of people in the street, and Tamara couldn't see any that looked like her father. There was one man, some way off, who seemed to be coming towards the house, but he was too far for her to recognize. Mama appeared on the street beneath the window and ran towards him. As soon as he saw her, he broke into a run too. Then Tamara could see that it was

448

Papa. He caught Mama's body in his arms as they met and she swung around him, her feet lifted off the ground. He put her down, and she buried her face in his chest. His hand was on the back of her head. Then she looked up and they kissed. It lasted for ten seconds, though Tamara hadn't started counting right away. Then they separated and began to walk arm in arm back towards the house.

Mama pointed towards the window where Tamara stood, and Papa looked up. He grinned and began to wave. Tamara waved back. Then Papa started to run to the door, leaving Mama walking alone in the snow. Tamara jumped up and down with excitement for a few moments and then realized that she too should run.

She turned and raced out of the bedroom, through Papa's study and into the hallway. There she brushed past somebody, but she didn't look to see who it was. It was Valentin Valentinovich's voice she heard shouting after her, but she ignored it.

Papa was just coming up the stairs – two, sometimes three at a time – when she reached the top. He picked her up without seem-ing to pause, but slowed his pace down to a walk. He hugged her close to him – she could feel his heart pumping, and his chest rose and fell rapidly as he breathed.

'And how's my little Toma?' he asked.

'I'm very well,' she said. 'And I've grown almost half an inch.'

'That's very impressive. And have you looked after Mama?'

Tamara knew that this was when she was going to have to lie to her father so as to keep her promise to her mother. 'Yes, I have,' she said. She decided she was good at lying.

They had arrived back in her parents' bedroom, and Mama had joined them within moments. Her father put her down and looked at her.

'You *have* grown,' he said. She grinned up at him. Mama slipped her arm through Papa's.

'Will you be here long?' Domnikiia asked. Tamara thought it sounded like a rude question, though her mother seemed more concerned than nagging.

'I'll try,' said Aleksei, 'but things may be on a knife edge in Petersburg now that Aleksandr is dead.' He suddenly went pale. 'You knew, I take it?' he asked.

Domnikiia nodded, and Papa looked relieved.

'Papa,' said Tamara, 'were you there when the tsar died?'

Her father looked down at her and smiled. 'No, my darling,' he said, 'I was nowhere near.'

Tamara pressed her lips together thoughtfully. Papa was nothing like as good a liar as she was.

At times like these, some men drank, some smoked, some gambled, some whored and others got into needless fights. Dmitry played piano. Not all of Moscow's representatives of the Northern Society had assembled at the club off Lubyanka Square, but it could cater for most of the activities they employed to pass the frustrating hours – except perhaps the whoring.

Dmitry was playing Scarlatti, but he wasn't paying much attention to it. Moscow seemed desperately provincial at a time like this. True, they had received the news a few days earlier than Petersburg, but that was just a lucky consequence of where Aleksandr had chosen to die. They certainly knew in the capital now, and it was there that the decisions of the Northern Society would be made. Those in Moscow could only follow. Even the Southern Society was irrelevant for the moment. There was no point in seizing power anywhere but where the new tsar was. In reality, that meant Warsaw, but Tsar Konstantin would already be on his way to the capital. Then Ryleev and the others would decide what was to be done with him. After that there would be bickering. It would be the north that acted and the south that subsequently tried to sort out the new constitution. It did not matter – change was all that mattered. But for now, the waiting was corrosive.

The hand touched his shoulder at the same moment he heard the voice.

'How have you been?'

450

He stopped playing and turned. It was his father. He felt a momentary annoyance at the memory of his encounter with Domnikiia Semyonovna, but it really changed nothing about his relationship with Aleksei. He had known about the woman for a long time; the fact that he had now spoken to her made little difference.

He stood and embraced his father. 'I've been well,' he said. 'And you?'

'I've dealt with things.'

'Kyesha – is he dead?'

'He won't be a problem any more.'

Dmitry glanced around the room and then guided his father to one side. The matter of Kyesha was what had taken his father south, but that all seemed quite irrelevant. In fact, Dmitry had begun to wonder whether a lot of what he had seen had really happened. He feared using the word '*voordalak*' to his father in case it was met with laughter. But much more significant events had taken place in the south, which were now of national importance.

'Were you *there*?' Dmitry asked in a low voice. 'In Taganrog?' His father's letters had hinted that he had been in the south, but only now did Dmitry guess precisely where. He did not know why he was whispering; if his father had had anything to do with the death of Aleksandr, then everyone in the club would take pleasure from hearing of it. Within weeks – or at most months – it would be the entire nation that hailed him as a liberator.

'I was in Taganrog, but not for long,' said Aleksei. 'I went to the Crimea – that's where Kyesha was. By the time I got back to Taganrog, Aleksandr was already dead. I came straight back here.'

Convenient, thought Dmitry. His father had been in Taganrog before the tsar's death and after it, but not on the actual day it occurred. Either that was false, in which case he was trying to hide any connection between himself and Aleksandr's death, or it was true, in which case he had made a clear effort to absent himself from the tsar's presence at that vital time. Either way, he was clearly being circumspect; wise, for the time being.

'I see,' said Dmitry, avoiding an explicit wink, but trying to convey the same implication with the tone of his voice. He leaned forward and spoke into his father's ear. 'Don't overdo it though. People will never believe what you did if you only announce it after the revolution.'

Aleksei scowled at him, and Dmitry realized he had probably said too much. Perhaps his father would never reveal his role – that would be like him; not so much modest as secretive. It was hard to believe that his father had actually raised his hand against the tsar, but there were others in the south who would have been eager to do that. Aleksei had obviously helped them in some way. And that meant there would be at least a few in the Southern Society who knew, and so the name Danilov would eventually make it into the history books.

'What's the mood here?' asked Aleksei.

'Confused. Impatient. The news can only have reached Petersburg a few days ago, so there's been no time for us to hear anything back. We can only guess that they will start an uprising. There's a lot suggesting we should all go up there, and concentrate our strength. But others say we'll be needed here. If the new tsar takes flight, this is where he will come.'

'Konstantin isn't even in Russia at the moment.'

'That's why we should act now.'

'Is there any consensus?'

'For the moment, it's wait and see – at least till we hear from Petersburg.'

'And your personal view?' asked Aleksei.

'I'd rather be where the action is.'

Aleksei patted him on the shoulder. 'A chip off the old block,' he said. Dmitry was reminded of what Domnikiia had said to him, about his similarity to Dmitry Fetyukovich.

'Do I take after Uncle Dmitry at all?' he asked.

Aleksei frowned, and then laughed. 'Not at all. Whoever gave you that idea?'

Dmitry had never really thought Domnikiia would say anything to Aleksei about their meeting – now he was sure she hadn't, otherwise Aleksei would have made the connection. He was still curious to know what she had meant, though.

'You named me after him,' he said.

'Yes, but that doesn't mean you'll be like him.' He changed the subject. 'Anyway, how's the training going? Every day at the manège, I hope.'

'Most,' said Dmitry, 'but there are lots of other things to train in. They haven't given up square-bashing yet.'

His father glanced down at the piano. 'Not tempted to join the band?' he asked.

'It's not easy to march with a piano.'

'You're keeping it up though?'

Dmitry nodded.

'Good,' said Aleksei. 'Next time you're in Petersburg, there'll . . . well, you'll see.'

Dmitry was about to ask his father what he meant, but it was clear he was being deliberately enigmatic. 'So what do you think we should do, Papa?' he asked instead.

'About what?'

'About the revolution.'

'Like you said,' replied his father. 'We wait.'

Even in the Crimea it was turning cold now, especially at night. The crescent moon was low in the sky, but still cast a reasonable light. This was the third night in a row Iuda had sat out here. He hoped it would be the last. He'd chosen the spot some way to the north of Chufut Kalye. The hills were lower here, which helped with the cold. There was no snow as yet, but it could be seen on the mountain peaks to the south.

It was an ideal location. The trail he had left should be easy enough to follow. He had gone back to Karaite citadel and talked to several of the locals there. A few had recognized him from when he had first reconnoitred the land, years before, but none guessed how close he had been living to them in the meantime. Certainly, anyone who asked wouldn't have too much difficulty gaining directions to an inn in Simferopol where he – still under the name of Cain – had been staying.

At the inn, they'd learn that the Englishman, Cain, had presented himself as a keen geologist, interested in the cave formations in the region. They'd be told the area he'd been asking questions about, and the fact that he intended to set up camp there.

Not too obvious, he hoped. It shouldn't matter though; anyone – any creature – that followed the trail would have such an overwhelming sense of their own superiority – against all historical evidence – that they would not be looking for a trap. Even if they were, the worst it could do would be to scare them off.

On the other hand, it could be Lyosha who came after him. He might be buoyed by his victory over Iuda – however pyrrhic it had been, considering that it required the death of Aleksandr – and have decided to pursue him. Would he get lucky and actually manage to kill Iuda one day? The chances were that someone would – someone less squeamish about it than Aleksei, probably. It had become a growing concern for Iuda, and that was what tonight's undertaking was all about.

His worst fear was that it would be Zmyeevich himself that came, though more likely he would see such personal involvement as beneath him. Iuda regretted having made an enemy of him. Their alliance had begun in 1812, when Zmyeevich had first sent Iuda to Russia to contact the tsar, under the cover of a band of mercenaries whose mission had been, even in Zmyeevich's eyes, secondary, though the defeat of Russia would have done him little good. He would make a terrible foe, but better to be alive and faced with an enemy like that than to be dead. More and more recently, Iuda had been reminded of his own mortality.

Somewhere behind him, lower down the hill, he heard a sound. He reached into his pocket and drank from the small pewter flask he found there. It tasted foul, but he knew he had to drink it – not too much though. He almost gagged as he swallowed; there was little chance of overconsumption.

Whoever it was was skirting along the hillside, round to the right. Iuda could still hear them, though they had not yet climbed high enough to have come into view. It would seem they wanted to greet him face to face. Foolhardy, perhaps, but it was necessary for an avenger to be known to his victim. That was why Zmyeevich had insisted Aleksandr know most of what was going on. It had proved a mistake then; it would now.

A face appeared, rising up over the brow of the hill with the moon behind it, but illuminated by the single lamp Iuda had placed beside him. It was the face he had been expecting. There was no attempt at stealth. He came to a halt a few paces away.

'Good evening, Cain,' he said.

'Good evening . . .' Iuda pretended not to remember the name. 'Ruslan, isn't it?'

'It was once. I prefer Kyesha now.'

'Ah, yes! Maksim Sergeivich's poor little brother Innokyentii.'

'You knew I'd go to Saratov?' asked Kyesha.

'I knew it must have been you who gave my book to Danilov. The only link you could have with him was through Maksim Sergeivich.'

'So you set me up? Aleksei too?'

'I have to admit I had formed only the vaguest of plans,' said Iuda. There was no need for deceit. 'You really did all the thinking for me; though if I'd been organizing things, I'd have been a little better prepared for Lyosha when he arrived at Chufut Kalye – or I'd have made sure he arrived a few weeks later. One thing at a time is best, I always find.'

'And now you're starting all over again.'

Iuda looked around him at the barren hilltop. 'Here?' he said. 'No, I think my cave-dwelling days are over. I was just waiting here for you.'

'Just like you were waiting for Aleksei?'

Iuda decided it was time to show a little weakness. 'You learn quickly,' he said, with a self-effacing smile.

Kyesha took a step towards him. Iuda felt his heart quicken as he welcomed in the familiar sensation of fear. This was not the kind of fear he had experienced with Zmyeevich on *Răzbunarea* – this was the good kind, the kind that told him he was alive.

'Where are all the others?' asked Kyesha.

'Others?'

'From the caves.'

'Ah! Those others. Raisa Styepanovna has gone her own way. You are here. As for the rest – they're still there.'

'Still in the caves?' said Kyesha. Iuda nodded. 'Dead, you mean?'

'Why should they be dead? They have long lives to look forward to.' As he spoke, Iuda could see that Kyesha's temper was on the verge of snapping. 'Long, dull lives.'

'Unlike you,' muttered Kyesha. He launched himself into the air towards Iuda, covering far more ground in a single leap than any human could. The impact knocked Iuda backwards off the rock on which he had been seated. He felt a sudden panic fill him. Beneath his coat he had a dagger made of wood – a copy of the one he had seen years before in Aleksei's hand. It would be so easy to use it now, so safe, but he resisted. Any safety such an action brought would only be for the short term.

He felt his back hit the ground. Kyesha was already on top of him and had him pinned down. Iuda knew how immense the strength of these creatures was, but it always shocked him to feel it directly.

Kyesha bared his fangs. 'I'm sure I don't have to tell you this,' he said, 'but there are two ways that an *oopir* likes to consume its prey. The quick way involves biting away the flesh of the neck. The slow way involves the gradual but ultimately total draining of the blood.' He paused, and Iuda saw the lustful hunger in his eyes. 'I hope you're not in any hurry,' he said.

Kyesha would not have seen the look of relief upon Iuda's face, even had Iuda not successfully repressed it. His head went down on to Iuda's throat and his fangs found their way through the skin. The entire length of his body began to pulsate in time with the slurping sounds that emanated from his mouth.

It was a fascinating experience. There had been no pain at the initial penetration. He had not yet isolated the chemical the vampire secreted to stop this. He did feel the sensation of blood being drawn from his body, but not enough yet to affect him. The strangest thing was – as Zmyeevich had described happening with Pyotr – the sense in which Iuda began to know Kyesha's mind. He could see what he saw and know what he knew. It was a good job the reverse wasn't the case, or Kyesha would have fled the mountains that instant.

Iuda could now see through Kyesha's own eyes. In truth, there was not much to see; just the bottom of his own earlobe and the side of his neck. More delightful was the fact that Iuda could taste what Kyesha tasted – he could taste his own blood. There was nothing new in that – Iuda, like any human, had sucked his own cut finger more than once, but to drink down great mouthfuls at a time was glorious, refreshing, invigorating. Clearly there were some compensations to being a vampire. In a way, he was sad that Kyesha would soon have to stop, but stop he would, and the sooner the better, for Iuda would still need his strength.

Then he felt it, a tightening pain in his stomach which he knew was in fact a far greater pain in Kyesha's stomach. The vampire pulled away from his body and raised his head upwards, screaming at the sky and clutching his belly. With a swift kick, Iuda was free of his weight and back on his feet. He felt a little dizzy – more from what he had been drinking than from the blood loss, he hoped. He grabbed the bandage he had placed on the ground beside where he had been sitting and pressed it against the wound on his throat. He held it there for a moment, and then tied it around his neck. He had little time. He reached into his bag for the few items he would need.

Kyesha had raised himself to his feet and was staggering across the rocky landscape like a drunk. Iuda caught up with him from behind and kicked him hard in the back of the leg. Kyesha collapsed to the ground in a kneeling position, his upper body gyrating in a small, slow circle, but never falling.

'What have you done?' he slurred.

'I've improved on a master,' explained Iuda. 'Your Pyotr certainly was great if he could fool Zmyeevich, but he did it in a very haphazard way. I need no troop of men to rescue me. What you drank was your own undoing.'

'Po—' muttered Kyesha.

'I'm sorry?' said Iuda, leaning forward to better hear him, and also tucking his dark hair behind his shoulders.

'Poison?' It took Kyesha an effort to say even that one word.

'For you more than for me,' explained Iuda. He straightened up and had to steady himself on Kyesha's shoulders. 'A concoction of my own, devised and perfected after much experimentation. The effect on me, having drunk it, is – I now discover – not unlike the inebriation caused by alcohol. The effect on you, drinking my blood, is far more debilitating.'

'Will I . . . die?' gasped Kyesha.

Iuda cocked his head to one side and smiled. 'A silly question. But my infusion won't kill you. You creatures are – as you know – very exclusive in the methods by which you can be destroyed.'

'So . . .'

'Sh!' said Iuda gently. 'Now I'm just going to take back a little of what you've taken from me. That's fair, isn't it?'

He grabbed Kyesha by the hair and pulled back his head, bringing his knife round so that the vampire could see it. He pondered which side of the blades to use, the smooth or the serrated. The razor-sharp edge of the smooth side would be tidier, but probably less painful, and though he had no qualms about inflicting pain on Kyesha – quite the reverse – he had other more important concerns for now. He brought the two sharp, parallel

458

blades close in until he felt them press against the skin, then he tugged the knife back firmly towards himself and across Kyesha's throat.

Kyesha's head moved back palpably under the strain of Iuda's hold as the knife tore through neck muscles that had been trying to resist. Two wide, dark gaps opened up between his chin and his collarbone, out of which blood began to vomit. Calmly but quickly, Iuda put down the knife and picked up the small bowl he had brought for the task. He held it in front of Kyesha and let the blood cascade into it. The flow was slowing already, but it didn't take long to fill the receptacle.

He let go of Kyesha's hair and put the bowl down carefully some way away on a flat piece of ground. It would be ridiculous to risk spilling it now. Then he returned to Kyesha, reaching inside his coat as he walked.

The vampire had managed to crawl a little way away, in a hopeless attempt at escape, but he scarcely had the strength to move. Iuda strode over to him. His chest was matted with blood, and the ground around him was stained. Iuda grabbed his hair again and lifted his head. The two parallel lines across the neck where the blades had cut gaped open, but even as Iuda watched, he could see they were beginning to heal. He let go, but Kyesha's head remained lifted under his own volition. The eyes opened and looked blearily in Iuda's direction. The lips moved, but no sound escaped them.

Iuda knew that he was decades old, but now, in this battered, vulnerable state, Kyesha looked more than ever the boy he had been when he had first allowed a vampire to drink his blood. Iuda would have loved to let him recover just a little more. Inside his overcoat he felt the handle of his wooden dagger, but then he hesitated. It would be too easy, and Iuda was in the mood for some fun.

He picked his knife up off the floor again and examined it, walking contemplatively around behind Kyesha again. This time there was no need for neatness or precision. He flipped the knife over so that the jagged, toothed edge faced Kyesha's neck, and grabbed his hair once again.

The blood spilled forth with the same eagerness as before, but now it was of no especial interest to Iuda. He felt its warmth flowing over his hand, but it was hard to distinguish from the folds of flesh that caressed him as his hand moved deeper into the gaping wound. Muscle and sinew yielded easily. Kyesha did not scream, but that was unlikely to be the result of any bravery. It was difficult for a man – or a vampire – to utter any sound with his windpipe severed and his voicebox lolling on his chest.

The bones of Kyesha's neck proved more tricky. Iuda grabbed the hair tighter and pressed his knee into the back of the neck to brace himself. He could still feel pain in his own neck, where Zmyeevich had tried to kill him, but it was healing. He twisted and sawed with the knife, searching for a way through, but still the bones were too strong. Then suddenly one of the blades found a gap between two vertebrae, and he was through. He felt no more resistance.

Iuda looked down at the creature, but did not see what he had expected. Beheading should have led to instant death and the predictable collapse of the corporal remains to dust. But what Iuda's eyes saw and what his hands felt was still flesh and blood. He realized he had been too slow. In the time it had taken him to cut through the neck bones, the front of Kyesha's throat had begun to regrow. The decapitation had to be complete.

It was of little consequence. Iuda reversed the direction of his pressure and, with a flick of his wrist, the opposite edges of the blades cut back through Kyesha's new-grown flesh with ease. At the same moment his right hand flicked forward as the knife became free, so his left lurched into the air, holding the severed head by its hair. He turned to look at it, but already the face was unrecognizable, falling away as it decayed and revealing a skull which itself crumpled and tumbled to the ground, its broken fragments retaining some slight vestige of shape as they lay in the grass. The hair entwined round his fingers broke apart and was scattered by the breeze.

Iuda felt a moment of exhilaration, but it was immediately followed by a wave of exhaustion. He was still weak from what he had drunk and what had been drunk from him. He picked up his bag and went over to where he had left the bowl of blood, sitting down on the ground beside it. It was a joy to have the weight off his feet, but his arms still felt heavy as he moved them. He picked up the bowl and swilled its contents around. The blood was still liquid – the only part of a vampire's body that remained in its original form after the creature's death, and even then, only if extracted before death.

He reached into his knapsack and pulled out a handful of glass vials. Each already contained a few drops of the liquid – itself extracted from the saliva of a vampire – that would stop the blood from clotting. He poured blood from the bowl into each of them in turn, watching it glisten, almost black in the moonlight. A little of it spilled on to his fingers. The taste for blood he had acquired in those few moments in which he had shared Kyesha's experience still lingered, but he resisted it, wiping his fingers on the grass instead. He filled almost four of the vials. He should only ever need the first, but one could never tell. He wrapped them carefully in scraps of rag and then put them back in his bag. He still had one dose of Zmyeevich's own blood, left over from the several he had taken during their plans to induct the tsar. But that blood would not suit his purposes, and might yet be needed to save him from his former ally once again.

He went back over to Kyesha's remains, now scarcely visible. Only his clothes were left. It would be ridiculous not to take the opportunity to pilfer. He felt through the pockets of the coat. There was a watch, which seemed to be of reasonable quality, and a small number of gold coins. Then, in the side pocket, Iuda found something he could not comprehend. Six roughly shaped items he first took to be stones and then realized were made of bone. What their purpose might be, he could not fathom, but they had clearly had some significance for Kyesha. He slipped them into his pocket, along with the money and the watch. He could work out what they were for later.

He felt a sudden pain in his neck. He reached up and touched his finger to the bandage. The wound felt sore beneath. The bandage was damp, but not wet. The bleeding had stopped. He reached into the bag again and brought out a small package, wrapped in paper. He opened it. Inside was a small, dark lump of meat: *kishka* – another trick he had learned from Pyotr. To say it was meat was a misnomer; it was a sausage made from congealed pig's blood. Normally, Iuda would not have willingly chosen to eat it. He was not squeamish about blood in general, but to consume it was a different matter. That was always one of the hardest things about passing himself off as a vampire.

But today, he had to eat it – it was good for him, as his father used to tell him, a long, long time ago. And besides, now that he thought about it, blood didn't seem unappetizing at all. He wolfed the sausage down in a few bites and followed it with a second. He felt a little better, but still tired. He packed up his things and prepared to set off; a short trek back to Simferopol, thence to hire a horse, and northwards. There were two further matters to be attended to: one might help rebuild his relationship with Zmyeevich; one was purely for himself.

He dragged himself up on to his feet, but instantly felt ill. The loss of blood and the potion he had drunk beforehand combined to make him feel dizzy. He lay back on the frosty grass and let his eyelids droop. A few hours' sleep there would do him good, despite the cold. He was in no hurry.

It was almost eight o'clock, and the sun was still an hour from rising. Tamara had woken Aleksei early and he had been happy to talk to her alone, letting her mother sleep in. He had spent as much of his time as he could with her in the four days he had had in Moscow – and most of the rest with Domnikiia. Domnikiia had now woken, and was playing with Toma. Aleksei decided it was time to do some work.

He still had a job to do. Aleksandr was – to all the world – a dead man, but there was still a tsar. Konstantin might not want to carry on using Aleksei in the role his brother had, and Aleksei wasn't sure he wanted to continue it, but he at least had to put together some sort of documentation summarizing what he knew about the Northern and Southern societies.

He went through to his study and sat at his desk, assembling piles of papers in front of him, but not looking at them. Ever since he had left Taganrog, he had wondered whether it might not be better to let the revolutionaries have their way. A republic might not be the best form of government for Russia, but it would be one in the eye for Zmyeevich – a way of cutting the Gordian Knot. Whatever influence Zmyeevich could then exert on subsequent generations of Romanovs, unpleasant though it might be for them, would have no bearing on the fate of Russia. If that was lost, Zmyeevich might not even bother with his revenge. Even if the revolutionaries went for the most moderate of their options – a constitutional monarchy – it could so weaken the role of the tsar that Zmyeevich would find him useless.

The problem was, not all of them were so moderate, particularly not in the south. There might not *be* subsequent generations of Romanovs – certainly not from the core of the family. Look what had happened to the Bourbons, those who had not got away. Aleksei had been eight years old when the French Revolution began. Four years after that marked the start of the Reign of Terror. The French themselves called it, more succinctly, *la Terreur*. That was when Petersburg had started to fill with émigrés fleeing for their lives. It was not their sudden poverty or their fall from grace that had terrified the young Aleksei; it was the stories they told. Tens of thousands were slaughtered by the bizarrely named Committee of Public Safety, which believed that somehow the safety of the public was an issue unconnected to the safety of individual members of that public.

They saw the guillotine as a clean, efficient, modern way of carrying out their year-long massacre, with an efficacy which only lawyers the likes of Robespierre could achieve – and take pride in. In Russia, the revolutionaries were more poets and soldiers than lawyers, but Aleksei knew what would follow them. At best, it could only mean their killing would be less well organized, but still they would massacre any they thought to be enemies of the state, and since they *were* the state – wasn't it a French king who had said that? – that made them free to kill anyone they regarded as an enemy of themselves.

Perhaps the very inefficiency of the current batch of Russian revolutionaries would mean they could not kill so many with such a degree of sanitization, and that therefore the people, literally revolted, would turn against them. The French idea of death carried out by a machine was vital to the success of the whole venture. But compared to a Russia like that, being ruled by a tsar who was himself ruled by Zmyeevich seemed almost desirable – at least a sane form of tyranny.

Aleksei laughed out loud. It was a sorry state of reasoning that led him to such a conclusion. But the fault was in assuming there could only either be one outcome or another. There were two much more desirable possibilities: either to let the revolutionaries found a constitutional monarchy; or to defeat them, let Konstantin reign as tsar, and go on to defeat Zmyeevich when the time came. He'd beaten him once, when he had only just discovered what it was Zmyeevich was attempting. In future he, or whoever he chose to pass his knowledge on to, would be better prepared.

But who would that person be? It was a cruel chalice and a bitter poison to pass on to a child. Could he do that to Dmitry? He would have no desire to protect a tsar. But in any case it was not a matter that needed considering now. What mattered now was the immediate threat to Konstantin.

Aleksei pulled the papers towards him and started sorting through them, choosing which he would hand over intact to the representatives of the new regime, which he would summarize

464

and which he would leave out. It would take all day just to do that.

'Can you come and play?'

He turned. Tamara's face was grinning through the door. It would be so easy to say yes, but this had to be done – and she had to learn that sometimes she couldn't have what she wanted.

'I'm sorry, my darling,' he said. 'Not just now.'

Toma ran back into the other room. Aleksei heard her voice as she went, speaking to her mother. 'I told you he'd say no,' she said, with an air of smugness. It looked like she wasn't the only lady in the family who had yet to learn she couldn't always have what she wanted. He turned back to his papers.

The one on top concerned the poet Aleksandr Sergeivich Pushkin. Aleksei moved it swiftly into a pile he would not be showing to anyone – he would burn them, most likely. Pushkin had a revolutionary spirit, but it manifested itself only in what he wrote, never in what he did. He was a better poet than Ryleev and a worse rebel – he would not have managed to kill a dozen in twenty years, with or without a guillotine, unless each one had challenged him to a duel.

Underneath that was a small paper envelope. Aleksei wondered for a moment what it was, and then remembered with a shudder. It was where he had placed the two fingers Kyesha had given him, the last time they had met in Moscow. It seemed a little crushed by the papers on top of it. Would a sensation as mild as that be transmitted to Kyesha, wherever in the world he might now be?

He picked up the envelope. It felt surprisingly light. He opened it and looked inside. There were no fingers. God forbid Tamara should have found them. But the desk had been locked all the time Aleksei had been away – and Domnikiia would not have let the little girl near it. What if Valentin Valentinovich had taken them? It was he who had allowed Aleksei the use of his desk – along with this section of the house – and had given him the keys. He might well have kept a spare set. Aleksei could only laugh at what his host might think at finding a pair of severed fingers in his desk. What if he had taken them out into the sun?

But when he looked inside the envelope once again, he saw that it was not empty. He tipped the contents out on to the desk. It was a dusty, grey powder – not a huge amount, but instantly recognizable for what it was: the final, rotted remains of a dead vampire. It had been over fifteen years since Kyesha had abandoned his humanity and become a *voordalak*. Now that he was dead, those years of decay had acted upon his remains in an instant. There was little left of him. It was hard to mourn his passing, but it was difficult, unlike with most of them, not to regret his becoming a vampire. Clearly Kyesha had chosen the path he had taken, but in their conversations there had been no sign of the base malice Aleksei had known in the Oprichniki. Even so, he knew Kyesha had killed, and would have killed again, and so ultimately his death had to be applauded.

There was one concern though. Aleksei could not be sure – there were a hundred ways in which he could have died, at the hands of any righteous Christian he might have chosen to attack – but Aleksei felt it in his bones. Wherever it had taken place, it had been brought about by the man for whom Kyesha had himself been searching.

It had been done by Iuda.

CHAPTER XXXII

ALEKSEI HAD BEEN IN MOSCOW FOR NINE DAYS, UNDECIDED as to what to do. It was easy to assert that action must be better than inaction, but to do the wrong thing now could bring disaster, and change the future of Russia for ever. Even if he simply went to the wrong place, he might find himself too distant from events when they finally occurred to have any influence over them. True, little was likely to happen in Moscow, but Moscow was at least reasonably central. The seat of government was to the north, in Petersburg; Tsar Konstantin was to the west, in Warsaw, though presumed to be preparing for his return, if he hadn't already set out; the Southern Society, and its revolutionary fervour, was to the south, around Kiev. Minsk was the city most ideally positioned between those three potential powder kegs, but Aleksei was damned if he was going to Minsk.

And that was the point on which his judgement might have been a little more subjective. Moscow meant Domnikiia and Tamara. They were reason enough to stay, particularly when there was no good reason to leave. He was reminded of the winter of 1812, after Bonaparte's hasty retreat from Moscow. Then he had lingered in the city with Domnikiia, awaiting events. Then, the event had been a letter from Dmitry Fetyukovich, announcing that he was on the trail of Iuda and the last remaining Oprichnik, Foma. This time, he would be summoned . . . how?

There was a polite knock at the door. Aleksei opened it. A footman stood outside.

'A gentleman to see you, sir.'

'Send him in.'

'He's in a great hurry and says you must accompany him,' the servant replied.

Aleksei put on his coat and grabbed his hat, heading out to the front door. Waiting for him was Lieutenant Batenkov, that young stalwart of the Northern Society in Moscow.

'I have a message for you, Colonel,' he said, 'from Dmitry . . . from Lieutenant Danilov. You must come at once.'

They walked briskly through the snow, towards the Kremlin and then past the manège and the Bolshoi Theatre before heading up to Lubyanka Square. The club was as busy as Aleksei had ever seen it. He saw Dmitry across the other side of the room, and forced his way through to him, half listening to the hubbub of conversation that filled the air. Three names stood out – the brothers Romanov: Konstantin Pavlovich, Nikolai Pavlovich and Mihail Pavlovich.

'What's happened?' asked Aleksei as soon as he and Batenkov had reached Dmitry.

'Grand Duke Mihail,' explained Dmitry. 'He reached Petersburg five days ago.'

Of the surviving brothers, Mihail, the youngest, was the only one whom Aleksei had met personally. Aleksandr had briefly introduced them six years before, and had recommended the soldier to the grand duke. The news that Mihail should have gone to the capital at this time was no surprise. 'And Konstantin?' Aleksei asked. It seemed the obvious question.

'No,' said Dmitry. 'That's just the thing, but worse than that, Mihail is refusing to swear allegiance to Konstantin.'

'What?' That was news – or more likely, rumour. 'Are you sure?'

'We've heard it from three sources.'

'Why should he refuse?' asked Aleksei.

'It's a *coup d'état*,' said Dmitry. 'Nikolai is trying to take over.'

'But Nikolai swore allegiance to his brother days ago – as soon as he heard Aleksandr was dead.'

'He would do, wouldn't he?' Dmitry seemed very sure of what was going on. 'That way no one suspects him, and he can see which way the wind is blowing. And see what his agents could do in Warsaw.'

'What do you mean?'

'Konstantin is being held prisoner – that's why he's not back in Petersburg.'

'Oh, come on!' Even as he spoke, Aleksei wondered if his scepticism was a reflection of his naivety. It would be a very Romanov way of doing things. Both the father and the grandfather had had power ripped from them by other members of the family. Why should this generation be any different? 'What do our friends in the Polish Society say?' he asked.

'There's no news,' said Dmitry. 'I'll be honest – what we're hearing from Warsaw is vague so far.'

'The plan was for them to rise up at the same time as we did,' said Batenkov, who had been listening intently to the conversation.

'Exactly,' said Dmitry. 'And if they see that Konstantin has been arrested, who are they to know that it's not as a result of a direct order from us, having taken charge here.'

Aleksei nodded. 'So what's the mood here?' he asked.

'We have to liaise with Petersburg, but the obvious plan is to back Konstantin. If we ensure he takes the throne, then he'll have to repay us by delegating much of his power to us.'

'A constitution, you mean? That's less than we'd hoped for.'

Dmitry touched his father's arm. 'You're such an old idealist, Papa. We have to grab what we can get when the chance arises. Who knows what may come of it in the end?' His patronizing manner cut Aleksei to the quick, but not for the obvious reason. What really hurt was how utterly deceived Dmitry was as to his father's motivations.

'Why side with Konstantin though?' Aleksei asked. 'Why not with Nikolai? He'd be just as grateful for the victory, and he's younger – maybe more in tune with our views.' To be honest, it didn't sound like the Nikolai Aleksei had heard descriptions of.

Batenkov nodded. 'And he's in a stronger position,' he added, 'being in Petersburg.'

'That's exactly why we have to support Konstantin. Nikolai is *too* strong. He'll win and be under no obligation to give us anything.'

Dmitry was right, Aleksei knew it. There was another reason too. 'Plus, we'll have right on our side – in the sense of supporting the correct succession,' Aleksei explained. 'Anyone loyal to the crown will be loyal to Konstantin.'

'I don't like standing around waiting, though,' said Dmitry. 'We should act.'

Aleksei couldn't help but agree. His mind was in turmoil. As a loyal Russian, he had to support Konstantin as the next in line to the throne. But if the Northern Society threw its hat into the ring with Konstantin, then whose side did that really put him on? And in his heart, didn't he believe that a constitutional monarchy – what Aleksandr had seemed to promise in the early days – was best for Russia? On top of all that, there was the question of Zmyeevich and the next generation of Romanovs. Aleksei had already decided that a constitution would be a good way of blunting that threat. If a constitutional monarchy it was to be, Aleksei's new ambition must be to keep it from descending into a French-style bloodbath.

'What had you in mind?' he asked.

'Go to Warsaw,' said Dmitry. 'Free Konstantin.'

Aleksei shook his head. That would be a waste of time, whatever outcome they were seeking. 'It's too far. Konstantin may already have left – or may be dead. The Polish Society is best placed to deal with it.'

'But someone has to communicate with the Poles,' insisted Dmitry.

470

'True – and that communication will have already been sent from Petersburg. They're in charge and they've got a clear picture of what's going on.'

'So we go to Petersburg.'

'Exactly,' said Aleksei. 'We have to stop Nikolai seizing power, or at least object to it. That will give Konstantin time to arrive.'

'And if Konstantin is dead?'

Aleksei considered. If one brother had slain another for the throne, then none of them could be trusted. It would be the end of the monarchy. 'Then God help Russia,' he said.

But the thought of fratricide brought the name Cain back to his mind. Power moving from Konstantin to Nikolai brought it one step closer to Nikolai's son, Aleksandr. That would be in Zmyeevich's, and therefore Iuda's interests. Could Iuda have played some part in what was happening? Aleksei dismissed it – it was paranoia. But where Iuda was involved, paranoia was a healthy trait.

'When do we leave?' asked Dmitry.

'Today,' said Aleksei.

'Can I come, sir?' asked Batenkov.

Aleksei looked at him, and then at Dmitry. Batenkov had a certain earnestness that it was hard not to admire, but there would be little benefit to his company. And now that their goals were concurrent – albeit from different points of view – Aleksei felt an unaccustomed closeness to Dmitry that he did not want to share. 'No, you stay here, Lieutenant,' he said. 'We'll be sending any information we get back to Moscow through you.'

The lieutenant saluted, and Aleksei and Dmitry left. Out on the street, it seemed even colder than when Aleksei had arrived.

'We'll meet in two hours,' he said. 'That should be enough time to pack. We'll meet outside my hotel.'

'Your hotel? Shouldn't you be saying goodbye to Domnikiia Semyonovna?'

Aleksei froze. He should have expected it – his son was no fool.

It was hard to judge his mood. There was a certain bitterness to his voice, but the very fact he mentioned it must indicate some acceptance. And was there a hint of friendly advice in there – a suggestion that Aleksei should do the right thing, and that meant saying goodbye to his mistress? Aleksei hoped so.

'OK,' he said. 'Let's not waste time. I'll meet you at the Lavrovs' house.'

They parted. Aleksei put his head down and forced his way through the blustering snow. It was impossible to judge Dmitry's attitude over Domnikiia – the boy probably didn't know it himself. The one consolation was that he was apparently quite unaware that living there in the Lavrovs' house, along with her mother, Dmitry had a little sister, Tamara.

'Well, I suppose if you *have* to go.'

Aleksei wondered who Tamara had been listening to, to come up with a sentence like that.

'I'm afraid I do have to,' he said. He was squatting down at Tamara's level, looking into her face, but he knew he was address-ing Domnikiia. 'It's only to Petersburg this time.' He glanced up at Domnikiia. It was no consolation to her. Petersburg meant his other home – his other wife. His only wife as far as Domnikiia was concerned, however he might tell her he felt.

'How long will you be?' asked Tamara.

'I don't know. I'll try to be home for Christmas.'

'Will you bring me something?'

'Of course.' Almost immediately, Aleksei understood what was behind the question. He hadn't brought her back anything from his journey to Taganrog. He thought quickly. 'Don't you want something now?' he asked.

'What?'

It was a good question. 'What would you like?'

She pointed to his chest. His shirt was buttoned up tight against the cold, but he knew what she meant. He reached inside and fished it out, pulling the chain off over his head.

'This?' he asked.

Tamara nodded. Aleksei cradled it in his hand. The fine silver chain hung down. He could see the knot where he had once hastily repaired it, a long time ago. The icon itself was oval; the face of the Saviour looked back at him.

'Do you want it?' he asked. Tamara nodded again. He held the chain wide open with his fingers, slipping it over her red curls and sliding it down to her neck. Then he pulled at her hair so the chain disappeared under it. She picked the icon up off her chest, tilting her head in one direction and the image in the other so that she could see it the right way up.

Then she dropped it and flung her arms around Aleksei's neck, squeezing tightly.

'Thank you, Papa,' she said. Aleksei hugged her back, feeling her heartbeat against his, and the tiny strength of her arms that was everything she had to offer. At last he let go and stood up. Her arms tried to hold him a little longer, but could not. He bent down one final time and kissed her. Then he picked up his bag and went to the door. Domnikiia followed him.

'Did you have to give her that?' she asked, once they were alone in the hallway.

Aleksei had guessed she might not be happy. Originally the icon had been a gift to him from Marfa. He touched Domnikiia's arm.

'It may have been my wife who gave me it, but it was you who insisted I wear it.'

'I suppose so,' she said. 'It was never much protection, anyway.'

'There're no vampires where I'm going,' he said.

'*She*'s there, though.'

Aleksei avoided the issue. 'I was originally intending to give it to Dmitry, because of Dmitry Fetyukovich.' The image came clearly to his mind; him breaking open the frozen, dead fingers of Dmitry's hand to get hold of the icon he had once given him as a sign of their friendship.

473

'No,' she said, firmly. 'It's best you give it to Toma.' She raised her hand to her cheek and thoughtfully rubbed the corner of her mouth. 'Won't Marfa expect you to stay with her for Christmas?'

'I'll make up some excuse.' Marfa would need little persuading, he was sure. It would give her more time to spend with Vasiliy. He had almost forgotten about his wife's lover. If the man's very existence could slip from his mind so easily, how could he claim truly to care?

He held Domnikiia close to him. She did not put her arms around him; they were trapped between them, pressed against her bosom and his chest. He kissed her, closing his eyes and leaning against her, as if falling into her beautiful, sweet mouth. Eventually, she was forced to step back rather than lose balance. She giggled and slapped him lightly on the arm, then pushed him towards the door.

'Go on,' she said. 'I'll see you soon. Christmas, remember? You promised.'

He let her herd him towards the stairs, then turned and kissed her once more, briefly, on the lips.

'Christmas,' he said.

Every day, Tamara knew, she got a little taller, and that meant that, every day, it was a little easier for her to look out of the window and on to the street below, pulling against the window-ledge with her fingers to raise herself up and see over it. It was already starting to get dark, and the snow in the street looked grey. She looked as straight downwards as she could and saw the top of Papa's head – or at least the hat on it. He was standing just outside the front door, not going anywhere.

Then he moved, reacting to something. Tamara looked and saw another man, walking over to her father, who patted him on the shoulder. They walked off down the street together. That was very strange. Why should Papa be so friendly with the man who had hit Mama? Did he know what the man had done? Did Mama

474

know that they were friends? Should she tell Mama what she had seen?

Her father didn't turn and wave like he usually did when he left, particularly if he was going a long way away. Tamara wished he had. But he would be back at Christmas. And he'd given her the picture of Jesus.

She ran over to the bed and lay down on it, holding the icon so that she could look at the picture. Jesus looked like a very kind man, though a little stern. If He hadn't had a beard, perhaps He would have looked a bit like Papa. She would ask her father to grow a beard when he came back; then she'd know. In the meantime, she had the icon, and she could look at it whenever she needed to be reminded of him.

CHAPTER XXXIII

FOUR DAYS LATER, DMITRY AND HIS FATHER WERE IN PETERSBURG. Dmitry's first instinct was to go to the house and let his mother know that they were home, but Aleksei felt that political matters were more pressing. He was afraid to look into his wife's face, Dmitry suspected – though he had not been hindered by any sense of guilt in the past. Neither man had raised the subject of Aleksei's infidelity on the journey north.

Once in the city, they made straight for Prince Obolensky's house, but he was not there. The butler recognized Aleksei and told them to try Ryleev's home. There they found Ryleev, Obolensky and a number of others.

'Colonel Danilov,' said Ryleev enthusiastically as they entered, coming over and shaking him warmly by the hand.

'Kondraty Fyodorovich,' responded Aleksei. 'This is my son, Dmitry Alekseevich.'

'We've met already,' said Ryleev, shaking Dmitry's hand. There was general greeting all round.

'We've just today returned from Moscow,' explained Aleksei.

'What's the mood like there?' asked Ryleev.

Aleksei looked to Dmitry, who realized that – since his father had only been in Moscow for about a week – he was in a better position to explain.

'There's a great deal of expectation,' he said. 'We've heard that Mihail Pavlovich has refused to swear allegiance to his brother, and also that Konstantin Pavlovich is still in Warsaw – perhaps a prisoner. Is Nikolai really trying to take command?'

'We're not sure,' said Ryleev, 'but that's the way we're going to tell it. Restoration of the rightful order of things will be a lot easier to sell to the masses.'

'The slogan will be "Konstantin and Constitution",' added Obolensky.

'And after a little while, we drop the "Konstantin",' said the man who had just been introduced to Dmitry as Kakhovsky.

'But what if it turns out that Nikolai isn't trying to take over?' asked Aleksei, ever cautious.

'It will be too late by then,' said Ryleev. 'If not, no one will blame us for trying to support the rightful tsar, even if it was based on a misunderstanding. Carry on with the news from Moscow, though.'

'All those who are friendly to our cause are ready to rise up,' continued Dmitry, 'but they await a signal from you – or an event that will force them to act.'

'The latter is unlikely in Moscow, I think,' said Ryleev. 'And what of the ordinary people?'

'They mourn Aleksandr and accept Konstantin.'

'So they suspect nothing of Nikolai's actions?'

'Not when we left. Many have already sworn allegiance to Konstantin, so they may be on our side when they hear.'

'Good,' said Ryleev.

'So, what's the plan?' asked Aleksei.

'We wait.'

'More waiting?' Dmitry was horrified. Aleksei raised a hand, indicating that he should listen.

'Wait until Nikolai declares himself tsar,' continued Ryleev. 'It will be a few days, at most.'

'How can you be sure?' asked Aleksei, quite prepared now to speak rather than listen.

'Trust me, we are certain. We already have agitators in the streets and in the barracks. Once the news of Nikolai's announcement spreads – even if we have to spread it ourselves – then the focal point will be the Winter Palace. We'll demand the proper reinstatement of Konstantin and a formal constitution to stop such an outrage from ever happening again.'

'But Konstantin will still be days away from Petersburg,' said Aleksei.

'Exactly,' replied Ryleev, with not a little pride, 'and that is why we will suggest the appointment of an interim dictator.'

'You?'

'Goodness, no. Prince Troubetzkoy has been elected to the role.'

'Is he happy with that?' asked Aleksei.

'Sergei Pyetrovich is a moderate,' said Ryleev. 'He sees the position as a way of preventing things from getting out of hand.'

'Does Nikolai suspect?' asked Aleksei.

'We must presume that he does,' said Ryleev. 'That may be why he has hesitated to move. But every day he waits, the confusion grows and with it we grow stronger. In the end, he may be able to command more men than we do, but they will not fire upon their fellow soldiers.'

'What can we do?' asked Dmitry.

Ryleev looked at Aleksei. 'Your brigade is the Life Guard Hussars, is it not, Aleksei Ivanovich?'

Dmitry's father nodded.

'You are in a minority there – they have been amongst the hardest to persuade to our cause. Do what you can to bring them round, or at least, keep them away if Nikolai calls on them.'

'My regiment's in Moscow,' Dmitry told them, fearful of the implication.

'I would not send you back there at a time like this,' replied Ryleev. 'We'll find a role for you.'

Dmitry was thrilled.

Nikolai Pavlovich wondered if he didn't hate his brothers. All except Mihail. Mihail was the only one of them younger than

478

Nikolai, and he was loyal. Konstantin was a wastrel – he didn't deserve to be tsar, and it was a good thing he wasn't going to be. But that he should refuse even to come to Petersburg and acknowledge his brother as rightful leader threatened to throw the whole country into chaos. It was typical of him.

It was Aleksandr who was currently the object of his brother's greatest wrath. The emotion disgusted him, and he was certain – and prayed for that certainty to transform into reality – that in a few weeks or months he would feel different. He had loved Aleksandr all his life, almost as a replacement for the father who had been taken away from him when he was only four. He had disagreed at times with some of Aleksandr's earlier liberal attitudes to the modernization of his country, but Aleksandr had seen the error of his ways. Above all, Nikolai could only regard his brother as a hero – a world hero – for his stand against Bonaparte.

But Aleksandr could not have picked a worse time to die. That was not fair – nor was it ultimately Nikolai's complaint. Aleksandr could not choose the time and place of his death, but as emperor, he should have been prepared for it to happen at any moment. As it was, he had left his affairs – the nation's affairs – in a terrible state.

For a start, there was the shocking vagueness over the succession. The decision that Nikolai should become tsar was clear and sensible, but why had that clarity not been conveyed to the very people he was intended to rule? It was not their place to decide who governed them, but it was a matter of simple practicality that they should be aware of who that person was. On top of that, Nikolai now discovered, there was the fact that Aleksandr had been aware for several years of groups within the army that were plotting against him. Had he not understood that the very idea of 'plotting against him' did not mean 'plotting against Aleksandr', but 'plotting against the tsar', whoever that might be? And now – *de facto* if not yet *de jure* – Nikolai was the tsar. The plots had not stopped with Aleksandr's death; if anything, they were likely to intensify.

Nikolai had to concede that he had not been completely unaware of what was going on, but he had assumed that his brother had things under control. Now, here in front of him, sat Baron Frederiks, fresh from Taganrog, with news that should have been known in Petersburg long before.

'I cannot but apologize for the delay, Highness. His late Majesty told me to leave with all haste, but upon his death I delayed. Then when Baron Diebich heard of the dispatches I had, he told me to depart immediately.'

'The fault is not entirely yours, Baron,' replied Nikolai. 'You were but the final link in a chain of delays.' It was as close as he could bring himself to criticizing his brother in front of another. He did nothing to correct the way Frederiks addressed him. The announcement of the fact that he was tsar would have to be handled with care.

'What action has been taken against the Southern Society?' he asked.

'When I departed, nothing,' said Frederiks, 'but much was planned. Arrests may have been made already; if not, then in the next few days. Pestel will be detained for sure.'

'And without him, the rebellion in the south will collapse?'

'It will be greatly hindered.'

Nikolai nodded curtly. Frederiks was wise not to employ hyperbole, however much he might be tempted. There was one document amongst the papers of the greatest interest, made up of just five sheets of paper, with the briefest of notes attached in his brother's hand.

Membership of the Northern Society – for NPR only

Nikolai's attitude momentarily softened as he saw this reminder of his brother, possibly one of the last things he had written. He touched the paper with his thumb, making sure that Frederiks would not discern the action, and felt the whisper of a connection. He sat down and glanced through the list. Many names were unfamiliar to him, some he could easily have guessed, others were horrifying. Troubetzkoy was a shock; Volkonsky a greater one. He checked carefully. It was S. G. Volkonsky – Sergei Grigorovich. It would have been unthinkable to see Pyotr Mihailovich on the list.

Perhaps more shocking than the names of the élite were those of the high- and middle-ranking officers; men with whom the royal family should have been able to trust their lives. A. I. Danilov, for example. He was a colonel in the Life Guards, wasn't he? Nikolai couldn't picture the face, but he remembered Aleksandr specifically commenting on some action he'd carried out. It was horrible for his brother's trust to be so brutally betrayed, but it was his own fault. He'd been too soft-hearted; too ill disciplined. Well, that wouldn't happen in the reign of Nikolai I – and this list would make a good start for showing everyone who needed reminding that treachery was the greatest sin of all.

Dmitry had chosen to stay a while longer at Ryleev's, but Aleksei thought it was best that he himself returned home. It had been an excuse to visit the leaders of the Society first – he had simply been shying away from the encounter with his wife. The fact that Dmitry now knew about him and Domnikiia didn't change anything – not with regard to Marfa. Aleksei felt certain Dmitry hadn't and wouldn't tell her. He could have asked him about it on their journey home, but he was always a coward when it came to things like that. Even so, he felt confident his son would keep his secret. How would it help to let Marfa know?

Aleksei's apprehension about seeing his wife after over two months was not related to his infidelity, but to hers. He had only just discovered the existence of Vasiliy – Vasya – before his departure. Now he had had time to consider it. Many men were hypocrites. They were happy to screw their own mistresses, but appalled at the idea that someone else might be doing the very same thing to their wives. In fact – as with most hypocrisies – there was a logic to it, deep, deep down. Men did not care so much that their wives had lovers as they feared other men might discover the fact. They did not fear the discovery of their own infidelity – most would admire them for it; most men at least.

Did Aleksei not fear such a discovery? Not greatly – not for himself. He had been so many things in his life – a Jacobin to the French, a Bulgarian to the Turks, a rebel to the revolutionaries – that he had almost completely managed to fortify himself against any consideration of the ill the world in general might think of him. There were four people on the planet whose good opinion he cherished, positioned with an obvious symmetry; two companions, two children: Marfa, Dmitry, Domnikiia, Tamara. There were a few others whose estimation he valued: Yelena Vadimovna, perhaps; Dr Wylie – he was too recent an acquaintance to judge; Tsar Aleksandr – undoubtedly, but the good opinion of the dead was worth little.

He stopped briefly in the street and uttered a single, abrupt laugh, causing a number of his fellow pedestrians on the Nevsky Prospekt to look. Aleksandr was not dead. He had managed, however momentarily, to fool himself. It was a good sign; if he believed it, how many others might? He smiled. The most important thing was that Iuda and Zmyeevich believed it. He cared little for Zmyeevich, but it dawned on him how much pride he felt to have fooled Iuda – Iuda, who had so often played him for the fool. It was a shame Iuda could never know.

Aleksei began walking again, through the snow. It was dark now, as it was for the vast majority of the day in Petersburg at this time of year. He was still a few blocks from home, and he returned his thoughts to the matter of his – and Marfa's – reputation. If he admitted that he desired the high opinion of the dead then the list grew longer. Maks and Vadim were both men whose low esteem of him would have shattered Aleksei. Dmitry Fetyukovich? – No, not in the end. Perhaps it was those early deaths, of two people who had truly mattered to Aleksei, that explained why he was so selective now in whom he gave a damn about. Or perhaps he had simply been thick-skinned since he was a boy, and that was what made him someone who could survive as a liar, a cheat and a spy.

But the fact that he did not care for his own reputation did not mean he had no concern for that of his wife, or his son. The revelation of Marfa's infidelity would do infinitely more harm to her standing in Petersburg than it would to Aleksei's. Even Dmitry risked becoming a laughing stock if his comrades discovered such a story about his mother. But that was not a reason to chastise Marfa for her behaviour – simply one to help her keep it secret.

Ultimately, Aleksei felt relieved. He and Marfa were on an equal level once again. He could not object to her having a lover when he had one – even if she had been unaware of the symmetry. Now at last, they could again be the friends they had once been. The passion – mostly – was long past, but now Aleksei did not need to feel guilty about it. She had her own recourse for passion, as did he. There was no need for Marfa and him to discuss it, but nevertheless his attitude could change. She did not know his secret, and never needed to be aware that he knew hers. And yet he was afraid that the moment she saw him, she would read the whole thing on his face.

He had arrived at their home. He let himself in and went up to the salon. There was no one there. There was no light in any of the rooms. He climbed the stairs to the second floor. There he could see a light emerging under her dressing-room door. It was not yet seven o'clock, so she would not be preparing for bed. More likely she was getting ready to go out – or to receive a guest.

He knocked softly on the door, but there was no reply. He turned the handle and went in. The dressing room was empty. On the other side, the door to their bedroom was ajar. He walked over to it. Through the gap, he glimpsed the mirror, and in it, the image of pink, amorphous flesh, writhing in shared pleasure.

Aleksei took a rapid step back and pressed himself against the wall. He couldn't help but grin. He'd come to terms with his wife's infidelity, but it was a cruel God who immediately presented him with the fact of it in all its wanton glory.

He listened – he would only stay for a moment, or two. Even though Marfa articulated no specific words, her tone was unmistakable in her halting, voiced breaths and short, eager sighs. Her partner was quieter. Aleksei heard the low murmur of a male voice, to which the instant response came, '*Da, Vasya! Da!*'

So there was no doubt – as if there could have been in the mind of any husband with enough respect for his wife to assume she would limit herself to a single lover – that the man who currently occupied the Danilovs' marital bed was Vasiliy. He heard Vasiliy's laugh. He knew he should have been outraged, but he was not. There was even a certain excitement in listening to his wife being fucked by this stranger – one more reason he should leave soon. It was enthralling to know that Marfa could respond in such a way, could so enjoy it. Their marriage had started out something like that, or so Aleksei hoped, but the passion had quickly faded. He thought she had been uninterested, but now he realized that perhaps it had been him – or both of them together. It was thrilling to hear his wife so enjoying the act of sex, even if it was not and never would be the case that she enjoyed it so intently with Aleksei himself. It was simply a pleasant surprise to know she had within her depths of carnal desire not often revealed in a woman, desires which put her on a level with – well, to be honest – Domnikiia.

The voices of Vasiliy and Marfa began to merge into a succession of rhythmic, guttural grunts, and Aleksei realized it was time to leave. He would come back later tonight, or even tomorrow, having worked out some way to announce his presence well in advance so that no embarrassment need be felt by either of them. Even so – disguise it though he would try – in future he would look at Marfa in a slightly different way. He would look at her with a certain feeling of – God help him – pride.

As he departed, he glanced around the dressing room. The signs that there had been a man there were all too obvious now that he looked for them. Marfa's own clothes were strewn about in a way that was quite out of character for her, but mixed in with them, Aleksei could easily spot the coat, the boots, the breeches of a man. There was even a leather bag on the chaise longue, which he knew was not his own. On top of it was what he took to be a cardboard box – a shirt box or something like that. He felt mildly peeved at the idea that Vasiliy might be taking advantage of the account Aleksei held at his tailor's – a minor insult in the circumstances.

But as Aleksei moved closer, he realized that what he had seen was not a box, but a book – a book that was not properly bound, but which had a cover made simply of cardboard. There was no writing on the front of it. Aleksei flipped it open and examined the first page. The text was remarkably familiar for something written in an unfamiliar language. Then he looked at the inside of the cover. What he saw there told him everything; absolutely everything.

Richard L. Cain F.R S.

CHAPTER XXXIV

'AS I THINK I TOLD YOU, LYOSHA, I AM KNOWN BY *MANY* NAMES.' Iuda had emerged from the bedroom. He was naked, as if deliberately to disgust Aleksei. 'But here in Petersburg I am Vasiliy Denisovich Makarov.'

'You really must hate me,' said Aleksei.

'No,' said Iuda thoughtfully, 'no, I don't think I hate you. But don't feel flattered – I don't hate anyone, any more than I love anyone. You really do interest me, though.'

'How kind.'

'I'm being honest, Lyosha.'

'And Marfa – does *she* interest you?'

'She does her best to entertain me,' Iuda replied. 'And I do like-wise – which is more than you do.'

'So which came first?' asked Aleksei. 'Your plan to tempt me with Kyesha and your book, or your plan to make me a laughing stock by screwing my wife?'

'A laughing stock? That's not you at all, Lyosha.' Iuda knew Aleksei as he knew himself. 'It doesn't hurt you that your friends will know your wife opened her legs for some passing stranger, or that her love for you is not so consuming she cannot even contemplate the idea of being with another man. What you object to is that it's me; that I can wander into your own bedroom without you having the slightest knowledge, and that I've been

486

doing it for years. What you're asking yourself now is, whither else have I wandered?'

'For years?' said Aleksei.

'Several,' confirmed Iuda.

Aleksei tried to think how long 'several' might be. Was there any moment in his marriage when there had been a noticeable change? When Tamara was born? When he returned from Paris? They were all times of change, but all had their explanations. But he was forgetting the golden rule: never believe Iuda. The earliest evidence of 'Vasiliy' being on the scene dated back only a few months. That was the limit he would give with any confidence to the time over which Iuda had been sleeping with his wife.

And it occurred to Aleksei that there were other, much more basic areas in which he should verify the facts for himself rather than believing Iuda. The words *Nullius in Verba* were no longer visible on the notebook, but they rang just as true as they had ever done. He leaned and tried to peer in through the bedroom door, but Iuda took a side step to block his view.

'How ungentlemanly, Lyosha,' he said. But then he seemed to read Aleksei's thoughts. 'Don't fret; it is Marfa Mihailovna in there, for sure. I'm playing no is she-ain't she, Dominique-Margarita tricks here tonight. Though I will admit, I did at first toy with trying that one with the lovely Marfa.'

'What?'

'I considered whether it might not be entertaining for you to see me at some window in the arms of your wife rather than your lover – or your lover's colleague; we still don't know, do we?'

'In 1812?'

'Yes,' said Iuda.

'But Marfa was in Petersburg in 1812. We were in . . .' Aleksei tailed off. He already knew where Iuda had been for part of that autumn. He had paid a visit – in the guise of Richard Cain – to Tsar Aleksandr, as Aleksandr himself had told Aleksei. And the tsar had been in Petersburg. It could have been no great additional effort to locate Marfa and pay a visit to her in the guise of Vasiliy Denisovich Makarov.

'What did you think I'd be doing while you were in Yuryev-Polsky hiding from the French?'

Aleksei was about to point out that it had not been the French he had been hiding from but Iuda and the other Oprichniki, but he decided it would do him little benefit.

'So it's been going on all that time,' he said instead.

Before Iuda could reply, a call came from the bedroom. 'Vasya!' Aleksei could detect a timbre of repressed panic in his wife's voice. Iuda went back inside, returning almost immediately.

'Your wife would like to get dressed, Lyosha,' he said. 'Perhaps we should retire.' He picked up a robe – Aleksei's robe – and put it on, then opened the door and invited Aleksei to step through it first. Aleksei was being made a guest in his own house, but now that he was in front of Iuda, at least he could decide where they would go. He led the way downstairs and chose the salon. Dmitry's harpsichord had been pushed to one corner of the room. Where it had stood there was now a pianoforte – the instrument Aleksei had ordered as a gift for his son before they had left. It had not yet been fully removed from the wooden crate it had come in. Even in the present circumstances, Aleksei found time to hope his son would be pleased with it. He sat down in an armchair. Iuda seated himself opposite.

'Since 1812,' said Aleksei, picking up where he had left off.

'Not as lovers, but as friends, at first.'

'How did you find her?'

'Oh that was no problem. The wife of Captain Danilov? They were all proud of their soldiers back then. I introduced myself as a friend of yours – at the time I still may have been, I can't recall.'

'You weren't,' growled Aleksei.

'I'll bow to your opinion on that. She was very friendly – not in any untoward way, I assure you – and by the time I left, I'd only dropped the fewest, lightest hints that you might have a lover in

Moscow. But I presume it was enough to ensure she never mentioned me to you.'

He paused, waiting for Aleksei to confirm his side of the story. It was true enough, Marfa had not mentioned meeting Vasiliy, or any friend of his from Moscow, but he wasn't going to give Iuda the pleasure of hearing him say so.

'Then, of course, events intervened,' Iuda continued. 'I almost died in the Berezina – I really did – but I was washed up on the far bank, and some kind French *soldat* dragged me to my feet and forced me to march on with them. I was in Warsaw before I could get away.'

'But you came back,' said Aleksei.

Iuda nodded. 'It was over a year before I managed to. By then you were marching across Europe in the opposite direction, and poor Marfa was all alone. She asked me directly whether you had a lover and – well, if you'd looked into that poor, confused woman's eyes, you'd have had to tell the truth – I told her about this pretty young thing in Moscow called Dominique. I told the story backwards really. First how you'd set her up in a small home, then how you'd met her at a brothel and how she'd been working there since really just a child, then how you'd spent your free hours wandering in and out of such establishments and how I thought it was probably a good thing you'd settled down with just one whore rather than flitting to a different one every night. She teased it out of me, Lyosha.'

'And you were there to help her find . . . restitution?'

'Not then, Lyosha, no. That wasn't until 1818, I think. She knew I was your friend – still your friend, even knowing what you were – and so it would be inappropriate for me, however much she begged.'

'What changed?'

'I don't suppose you even noticed. It was 4 June. Mean anything to you?'

'Marfa's name day,' said Aleksei.

'And do you know where you were?' Aleksei could guess, but

he said nothing. 'You had an "urgent appointment in Moscow" apparently. All three of us know what that meant. It was pure chance I was in Petersburg, and I finally took pity on her.'

'Seven years of screwing my wife – just for this moment?'

'This moment?' asked Iuda.

'The moment I would find out.'

'Oh, you do have a high opinion of yourself, Lyosha – and of my foresightedness. I had no idea how I was going to use our relationship when we first formed it. I will admit that the thought of you discovering us was – throughout – an added excitement, though not, I think, so much for Marfa. Not at first. Early on, I imagined the possibility of you rushing in on us and smothering her in some jealous rage, like that Moor, and then you would go to prison for it, but I quickly realized you don't have that kind of mettle.'

'I might have killed *you*,' said Aleksei, with the intended implication that he still might.

'Then you would still have been convicted as a murderer. But that is why I've obtained a little protection.' He tapped his chest lightly with the flat of his hand, but Aleksei did not understand what he meant by the gesture. 'It seemed that was unlikely too though, so I've been forced to live merely in the hope of the sense of betrayal you would feel on your discovery.'

Aleksei smiled. He didn't feel so betrayed. 'You must be disappointed,' he said.

'Time will tell.'

Aleksei might have dismissed the comment as bravura, but he knew Iuda well enough to fear there might be more behind it.

'So what do you plan to do with Marfa now?' he asked. 'Kill her?'

Iuda laughed. 'Why should I?' He leaned forward and spoke confidentially. 'You and I are both fortunate, Lyosha. Men of our age seldom get the chance to enjoy the body of a beautiful, sensual woman. I would be a fool to put an end to it.'

He stood up, seemingly impatient, and walked over to the piano. He sat down and began to play. Aleksei did not recognize the piece, nor did he like it, but there was no doubting Iuda's talent. He noticed for the first time a scar on Iuda's neck – almost healed. He felt his heart jolt as he wondered briefly if Iuda had at last become a *voordalak*. But the fact he could see the wound proved no such transformation had occurred. If Iuda were a vampire, his flesh would have healed. Besides, his reflection was clear in the mirror that hung on the wall behind the piano, as it had been in the bedroom mirror. Iuda was as human as he had ever been, but clearly he'd had some kind of falling-out with a vampire – perhaps even Zmyeevich. Aleksei began to formulate a question on the matter, trying to find the words that would most rile Iuda. At the very least it would interrupt him from playing that strange, discomforting music.

But before he could say anything the door opened. It was Marfa. She had dressed, but not formally. Her cleavage was deliberately obvious, as were her ankles and calves. She walked over to Iuda and placed her hands on his shoulders. She looked more alluring than Aleksei had seen her since they were first married. She was just turned forty, and getting a little plump, but not excessively. That evening, her skin seemed to glow. That was thanks to Iuda. Aleksei pushed the thought from his mind.

'That's beautiful, Vasya,' she said. Her voice still sounded nervous, but she hid it well – not as well as Iuda, but he was practised at extemporization. As much as they both might try to appear confident, Aleksei guessed his arrival had taken them by surprise, though Iuda at least had known it would happen one day.

'Thank you, my dear,' Iuda replied. He stopped playing and reached for her hand, placing it against his lips.

'I'm not sorry, Aleksei,' said Marfa, turning to her husband. 'There's no reason I should be. I'm not even angry any more.'

'Angry?'

She frowned in annoyance, and raised her voice just slightly.

'With you, for being with . . . that woman. You should have told me if you weren't happy.'

'I was happy,' said Aleksei, but he realized his explanations were not going to help. He was happy with Marfa, then he had met Domnikiia and he became even happier.

'Good,' she said. 'And we're both happy now. You can't object to me taking a lover, can you?'

'I object to it being *him*.' Iuda gave a look of mock indignation as Aleksei spoke.

'Because he's your friend?' asked Marfa.

Hardly, thought Aleksei, but what could he explain of Iuda to Marfa? What he had done in Moscow in 1812? What he had done in Chufut Kalye just weeks before? It would sound less like the pathetic excuses of a cuckold and more the ravings of a madman. Neither would achieve anything.

'He's not my friend,' he said simply.

Marfa frowned and looked down at Iuda. 'I'm sorry if I've been the cause of that. Vasiliy Denisovich is a fine man.'

Aleksei leapt to his feet. 'I can't stay here,' he said. He headed for the door. Marfa caught up with him just as he was stepping out into the street. He turned and looked at her. She was shivering from the cold. It was ridiculous for her to stand at the open door in the winter weather dressed like that, but Aleksei relished the sense of vulnerability it gave her. He remembered how much he had once loved her. He still loved her, but he loved Domnikiia more. It was she that was forcing him to choose.

'You can't leave,' she said.

'I'm not leaving,' he replied. 'I'm just going.'

'We have to think of Dmitry.'

'I know. I know. But I can't think now.'

'Nothing really has to change,' she pleaded.

He paused. He really couldn't think, but he had to. 'That's what I thought,' he said, 'until I found out it was *him*.'

She looked bewildered – not the strong, confident woman of moments before. In Iuda's absence she was lost. And that was why Aleksei knew he could not abandon her – because, one day, Iuda would.

'We'll find a way,' he said, 'but not right now. Give me a few days.'

He kissed her and then put his arms around her, squeezing her briefly, but tightly. Even after, he liked to think he'd felt her hug him back.

CHAPTER XXXV

ALEKSEI HAD TURNED ON TO NEVSKY PROSPECT AND WAS heading he didn't know where; to the west, towards the river, but that was merely a direction, not a destination. The city was busy, despite the snow and the early dark – these were things the people were used to. Aleksei walked briskly, his head down, ignoring those around him. He felt the road slope upwards and then down again as he crossed the bridge over the Moika, but he did not look into its frozen waters.

Iuda must die. That was the only solution – and the solution to many problems. He could see no prospect of Marfa abandoning her lover, and if she stayed with him . . . it was too insane to contemplate. At worst, Aleksei would have to leave her. It would cost her her reputation and eventually far, far more. Iuda would find some abominable way to treat her; there was no doubt about that. He was like the scorpion Aleksei had discussed on the hilltop of Chufut Kalye – it was his nature. Aleksei could not leave his wife to that. He would have known that anyway, but he had felt it as a certainty since he had looked into her eyes just now on the threshold of the home they had made together.

And so he would have to kill Iuda – not in the way he had tried so often before; this would be simple murder. In 1812 there had been a war, and one more body would have made no difference. In the caves of Chufut Kalye, there would have been no remains – he would have been devoured by his erstwhile captives, if only

Aleksei had had the guts to stay and ensure that it happened. Even on the beach in Taganrog, where a single thrust of his blade would have destroyed the monster, he would have got away with it – he was a member of the tsar's personal bodyguard, defending His Majesty as was his duty.

In all of those circumstances – had he succeeded – he would have got away with it not only in terms of there being no legal retribution, but in that Marfa would have had no idea it was her husband who had killed her lover. Even if she heard the story that Aleksei had stabbed Richard L. Cain in Taganrog, the name would mean nothing to her – at least, Aleksei presumed Iuda had not told her any of his various other *noms de guerre*. But after their encounter that evening, even if Aleksei were to commit the otherwise perfect murder, Marfa would instantly connect the disappearance of her lover with the actions of her husband. Even so, it would be better than letting him live. If Marfa never spoke to him again, he would at least have saved her. But ideally, Iuda would not simply disappear. He would have to die obviously, either in an accident or at the hands of some other – but who could Aleksei find to put in the frame for that? It would not be easy to kill any man that way – with Iuda, it might prove impossible.

He looked up. Ahead of him were the yellow walls of the Admiralty and, beyond them, the frozen Neva. He felt a hand on his arm. For a moment, he thought Marfa had pursued him, but the grip was much firmer, pulling him round.

It was Iuda.

'Aleksei,' he said in a conspiratorial whisper, 'I appreciate we have our domestic disagreements, but we have other matters to discuss of more national significance.'

'What?' spat Aleksei, knocking Iuda's hand from his arm.

'Concerning the tsar.'

Aleksei felt the sudden urge to smile victoriously and, beyond that, to tell all, to explain to Iuda how they had all fooled him, that the tsar – Aleksandr – was alive and well and free of his machinations, able to live in peace without ever hearing of

Zmyeevich or Iuda again. It would be delicious to reveal it all, and might almost compensate for much of what Aleksei had felt that evening, but in the very telling, the victory would evaporate. Iuda would tell Zmyeevich and the pursuit of Aleksandr's soul would begin again. It was a tragedy, but Aleksei knew he could not speak. That was where Iuda's intrigues outdid his – Iuda could trick him, and had done so many times, even with all the facts out in the open.

Of course, there was one variation that would fit in very well with Aleksei's other problem. It would be safe to let Iuda know he had been duped – taken for a *prostak* – if he did not subsequently have the chance to tell Zmyeevich; if, for example, he learned the fact just moments before his death. That would make the revenge complete. It added one further layer of complexity to what Aleksei had to achieve when devising Iuda's obliteration. But it would be a pleasure to rise to the challenge.

Meanwhile, he couldn't help but be intrigued by what Iuda had said.

'The tsar?' he replied.

'Who do you think *is* the tsar, Lyosha?'

Aleksei felt his stomach tighten. So it seemed Iuda already knew of the deception foisted upon him. It was like him to allow Aleksei to feel that sense of victory, before deflating it utterly. Even so, it was best that Aleksei maintained his bluff until all was lost for sure.

'Konstantin Pavlovich, of course,' he said.

Iuda shook his head with a smirk. 'No,' he said. 'It's Nikolai Pavlovich.'

So it seemed that Iuda had heard the same rumours that had reached the Northern Society. He had a simple answer for it. 'Nikolai might like to be tsar, but that doesn't make it so.'

'It's not what Nikolai likes; it's what Konstantin doesn't,' said Iuda. 'He's refused to accept the crown – or abdicated within moments of taking it. It amounts to the same thing.'

'What?'

'It's true. Believe me, Aleksei, it is.' Iuda paused briefly. 'I concede that's not something you're very likely to do, but check it out for yourself. Nikolai is the emperor.'

Aleksei considered. He would check, though he doubted Iuda would lie about something that could so easily be verified. Even so, Iuda would have needed a better reason for telling him the information than the simple fact that it was true.

'Why should *you* care?' he asked.

'Because if people believe that Nikolai is usurping the throne, they'll rise against him. It could mean the end of the Romanov monarchy.'

'Zmyeevich may care about that, but why do you?'

Iuda smiled to himself. 'I have more reason than ever to see that Zmyeevich gets what he desires,' he said. 'But for now, my goals concur with yours. You helped to kill one tsar in order to save his dynasty.' Aleksei's expression remained sceptical. Iuda pressed the point. 'Look, Lyosha, I'll be honest. The reason I came up here, apart from the desire to visit your lovely wife' – he couldn't resist, even when trying to cajole Aleksei – 'was to try to ensure that the crown skipped through the generations as quickly as possible. It turns out that Konstantin has helped do that for me. I'm happy to settle at that – Aleksandr Nikolayevich would have a regent if he became tsar now; that wouldn't help our cause.'

Aleksei considered. Iuda's reasoning was sound. Nikolai becoming tsar would force him and Zmyeevich to pause for at least a decade, if not more, until young Aleksandr came of age. And even then, they would first have to kill Nikolai, which would be no easy thing given the protection he would enjoy as tsar. Unless, of course, the revolutionaries got their way. If they were to succeed in killing Nikolai, then there were two possible consequences: a republic, or a quick accession of Aleksandr II. Was Iuda instead choosing the safer option of letting Nikolai live, or was this just another bluff?

'Think about it,' Iuda said, and then vanished into the billowing snow.

Aleksei slept that night in a tiny, cramped room underneath the rafters of a run-down tavern. It was the first time in two decades he had spent a night in Petersburg other than in his own home. On waking, he had at first felt confused by his surroundings, but that had only lasted a moment. Then he had been aware that there was some problem in his life that he had to resolve – a serious problem, but one he could not quite discern; perhaps that implied it was not significant. Then he remembered Marfa.

There was little else in his whole life – since the death of his parents – that had so unnerved him. It seemed a ridiculous thought, given that he had in his time fought battles against men, stalked *voordalaki* by night, and conspired to convince the whole world that the leader of a nation was dead. And yet in all those things, he had known that it was he who must take charge of things, organize them, survive. Even in the thankfully occasional tribulations in his relationship with Domnikiia, he had always felt in charge of his own destiny. And why? Because throughout all that, he had been aware of Marfa Mihailovna sitting in Petersburg, always waiting for him, always loving him. She was his foundation, and now she was gone. And yet there was still hope. Iuda had to die for that hope to flourish, but that very thought gave him the energy to face the day.

But there was another matter to occupy him today, of higher precedence: the crown of Russia. He suspected that what Iuda had told him about Konstantin and Nikolai was true, but it had to be verified, and he could think of only one man in Petersburg whose word he would trust on the subject – and that man would be difficult to reach. He headed over to the Winter Palace.

Yevgeniy Styepanovich was surprisingly easy to get hold of. The Lieutenant General emerged from the Winter Palace almost as soon as Aleksei asked after him. His mood was curt.

'What is it, Danilov? This is not a good time.'

'I need an audience with the grand duke,' said Aleksei.

Yevgeniy seemed flustered, and Aleksei could well guess the

reason. To the outside world, there were two grand dukes in the palace – Nikolai and Mihail. To the cognoscenti, there was only one, the other having been recently promoted to the rank of tsar. Aleksei allowed Yevgeniy a few moments of confusion before providing a clarification.

'I mean Grand Duke Mihail,' he added.

'Some hope! He's gone back to Warsaw.'

Aleksei looked over at the Lieutenant General. He was a big man, but Aleksei knew him to be weak. 'No, he never made it to Warsaw. He got as far as Neenal and then was told to turn back.' The information had been simple enough for Aleksei to pick up. 'He arrived here earlier today.'

Yevgeniy considered for a moment. 'Wait here,' he said at last, and marched off back towards the palace. Aleksei leaned out over the Neva. The bridges that spanned it were almost meaningless at this time of year. A thick crust of ice covered the river, though the water beneath flowed as quickly as ever. Most who needed to cross to the northern islands of the city could walk straight over. Only those on horseback or with heavy cargos that risked cracking the ice stuck to the bridges. At this time of the morning, when the sun was as hot as it would get, a mist rose off the river. The sun's heat probably did little to weaken the strength of the ice-sheet, but if Aleksei had needed to go across, he would still rather use a bridge.

He was on the English Quay, between the Admiralty and the Winter Palace, a little further east than where he had last met Yevgeniy Styepanovich. He did not have to stand there for very long.

'Three o'clock,' said the Lieutenant General on his return. 'His Highness will allow you five minutes.' With that, he was gone once again. Aleksei had four hours to wait.

Aleksei ate, and then drank, and then drank some more. It was still only one o'clock. It would not do to appear in front of Grand Duke Mihail in any but the most alert state of mind, so he decided a walk through the cold winter streets would refresh him. He'd gone to his barracks and changed into his full dress uniform. It would impress the grand duke and, moreover, it was well made – it kept him warm. He glanced at his gloved hands. On the left, the two redundant fingers had been folded over and sewn neatly into the palm. It was the same with all his gloves – Marfa had done that for him.

In total, he walked past the front of his own house seven times. He glanced up occasionally, but saw no sign of her. His own servants might have seen him, but they would be discreet – they had been discreet enough over the years about what their mistress had been doing. Twice he almost went in, but never quite made it. The previous evening he had told her they would find a way of working things out, and he was convinced that she accepted it. To go to her now would not change that – what it might change was precisely where the advantage lay in their relationship once they had sorted things out. It would make him seem weak, and even she would not be happy for him to have that status in the long run.

The sun was already setting when he arrived back at the Winter Palace. Yevgeniy Styepanovich took him through corridors and hallways, until they eventually arrived at a first-floor room that overlooked the river. Mihail Pavlovich was in conversation with two other men when Aleksei arrived, so he stood quietly in the shadows and waited. When the others had left, the grand duke beckoned him over.

'Colonel Danilov,' he said. 'It's good to see you again.'

'May I offer my condolences on your brother's death, Your Highness,' replied Aleksei. He looked at the grand duke. It had been a few years since their first and only brief meeting. Mihail was now twenty-seven. Between his fingers, as always, he clutched a foul-smelling cigar. He did not look like any of his brothers. Aleksei wondered if he really was the son of Tsar Pavel, though he had never heard even the slightest rumour to the contrary.

'Aleksandr Pavlovich set great store by your abilities,' said Mihail, 'and therefore so do I. What is it that brings you here?'

He sat down and offered the seat opposite to Aleksei, who took it.

Aleksei knew there was no option but to speak frankly. 'Why have you not sworn allegiance to your brother as tsar?'

'To my brother?'

'To Konstantin Pavlovich.'

'Konstantin Pavlovich is not tsar; Nikolai Pavlovich is,' the grand duke explained simply.

'So it's true that Konstantin has abdicated?'

'He was never in line of succession.'

It seemed clear enough to Mihail, but Aleksei was dumbfounded. Perhaps it was Konstantin who was not his father's son – but that was absurd. 'Never in line?' was all he could manage.

'"Never" is an exaggeration; not since 1823, though some of us suspect that Aleksandr had it in mind much earlier. He decided his brother could never become tsar, and Konstantin, so it seems, was more than happy to agree.'

'But why?'

'From Konstantin's point of view – because he loathes responsibility. From Aleksandr's, it's more a legal matter. Konstantin married beneath him. Our father changed the succession laws in 1897, and by most interpretations Konstantin could not become tsar. The decision of Aleksandr was merely a formality.'

'So Nikolai Pavlovich has known for two years that he would be tsar?' Aleksei's voice revealed his astonishment.

'Indeed.' Mihail ran his hand through his hair before resuming. 'But he feared that no one would accept the news if he simply announced it, so he awaited Konstantin's arrival. But Konstantin refuses to come. Half the army has already sworn allegiance to Konstantin – as has Nikolai. Now if he attempts to set things right, they'll call him a usurper.'

'What does he plan to do?'

'Tomorrow he will ask the senate and the army to swear their allegiance to him. Enough people have now heard of Konstantin's refusal, even if some don't believe it.'

'You think the men will comply?' asked Aleksei.

'I believe that is the sort of information my brother used to rely on you for.' The grand duke was more wily than his years suggested.

Now Aleksei had to decide. In reality, he doubted whether what he said would make much difference, but it would show the world – and himself – where his heart lay. If Konstantin was unwilling to be an absolute tsar, then it was unlikely he would become a constitutional one. Nikolai would never compromise with the rebels, so the options were either a republic, or Tsar Nikolai. A republic, Aleksei was convinced, would lead to chaos and a bloodbath. Tsar Nikolai I would lead to Tsar Aleksandr II and the risk of Zmyeevich once again seeking his revenge against the Romanovs. That was the more remote possibility, and the one Aleksei would rather live with. He would tell Mihail all he knew – most significantly that the attempt to make the army swear allegiance would almost certainly be the flashpoint. After he had betrayed all their secrets, then all he had to do was to save one particular member of the Northern Society – his own son.

He took a deep breath and began. 'Highness, as far as I know . . .' The door opened and in walked a figure that Aleksei could recognize only from portraits. It was Grand Duke Nikolai. A second later, he corrected himself; it was Tsar Nikolai. He leapt to his feet, as did Mihail.

'Good evening, Brother,' said the tsar, somewhat formally, presumably because he was in the presence of a stranger.

'Good evening, Your Majesty,' said Mihail. 'May I present a gentleman who was a loyal servant of the late Aleksandr Pavlovich.'

Nikolai held out his hand, and Aleksei bent to kiss it. He was not a man to be affected by grandeur and status, but he felt a swelling of pride within him as he considered the honour of this early introduction to the new tsar – before many Russians even realized that Nikolai *was* tsar. He could not tell whether he would ever love him as he had Aleksandr, but he felt profoundly sure in the knowledge that it was his duty to serve him.

'Colonel Danilov, Your Majesty,' he said, his head still bowed. 'Aleksei Ivanovich.'

Aleksei felt the tsar's hand suddenly withdraw. He looked up and saw Nikolai backing away, with an utterly unconvincing pretence of casualness. With every step he took, the look of horror on his face grew. Aleksei could not fathom what had caused it. He glanced over his shoulder to see what it was that had so shocked the new tsar, half expecting to find that Iuda had broken into the palace, but there was no one there. He looked back at Nikolai.

'Kolya?' asked the tsar's brother. 'What's the matter?'

The tsar raised a trembling hand and pointed at Aleksei. 'That man,' he said, 'is a traitor.' He had reached the door and opened it to shout through. 'Guard! Guard!'

'You must be wrong,' insisted Mihail. 'Our brother put great faith in him.'

Nikolai remained by the door, moving the line of his gaze between Aleksei and the guards he was hoping to see outside. 'Only yesterday I received a letter from Aleksandr Pavlovich declaring this man a turncoat, along with the whole of their damned society of rebels.'

It took Aleksei a moment to realize what Nikolai meant. It was a simple misunderstanding to clear up – the very list the tsar referred to was written in his own hand. At that moment, the guards arrived. There were three of them. Aleksei realized that he might prove his innocence, but that it would take time, which for now he didn't have; not if he was to save Dmitry.

He grabbed hold of one of the long, sleek velvet curtains that hung from the window and jumped into the air, pulling himself up on it. The curtain swung back towards the window, and with it went Aleksei. He held his feet out in front of him and heard the sound of shattering glass and splintering wood as they made contact. He closed his eyes momentarily to avoid them being hit by any shards, and when he opened them, he found himself suspended above the snowy street below, at the very limit of the curtain's swing, before he slowly began to fall back towards the palace.

He let go just before reaching the broken window and landed on the ledge outside. The snow was halfway up his calves and felt slippery under his feet. Inside, the guards were almost up to the window, swords drawn. Aleksei edged along the ledge as fast as he dared, and soon found his way blocked by one of the towering Corinthian columns that decorated the walls of the palace. He began to climb down, lowering himself from the ledge and scrambling with his feet for the ornate golden leaves of the capital of the column below. He found them and allowed himself to slip a little further downwards.

Suddenly, there was a shot. He looked over to the window and saw one of the guards leaning from it, smoking pistol in hand. Even as Aleksei looked, he saw the guard withdraw so that another might take his place. Aleksei let himself fall, and then grabbed the tiny ridge that ran above the next row of windows, scarcely able to grip it through the snow. He dangled there, wondering whether to let himself drop or try to climb further down.

The decision was taken from him. Another shot rang out, and he felt a sudden burning pain in the middle finger of his left hand. He snatched it away instinctively, but his right hand could not take his weight alone. He fell to the ground and immediately found himself in blackness and unable to breathe. He pawed the snow aside with his hands until he saw light and felt the cold night air fill his lungs again. The snowdrift had to some extent broken his fall, but he could not waste time determining whether he was injured. He scrambled to his feet and ran along the quay to the east, keeping close in against the palace wall.

Another shot was fired at him, but came nowhere near. Now all three guards had fired, and Aleksei felt safer. He forgot about hugging the wall and ran with all his strength, his aging lungs and legs straining for life and freedom. When he did stop, he fell down exhausted in the snow.

CHAPTER XXXVI

Monday 14 December 1825

I T WAS MORNING – AS DARK AS ANY WINTER MORNING IN PETERS-
burg; the solstice had occurred just five days before. Aleksei
had slept in the same tavern as the night before. His one goal
since fleeing the Winter Palace had been to find Dmitry, and so
far he had failed. He had gone first to his own home, but the
footman had informed him that neither Marfa Mihailovna nor
Dmitry Alekseevich was there. The man had bandaged Aleksei's
finger, which was a relief. In future he would be known – amongst
those *voordalaki* who cared – as the two-and-a-half-fingered
man. The bullet had gone clean through between the first and
second knuckles, leaving a reasonably neat stump. The cold had
numbed it, but once he had got into his house, it began to throb
with pain. He could not stay. His address was registered. Soldiers,
under Nikolai's orders, would soon arrive there.

He had gone to Ryleev's house and found it bustling with
officers, each with the same thought on his mind: tomorrow was
to be the day of revolution. But Dmitry was not among them.
Someone suggested he should try Obolensky's, but that had been
his next port of call anyway. The prince's house was quieter than
the poet's had been, but amongst those who were there, the mood
was the same. There was still no sign of Dmitry.

Aleksei had wandered through Petersburg searching the streets,
the taverns, even the churches. He was aware there might be

troops out looking for him, but they wouldn't recognize his face, and it was a chance he had to take. None of it proved to be of any avail. It was after midnight when he trudged back to the tavern.

In the morning he awoke feeling refreshed. It was still dark outside, but he had more desire to rise than he had done for many months. Today was simple – simpler than any other day of his life had been. He must get Dmitry away from the rebels. They would fail; that was obvious. Nikolai was far too well prepared. Aleksei had done his son a service by erasing his name from that list, but it would all be meaningless if Dmitry was caught in the act with the other revolutionaries. As for his own fate, Aleksei cared little – at least for today. Tomorrow he would see whether he could save his own neck; today was about Dmitry. Still, his own survival was important – if dead himself, how could he ensure the death of Iuda?

Aleksei left the house and headed once again up Nevsky Prospect, towards the Admiralty, or the Winter Palace, or wherever in that area of the city the uprising might begin. He still wore his full uniform. It was all he had to wear, but he knew that most of the rebels – those who were soldiers rather than poets, at any rate – would do the same. His sword was at his side and his gun was in his pocket. The city was eerie in the morning twilight. The streets were as busy as they might be on any Monday morning, but Aleksei saw in the eyes of all he passed the sense that something of unspeakable enormity was about to happen. Before he reached the Admiralty, he saw someone he recognized; a young captain by the name of Yekimov – a keen member of the Society.

'What's the news?' Aleksei asked. There was no one near them who might eavesdrop.

'The senate has assembled already,' said Yekimov. 'They're going to swear loyalty to Nikolai Pavlovich.'

In reality, it didn't much matter. The senate had no power – less even than its Roman namesake at the height of imperial ascendance – but the symbolism might prove significant.

'Have any of the regiments marched on the Winter Palace yet?' Aleksei asked.

'I don't know, but when they do, it will be Senate Square, not the palace. Troubetzkoy thinks that if we can sway the senate, everything else will follow. At least that's what he said last night. No one's seen him today.'

'Thanks,' said Aleksei. 'Where are you headed?'

'To the fortress. Ryleev's told me to see what can be done about raising the battalion there.'

'Have you seen Lieutenant Danilov? Dmitry Alekseevich? My son?' Aleksei realized that his intensity risked frightening the captain.

'I'm sorry, sir. I haven't.'

They walked a little way together, then Yekimov headed off to complete his task. When Aleksei reached Admiralty Boulevard he looked west towards Senate Square. Even at this distance, it was clear that a crowd was assembling. Between him and them, outside the Admiralty, stood a group of concerned-looking men on horseback. Aleksei could only guess that they were loyal to the tsar, keeping an eye on how events unfolded. It would not be safe for him to approach the square directly. Instead he slipped north, between the Admiralty and the Winter Palace.

The Neva was a stunning sight – not just because it was a vast, wide, gleaming sheet of ice, but because of the soldiers, converging from all directions on to Senate Square. In the middle of the widest part of the river, opposite the Peter and Paul Fortress, just before the Great and Lesser Nevas split, the crowds separated, avoiding the invisible but potentially deadly weak spot in the centre of the ice. How many hundreds were there altogether? It was impossible to count. There were typically around twelve thousand soldiers stationed in the city in total; both sides would be considering how those would divide. If the split were balanced, it would probably mean a victory for the rebels, as a drift would begin from previously loyal troops. But they were unlikely to get half – how many fewer would still be enough? It was possible that

Nikolai had brought in additional troops, but he could not be entirely sure which side they would take.

Aleksei stepped down on to the frozen river. He would far rather have walked along the paved embankment, but that would mean passing close to the Admiralty, where loyal soldiers would be stationed. His fear of them was more rational than his fear of the ice, and so he overcame the latter. The Neva allowed him to give the building a wide berth. It was slippery, though most who crossed seemed to be dealing with it better than Aleksei was. He was reminded of two previous occasions when he had been forced to travel on foot across an icy plane. Both of those had been in battle – once on Lake Satschan, after the Battle of Austerlitz, and then seven years later as the French fled across the Berezina. Then cannonfire, and slightly warmer weather, had meant that the ice was unstable. Today at least, as during every winter in Petersburg, it was as reliable as any other thoroughfare.

His way was eventually blocked by the Isaakievsky Bridge, but it marked the point Aleksei wanted to reach. The pontoon bridge stretched out from Senate Square, across the Great Neva towards the Twelve Colleges on Vasilevskiy Island. With the river frozen, it was impossible to crawl under it, and it would be difficult to climb up on to it, but along the embankment, steps that in summer led up from the water's edge now led up from the ice. From the river he was too low down to be able to see into the square – all that was visible was the top half of the statue of Pyotr the Great – but he could sense from the murmuring noise that a vast crowd had assembled.

As he ascended the stone steps away from the ice, the whole scene became clear to him. In the background stood Saint Isaac's, the scaffolding already in place for its planned demolition, but the crowds were keeping well away from there. They were clustered around the statue of Pyotr – an odd choice for rebels in a republican cause, but Aleksei doubted if many truly knew what their leaders had planned for the country. There were over a thousand there, and more flocking in all the time.

Aleksei stood on the quayside, a little way from the crowd, watching. He was about to cross over to the square when a sudden chill came over him – noticeable despite the winter cold. He remembered a story he had heard about what had happened on that very spot, one hundred and thirteen years before. The landscape would have been different then. The embankment would not have been built, and there would have been no statue of Pyotr. Saint Isaac's was just a church, small compared with the current building and minuscule in comparison with the new one that was planned. The Admiralty would have been there, but nothing like as grand.

In Aleksei's mind, Pyotr had approached from the east, emerging from the Admiralty. Zmyeevich stood there waiting. Where could Colonel Brodsky and his men have been hiding? How had they been strong enough to subdue a creature like Zmyeevich? It was all the stuff of myth, handed down from generation to generation of the Romanovs and embellished at every step. Could the whole thing have been invention? *Nullius in Verba*. There was little concrete evidence that there was anything in Aleksandr's blood. He claimed that he sometimes saw through Zmyeevich's eyes, but that could be simple hallucination, brought on by the fear of the tales his grandmother had told him. Zmyeevich believed it though – or at least Iuda claimed he did. Zmyeevich had been there – here – so the story went. It may not have happened the way Aleksandr described it, it may not even have happened here, but there had been a meeting between Pyotr and Zmyeevich. And Pyotr had come out on top. If not, why had Yekaterina ensured that his statue, close to that very spot, depicted him trampling a serpent?

Aleksei crossed over to the square and joined the crowd. There seemed little coherent purpose to their presence. They simply stood and waited. Occasionally a shout could be heard: '*Konstantin ee Konstitutsiya!*' But at whom they were shouting was not clear. Aleksei spoke to the first officer he came to.

'What regiment are you with?' he asked.

'The Moskovsky,' he said, 'but there are Grenadiers here too, and some of the Marine Guard.'

'Who's in charge?'

'Bestuzhev led us here, but we're waiting for Prince Troubetzkoy. He's going to take charge until Konstantin Pavlovich can be freed.'

'Freed?'

'It's all a lie that he's abdicated – Bestuzhev told us. They have him in chains in Warsaw on Nikolai's orders. It's an outrage. Even the senate's fallen for it.'

'They've already sworn allegiance to Nikolai?' asked Aleksei.

'Apparently. They took the oath at seven this morning. They already left.'

It was almost laughably disorganized. Perhaps Aleksandr had done his brother a favour by bringing on the succession so suddenly. If the rebels had been able to stick with their plans of acting the following year, they would have had more time to prepare. But any comedy that there was would vanish if this crowd continued to grow. Loyal troops would have to do something to disperse it – and that would mean a massacre. But none of that was Aleksei's immediate concern.

'Do you know a Lieutenant Danilov?' he asked. 'Dmitry Alekseevich.'

The man shook his head. Aleksei moved on through the crowd, asking for Dmitry, but of the few who had even heard of him, none had seen him. It seemed hopeless that he would ever find him; his main hope lay in his son's height. He would stand out from the crowd, but only by a little.

Over to the east and south, Aleksei could see more troops assembling, many on horseback. There was no indication that they were part of the rebellion – they were here to put it down, and were merely awaiting the order so to do. Aleksei again saw the group of horsemen that he had noticed outside the Admiralty. Now they had been joined by Tsar Nikolai. At that distance it was impossible to see his expression, but on his decision of whether to end the rebellion by persuasion or by force lay the fate of thousands of men.

Aleksei turned back and scanned the crowd. He still saw no sign of Dmitry and – as the numbers swelled – had little hope of finding him. Then he noticed movement around the statue of Pyotr. A figure was climbing up on to the Thunder Stone, preparing to address the rebels. It was Ryleev. Aleksei ran over to listen.

Dmitry looked up into the sky. The face of Kondraty Fyodorovich Ryleev looked down on him and the whole crowd. Behind him, Pyotr's bronze horse reared into the air. Dmitry felt elated. Ryleev had been a hero to many at the Cadet Corps College, and though there had never been any official path of recruitment, a number of the youngest members of the Northern Society – those, like Dmitry, who had never seen battle – had joined on the basis of his reputation. In all there were at least three thousand here, he'd heard, with more on the way. Those soldiers who remained loyal to Nikolai – fooled into thinking he was truly tsar – would never fire on their comrades. Nikolai would have to relinquish power and let Troubetzkoy take over, if only Troubetzkoy would arrive soon. Perhaps they had already arrested him. Then Ryleev would have to lead. Maybe that wasn't such a good idea.

Dmitry had arrived at Ryleev's house the previous night, to be told that he had missed his father by less than an hour. It was a disappointment, but he knew Aleksei would appreciate that forthcoming events would take precedence over kinship, at least for the day. He had stayed at the house, and in the morning all had been in chaos.

First, Bestuzhev had arrived with news that Kakhovsky had promised to assassinate Nikolai at the first opportunity. Ryleev paused at the news, and then said, 'Remember the *garde perdue*. He must not be linked to us.'

'He knows,' Bestuzhev had replied.

The conversation had taken place as a shouted exchange through Ryleev's bedroom door as he prepared himself. When he finally emerged, Dmitry was shocked at what he saw – too shocked even to laugh. He was not alone in his emotions. Ryleev himself described what he was wearing – and the motivation behind it – far better than Dmitry ever could have.

'I'm dressed as a peasant, you see,' he explained, indicating his rough clothes and knapsack. 'But' – the word was long and drawn out – 'I'm also carrying a rifle – like a soldier. That's what today is all about; the union between the soldier and the peasant – the first act of their mutual liberty.'

Dmitry would have observed that Ryleev was neither a soldier nor a peasant, but he bit his tongue. Bestuzhev had been more outspoken.

'There are *only* soldiers with us today – no peasants,' he said. 'They won't understand any of this sort of patriotic symbolism. All they believe is that Nikolai should not be tsar.'

Ryleev had eventually agreed and had gone again to change, with the words, 'Perhaps I was being a little too romantic.' Bestuzhev left the house to search the city's barracks for more support. Ryleev had dressed once more and was about to leave when his wife rushed out to him and grabbed his arm.

'Don't stir from the house today,' she begged.

'Don't be silly,' he had replied.

'You will die,' she shouted.

Ryleev had pulled himself away from her, and she shouted up the stairs, 'Nastenka! Nastenka! Beg your father to stay.'

A little girl had appeared – Ryleev's six-year-old daughter – seeming as upset by her mother's shouting as by her father's departure. In the end, she had to be dragged away from her father's legs, to which she had clung desperately. His wife had swooned on the couch. Ryleev left hurriedly, accompanied by Dmitry and several others. It was a terrible way for a man to part from his family on a day that carried such risk, but if he had stayed, he might never have got away. Again, there were times when the affairs of the nation had to be placed above those of the family.

They had arrived at Senate Square to the news that Troubetzkoy had not arrived and that the senate had already sworn allegiance to Nikolai. Ryleev decided that he must speak. They had helped him up on to the plinth that supported the statue of Pyotr, and he had addressed those that could hear him.

'Let them read Aleksandr's will,' he shouted. 'They've got the parchment sealed there in the senate.' He pointed over to the building. 'That will tell us whom His late Majesty wanted to succeed him.'

There were cheers in the crowd. Dmitry had never felt more convinced of their victory. He stood and listened to Ryleev's words and to the roars of the crowd. When the speech had finished, a familiar chant rose up.

'*Konstantin ee Konstitutsiya! Konstantin ee Konstitutsiya!*'

After that, Ryleev climbed down and Dmitry lost sight of him. Then came disappointment. Dmitry overheard a conversation between Obolensky and Bestuzhev.

'Troubetzkoy's not coming!' snarled Obolensky.

'What?'

'The man's turned chicken.'

'He'll be here,' insisted Bestuzhev.

'He's already been here. He didn't like the look of what was going on, so he nipped along to the office of the chief of staff and asked where he was supposed to go to swear allegiance to Nikolai. You know where he is now?'

Bestuzhev shook his head.

'Hiding in the Austrian embassy.'

For the first time, Dmitry felt doubt. What kind of men were they led by? Ryleev made no claim to be a commander, but the farces of that morning proved that his poetical head was irredeemably in the clouds. Troubetzkoy had been a brave soldier – not least at Borodino – but that had been years before. Here they were – thousands of brave men with hope of a new future for Russia – brought to the square like sheep and then abandoned. Just a little leadership could make all the difference, but there was nowhere for it to come from.

Obolensky and Bestuzhev began to bicker about who should take charge – each trying to pin responsibility on the other. Bestuzhev insisted that he only had naval experience, which would be no use here; Obolensky argued that he was no leader of men. But Dmitry had stopped listening. He had seen someone through the crowd, approaching him.

It was his father.

Aleksei rushed through the crowd and embraced his son.

'Thank God I found you,' he said. Then he saw Dmitry's face. 'What is it?'

'It's falling apart, Papa. There's no one to lead us.'

'What about Troubetzkoy?'

'Troubetzkoy made a run for it,' said Dmitry, 'and none of the others has the wit to take charge.'

Despite himself, Aleksei felt some of Dmitry's disappointment. There was a dignity to the rebels, or to many of them – those involved at Dmitry's level, chiefly. The ordinary soldiers here knew nothing. They had been deceived into thinking they were here to support Konstantin, when in reality Konstantin wanted no support. The men at the top were a mixture of politicians and dreamers – the former in the south and the latter in the north, to make a broad generalization. It was men like Dmitry who truly wanted a better Russia, and might have created one, given the opportunity.

'You could lead us,' said Dmitry suddenly.

Aleksei gave a curt laugh and then saw his son was in earnest. 'Me?' He laughed again. 'I'm a colonel. I have no nobility in my blood, and no ability to make pretty speeches. More than that, it's my profound belief that this day is beyond salvation. If I were to lead them anywhere, it would be back to their barracks.' Aleksei did not have to lie for any of it. He had no need to admit to his son that he wanted the uprising to fail, because he could see now with certainty that it would fail.

Dmitry looked at him with a gaze of utter disappointment. He shook his head slowly and turned away, saying, 'I never took you for a coward, Papa.'

At that moment, a silence settled on the crowd. Aleksei looked around and saw a figure on horseback riding boldly towards the centre of the square, where Bestuzhev and Obolensky stood. Aleksei recognized the man immediately – it was Mihail Andreevich Miloradovich, the governor general of the city. Aleksei remembered him from Austerlitz and more recently his heroic efforts to save lives in the floods the previous year. He also remembered that Miloradovich had submitted to Aleksandr a practical plan for the abolition of serfdom – and there was no man working on his own estates who was not free. Was it possible that he was coming here to join the rebellion? If so, Dmitry's fears would be transformed. This would be a man to lead them.

Aleksei stepped forward and put a hand on Dmitry's shoulder. Dmitry glanced at him and Aleksei could see in his eyes that sense of hope he had anticipated. They moved closer to hear what the governor general had to say. As soon as they were in earshot, it was evident that he had not come to succour the rebels.

'And so I implore you,' he was saying, 'return to your barracks. You have my word; Nikolai is rightfully tsar. Those of you who have been deceived will not be punished for misplacing your patriotism. I've fought alongside many of you. I hope you've found me to be a man you can trust. I in turn trust our tsar, as appointed by his predecessor and by God – Nikolai Pavlovich.'

There was no cheer of support, but his speech was met with a thoughtful silence. Aleksei's heart leapt at the prospect of a peaceful outcome, though the tension in the square remained a physical presence. Obolensky stepped forward to speak. Beside him was that odious figure, the volunteer for the *garde perdue*, Pyotr Grigoryevich Kakhovsky.

'You have no friends here, Mihail Andreevich,' Obolensky said. 'You may support this despot, but these men love their country. I suggest you leave. If you remain, you may find yourself in danger.'

Miloradovich glanced from man to man of those who had gathered round, avoiding the gaze of Obolensky.

'Miloradovich is right, Mitka,' Aleksei murmured to his son. 'You must leave. Now.'

'Never!' whispered Dmitry in response.

The governor general spoke again. 'I'll leave you all to consider matters,' he said. 'There may not be much time to end this peacefully.'

He turned his horse and rode back through the crowd, which parted to let him pass. There was a movement behind him. Aleksei saw the raised pistol. He threw himself towards Kakhovsky with a shout, but it was too late. The pistol fired with an explosion of smoke. The hole in Miloradovich's back was small, but he fell forward in an instant. There were shouts all around, some of approval, others of anger. Cavalrymen galloped to rescue the governor general, but Aleksei did not see what happened to his body as the crowd surged forward.

Somebody began a chant of 'Konstantin ee Konstitutsiya!', which was soon picked up by the rest. Whatever contemplation Miloradovich might have inspired was quickly forgotten. Now there was no hope of a peaceful ending to the day. There were ten thousand soldiers out there with rifles, horses and cannon. It would be carnage.

Aleksei felt hands lifting him up from the ground. It was Dmitry. Holding his father's arm, he seemed to notice for the first time the bandage which covered Aleksei's left hand.

'That was needlessly cruel,' said the boy. 'And you're no coward, Papa.'

Aleksei had no time to ponder whether the last comment was inspired by his actions or by his latest wound. As he pulled himself up to his feet, the crowd around them thinned, and walking slowly towards them, looking calm and serene in civilian clothing, came Iuda.

Shock and loathing welled up in Aleksei's stomach at the sight. Of all places and times, this was not one at which he wanted to be concerned with Iuda. But Aleksei's reaction to the sight was quite different from that of his son.

Dmitry let go of his father and strode over to Iuda, his hand held out in greeting.

'Vasiliy Denisovich,' he said, smiling broadly. 'What an honour.'

CHAPTER XXXVII

'WHY HAVE YOU COME HERE?' THE QUESTION THAT DMITRY spoke was identical to the one on Aleksei's mind, but he uttered it with none of the bile which Aleksei would have injected.

'I came to see you, Mitka,' replied Iuda. 'Your mother is very concerned.' He turned his attention to Aleksei, who had now caught up and stood beside his son. 'It's good to see you, Lyosha,' he said, holding out his hand. 'It's been many years.'

Aleksei's mind raced to understand what on earth Iuda could mean. Clearly, his words were for Dmitry's benefit.

'Good Lord, yes,' said Dmitry, with a hint of surprise. 'I'd almost forgotten you two actually knew one another. It must be a long time.'

'1812,' said Iuda. 'You were just a little boy. And a good boy, too – though it was hateful of me to ask you to deceive your father, and for so long.'

'I think I've deceived him no more than he's deceived me,' said Dmitry. 'I saw her, Vasiliy, in Moscow, just like you said.'

'So it wasn't only Marfa you introduced yourself to,' said Aleksei. He couldn't take his eyes from Iuda, much as he wanted to gauge his son's reactions.

'Mama's told you already?' asked Dmitry. 'Vasiliy's been a great friend to both of us – particularly when you've been away.'

Aleksei perceived the slightest shake of Iuda's head, as if to tell him, no, Dmitry did not know just how close a friend Iuda had been to his mother. That certainly fitted the boy's tone. No son could speak so lightly of the man who had turned his mother into an adulteress. And what would be the benefit of revealing the truth, even if it were to be believed? Dmitry had clearly been robbed of much of his respect for his father. Would it be fair to take away his opinion of his mother too? But on the other hand, it might be worth it if it would also strip away any regard in which he held Iuda.

'Almost like a father,' Dmitry continued. There was no suggestion of any artifice in his voice, but that did not change the fact that he believed what he was saying. Now Iuda's eyes smiled in victory. Aleksei felt weak.

'I'm a soldier,' he said. 'I couldn't always be at home.'

'God no, Papa,' said Dmitry, stumbling over his words as he realized what he had said. 'I didn't mean anything of that kind.' But it was too late for him to take it back.

Iuda was characteristically two-faced. 'Nor did your father think it, Mitka. I couldn't begin to take Lyosha's place in your heart, any more than I could in your mother's. I'm just someone who's kept a benign eye on you when he's been away. I'm sure you'll have much less need of me now you've grown up and flown the nest.'

Iuda had played it so simply – Dmitry was forced to disagree. 'No, Vasiliy,' he said, gripping Iuda's shoulder, 'you've been far more to us both than that. And always will be.'

Iuda patted Dmitry's hand and smiled kindly. 'Thank you for that, Mitka,' he said. 'I will try to live up to your expectations. But we have chatted long enough. We must turn to the reason I am here.'

'Go on.'

'Your mother has sent me. I've told her what you've been planning for today.' Iuda raised a hand as he spoke, as though to stop any objection from Dmitry. 'I'm sorry, but I hold you both in too much regard to keep it from her.' With the clear implication that Aleksei did not. 'She begs you to leave, before you are killed.'

Dmitry did not even need to think about his answer. 'As does the mother of every man here,' he explained. 'No freedom would ever be won if women ruled the world; they all love their sons too much.'

Iuda nodded. 'That is much what I told her you would say, but at least I have done what she asked of me.' He paused, lifting Dmitry's hand and holding it in both his own. 'This appeal, however, comes from me. Leave the field. You can do nothing here. Nikolai is tsar; you cannot change that.'

'I can die trying,' insisted Dmitry.

'You will die failing,' said Iuda.

Iuda held the pose for several seconds, looking up into Dmitry's eyes. Neither spoke. It was Aleksei who broke the silence.

'Listen to him, Mitka,' he said. It revolted him to urge anyone to take Iuda's advice, and to be deferring to him, rather than to take the lead in imploring Dmitry to go, but none of that mattered if it succeeded in saving the boy's life. Aleksei loved Dmitry as a person more even than he loved him as a son. He was prepared to lose the relationship in order to save the man.

Finally, Dmitry was resolved. 'Very well,' he nodded, 'but you'll both come too.'

'Of course,' said Aleksei. 'But Vasiliy and I have an important matter to discuss first.'

Iuda raised a questioning eyebrow at Aleksei. There was a hint of admiration in the smile that crossed his lips.

'Here?' exclaimed Dmitry. 'Surely it can wait.'

'No,' said Iuda, 'your father is quite right. Besides, if we all three leave together it's more likely we'll be stopped. We'll see you soon. We both will. And don't worry, I'll be quite safe.' He tapped his chest again in the same way Aleksei had noticed two days before. If Dmitry observed it, he made no comment.

Instead he gave Aleksei a brief hug, then did the same with

Iuda. He headed off to the east, pushing his way through crowds of rebellious soldiers who did nothing to stop him.

'What is it that we have to discuss?' Iuda's voice spoke in Aleksei's ear as they watched Dmitry depart.

The truth was there was only one thing Aleksei wanted to talk to Iuda about, and that was to tell him that he had been taken for a fool and that Aleksandr was not dead. But he had already decided that he would do that only in the moments before Iuda's death. Now he had the perfect opportunity to kill Iuda, or at least to see him die.

Iuda – Vasiliy Denisovich Makarov – Richard L. Cain – all would die by a single bullet, fired from the gun of a soldier loyal to Tsar Nikolai I. There were plenty of them about, the square was almost surrounded by now, and if none of them managed to fire a fatal shot, then Aleksei had a loaded pistol in his pocket, and was as loyal to Nikolai as any. Neither Marfa nor Dmitry could lay any blame at Aleksei's door for the death. There would be hundreds killed here today, it was inescapable. No one would be suspicious if one of them was Iuda. Dmitry had heard for himself that Iuda was prepared to stay a while longer. Perhaps there would even be witnesses who could attest to seeing Aleksei desperately attempting to save his old – and so recently reconciled – friend's life. He felt sure he could stomach a little play-acting for that.

'You play a long game, Iuda,' he said.

'You're too generous, Lyosha. You see structure in the present and assume that my every action in the past was working towards it. In reality, the reverse is true. I do things that seem interesting at the time and then decide later what I can make of them.'

Aleksei was only half listening. His eyes were scanning the square. Dmitry was not yet out of sight. To the south, he could see a definite, organized movement of the troops.

'Do you really think,' Iuda continued, 'that in 1812 I ingratiated myself with your wife and son with the intention of revealing the fact to you in 1825?'

'You planned to reveal it some time.'

'How could I even know how they would react to me? I couldn't have guessed that your wife would be so eagerly accommodating; nor how much your son would search for someone to fill the gap left by his absent father.'

Aleksei glanced at him. It wasn't so surprising that barbs concerning Dmitry stung more than those about Marfa, and it wasn't just that one was a fresher wound. 'I don't think Dmitry would be too fond of you if he knew what you and his mother had been doing.'

'Her thoughts exactly,' said Iuda. 'To him I'm just an old family friend – a sort of uncle, whom he has known longer than he can remember.'

'You had to make sure he never mentioned you to me.'

'Again, you see patterns after they have emerged and assume they are part of some grand design. Do you play chess, Lyosha?'

Aleksei's mind jumped back to a frozen army camp where – as now – he had believed he had Iuda at his mercy. 'You know I do,' he said. 'Last time we spoke of it, you described how disappointed you got whenever I fell for one of your little traps, because it meant you wouldn't get to spring the bigger trap you'd been planning all along.'

'I did say that, didn't I? Well, I lied – it's a vile habit and I apologize for it. But the big trap is not the one that was designed to be big; it's the one that grows that way. I never told Marfa or Mitka to avoid telling you about me. The boy was only five at the time – how could he have understood? And what would it have meant to you to hear of Vasiliy Denisovich? But then, when I learned later that you knew nothing of me, that's when I decided to encourage the idea. I was already fucking your wife as often as she could take it, so she wasn't going to tell. And Dmitry wasn't too pleased with you at the time, thanks to your failure to take his piano playing seriously – it was I who first taught him to play, incidentally.'

Aleksei let the words bounce off him. It was all true, but it did not matter. Whatever Iuda might have attempted, Dmitry had grown up to be a good man – a man who did not get on with his own father, but that could be remedied, once Iuda was out of the way.

Iuda himself seemed to have detected Aleksei's lack of interest, and had changed tack. 'I'm glad we persuaded him to go though, Lyosha. That was teamwork, you'll have to admit. Neither of us wants him to die here amongst these failures.'

'Failures?'

'Oh, come on. You know it as well as I do. The leaders are romantics and the men are dupes. Listen to them.' He paused, cocking his ear to the air with his usual theatricality. Various shouts filled the square, but one phrase which had become the rallying cry of the rebels stood out.

'"*Konstantin ee Konstitutsiya!*"' he repeated. 'I asked one of them what "*Konstitutsiya*" meant. You know what he said?'

'What?'

'He said it was the name of Konstantin's wife. These people don't deserve liberty.'

Aleksei was still eyeing the square. Dmitry was almost out of sight. He could hear shouted orders flying back and forth in the distance. Soon they would open fire. Iuda needed to be prepared for what Aleksei planned to tell him – it was time to do a little knife-turning of his own.

'You think that's Zmyeevich up there?' He nodded towards the bronze statue. 'Vanquished by Pyotr – crushed under his horse's hooves?'

Iuda looked up at the serpent. 'It must have been around here, mustn't it?' He sounded as though it had genuinely only just occurred to him. 'Yes, I suppose it is.'

'Do you think they'll do one of Aleksandr in a similar pose?' asked Aleksei. 'Of course, it won't just be Zmyeevich they show him defeating. How would you like to be depicted? A cockroach must be very tricky to carve.'

Iuda smiled tightly. 'I don't think Aleksandr's victory was all

523

that brilliant. To triumph by dying? Did he perhaps never get as far as the end of the Bible? Saw what the Son of God did and decided to emulate it, not realizing that he needed to manage resurrection as well as crucifixion? Pyotr was the true genius. To have his blood drunk by a vampire and to live through it into old age – that's a feat that would be almost impossible to surpass.'

Aleksei had to hide his excitement. Soon Iuda would know the truth of what he was saying. It would be a joyous moment.

Dmitry had forgotten to thank his father for the piano. It was a small thing, but it mattered. It was Vasiliy who deserved the real thanks, for the encouragement, the advice, the first inspiring lessons. All Aleksei had done was to spend some of his money; a lot of his money. But it was money well spent, and Dmitry felt it indicated a change in his father's attitude. He would have time to thank them both later, he hoped.

He stepped over the tiny low fence that marked the boundary of Senate Square. For the crowds on both sides, it was as good as a thick, solid brick wall. On the inside stood the rebelling soldiers. They had been told to assemble in Senate Square, and assemble there they did. One foot placed outside would have ruined the plans so carefully laid down by their diligent, absent leaders. On the outside, it was all civilians, by now quite a number of them. It was coming up to three in the afternoon – almost sunset – and news of what was happening had spread through the city. The citizens had gathered to watch. But just as the rebels knew their place, the onlookers, even without explicit instruction, knew that to step over those small slats of wood and into the square would transform them from observers into participants. It was as invisible and as impenetrable a barrier as that which separated a stage from an auditorium.

From over by the cathedral, Dmitry heard a shout. He looked. It was Nikolai himself who had given the order. In a second, a dozen cannons roared and their mouths spat canister across the square. A wave of men at the front of the crowd collapsed. Dmitry whirled on his heel and looked back towards his father and Vasiliy. Around them, some men fled and others stayed rooted to the spot. The men he was looking for stared back in his direction.

Aleksei was gesticulating with exaggerated arm movements, pointing at Dmitry and at himself and Vasiliy and in other directions too. The message was clear enough. Dmitry should carry on in the way he was heading; they two would try to escape across the other side of the square. Still Dmitry hesitated. He should go back and help them, though there would be nothing he could do but encourage them to run faster. They were both the type of men who knew how to survive. His father was, anyway. Vasiliy always had a slightly spiritual, unworldly air to him, a sense of benign impracticality, which Dmitry loved, but caused him worry as to the dangers it might bring upon its bearer.

But Dmitry knew he need not be concerned. However little experience Vasiliy might have under fire, Aleksei was an old professional, and Dmitry knew that his father, whatever differences he and Vasiliy might have had in the past, would not leave the square without first ensuring his friend's survival. It was Vasiliy himself who had taught Dmitry that much about his father – taught him more than he had ever had the chance to experience for himself.

Dmitry took one last look towards the two of them, still in a state of indecision. Aleksei repeated his gestures once again, as if Dmitry had not understood them, but surprisingly it was Vasiliy who appeared the more calm. Standing just behind Aleksei, his only movement was a slow nod, but Dmitry understood entirely what Vasiliy meant. He always did.

Dmitry Alekseevich turned and fled into the twilight.

Aleksei turned back towards Iuda the moment he saw Dmitry at last depart. There was no one there. He heard a second volley of cannonfire. This time, panic spread through all assembled.

Those who had stood their ground in the face of the first barrage now ran for their lives. Through the crowd, Aleksei caught sight of Iuda; he was past the statue of Pyotr and heading for the far corner of the square. Aleksei set off in pursuit. Most of the crowd was flowing in that direction, and Iuda soon became lost from sight again.

Aleksei kept on running. Iuda was easy to spot as one of the few in civilian dress. He had reached the corner of the square and had stopped, deciding which way to go. Half of the crowd was pouring into the narrow gap between the buildings that was the entrance to Galernaya Street, hammering on doors which refused to open, whilst the other half – more than half – were heading for the river. Some were making for the Isaakievsky Bridge; others ran straight out on to the ice itself. Iuda chose the river. His indecision had allowed Aleksei to catch up with him a little, but he was still not close.

Now, there were more civilians. Those crowds that had gathered to watch the stand-off as though it were some public spectacle had suddenly found themselves a part of the entertainment at which they had come to gawp. Soldiers showed them no more respect than they did their comrades, and many – men, women and even children – were trampled underfoot.

Iuda was out on the ice now. He would have been a fool to take the bridge. It was already overflowing with fugitives and many were forced to leap off its sides and on to the flat, white surface below. In summer, the entire bridge might have capsized, but the ice that locked its pontoons into place allowed no movement. Aleksei was on the rim of the stone embankment. He had the advantage of height over Iuda and was within range, but he did not want to shoot him in the back; that would be no fun. He drew his pistol.

'Iuda!' he shouted.

Iuda turned and saw the gun in his hand. He stood still and upright, his head slightly to one side. He seemed shocked – as if Aleksei had cheated. And it was true, if Aleksei were to shoot him stone dead now, it would be to cheat them both. But Aleksei was a pretty good shot, and Iuda would live long enough to hear what he had to tell him.

There were a hundred witnesses, but none would bother to look in the direction of the two men who faced each other across the ice. Even if they did see, they would not volunteer any information. 'And what were you doing in Senate Square that evening?' would not be a question for which many could find a satisfactory answer. For the same reason, many broken limbs that night would go unset, many wounds unbound; many who might have lived would die.

Aleksei took aim and curled his finger around the trigger. Above him, he heard a whistling sound. It was a cannonball. At almost the same instant he heard a second. Some of the fools had loaded their guns with round shot rather than canister. It would do nothing but shatter the ice of the river – unless that had been their intention. The first shot sailed over the river and landed somewhere on the Vasilevskiy Island. The second smashed through the Neva's frozen surface close to the far bank. Iuda was thrown from his feet on to his back. Aleksei tried to adjust his aim, but it caused him to lose his balance. He jumped down on to the ice and managed to remain on his feet. He walked towards Iuda, holding the pistol out in front of him.

'We should do this in summer next time,' said Iuda as Aleksei approached.

'There won't be a next time,' replied Aleksei.

'Doesn't it seem to you like fate? The bridge? The icy river? The cannonfire?'

'The difference is I have a gun this time,' said Aleksei.

Iuda pulled a face that acknowledged Aleksei's point. Aleksei took aim. He remembered the advice of Kyesha's letter: no poetry, just certainty.

'Can you do it, Lyosha?' Iuda asked. 'Can you really kill me with such callousness? Not leave me in a burning building? Or thrust my head under the water of a freezing river? Or abandon me in a cave with a horde of ravenous vampires who despise my very soul? You have to leave me some way out.'

Aleksei thought about what Iuda was saying. Was there really some weakness, some sentimentality in Aleksei's make-up that meant he had to give Iuda a fighting chance, or that he had to let God decide his ultimate fate? History might indicate it, but that said nothing for the future, or the present. He allowed a parade of faces to pass in front of him: Maks, Vadim, Margarita, Major Maskov, Captain Lishin, countless unnamed others, even the vampires that he had tortured, even Kyesha. And what of what he had done to Marfa and Dmitry; to Aleksei himself? If Aleksei had given Iuda a chance before then he had been a fool. But that could be remedied. He was older now, and wiser.

He pulled the trigger.

The pistol recoiled in Aleksei's hand and Iuda's body jerked with the impact of the pellet. Blood spurted from the centre of his chest, but Aleksei knew he had missed the heart. Iuda had to be alive to be able to listen.

Now for the play-acting – just in case somebody chose to bear witness to this event, to report it back to Marfa or Dmitry.

'Oh my God! Vasiliy!' shouted Aleksei. He ran over to the prostrate figure and knelt beside it. Looking back towards the square, he saw government troops begin to arrive at the river-bank. Behind them rode Pyotr in triumphant bronze, silhouetted against the moonlight. Aleksei grabbed Iuda under the arms and dragged him out further towards the middle of the river, as if to protect him from those terrible men who had shot him, but he still made sure that they were in a place where Pyotr's bronze eyes could look down upon them.

'You surprise me, Lyosha,' said Iuda. His voice was croaky and punctuated by coughing. Blood showed on his lips, flowing out down his chin each time he spoke. 'But I suppose you have won. A checkmate is a checkmate, however dull.' His fingers scrabbled at his coat buttons. Aleksei helped to undo them, knowing that he had to breathe in order to hear what Aleksei had to say.

'Oh, this is no simple checkmate, Iuda,' said Aleksei. 'You've been fooled – played for a *prostak* – and now I'm going to tell you all about it.'

Iuda's hand slipped inside his coat. His fingers worked at the buttons of his shirt and finally found their way inside. For a moment Aleksei was fearful that he had his own gun, but he doubted he would have the strength to use it.

'Do go on, Lyosha,' said Iuda. Any pretence he made at encouragement was lost in the gargling of blood in his chest. He really didn't seem interested in what Aleksei had to say. Aleksei thought he had been pretty smart – finding a way of solving all his problems and of puncturing Iuda's ridiculous ego at the moment of his death. But when the moment came, Iuda was refusing to play the game. His hand reached inside his shirt and finally caught a grip on whatever was within. He sighed and closed his eyes, breathing more easily. In any other man, Aleksei would have suspected that he had taken hold of a crucifix.

Iuda opened his eyes again. 'Go on, Lyosha,' he said.

At last, Aleksei understood the difference between them. It was not that Iuda was better at devising a deception than he was. He probably was, but that was not the point. The real difference was that Iuda did not so eagerly play the victim as Aleksei had always done. He managed to keep up the veneer of being in control even as he lost everything – his life included. It did not matter. Iuda would die and Aleksei would have the pleasure of telling him that Aleksandr was alive. Iuda might pretend not to care, but Aleksei would know, and that would be enough.

'Iuda,' he said, patting him consolingly on the chest, 'I have beaten you.'

Iuda's body was ripped by convulsive coughing. Aleksei realized he would have to hurry things along, but Iuda seemed to appreciate that too. He pulled his hand from inside his shirt. Two strands of a leather cord emerged from it, by which whatever he was holding had been hung around his neck. He opened his hand and in it Aleksei saw nestling a small glass vial, containing a dark liquid. With a jerk, Iuda tugged at it. The stopper, attached to the leather band, came loose, and in a moment Iuda had the vial to his lips. He drank very little and then his arm fell to one side. He breathed more slowly now, as a contented smile spread across his face.

'Carry on, Lyosha,' he said. 'Tell me what it was you were going to say.'

Aleksei didn't speak. He looked down at Iuda's hand. The glass vial had rolled out of it on to the ice, spilling the remainder of its contents. A small, dark stain spread out across the ice – black in the moonlight, but Aleksei knew well enough not to trust that fickle illumination. He picked up the vial and sniffed it. The scent was unmistakeable – blood.

'Please, Lyosha, grant a dying man his wish.'

Aleksei said nothing. Iuda's words from earlier that day echoed in his mind.

'Pyotr was the true genius. To have his blood drunk by a vampire and to live through it into old age – that's a feat that would be almost impossible to surpass.'

But Iuda had surpassed it. He had had a vampire drink his blood – the scars Aleksei had seen on his neck proved that – and had kept in that bottle which he hung around his neck blood from that same vampire; an insurance policy – a lifesaving elixir he could consume whenever his life was at risk. Perhaps Kyesha had been the *voordalak* from whom he had taken that blood, perhaps another. It did not matter.

'Please, tell me. How did you fool me?'

Aleksei smiled. 'I didn't, Iuda. I was pretending, but I won't lie to you. I could never devise a trick clever enough to fool you.'

'I thought perhaps you'd finally discovered it was Dominique you saw me with at that window in Moscow.' His lips curled into a grin. 'Or equally, that it was Margarita.'

'No, Iuda,' said Aleksei. 'You've still got me there.'

Iuda coughed again. His stomach contracted and his upper body rose up towards Aleksei. His eyes stared out at him, and tried to smile, but it only meant that more of his own blood spewed from his mouth. His eyes lost their focus and his body went limp, falling back on to the ice. On last, great, bloody cough issued from him, but Aleksei knew it was only the wind escaping from his body.

Iuda was dead, but not dead. He was undead. How long it would take for the full transformation – the induction, as Iuda had termed it – to be complete, he did not know. But it would happen. Iuda had preferred to live as a man for as long as he could, but in the end had chosen to live as a *voordalak* rather than not live at all.

Unless Aleksei could do something about it.

He had not brought his wooden sword with him – he had not thought to encounter any *voordalaki* in Petersburg. But he had his sabre, and although he knew he could not use it to stab Iuda's lifeless body through the heart, he could still make use of it to sever Iuda's head.

He rolled the corpse over on to its front and then stood up. He drew his sword, raising it up above his head and squeezing the handle tight. He felt pain in his left hand, where his newest wound had scarcely begun to heal, but he ignored it, focusing all his hatred upon the back of Iuda's inert neck.

'Halt!' came a shout from the riverbank. 'You there! What the hell are you doing?'

Aleksei ignored the soldiers and brought down the blade. A shot hit him in the arm, but it did not hamper him as he swung the steel inexorably towards Iuda's undefended neck. Then the ice shook beneath his feet. A cannonball landed in front of him, just beyond Iuda's body. Aleksei was thrown back. He felt his sword briefly connect with Iuda's flesh, but it would have been no more than a scratch. He landed on his back, but was soon sitting up again.

It was too late. Even as he watched, Iuda's inanimate body slipped into the hole in the ice the round shot had created. There was barely the sound of a splash as it vanished. Aleksei was reminded again of Satschan and even more of the Berezina. It was ever the same in Russia – snow and ice and freezing cold. This time, though, things were different. There was more certainty. This time he knew for sure that Iuda was dead. But though, like his namesake, Iuda would be entombed in ice, and though he had chosen a fate that ensured he would encounter Satan himself, neither would be permanent. This time Aleksei was confident that, when the ice melted, Iuda would live again.

Aleksei turned over on to his front and raised himself to his feet. He began to run across the ice, towards Vasilevskiy Island and – perhaps – freedom.

Nikolai's loyal troops ran after him in close pursuit.

Aleksei remained imprisoned in the Peter and Paul Fortress for seven months. He'd made it across the river, but there were troops already waiting on the other side, rounding up the fleeing rebels. Aleksei opted for arrest rather than a bullet.

Prince Volkonsky – Pyotr Mihailovich – had been his most frequent visitor and greatest supporter, but there was nothing he could do to get Aleksei off the hook. He'd been a favourite more of Aleksandr than of Nikolai, and any sway he might have had was reduced by the involvement of the other Prince Volkonsky – his brother-in-law, Sergei Grigorovich – in the plot itself, which had taken on the appellation of the 'Decembrist Uprising'. Even if none of that had been the case, there was little hope for Aleksei; he had infiltrated the movement too well. His name – in his own hand – was on the list in Nikolai's possession, many of the rebels could identify him personally, and he had fled arrest from the tsar himself at the Winter Palace. Any defence would risk the true story of what had happened in Taganrog coming out, and exposing Dmitry as one of the plotters. Neither was worth Aleksei's freedom. They tortured him, but they were amateurs compared with what Aleksei had experienced. Other prisoners did not stand it so well; Colonel Bulatov, so the grapevine had it, had committed suicide – by cracking his skull open against the wall of his cell.

The greater help that Volkonsky could offer was the promise that he would ensure the financial security of Aleksei's family – both his families – and the spiritual security of the Romanovs. Aleksei did not know whether his trial would lead to death, prison or exile, but there was a strong likelihood he would not be in a position to do anything useful when Aleksandr Nikolayevich came of age. He told Volkonsky that Cain was now a vampire, and told him all his aliases – all those he knew.

The thaw came as usual in spring and the ice on the Neva melted. Hundreds of corpses began to be washed up on the riverbanks, of both rebels and bystanders, but there was no sign of Iuda. Volkonsky argued that the corpse could well have floated out into the sea and sunk to the bottom, or could have been misidentified – easy in the case of a man with so many names – but Aleksei knew that, like Christ, like Caesar's dynasty, Iuda had required his own death in order to rise again and become the thing that in his heart he had always been: a vampire.

Letters from Dmitry and Marfa made no mention of Vasiliy Denisovich, either in terms of his disappearance or his continued presence, but to discuss him would be to kick Aleksei while he was down.

On 13 July 1826, the sentences were carried out. There were 289 convicted. Suspiciously, 290 of those who had gone on trial were acquitted. It seemed that Nikolai was being mathematically precise in his demonstration of erring on the side of leniency. Many of the men had taken part in a revolt in the south, some weeks after the events in Senate Square. It had been better organized and better supported, but so far away from the seat of power it had meant nothing, and the strength of Nikolai's loyal armies had proved the greater.

It was three in the morning when they began to be led out of the dingy cells – still damp from the floods of two years before. Whereas at the time of the uprising there had only been six hours of daylight, now there were only the same of darkness. It was a bright morning twilight that Aleksei and the others emerged into, though the full moon still hung in the air. At least he would have the satisfaction that Iuda could not be there to witness his undoing.

Aleksei stood stiffly to attention as the insignia were ripped from his uniform. There were so many prisoners they had to queue, but none was allowed to see what was happening to the man in front of him. Aleksei had been proud to be made a colonel, and many people now long dead – his father, his mother, Vadim Fyodorovich – would have been proud of him too. But if they were now in a position to know he had become a colonel, and to know that he had been stripped of that rank, then they must also know the reasons behind it; he felt no shame.

He was moved on and next instructed to remove what was left of his uniform and change into a simple peasant robe, but then, strangely, he was issued with a sword. It was not his own, but he could guess the symbolism that led to its being issued to him. He was brought out into the early sunlight. It had been raining overnight, but it was clear now, though the ground was still damp. In front of Aleksei stood five gallows, empty for the time being, and beside them a raging fire.

The sword he had just been given was taken from him. The officer who had taken it raised it above Aleksei's head, holding its handle and its tip, and began to bend it. This was the symbolic degradation that was applied to a traitor. Aleksei himself had once before been on the other end of the ceremony, when he had held Maksim Sergeivich's sword above his head and snapped it in two. Then he had believed Maks to be a traitor and Maks had known that, ultimately, his treason was justified. Aleksei could not feel sorry for himself. There were people alive who knew what Aleksei had done – not many, but enough. He would die in the knowledge that somewhere out there, those that he cared for most still loved him. Maks had only regained that love after he had died, and for him that was too late. He remembered Maks' tearful eyes as the sword shattered, and the surrounding circle of *voordalaki*, with Iuda gloating as he looked on.

The sound of the sword breaking – that same metallic scream, which he had not heard for thirteen years – awoke him from his thoughts. The two halves of the blade were thrown on to the fire to melt, and Aleksei was led to a group of his fellow traitors who stood and waited before the gallows. That was the worst affront of all. Russia did not sanction capital punishment, not for the last three quarters of a century. It seemed that Nikolai, like his brother before him, had plans to modify the constitution. Once all the officers – now officers no more – had gone through the process of degradation, the hangings began.

The names of the five ringleaders were read out and they were led up to the gallows; Pestel, Muriev-Apostol, Ryleev, Bestuzhev-Riumin and the murderous Kakhovsky. Each man climbed the ladder and had a noose placed around his neck and tightened. The hangman struggled with the ropes, wet from the overnight rain, but eventually all five men were ready. They were kicked away from the ladders.

A groan was uttered in unison from the watching crowd and heads were turned away. Three of the men slipped from the ropes and landed on the ground below; Muriev-Apostol, Ryleev and Kakhovsky. While the other two men kicked at the air with ever decreasing vigour, the process began again for the 'lucky' three. This time there was no mistake. In Aleksei's mind, only Kakhovsky deserved it.

Another list of names was read out – around thirty in all – Aleksei's amongst them. Then the sentence was declared. It was not to be hanging. Aleksei could not tell whether he was relieved. To die would have made a quick end of it, but life meant hope, and Aleksei was in need of hope.

A few hours later he was led, in amongst a small group, out of the Neva gate of the fortress and along the short, stone pier to a waiting barge. He looked across the broad, flowing river at Saint Petersburg. He could see the Winter Palace, and a little of the Admiralty, but Senate Square and the statue of Pyotr were out of sight. He stepped down into the boat and within minutes it

535

pushed off, taking him, and his fellow rebels, to a new life, from which there would be no return: a life of exile.

He looked once again at the city's skyline. As they moved upstream, he just caught a glimpse of the monument to Pyotr's proud victory, where once, like Saint George, he had defeated a serpent. If only, like George, he had managed to kill it. The statue disappeared from view. It would be the last he saw of Petersburg, or of any real civilization, but he would get used to it.

Even so, he wished his final glimpse of a city could have been of Moscow. He'd always preferred Moscow.

EPILOGUE

SIBERIA. ON THE BANK OF A WIDE, REMOTE RIVER STOOD THE town of Irkutsk, fifty versts from Lake Baikal, five thousand from Moscow. It had been almost twenty-nine years since the day of the Decembrist Uprising.

Domnikiia toyed with the iron bracelet that encircled her wrist. She had worn it since 1828. Most of her friends – a small and exclusive circle – wore one. 1828 had marked one of the first, slight relaxations that the Decembrist exiles had been allowed – the removal of their leg-irons. It had been Pauline Anenkov who had come up with the idea of having the fetters reforged as a symbol of . . . who knew what? Some of the women had also had wedding rings made from the metal, but Domnikiia had not. As far as they knew, Marfa Mihailovna was still alive.

Many wives, and a few lovers, had come out to Siberia to support their exiled men. Originally, they had been a lot further east than this, and conditions had been indescribable. Aleksei and those others allocated to the second rank of conspirators – those who avoided the death penalty – had been sentenced to various periods of hard labour, followed by permanent exile. Aleksei was ordered to dig in the mines for twelve years; it was neither the longest nor the shortest sentence.

After that, life had become more tolerable, certainly for those men who had female companionship. There had never been any question of Marfa coming to join him, Aleksei had assured

Domnikiia of that even before he left Petersburg. She had written, intermittently, for a few years, but after a while, there had been nothing. The same was true of Dmitry Alekseevich. Aleksei told Domnikiia all about Iuda – in his alter ego Vasiliy Denisovich – soon after she had come out east to join him.

Prince Volkonsky – Pyetr Mihailovich – had made everything possible. He seemed to show more concern for Aleksei than he did for his own brother-in-law, Sergei Grigorovich, though he knew Aleksei not to have truly been a supporter of the cause. Pyetr Mihailovich had ensured that money came to them out in Siberia, and – apparently – to Marfa and Dmitry, and, most importantly, to the Lavrovs.

It had been the most appalling decision that Domnikiia or Aleksei had ever had to make, tearing their hearts in two, but for Tamara's own sake, they had abandoned her. It would have been misery for her to live in the conditions they at first suffered – though children had been born out here to the wives of exiles – and to live and grow in Moscow, stigmatized as the child of a Decembrist, without any hope of ever seeing her parents again would have been a pointless cruelty. Fortunately, the seeds of deception had already been sown.

Toma would grow up as Tamara Valentinovna Lavrova, daughter of Valentin Valentinovich and Yelena Vadimovna. Aleksei had smiled at the thought she would be Vadim's granddaughter, but it was little compensation. Yelena had been saddened but supportive when the idea was put to her. Valentin had been surprisingly accommodating. He was not a cruel man and he loved Tamara as he loved any child. In his mind, she would be far happier as his own than as the daughter of Aleksei and Domnikiia. The regular payments from Volkonsky had been persuasive too.

As for Tamara herself, both hoped – and feared – that she had been young enough to forget them. They would never know if some memory of them lingered in her heart, but years of life under the name of Lavrova would obscure whatever of her true parents remained with her. And it was not simply the shame of having a Decembrist father they were protecting her from. If Toma had stayed with Domnikiia, in Petersburg, Siberia or anywhere, Iuda would eventually have made the connection. Would he have pursued the daughter, seeking revenge on the father? Aleksei had been certain that eventually he would. It wasn't a risk they could take. At least Aleksei had been lucky enough not to have had the opportunity to say goodbye.

Volkonsky had written to them regularly. Letters in both directions were censored, but both Aleksei and the prince were wise enough to be able to write a great deal with few words. Almost every letter from Volkonsky contained a phrase along the lines of 'Tsar Nikolai and Tsarevich Aleksandr are both in the rudest of health,' or – less frequent but not uncommon – something like 'The tsarevich was seen today inspecting the guard under the glare of the midday sun.' Aleksei had not been so forward with Domnikiia over affairs of state as he had with regard to his home life, but she could make some vague guess as to the significance of the midday sun.

Since their periods of hard labour had expired, the Decembrist families had moved from town to town, but always with a tendency to head back west – and always having leaped through the hoops of bureaucratic approval. Tsar Nikolai was vindictive in his attitudes towards his would-be usurpers, but none of them could honestly swear that they would have behaved any differently in his shoes – a few of them swore it dishonestly. Many of them – Aleksei included – tried to better the lot of the Siberian peasants, through improvements primarily in agriculture and education. Aleksei knew nothing of farming, though he learned much, but he taught the local children Russian, French, Italian, German and even some mathematics. The fact that most of his mathematical examples involved predicting the trajectory of a cannonball did not discourage him, and the better of his students worked out how to transfer that knowledge to the problems they themselves faced in building, farming, fishing and so forth.

Volkonsky had died two years before. He had continued writing

– and sending money – to the last, but it was through his brother-in-law that they had heard the news. He had been seventy-six – just five years older than Aleksei, and the news had been for him a *memento mori*. It was sad, but in terms of the practicalities of lessening the misery of their exile, he had already done his duty. There was no need for more money. Dmitry was a major, last thing they had heard. They knew nothing of Tamara – they had specifically instructed Volkonsky not to tell them; it would have been too painful – but she would be thirty-three by now, happily married, and no doubt with children of her own.

Domnikiia and Aleksei had themselves saved much of what Pyetr Mihailovich had sent them. They owned this house, never mind that it was made of wood and not stone. And they owned land, which Aleksei farmed. 'We must cultivate our garden,' Lyosha always said to her, and then told her she should read Voltaire – but she never did. What mattered was that they were contented, even if it was a life that neither had envisaged. True, it was horribly cold here in the winter, but that only reminded them they were in Russia. In the summer, it was usually pleasant – rarely too hot. Now it was somewhere between summer and autumn, and still comfortable to sit out in front of the house and gaze down to the river, even after sunset. Today it was particularly important that she could sit outside, because Aleksei had a visitor.

The old starets – a few years older than Aleksei, she would guess – had arrived on horseback. He looked in some strange way familiar to Domnikiia, but she could not place him. He had given her his name and she had, with ridiculous but somehow appropriate formality, gone to announce him to Lyosha. The old man had followed her into the house and Aleksei had seen and recognized him. He had rushed over – as best he could – and hugged the old man like a long-lost brother before she had been able even to repeat the name she had been given – Fyodor Kuzmich.

She had sensed that Aleksei and the old man – the *other* old man – had things to discuss and had left them alone, despite both their protestations. Now they had been together for almost half an hour, and she was tempted to go back in. She peeked through the window and Aleksei saw her. He beckoned her in enthusiastically, and she complied.

Aleksei was sat in his favourite chair, a rug over his knee despite the warmth. He was seventy-three now – to her sixty-one – and showed many of the superficial indications of aging that one might expect. The hair of his head and beard was white. His skin was thin and pale, but not excessively wrinkled. His body was wizened, but not weak – the years of forced labour in the mines had helped with that. His hearing was poor, as was his eyesight, but he had a pair of eyeglasses that he used whenever he wanted to read.

The man who sat opposite him – Fyodor Kuzmich – seemed wiser, but less contented. Age had affected him similarly, except that the top of his head was completely bald. Aleksei still possessed a full head of hair, but for a tiny gap on the crown that Domnikiia had only recently noticed.

'And Cain never knew?' Kuzmich asked just as Domnikiia entered. She shuddered silently at the name.

'No – much as I was tempted to tell him.'

'You think he still lives?'

'I'd be a fool to make any other assumption,' said Aleksei.

'So our deception – your deception – remains a victory; a suitable reimbursement for the times he deceived you.'

'He never deceived me,' said Aleksei. 'He just persuaded me to deceive myself.' His eyes flicked up and looked straight into hers. 'But I've understood the truth for a long time. Some things don't need faith – some things you just know.'

Domnikiia had no idea what he was talking about, but she saw the look of love in his eyes, the same look she had seen every day since she had climbed out of that troika after a journey of thousands of versts and their eyes had met for the first time in two years. She did not care to listen to their conversation any more; she did not need to.

541

She went back outside and walked slowly, with a little pain in her knees, back to her chair. She sat down and gazed up above her. There was no moon tonight, but the sky glittered. It was strange, but she sat out there most nights – when it was neither cold nor cloudy – and gazed at the constellations, most of which Aleksei had taught her. He was smart enough to know that the patterns were just random, not icons set into the sky by the gods, and she was smart enough to believe him, but it wasn't for that that she gazed at them.

Her reasoning was simple. It wouldn't be every night, it probably wasn't tonight – it might only be one in a hundred or even a thousand nights – but just occasionally, Domnikiia was sure, as she looked up at Pegasus or Orion or Cassiopeia, that somewhere, across half a continent, her daughter would be walking along a street, or sitting in a chair, or lying in a bed with the man she loved, and lifting her eyes skyward to gaze, like her long-forgotten mother, upon those same stars.

Historical Note

The official record tells us that Tsar Alexander I entered immortality in Taganrog on 19 November 1825, attended by his wife and his closest advisors. But almost immediately, rumours began to circulate that he had not died but had faked his own death, in order to abdicate a crown with which he had never felt comfortable. The tale was that he lived out the remainder of his long life in the guise of an impoverished holy man, by the name of Fyodor Kuzmich, dying finally in Tomsk in 1864. If Alexander and Kuzmich were one and the same, then he would have been eighty-six years old. While many historians regard these stories as worth little more than a footnote, within the Romanov family itself they were widely held to be true. As recently as 1958, the Grand Duchess Olga Alexandrovna, sister of the last tsar, Nicholas II, is quoted as saying, 'I am old and not long for this world; you are young and apparently have understanding of these things. You should know that we have no doubt that Fyodor Kuzmich *was* the emperor.'